A PLACE IN THE DARK

GUERNICA WORLD EDITIONS 27

A Place
in the Dark

A Novel

Frank Lentricchia

GUERNICA
World
EDITIONS

TORONTO—CHICAGO—BUFFALO—LANCASTER (U.K.)
2020

Michael Mirolla, editor
Cover design: Allen Jomoc Jr.
Interior layout: Jill Ronsley, suneditwrite.com
Guernica Editions Inc.
287 Templemead Drive, Hamilton (ON), Canada L6M 2Z7
2250 Military Road, Tonawanda, N.Y. 14150-6000 U.S.A.
www.guernicaeditions.com

Distributors:
Independent Publishers Group (IPG)
600 North Pulaski Road, Chicago IL 60624
University of Toronto Press Distribution,
5201 Dufferin Street, Toronto (ON), Canada M3H 5T8
Gazelle Book Services, White Cross Mills
High Town, Lancaster LA1 4XS U.K.

First edition.
Printed in Canada.

Legal Deposit—Third Quarter
Library of Congress Catalog Card Number: 2019949199
Library and Archives Canada Cataloguing in Publication
Title: A place in the dark ; The glamour of evil : two novels / Frank Lentricchia.
Other titles: Novels. Selections (Guernica) | Glamour of evil
Names: Lentricchia, Frank, author. | Lentricchia, Frank. Glamour of evil
Description: Series statement: Guernica world editions ; 27 | Two separate works printed
back-to-back and inverted (tête-bêche format).
Identifiers: Canadiana (print) 2019017451X | Canadiana (ebook)
20190174595 | ISBN 9781771835312
(softcover) | ISBN 9781771835329 (EPUB) | ISBN 9781771835336
(Kindle)
Classification: LCC PS3562.E57 P53 2020 | DDC 813/.54—dc23

For Neal Bell

CHARLIE AT MY LAI 4

MANY YEARS AFTER YOU LEFT Los Angeles, a failed Ph.D. candidate, you open again the issue of *Life* that you purchased for 40 cents on December 5, 1969. To the article entitled "The Massacre at My Lai," with color photos, and once again you are engrossed by the large photo (recto) facing the opening page. An artistic arrangement, so you wanted to think, but you knew then, draft-deferred Eliot Conte, as you know now, that it was not artistically arranged.

Seven Vietnamese huddled together, bare-footed and filling the frame. At the front, with six tightly grouped behind her, as if in deference to her authority and courage, an old woman—the matriarch, no doubt—lips together, corners of her mouth turned severely down in cold contempt. If she is afraid, she will not show it. Directly behind and snug against her—hiding, clinging—a young woman with her face buried behind the matriarch, her arms around the old woman and hands loosely clasped at the old woman's waist. Loosely clasped: as if in resignation.

Behind and to the left of the old woman, a girl. You once guessed late teens, until you learned that she was 13. On her hip, a boy-child of perhaps 3. The 13-year-old, who seems older, is looking down at her waist, lips slightly parted—hers is the look of consuming concentration. She is fussing with an open button at the waist of her black blouse. Slight nakedness of midriff. You feel, and are a little ashamed to feel, a quick erotic charge. She is trying to do the difficult task of re-buttoning her blouse with one hand. What is that dark smudge across her forehead? You learned not long ago

1

the truth of the dark smudge: she had been thrown to the ground by an American soldier, who opened her blouse, but decided not to rape her because he judged her too dirty to rape. The child she holds at her hip is looking out into the middle distance. The innocent gaze of a 3-year-old's curiosity. What does he see? Standing beneath the child on her hip, a little behind her, with his arms around the dangling leg of the hip-child, a boy of 7 or 8, in white pajamas with broad blue stripes. He is looking hard left with keen interest into the far distance, away from what it is that the matriarch stares at unflinchingly. Something is going on in the far distance. What does he see? The boy of 7 or 8 will not be distracted by the American soldiers standing around, relaxed and ready, toward whom the matriarch directs her withering gaze.

At the left edge of the photo, yet another girl, 8 or 9. She stares at the soldiers—mouth open wide, corners turned severely down. Screaming? Crying? Both? You can't hear her. This is a photo. This is only a photo, and you were never there. Try to feel grateful that you were never there. Because who, including you, knows what you would have done had you been there.

Alongside the silent screamer, his body hidden except for his bald dome and one arm lifted from his elbow, poised over the head of the screaming girl. The grandfather? Husband to the matriarch? His hand is angled down with purpose, about to descend and caress the silent screamer's head—or maybe to cover her eyes, so that she will not see what causes her to scream. The consoling hand, frozen in time forever. Did it reach its goal before it was too late? You need to believe that it did. At least that. But you do not believe it.

The Army photographer, there at My Lai to do his job, asked the soldiers to wait, so that he could take his shot. They complied, he took his shot, turned and left. As he walked away, the soldiers did their job. The photographer said that he glanced briefly over his shoulder, saw the falling bodies, then never looked back.

And you, Eliot Conte, lover of poetry and painting, will think, years after seeing again the *Life* photo, of two paintings. A famous one by Peter Paul Rubens, "The Rape of the Sabine Women," and an obscure one by Giorgio Vasari, "Christ Carrying the Cross." But most of all, you will think of a poem by W.H. Auden, "Musée des Beaux Arts." The opening of that poem penetrates you now as it never did before: "About suffering they were never wrong/The Old Masters." You add in homage to Auden: How it takes place while someone, a child/At her hip, fumbles with a button.

* * *

At 7:22 a.m., on March 16, 1968, a platoon led by 24-year-old Second Lieutenant William Laws Calley, Junior, of Miami, Florida, enters what is called My Lai 4, 521 miles north of Saigon on Vietnam's south central coast, province of Quang Ngai. My Lai 4 is called My Lai 4, rather than simply My Lai, because it is part of a patchwork of six My Lais—hamlets and subhamlets, rice paddies and irrigation ditches, dikes and dirt roads. Second Lieutenant Calley will soon find the deep irrigation ditch at the eastern boundary of My Lai 4 to be especially useful for achieving the mission designated "Search-and-Destroy" by Military Assistance Command, Vietnam, whose supreme leader, General William Westmoreland, who liked to be called "Westy," had himself baptized "Search-And-Destroy."

By mid-day, Calley's platoon will have destroyed—"wasted" was his word—504 unarmed civilians. Old men, old women, teen-age girls, children, babies and an unknown number of ducks, cows, calves, pigs, piglets, goats, chickens, dogs, cats, and two water buffalo. They will have burned food supplies. Burned thatched huts. Exploded brick houses because they suspected, not irrationally, that the brick structures served as Viet Cong bunkers. And they will have hurled freshly-killed and partially disemboweled residents to the bottoms of wells in order to ensure their pollution.

At Miami Edison High School, William Calley called himself—and liked to be called—"Rusty." His commanding officer, Captain Ernest Medina, called him publicly and routinely Lieutenant Shithead. Before enlisting, Calley briefly attended Palm Beach Junior College, where he earned one 'C,' two 'Ds,' and four 'Fs,' then dropped out and drifted to dishwasher, train conductor, and bellhop. Through his days of romantic desire in high school and college he had no success in dating, but in Vietnam he had his pick of the prettiest prostitutes, who frequented the camps, and who never refused him, as he suspected those Florida girls had, because of his twig-like stature—he stood 5'3" and weighed 128 pounds—or because, already, in his early 20s, he was half bald and occasionally sported what must be called a reverse pony-tail, which descended from the middle of his dome down over his forehead.

After basic training William Calley qualified easily for Officers Candidate School, where he was remembered mainly for his passion for pizza. The much-circulated picture of him taken at his court-martial for 22 counts of murder, with his dress hat pulled low over his forehead, pleased him greatly. He felt that he definitely looked like Montgomery Clift in *A Place in the Sun*, who was himself twig-like in build and whose mouth, with its down-turned corners, Calley felt, quite strongly, looked precisely like his own.

At the trial it was established that there were many sexual assaults committed on the morning of March 16, 1968, but Lieutenant Calley witnessed only one of them, which he could not, and would not, abide: a soldier with a teenage girl on her knees before him, rifle muzzle to her head, his pants down. After being ordered by Calley in the sternest tones to "cease undergoing oral sex and pull up your pants, soldier," the soldier obeyed, rather than turning, pants still at his ankles, fully erect, and killing Calley for the crime of blow-job interruptus. Calley would later explain: "If a G.I. is getting a blow-job, he isn't doing his job. He isn't destroying communism."

Not far from the slaughter at My Lai 4 lies the long and dazzling white beach of the South China Sea, a favorite in-country site of R & R for mentally and physically distressed U.S. Military personnel, who name it China Beach—who, when bored with surfing and gazing at the monotony of waves, shift their gaze with a slight turn of the head and enjoy, in the near distance, the cloud-flecked green and gentle mountains called Truong Son. Gentle, like nothing else in Vietnam.

* * *

On the morning William Calley enters My Lai 4, Eliot Conte—teaching assistant in the Department of English at U.C.L.A. and promising Ph.D. candidate there—awakens at 5 a.m. in panic to prepare and overprepare Hemingway's *In Our Time* for English 1A, section 64. Before demonstrating the power of close textual analysis (his power), he will give his students an overview and tell them that Hemingway's linked series of stories chart the relentless formation of a young boy, Nick Adams, in the School for Violence, from age 5 or so through young manhood and radical psychological instability in his early 20s, a newly returned World War I veteran barely holding himself together, while trout fishing alone in idyllic Upper Michigan.

With the finest precision, Conte levels off 2 teaspoons of sugar which he stirs—counting exactly 5 revolutions per teaspoon—into his fourth cup of coffee. Reviews his notes. Makes notes on the notes. Reviews the key moments in Hemingway's book. Underlines them in red as his anxiety is suddenly quadrupled by the memory of what he'd done the night before, when he'd proposed, drunk, utterly soused, to a woman he was not attracted to and who would not sleep with him unless and until he married her. Unlike William Calley, he did not seek out prostitutes, either in Los Angeles or back East in Utica, New York, his home town, where he had endured (like Calley) the romantic desert of high school, after which he was accepted at elite, nearby Hamilton College, where he majored in English and was known as T.S. Eliot Conte. Not T.S. for Thomas Stearns Eliot, in benevolent allusion to the poet, but T.S. as in Tough Shit. Tough Shit Conte. Never said in his company because at 6'3" and 235 muscular pounds with a hard stare, he was feared.

Perhaps it was the hard stare, or his hulking presence, or the shyness which made him speak awkwardly, at best, mostly not at all, with girls he found attractive. At Hamilton he dated only twice in 4 years—though dated is not quite the word to describe the events with Elsie—the 40-something who cleaned his dorm room and vacuumed his pipes, in his room, her mop and pail set into the corner.

In Conte's class at U.C.L.A. there were a few stunning California girls, but just one with a taste for danger—she was nubile, she was lubricious—who would have responded warmly if he'd made even the smallest move, but he didn't, though he thought of her often and masturbated to her image frequently, with the greatest pleasure, especially after he married the woman who wouldn't sleep with him until he walked her down the aisle in Santa Monica, and for whom on their wedding night he could not summon the desire, as they would say in his East Utica Italian-American neighborhood (men and women alike), to bury the salami.

Twenty-one days after the massacre at My Lai 4, Martin Luther King is assassinated in Memphis, Tennessee. When he learns of King's murder on April 5th, Tough Shit Conte predicts to his class, "Robert Kennedy is next"—said without a trace of emotion. Two months later, on the 5th of June in Los Angeles, Robert Kennedy was next.

Despite his fearsome presence, T.S. was a gentle guy who'd done violence just once when, at 13, in a school-yard altercation with a bully who'd gotten the best of him for a year, young Conte managed to pin the enemy to the ground, whereupon he commenced to choke the chubby prick and would have killed him had he not been pulled off just in time. Just once. But after the murders of King and Kennedy he harbored and cherished the thought that maybe bad people need to be taken out, outside the unreliable justice system, whenever necessary. He imagined, many times, doing it himself, with his bare hands. The pleasure. Second only, if that, to an orgasm.

* * *

Calley's platoon, with one exception, despised him. He lacked common sense. He read a map and compass incompetently. He led them into dangerous situations so many times that they felt compelled to call secret meetings to discuss "fragging" him—killing him before he killed them, by rolling a grenade into his tent as he slept. Nine hundred plus cases of fragging were reported in Vietnam between 1968 and 1972, when it became clear to the grunts on the ground that the fight was hopeless, so why should they be put in harm's way by this idiot Calley, especially now that the home front had turned against their service to their country. Fuck you for your service, soldier. Fragging was directed at officers, like second lieutenants.

The single exception among the despisers in Calley's platoon was his radio operator, a true friend, whose job meant that he needed to stay close to Calley, as he did on the day that a VC sniper put a bullet in his kidney and killed him. Had Calley been widely respected it is imaginable that his boys, the 18- and 19-year-olds, would say in response, Let's kill a gook for Calley! Rather than whispering desire to blow up this fuckin' midget. Fuckin' douche bag.

Charlie Company had been in-country for 3 months without contact with the enemy, except when the invisible snipers and mines took a number of its men to the grave, or physically compromised them permanently. Charlie Company was angry. The boys wanted revenge for their buddies and on the evening before they entered My Lai 4 Captain Ernest Medina promised that they'd have it. He told them that the My Lai complex of hamlets and subhamlets had long been established by intel as a VC stronghold. Its inhabitants, if not actual VC fighters, were supporters, sympathizers, sustainers. At Calley's trial, Captain Medina testified that on the night before the My Lai episode, when he gave his instructions, he was asked if he meant civilians, women and children. He testified, "No. You have to use common sense."

Twenty-one soldiers of Company C gave this sworn testimony:

"I said to Captain Medina, you mean everything? Captain Medina goes, Everything. Men, women, children, cats, dogs, everything."

"He said it was all VC and sympathizers."

"He said, Kill everything that moves."

"He told us everything, we was to kill it."

"He didn't want to see anything living but GIs."

"We were supposed to leave nothing walking, crawling or growing."

"He said everybody should be destroyed."

"I said, Could it be a woman? He said, Yes. Could this be a child? He said, Yes."

"There was no innocent civilians in My Lai. That was Captain Medina's point."

"Kill'em all."

* * *

"You don't know MGR? The Merely a Gook Rule. Slopes, dinks, slants, gooks. They're subhuman. Merely gooks you're wasting. Not people."

* * *

"We in the military of the U.S. of A. call all these VC and their supporters, we call them 'Charlie.' Isn't it funny that Company C, our Company, is called Charlie Company? Can our Charlie be as tough as gook-Charlie? Remember, unlike us Yanks, their Charlie don't get no R & R. Their Charlie's idea of R & R is cold rice and a little rat meat. Do we have the balls, *sufficiently* major, to properly deal with that?"

* * *

Conte's class on Hemingway's *In Our Time* was going well. He knew, as he lectured, that it was going well. It was a high to feel it and know it going so well as he was doing it, as if a part of himself stood outside of himself and smiled and nodded as it looked over his shoulder to observe his excellent performance and at the same time observed *her*, the nubile one, in the front row now where she'd never before sat—she, who never from the back row smiled and nodded, as so many eager-to-please students do—now there she is, in the front row, smiling a little, but not nodding. Yes. He was a very good teacher. A very good *sexy* teacher.

They burst in shouting—eight of them. Females and males alike with shoulder length hair, the greasy sheen and clotted strands of which indicated to him that they hadn't washed their hair for a month or more. Maybe never. Or their bodies. And they, West

Coast white bread all, call policemen pigs. Some braless, some of the males shirtless, unshaven. Some in tie-dyed T-shirts, all barefooted. None looking fit—soft, skinny, pudgy. Unshaven underarms and legs of the girls:

POWER TO THE PEOPLE!
HO! HO! HO CHI MINH!
HEY! HEY! LBJ! HOW MANY KIDS YOU KILL TODAY?
HEY! HEY! HO! HO! LBJ HAS GOT TO GO!
MAKE LOVE! NOT WAR!

The nubile one stands and joins the protesters who immediately, and as if in disciplined formation, take a step back, leaving her isolated at the front, whose state of dress and hygiene is conventional. She is The Leader. She is The Alpha Bitch. Silence in the classroom. She points at him, but does not speak.

He says, "Why?"

No response.

He says, "What is this?"

No response.

He says, "Why have you disrupted my class?"

No response.

He says, "What have I done to warrant this disrespect?"

She speaks, "Your shoes."

He says, "What did you say?"

She says, "Your shoes."

He gazes down at his wing-tipped brogues, which cost him more than he could afford.

He says, "What about them?"

She says, "Your tie. Your oxford shirt. Your hound's tooth sport coat with the pseudo-leather patches at the elbows. Was your hair cut at Brooks Brothers?"

He says, "You're here to protest my choice of barber?"

She says, "What you stand for."

He says, "What's that? Enlighten me."

She says, "Murder in Vietnam. Authority."

He says, "I'm a walking-talking symbol?"

She says, "You are."

He says, "I'm only Eliot Conte."

She says, "What are your views?"

He says, "What views?"

She says, "On Vietnam. Do your views match your shoes, daddy?"

He says, "You assume I have views on this war."

At that, the eight protestors leave without a word. Their leader, Cora Kaplan, returns to her seat in the front row.

* * *

She, Cora Kaplan, steps into Conte's office. Shuts the door behind her.

* * *

"There was about 45 people we gathered in the center of the village. It was like a little island, right there in the center of the village. Men, women, children. Babies. We make them squat down. Lieutenant Calley comes over and says, You know what to do with them, don't you? I say yes. I took it for granted he just wanted us to watch them. And he leaves and he comes back 10, 15 minutes later and goes how come you ain't killed them yet? I told him I didn't think you wanted us to kill them, I thought you just wanted us to guard them. He says, No, I want them dead. He steps back 10, 15 feet and starts shooting them. He tells me to start shooting them. So I start shooting them. I pour about 4 clips into the little island. I fire on automatic. You just spray the area, so you can't know how many you killed 'cause they were dropping fast, like flies. Then we round up more. And one of the guys holed up east over in the ravine, the ditch, told us to bring them over to the ravine, so we led them over and by that time we got about 75 people, all gathered up in the ravine, or ditch, whatever it's called, I doubt a ravine and a ditch are completely equal thoughts. So we throw ours in with them and Lieutenant Calley tells me, he says, Meadlo, Paul Meadlo, we got another job to do. And so we walk over to the gooks and he starts pushing them off into the ditch and starts shooting them. It wasn't a ravine. It was a ditch. We start pushing them all off and we start shooting. We just push them all off and just start using automatics on them. Babies in their mother's arms. And so we start shooting them and somebody tells us to switch off to single shot so we could save ammo. So we switched off to single shot and shot a few more rounds and saved ammo. I would say me and the Lieutenant, we shot off about 350 rounds each, and I was crying when we shot into those people in the ditch. The worst fuckin' thing, excuse my language, your honor, a live baby clinging to its dead mother, who had her insides on the outside."

* * *

Cora Kaplan walks over to his desk, leans into him, and says, "You want to fuck me, daddy?"

* * *

"He was a small boy, about three or four years old. He was clutching his wounded arm with the other hand while blood trickled between his fingers. He just stood there with big eyes staring at me like he didn't understand. Then Captain Medina's radio operator put a burst of fire into him."

* * *

Conte says, "What can I say?" She says, "Be honest." He says, "No, I don't want to." She says, "You lie."

* * *

"Just outside the village, there was this big pile of bodies. This really tiny little kid—he only had a shirt on, nothing else—he comes over to the pile, he was bare-assed, and holds the hand of one of the

11

dead. Probably his mother. A G.I. behind me drops into a kneeling position, 30 meters from the kid, and kills him with a single shot."

* * *

Conte says, "I'm going to open the door." She says, "Don't. I wouldn't want my comrades to see me here." It flashes through his mind: *With me on my knees going down on you.*

* * *

"I know you've got to destroy the enemy's resources. It's an old tactic and a good one. Sherman's march to the sea etcetera. You've just got to. They shot and stabbed all animals, which were, in effect, VC support units. One soldier was stabbing a calf over and over. Blood was running from the calf's nose. The calf tried to move toward the mother cow. The G.I. was enjoying it and stabbed again with a bayonet he took off his rifle. Soldiers stood around and watched. Others were killing the baby pigs and all the other cows. God, those cows died hard."

* * *

She says, "Let's talk about Hemingway." He says, "About his sexism, I presume?" She says, "No. Something worse."

* * *

"Eventually we reached the beach. We captured four suspects, one kid, one 15 to 25, one 40 to 55, and a girl in her 20s. They were being beaten hard and the kid named the older man as a North Vietnamese Army platoon leader. Captain Medina drew his .38, took out 5 rounds and played Russian Roulette with him. That's a fact, your honor, before that movie *The Death Hunter*, which people who saw it said made up that Russian Roulette thing. Then he grabbed him by the hair and threw him up against a tree. He fired

2 shots with a rifle, closer and closer to the man's head, then aimed straight at him. The guy starts rapping like hell. He turned out to be an NVA area commander. Then Captain Medina had a picture of himself taken while he drank from a coconut with one hand and with the other held a big sharp knife under the throat of the kid who was gagged and tied to a bamboo tree."

* * *

Then Conte says, "You want to fuck me, Cora?"

* * *

"I saw a G.I. chasing a duck with a knife."

* * *

She says, "The subject, Mr. Conte, is Hemingway. You identify with the mental-case hero of the book. Pathetic. Not tragic like you said this morning. Pathetic. Him and you."

"Pathetic?"

"Reactionary. Complicitous with the MIC."

"The what?"

"The MIC. Military Industrial Complex. Make it a part of your everyday vocabulary, daddy."

"How about another acronym? MACV? That too part of your daily vocabulary, Cora?"

"What's that, Professor Wing-tip?"

"Military Assistance Command, Vietnam. Embrace it. Make love to it."

"Give me a break."

"The MIC. The Pigs. You and your friends deploy abstractions like MACV deploys B-52s in Vietnam at 38,000 feet. You and your friends see nothing and nobody in particular. It's easier that way isn't it?"

"What's easier?"

"To obliterate particular things. Actual people."

"Poor, dad! Did I hurt your feelings when I told you what you represent?"

"When you have an abstraction in your arsenal, Cora, who needs an M-16? You're a killer, Miss Kaplan."

"Afraid of me? Your symbol of radicalism? Or is it something more particular that scares? Don't you want to touch me here, dad?" Slides her hand under her short skirt and moves it to her crotch. She says, "I have my finger in."

* * *

And Lieutenant Calley said: "We weren't in My Lai to kill human beings, really. We were there to kill *ideology* that's carried by—I don't know. Pawns. Blobs. Pieces of flesh. I wasn't in My Lai to destroy intelligent men. I was there to destroy an intangible idea."

* * *

"But I won't touch you."

"But you want to."

"The subject is Ernest Hemingway."

* * *

"Your name?"

"Dennis Conti."

"Present address?"

"Providence, Rhode Island."

"Occupation?"

"Truck driver."

"Do you know the accused?"

"Lieutenant Calley. Right there!"

"What did you do?"

"Lieutenant Calley told us take care of these people."

"What did the people do?"

"Just screamed and yelled."

"What was the condition of the people?"

"A lot of heads shot off. Pieces of heads. They was pretty messed up. Paul Meadlo fired a little bit and broke down. He was crying. He said he couldn't kill any more people. There were a few kids left alive. Lieutenant Calley killed them one by one."

* * *

She says, "Your tone this morning told me you identified with this basket-case Nick Adams, who makes a separate peace. He drops out. In our movement we drop *in*. We *engage*. We fight for *change*. I don't hate America. Do you give one shit about what we're doing in Vietnam?"

"I can't give you a yes or no answer."

"Why not?"

"It's more complicated than that."

"Typical academic. You dropped out."

* * *

"Isn't it a fact you were taking penicillin for venereal disease?"

"No … Oh yeah. You're right. I was getting shots."

"Weren't you under the influence of marijuana on March 16, 1968?"

"No."

"Didn't you smoke it the night before?"

"No."

"Weren't you a constant marijuana smoker?"

"No."

"Did you open your pants in front of a woman in the village by My Lai?"

"No."

"Isn't it a fact that you were going through My Lai that day looking for women?"

"No."

"Didn't you carry a woman, half-nude, on your shoulders, and throw her down and say she was too dirty to rape? You did that, didn't you?"

"Oh yeah, but it wasn't at My Lai."

* * *

In the office, the morning of March 16, 1968, Eliot Conte explained his views to Cora Kaplan, though it wasn't exactly a "view" that he explained so much as it was his strange distance from the war, those who prosecuted it, and those who protested it at home. "Distance," not "alienation," is the word. Had he been alienated he'd have felt something, rather than nothing. If he'd had a "view," it would have implied that he had a set of convictions from out of which he expressed his "view." She told him, after his explanation that did not explain, that she had no idea who he was and he confessed to her and to himself that he didn't either.

This is what he told her: that he watched the nightly news and saw footage of Napalm strikes, bodies, ours and theirs, though when he saw U.S. troops, in the fields of action, those living and dead and wounded, he felt no connection. Even the Vietnam Vet he knew passingly at U.C.L.A., a young man in a wheelchair, did not cause him to feel bonds of pity or sadness or fear. For some reason he thought he'd like to know the man in the wheelchair. Was that a feeling, and if so, what did it mean? He could not say that he supported or opposed the student protestors. He could not say that he supported or opposed the troops over there: "Now you know my so-called views, Cora. My father is a political kingmaker in Upstate New York and what I learned from watching this powerhouse father of mine is that wherever power is, try to hide yourself away from it. A futile effort, but you should try. Be careful, Cora."

She replied, "I was wrong, Mr. Conte. You are not Nick Adams. He rejects *something*. Like Huck Finn he wants no part of civilization. You don't reject or accept anything. Nick Adams finds his separate peace in the natural world, when his mind is plucked out fishing Big Two-Hearted River. He has moments where he becomes his body. The way you described those moments in class today showed me the beauty of Hemingway, and the way you talked told me you never had your mind plucked out."

She wrote a strong final essay on Hemingway and the Erotics of Nature. A year and a half later, when America learned about My Lai, she was gone, transferred to the University of Southern California. He would have liked to talk with her about My Lai and the spread of photos that appeared in *Life*, December 5, 1969—the photos more searing even than the searing text which accompanied them.

He wanted to see her again. She would've plucked his mind out. He was married disastrously, and never saw her again. When he heard from a fellow graduate student who had tried unsuccessfully to date her, that she was engaged to a dentist whose specialty was oral surgery, he took no bitter satisfaction.

* * *

Alongside the ditch of corpses. Around noon.

They remove their helmets. Some smoke. Some relieve themselves. A lone black soldier kneels, facing the corpses, and makes the sign of the cross. Others eat lunch.

* * *

December 12, 1969

The Sylvester Stallone look-and-talk alike—the Vietnam Vet in the wheelchair named Vincent O'Brien—is an undergraduate in the U.C.L.A Theater Department and he's rolling along now just ahead of Conte toward the Café inside the U.C.L.A. book store.

Conte says, "Hey, Vincent."

O'Brien looks up and says, "You remembered."

"What did I remember?"

"Not to call me Vince or Vinny. You'd be surprised how many do. They meet me once, the second encounter they go, How's it going, Vinny? I correct them: My name's Vincent. They immediately shrink in size and disappear inside themselves. A guy in a chair, criticizes a nonchair? They feel bad. I say to one of the shrinkers, Would you feel better in my company if you were also paralyzed from the waist down? So what's up, big guy? You want to talk about 'Nam? My Lai? Because of what came out last week in *Life*, in living color?"

"I do, Vincent."

"You think I hoard unique insight about everything painful? Thanks to the chair?"

"Do you? Coffee?"

"If you're buying. Care to push me? I'm worn out."

Conte pushes him to the café counter where Vincent says, "I could get used to this. You pushing, you buying. Plus it would give you a little guilt-relief. No-'Nam-Conte. Huh? Just a little relief, don't get excited. A spit in the ocean of your guilt for not being there. A cappuccino, Wanda, plus 2 of those chocolate-chip cookies. One for me, one for my pusher."

"A cappuccino, thanks, Wanda."

At the table Conte pulls a magazine from his briefcase. Last week's *Life*, December 5th, which shocked the country and turned public opinion decisively against the war. The student radicals were winning. But the country did not turn against William Calley, who would be the sole person convicted for the slaughter at My Lai 4. Calley was charged September 5, 1969 and would be convicted March 31, 1971 and sentenced to life at hard labor at Leavenworth. One day after arriving at Leavenworth, he is remanded to house arrest at Fort Benning, Georgia, where he enjoys private sessions with his girlfriend. Three and a half years later, he's pardoned by President Nixon, September 25, 1974: Thousands of calls and telegrams to the White House had demanded it. A public opinion poll reports upon his conviction that 70% of Americans believed he was a scapegoat for higher authorities, who had ordered his mission and many more like it—a view held by many Vietnam Vets. 12% said he was a stone-cold killer, not a scapegoat, and 18% had no opinion. A country-style singer out of Alabama cut "The Battle Hymn of Lieutenant Calley," the lyrics of which to the tune of "The Battle Hymn of the Republic" celebrated his patriotism. The new Battle Hymn quickly climbed high on the charts. Many years later, Conte would google it and the music and visuals gave him a disturbing thrill, which he's never been able to understand. Was he a knee-jerk patriot? Pro-Calley? Had he eaten of the grapes of wrath?

A *Time* magazine cover featured a dramatic drawing of Calley under the title, Who Shares the Guilt? The governor of Georgia at the time of his conviction, Jimmy Carter, asked all Georgians to drive with their lights on in the daylight hours for a week, in honor of Calley. When he finally gained his freedom, he married his girlfriend in Columbus, Georgia. The ceremony was the society event of the year.

* * *

Conte opens *Life* to the My Lai article and color photos. He says, "Look. These babies. Bare from the waist down. Those little asses. Look at this: A little boy, maybe 5 or 6 crawling wounded with his even littler brother under him, to protect him. Toward the camera. A soldier, it says, near the photographer, it says he blew those kids away."

Vincent says, "Yeah, but where are all the young men of fighting age, big fella? Ask yourself what that means before losing your shit."

Conte says, "All these people torn apart. What were the children and babies guilty of? Who believes in God after seeing this?"

Vincent says, "Amen to that. But the theory is, the little bare asses grow up to be VC."

* * *

Lieutenant Calley said: "Now what in the hell else is war than killing people? Destroying their homes, their farms, their way of life: that's war. And who in the hell is hurt besides civilians?"

* * *

"What were the children doing?"
"I don't remember."
"What were the babies doing?"
"They was in their mothers' arms."
"Had they made any move to attack?"
"Who, sir?"
"The babies."
"I assumed they was getting ready to."

* * *

Vincent says, "They'll crucify Calley for this."

* * *

Lieutenant Calley said: "A Christ. I heard of a play about me: *Pinkville*. The actor who is me comes to the front and center saying: 'I will not die for your sins again.' I agree with him. I am not a Christ, and if I can stay that way, I'm going to. It may be wretched of me to say this: America asks for a Christ, and I'm not willing to be it."

* * *

Vincent says, "Big fella, ask yourself this question, which how many people who read this *Life* article will ever ask themselves. This polluting of the wells. This burning of their houses. This destruction of food supplies. This killing of all livestock. Where do you suppose working-class soldiers just out of high school from Palookaville, U.S.A. and the big city ghettoes learned to do this?"

* * *

Lieutenant Calley said: "Do not blame the Frankenstein monster."

* * *

Conte says, "This black soldier, Herbert L. Carter, it says here he shot himself in the foot with his .45 because he couldn't do what Calley wanted him to do."

Vincent says, "Keep in mind what a destructive force a .45 unleashes. The pain is immense he was willing to endure in order not to kill that day."

Conte says, "Herbert L. Carter in this picture after he shot himself seems to be smiling."

Vincent says, "Keep in mind for that entire day no one else shot themselves in the foot. They followed the orders of their Lieutenant, who was following orders. Anyone who claims, as Calley's prosecutors will no doubt claim, that Calley went rogue is a liar protecting the upper levels. However awful what those guys did over there, the prosecutors and those they'll protect at the upper levels—you know, the college grads and the West Point types—they are worse: They all suck Satan's dick. Calley did not go insane."

* * *

"The mines that caused groin wounds were pressure released devices that if stepped on exploded vertically. VC soaked shards of metal in feces to promote infection. As if taking off our dicks and balls wasn't enough."

* * *

Conte says, "But following orders doesn't get us out of responsibility. You can't get away with murder because someone above you in the military chain told you to kill civilians."

Vincent says, "VC lived in the villages and hamlets and worked the rice paddies when they weren't killing us. They all look alike.

They all dress alike. Nobody denies this, Conte. The people of My Lai were the fathers, the grandfathers, the mothers, the grandmothers and sisters and little bare-assed brothers of the VC of My Lai. Their supporters. Why wouldn't they be supporters? They were just doing their best, these civilians, to defend home against us invaders."

Conte says, "But the Nuremberg trial established the Standard of Responsibility. If you do an illegal act you can't get off because you were following orders. We are responsible, Vincent."

Vincent says, "The Nuremberg trial established the Standard of Responsibility for the Germans. The losers. The Standard of Responsibility since Nuremberg has never been successfully applied to the U.S.A., and it never will. You're a good man, Eliot Conte. But war circumstances make everybody dirty. Including the good people. Lyndon Johnson? Richard Nixon? They will not go down for this. Calley alone, you watch."

* * *

Lieutenant Calley said: "I liked it in Vietnam. I knew, *I can be killed here*, but I could also be more alive there than in America."

* * *

Vincent says, "I'll tell you what you won't ask, but would like to know. We were walking through a series of rice paddies in water about a foot deep. The rice paddies have a stink. I still smell it. They were working in there as we went through, wearing those conical hats. They reminded me of those pyramids that contain Egyptian royal dead from the olden times. In their black pajamas. I never saw her, but a buddy of mine did when it was too late. A worker behind me had a rifle in a waterproof bag submerged at her feet. She opens up on me. I go face down in the water. Almost drowned. My buddy shoots her to pieces. This is why I'm in this chair. I made war. Now I can't make love. If I knew in advance that one of those workers was weaponized? If I knew, but not which one? I'd have said to my buddies, Let's kill'em all now, while we got the chance. Your coffee cold?"

"Yes."

"Mine too."

"I'll get us fresh cups."

"Thanks."

"Vincent?"

"Yeah?"

"I'm sorry."

"Way down the road some distinguished documentarian will produce a film on 'Nam. Calley and his boys are singled out and scapegoated as murderers. They alone will be called murderers. This distinguished documentarian will win major awards. But in 'Nam, big guy, take it from me. Many Calleys. Many My Lais."

"You're a prophet, Vincent O'Brien?"

"You'll see."

THE PRESENT

Jolted (1)

O N BLEECKER STREET, UTICA, NEW York, outside Café
Caruso, Eliot Conte sits in a beach chair, dozing in the sun.
A car brakes. The driver looks at Conte. Passes on. The same
car approaches from the opposite direction and stops alongside of
him. From the car, a light tenor voice, "Remember me?" Conte
wakes, looks. The man exits the car, careful to keep his distance. The
man says, "Remember me?" Conte shakes his head. The man says,
"Say something. You son of a bitch." The man says, "Seven years
ago. The train from Albany to Utica. I was arguing with the wife.
She was silent. You yanked me up out of my seat by the neck. You
dangled me in the air over my seat. You said, Stop or I'll kill you. I
lost control of my bowels. Say something. You don't look so tough
anymore. You look like shit. I hope you die tomorrow." Conte says,
"I remember." The man says, "I should drive over the sidewalk and
put you out of your misery, but I'm not as nuts as you." Conte nods.
He's nodding.

THE CONTE
VARIATIONS

1

L OOK THE BOOGEYMAN IN THE eye—don't flinch and the terror
will vanish in an instant. After consulting the internationally
distinguished surgeon in Syracuse, Eliot Conte was certain it was the smart thing to do. To glue himself to his computer
screen and watch eleven open-heart surgeries. Cardiomyoplasty.
Atherectomy. Heart transplant. Heart-lung transplant. Aortic valve
replacement. Ascending aortic arch aneurysm. Bypass (double, triple, quadruple.) Transmyocardial revascularization. (What words!)
How quickly it was accomplished, the heart transplant. Ninety minutes—out with the old, in with the new.

He had sat for thirty-five consecutive back-crippling hours of
YouTube on coffee and doughnuts and pizza, and a nap here and
there on the couch. As if that weren't enough, he requested and his
Utica doctor arranged for him to observe, live, an open-heart procedure—aortic valve replacement, the surgery he needed urgently
to undergo. Because he was short of breath walking from his back
door to the car 9 yards away. He couldn't wait to attend the live event
and there he is, costumed precisely like the various medical personnel in the O.R. and feeling like one of them, as he stands behind the
head of the anesthetized patient, a morbidly obese Caucasian male,
as he leans over within 24 inches of the surgical site. It begins: the
neat, initial incision (very little blood). Then the sawing through of
the breastbone and the odor (mild) of burnt bone and the pulling
apart and clamping of the rib cage and there it is, a sudden sea of

red. There it is: Exposed. The beating heart. Smaller than an adult fist. Quickly it's hooked up to the heart-lung machine. An infusion from the heart-lung machine. The beating heart ceases to beat. The defective valve is plucked daintily out: a whitish thing looking like a small blighted spring bloom, replaced by engineered cow flesh. It ends, 3½ hours later, with the pummeling racket of the staple gun, like a gleaming carpenter's tool, as the severed breastbone is put together.

He took in the videos like a coldblooded medical professional: feeling nothing. The up-close observation of an actual surgery was different. "Mind-blowing," he said to his wife. "I had no mind and I was nothing for 3½ hours as the surgical site passed into me and filled me to the brim and over the brim. That's what I was: the surgical site itself, and I never felt better. Like what I experienced 25 years ago in Venice at the Scuola di San Rocco. Those massive paintings of Tintoretto. The one I can't get out of my head to this day 25 years later—just after you pay to enter and you enter and there it is, the first one you see, on your left, the Angel flying with huge white wings through the open window to break the news to the shy young woman, who is not much more than a girl in her teens. In the O.R. and among the Tintorettos I was the Angel, I was the open-chest, the sea of red. I was the open window. Most of all, Catherine, I was the open window as the Announcing Angel sailed through."

She says, "Not the shy teenage girl? Who was wide open?"

"I was wide open. I was the teenage Virgin Mary."

The ravishing memory of Venice persists, but the high of the O.R. does not. Two days later, it gives way to contemplation of the interior meat of the obese Caucasian male—organs and all the rest of it at the edge of death. Observing the surgery was a grave mistake. "Grave" as in pointing directly to the gaping hole and a coffin, his coffin, placed at the bottom, six feet deep, eight long, five wide. The innards of calves and cows and pigs that he helped to butcher when he worked as a teenager in a slaughterhouse. His innards. The innards of the obese Caucasian male. His innards. He hears the thud, thud, thud of the first shovels-full hitting the coffin-lid. Or is it the door as the resurrectionists imagine it? The door that opens at the end of the world and the rotted body and the skeleton broken in so many pieces rising at the end of time: whole, healthy, beautiful, to be welcomed by the Lord and hosts of choiring angels.

He told Catherine that when she'd take their 3-year-old Annie to Albany to visit her parents for a long weekend, once every month, he imagined collapsing dead in the house shortly after she left. When she returned 3 days later she would open the door and be assaulted by the stench of his putrefying corpse. His rotted meat: "Mommy, why is Daddy sleeping on the floor? Wake up, stinky!"

One morning, staring out the window, but not seeing the birds flutter and forage in his backyard, he calculates: 240 cubic feet of dirt equals 16,000 pounds of dirt piled on top of his coffin. Who can heft it from the coffin door? Only the Lord, who he's sure does not exist. Better to burn at 2,000 degrees Fahrenheit for 3 hours. No dirt. No rot. Your flesh consumed in flames and your soul, whose existence you deny, levitating in smoke out the chimney and into thin air.

Those nice Roman Catholics he grew up with, he was one himself, believed cremation a mortal sin because it subverted the Lord's power of resurrection. Because there would be no bones and rot for Our Lord to make whole and forever happy, but the Vatican reminded Catholics that the greatest of all sins for which there was no redemption—a blasphemy worthy of atheists—is to deny the Lord's power to resurrect even out of nothing. For the Lord, son, to overcome cremation is a piece of cake, a walk in the park, a no-brainer for the Infinite Brain, saith the Pope. Our Lord creates *ex nihilo* and He resurrects *ex nihilo*.

Five pounds of ash, or less. A few fragments of bone. Let it all be tossed into the Mohawk, the river running through Utica—the Mohawk which near Albany empties into the Hudson, where the great river flows widening south until it empties into New York Harbor and your ashes and bone chips become far, far, far less than a trillionth of a trillionth of a trillionth part of the Atlantic Ocean.

But what is that? What is it? That red bird with a black band framing its eyes and face and covering the front of its neck and descending part way down its breast where it becomes a black bib, deep black against deep red. Those red feathers that stick arrogantly straight up on the head. What do you call those arrogant feathers? That fat beak looks like it could crack nuts. What is that bird's name?

When he asks Catherine, she says, "You must have seen a male Cardinal. In Lower East Utica? Is it possible? Who knew you could care?"

She was alluding to his bitter early morning grumbles, when Conte-the-bad-sleeper would be rousted at dawn in springtime by the chirping, the singing and the raucous calls of males protecting territory and broadcasting need for amorous contact.

"I hate birds," she'd heard him bitch, not infrequently, as he lurched into the kitchen to make the coffee. "Fucking birds," he'd say.

He tells her that he's ordered the National Geographic Society's *Field Guide to the Birds of North America*. He tells her that he felt "weirdly relaxed" when he saw the red bird.

She replies, "Because the red bird is like a Tintoretto, a new beautiful thing to make you forget yourself."

"You mean the Cardinal, don't you?

She replies, "Let's call it the red bird from now on."

"The red bird of self-forgetting?"

"The course is obvious. The cure."

"What course? What cure?"

"The cure for dwelling on what must come to pass."

He does not respond.

"It will come to pass. You. Me. Annie too."

"Don't say Annie."

"Want to drop the subject? Bury it out of sight?"

"Yes."

"It's not possible to bury it out of sight for good."

"I don't believe in God, but pray that Annie's not taken before we die."

"It happens."

"Do you know what that means, Catherine? Especially when by violence?"

"My God is a son of a bitch."
"Yet you pray."
"You do too."
He says nothing.

* * *

He too much imagines. Too much broods upon the father impotent to halt what fate may have in store for his daughter and he no longer hearing at the house on Mary Street: Again, daddy! Again! As he would hurl her—Annie—hurl her high, Save me, daddy! and catching her, and saving her, at the last second. Save me again, daddy!

One month to surgery.

2

TWO WEEKS BEFORE HIS CONSULTATION with the surgeon at the Upstate Medical Center in Syracuse, he did the relevant Internet research and decided on pig. He concluded that the consultation would therefore be a waste of time and communicated his desire for pig in an e-mail, and asked to have his surgery scheduled.

The distinguished surgeon responded, "Come see me soon or find yourself a butcher to open your chest."

"Butcher" was the doctor's standard description of all other Thoracic-Heart surgeons: past, present, and those yet to be born.

So he made the drive from Utica on the hottest day on record in August in Upstate New York, 109 degrees, the air conditioning in his aged Toyota Corolla out of service. Half way to Syracuse on the Thruway, a sudden violent thunderstorm, visibility zero, his windshield wipers working on slowest speed only. He believes that he's suffocating and opens the four befogged windows in hopes of clearing the windshield and the wind-slanted downpour whips through.

In Syracuse, he walks into the examination room, drenched, hair plastered and matted. A racially ambiguous nurse offers Dr. Frankenstein's Italian-American monster a towel. He declines, saying "I'm good."

The nurse hands him a form and a cheap ballpoint pen attached to a clipboard. The form says: CHECK ALL THAT APPLY. At the top he prints his name neatly: ELIOT CONTE. He reads slowly, thoughtfully reviewing the state of his bodily and mental health. He checks, first, under CONSTITUTIONAL: *chills* and *fevers*. Under EYES: *eye pain* and *visual disturbances*. Under GENITOURINARY: *painful urination, penile swelling, loss of stool*. Beside "penile swelling" he prints neatly: "but not an erection." Under NEUROLOGIC: *facial asymmetry* and *speech difficulty*. Under HEAD, EARS, EYES, THROAT: *ear pain* and *drooling*. Under RESPIRATORY: *choking* and *high-pitched wheeze*. Under CARDIOVASCULAR: *swollen ankles, palpitations*, and *waking up short of breath*. Next to "waking up short of breath" he prints neatly: "often screaming." Under MUSCULAR SKELETAL: *joint aches, problems walking*. Under GASTROINTESTINAL: *anal bleeding* and *nausea*. Beside "anal bleeding" he prints neatly: "More than once in a while. Much more." Under PSYCHIATRIC: *agitated easily, confusion, hallucinations, self-injury, suicidal thoughts*. Beside "hallucinations" he prints neatly: "especially of child-slaughter."

A man in a white coat appears. Fit, brisk, crew-cut. He takes the form, reads slowly, thoughtfully, then folds the form neatly in quarters and hands it, smiling, to the patient, who says, "You're supposed to keep that for the record of my health. Doctor."

The man in the white coat replies, "Under no circumstances."

Then, without prelude, the man in the white coat says, "I quickly slice you open—stem to stern. I saw through the breastbone, yank open the rib cage and gain access and total control. At which point, when I've done exactly what is done at the beginning of an autopsy, but *only* at that point—penile swelling? Drooling, you say?" The formerly robust man, sitting opposite the man in the white coat, sits back at his ease, unfazed.

The man in the white coat says, "Have you guessed my secret? As an undergraduate, I performed with ETG—the Extreme Theater Group. In starring roles. Relax. The incision will only be eight inches long. About like this:" Holds his hands apart a good thirty-six inches. "From here to here." He traces a line with his forefinger from his Adam's apple to his crotch. They laugh. The hollowed-out man, Eliot Conte, heartily—the man in the white coat, mirthlessly.

"Perhaps twenty minutes after we've put you under deeply—you don't want to know how deep—and after I've slashed and hacked and the resident anesthesiologist's heart is in her throat, your heart, Mr. Conte, is in my hands. As it were, Mr. Conte, as it were. At that point, we do it. We connect you to life: the heart-lung bypass machine, which takes over for the afore-referenced organs. Because I choose not to cut on your actual heart when it's actually beating. Hallucinations of child-slaughter? Anal bleeding, you say?"

"But should the heart-lung bypass machine," Conte says casually, with a small smile, "should it fail us catastrophically?"

"*Us*, Mr. C?"

They do a high-five.

"Let me assure you, Mr. C, that the detailed and definitive record of the causes and cures of all catastrophic failures of the heart-lung bypass machine in the United States and worldwide since 1953—when it was invented—including, but not limited to, failure of electronic components, electrical fires, power surges, power outages, brownouts, human error, Acts of God, and acts by medical personnel of premeditated malignancy—this grievous record of catastrophic failure was destroyed in a psychotic episode by the Director of the Mayo Clinic. High-pitched wheezing, you say?"

Conte reaches over to shake the surgeon's hand. The surgeon grasps Conte's hand tightly in both of his and says, with great intensity, "In our final hours, what do we have to shore up against the appalling thought of the Big Nothing? Have you any idea, Mr. Conte?"

"Comedy, doc. Only comedy."

"Farce, Mr. C. Only farce. I have been diagnosed with an inoperable malignancy which will press against and render the heart of this heart surgeon non-functional. Just another of life's shitty little ironies. I have two years. Perhaps less. Mr. C, at this time I'm good to go. Are you?"

"Doc," Conte says, "I look forward to going." He's thinking: all the way into the Big Nothing.

"Your aortic valve is severely compromised."

"Doc, I have no fears."

"You lie. But let that pass. Three choices for replacement. The gold standard, with certain nontrivial qualifications, is the mechanical substitute. According to current thinking, good for the remainder of what might remain of your so-called natural life, no matter how long you might survive the knife. The downside of mechanical, you'll be put on a powerful blood thinner, whose possible side effects include lethal internal—"

"I don't care about the side effects."

"You have nerves of steel? Balls of brass?"

Conte stares him down.

"Excellent! Because with mechanical, the truly maddening side effect is often—how often? You don't want to know. A ticking sound from inside the chest, easily audible at the family dinner table when there is no conversation. Let's be honest: silence at the dinner table is a frequent state of affairs in our families. In other words, the ticking is audible in any sullen context. Two days after your discharge from the hospital, the wife sleeps in the guest room, never to return to the conjugal bed, but for you, in the still of the night, no exit. Screaming, Mr. C? You awake screaming?"

"I don't care about the side effects."

"Excellent! You want mechanical."

"I do not."

The surgeon pauses, nodding: "You don't fear the side effects, but you have an *issue* with a replacement good for the life of the patient, and look forward to the *limited* life offered by options 2 and 3?"

"Yes."

"Let me tell you a story, Mr. C, worth recalling in our final hours on this wretched earth."

"What are my chances of dying on the table?"

"How shall I put this? The good news is that I am not a contract killer."

"My chances, doc."

"I love the feel of a cold scalpel at the break of dawn."

"Doc. My chances."

"Nontrivial."

"25/75 in favor of the Big Nothing?"

"You are elated at such a prospect?"

"I feel good, doc."

"You lie. But let it pass. Now listen to this: A former patient of mine, a bearded Muslim—oh, just another academic fraud—who had married a devout Israeli Jew a decade before and then renounced Islam in all its forms at the grandiose annual meeting of the Modern Language Association—"

"This Muslim terrorist, doc. Alive or dead?"

"The jihadist is dead."

"Under your knife, on the table?"

"On the table. Yes. But not the one in the O.R. At a dinner party, with distinguished colleagues in the Yale English Department. All left of center politically, of course, and full-throated scorners, each and all, of American Islamophobia, who in a curious lull in the conversation concerning all things football, and as the faculty wives and the emasculated faculty husbands sit there mum and hostile, knocking back glass after glass of mediocre wine—they hear it. The ticking. The secret terrorist points to his bulky 300-dollar Icelandic sweater and shouts, 'Allahu Akbar!' as he leaps to his feet and reaches quickly into his pocket for the detonator. The heroic liberal on his right, sensing what was about to occur, seizes the greasy big carving knife used on the succulent goose and stabs him through the jugular. The jihadist, gushering blood, collapses on the ravaged goose. Oh! This Muslim of unfortunate humor!"

The doctor pauses—deliberately, for dramatic effect.

"End of story?" Conte says. "Say it isn't so. Tell me more."

"Two weeks later, with the encouragement of the Yale legal squad and the New Haven D.A., the Grand Jury finds no cause for indictment. A prank turned lethal for the prankster, it is said on cable news. At a press conference, with Yale's president nodding at his side, the D.A. says in all but words, 'The bastard had it coming.'"

"You're making this all up."

"Mr. Conte, I don't do fiction."

"You know this how?"

The surgeon licks his lips slowly: "Mr. C, I heard it all from the Muslim's devout Israeli wife, with whom I was having an affair. I heard it 4 days after his death. In bed."

"Promise to tell this story again just before the anesthesia is administered, from which I may never emerge."

"You hope never to emerge?"

"Promise to tell it."

"Cross my heart and hope to die. Mr. C, options 2 and 3. A new aortic valve made of either cow flesh or pig flesh. Flesh of a pig heart."

Without a second's hesitation, Conte replies, "Flesh of a pig heart."

"The least desirable, sir."

"Pig."

"Cow might last twenty years. Pig ten to fifteen."

"*Might*, doc?"

"Until death, Mr. C, no absolutes."

"Pig."

"To be perfectly honest, Mr. C—"

"Why wouldn't you be, doc?"

"Major studies remain incomplete. Nevertheless, the current thinking is—no, we cannot say definitively—in truth, we may never say definitively that cow is strongly indicated. But I say, cow, cow, cow, with heavily qualified confidence."

"Pig, pig, pig."

"Not unless you wish to undergo a second surgery sooner rather than later, with the risks entailed in any open-heart procedure. If you want that, then, I suspect, that your mental—"

"Who," Conte says, "chooses pig, typically, and why?"

"Patients of surgeons, like me, who have major stock portfolios in North Carolina corporate pig farms. And now you."

"Why, then, did you push for cow?"

"Because, Mr. C, in your case 'C' stands secretly for 'contrary.' Had I said pig, pig, pig, you would have said cow, cow, cow."

"Oink."

"Unconvincing, Mr. C. Now listen to this:" The surgeon proceeds to imitate pig-voice, unlike Conte, authentically, like a pig. The surgeon snorts and roots in the imaginary muck of the pig sty. Very like a pig. Then the surgeon says, in his human voice: "I trust that you wish to live as long as possible in sound physical and mental health."

Conte's response is awhile in coming: "It would appear that the jury is still out."

The consultation is concluded. The surgeon offers a fist bump, "a terrorist gesture," he says, "in memory of the comical Muslim. Loss of stool, you say? The entire load?"

* * *

When Conte leaves the examination room for the parking garage, he heads first and urgently to the Men's Room, to push out there a thin and wobbly stream. He needs to get more out, but his prostate, so long inflamed and enlarged, will not relent and he'll experience a vague, though persistent, urgency to pee for several hours, for which there is nothing to be done. In the elevator now, down he goes into the semi-dark of the parking garage, where he removes his soaked shirt and is about to remove the clammy trousers and underwear, but recalling the elevated position of the African-American toll-taker, who will have an unimpeded view down into his lap, and imagining her saying, I've seen that thing before—or worse, much worse, looking at it and saying nothing at all—he sheds his pants, but not his briefs.

In the car, he taps out an e-mail to the surgeon: Film my surgery in living color. Begin: wide angle shot of you, various medical personnel, me on table unconscious, naked and uncut—nurse shaving genitals, sanitizing penis, inserting catheter. Then: extreme close-up extending thru duration of procedure. Opening of chest, your hands at work as your blue surgical gloves go red. I survive? Send me for post-operative viewing pleasure. Not survive? Keep for your post-mortem viewing of a patient lost. Do you grieve for patients lost, doctor? Would you grieve for me? Think twice of sending to my wife and child, lest they discover what truly lay hidden in my heart.

The doctor responds:

Yes, Mr. Conte, I do grieve. But only for the survivors. He hits "send" and thinks immediately of something he needed to say to Conte. Writes a new email: Sink into others. The only cure.

* * *

Just before the Thruway entrance, Conte pulls over onto the shoulder, reaches for his wallet and removes the photo he took of a beaming Catherine, just prior to undergoing an ultrasound, 3 months into the pregnancy. He replaces that photo and removes a much-folded piece of paper he'd stuffed behind the photo of Annie balanced precariously atop an uncut watermelon. He unfolds the paper: It's the print-out of the grainy ultrasound image of Annie *in utero*. The image that had rendered her a sudden reality and him a father. Forearms resting on his thighs, he drops his head slowly toward his midsection. Slowly, deeply, as if desiring to bury himself in himself, untouchable.

3

"INTIMATE RELATIONSHIPS," HE SAYS, "ARE zero-sum games. You, Catherine Cruz, young and in the pink of health, ever lifeward, while me, Eliot Conte, old, emaciated with heart disease, ever deathward."

"Did you just make that up," she says, "or are you quoting one of those self-lacerating things you enjoy scribbling into your notebook of self-regard?"

They would put Ann Cruz Conte down, a.k.a. The Fiend, at 7 p.m. (always at 7 sharp) and the child would be asleep within a minute or two after she, the mother, Catherine Cruz, would sing a nursery rhyme or two. And The Fiend would sleep without interruption until 5:30 a.m., when she would awake with guns blazing, come to their bedroom, climb up onto the big bed and begin jumping up and down—the bed become a trampoline as she demands "Oscar-Cookie," her way of saying that her father, Eliot Conte, set her up before the TV with the special-highlights video of *Sesame Street.*

She was most pleased, being a Fiend, with Oscar the Grouch, who lived in a garbage can. She loved the Cookie Monster too, who lived, as she would, by cookies alone. When her mother volunteered to set her up with the video, in order to give her semi-insomniac husband another hour of light and virtually worthless sleep, The Fiend would say: "No! Daddy!"

At 6:30 a.m., the video concluded, the child would return to her parents' bedroom, climb up onto the trampoline, jump up and down and demand that her mother "make me sautéed cheerios! Now!" She would accept no substitutes. Not even ice cream. Because she was a Fiend.

Three-year-old Ann Cruz Conte has been called The Fiend by her amazed parents since birth, when just emerged, blood-smeared, from her mother's body she was placed on Catherine's belly, where she proceeded to crawl, less than 3 minutes old, her tit-radar fully operative, directly to her mother's breast and the nipple on the right side—to root and suck. There would be no milk for 3 days, but The Fiend was undeterred from going at it with ceaseless vigor.

Catherine Cruz and Eliot Conte were thrilled by the Satanic fierceness of their daughter's will. Love for this child welled up so much that they sometimes called her The Arch-Fiend—that is, Satan himself. Her first word was BO!, which they thought cute and funny, even though it was expressed with more than a touch of hostility—much more—and directed at ma-ma and da-da. Soon they understood that BO! was the initial rejection, at 10 months of age, of their authority and even, they speculated, of their parentage: an attempt to say NO! in thunder. They were simply delighted, they could think of nothing better than to be resisted by their child, as Satan had rejected God Himself, and they were confident that in the life that lay ahead for her, in a too often difficult world, she would prevail. Catherine would say "too often difficult." Her emotionally-troubled husband would say "too often terrible." They wanted to make another Fiend or two, and turn their house into a veritable Inferno, but it didn't happen.

On this particular night, after the demon, the devil, has been asleep for 2 hours, Catherine tip-toes into her room, then tip-toes back out, hand over heart. Conte whispers, "All quiet on the Western front?" Catherine whispers in reply, "The coast is clear." Then they tip-toe into their bedroom, which shares a not-well-insulated wall with the room of The Fiend and proceed to slip under the covers to cuddle tight and naked. Because, in Conte's mind, "at least that," if nothing more, but maybe, but perhaps, who knows, possibly what in his mind he thinks of as "the main event." Twenty minutes later, Conte rolls over onto his back, stares at the ceiling and says, "Nothing again."

She resists, but barely, a near-overwhelming desire to sock him in the jaw and instead says, "What we were doing? Nothing?"

Both lie flat, uncovered and naked, and cannot see the demon-daughter standing at the threshold, holding her ravaged fringed blanket.

He says, "Death is a gift that I have not yet earned."

"You're eager to earn death? What we did was nothing?"

He doesn't respond.

She says, "Annie is something. I hope I'm something. The three of us together are something. Are we not?"

After a long pause, he says, "Do you think that I have a weak chin? I think that I have a weak chin."

"I asked you a serious question about our family. That's your answer? Have you lost your mind?"

"Uh, the one before me. Your first husband, according to what you once said had a weak—"

She cuts him off. "Asshole, not husband."

"You once said The Asshole had a weak chin."

"You do not. Idiot."

"Maybe, Catherine, you just don't want to say the words. May I suggest a politically correct alternative? How about saying, Eliot, you are differently chinned?"

"Christ."

"At the mall yesterday, a 3-way mirror told me the terrible truth. Is it not the case that I am the backup?"

"Backup for what? Idiot."

"For The Asshole. Because you're obviously drawn to chinless wonders, who suffer from a genetic abnormality signifying flaccidity of character."

She says, "Okay. I'll play along. There are weak—I mean, differently chinned women too. What does that say about a woman?"

"Much vocal sound and fury, signifying nothing."

"Bastard."

Ann has been taking off her clothes and now she's running to the bed. She climbs up. Eliot tries and fails to cover his nakedness. The Fiend is pointing at his penis and demanding to know, "What is that little BIG thing?!"

Conte says, "Uh."

Ann says, "I'm going to STEP on it! I want to KICK that damngod thing!"

Conte says, "Where did you learn that naughty word, sweetheart," as if he didn't know where her mangled curse came from. He and Catherine pull the covers to their waists.

"You learned me, Daddy. Mommy learned me too."

"We shouldn't say that word, sweetheart. None of us."

"Why?"

"Because it's naughty."

"Damngod!"

"Ann."

"DamnFUCKgod!"

"Oh, Annie."

Catherine says, "You taught her well, Conte."

"*Me*?"

She says, "We'll all be in a sh-boat load of trouble when she brings your mouth to pre-K next year."

"*My* mouth?"

"CONTE! CUNTY!"

"Please, Annie, don't say those words anymore."

"Daddy, why are you crying?"

"I am certainly not crying, sweetie."

"Yes you are!"

"Why do you think so?"

"Your FACE is crying! I'll shoot you!"

"Do you see tears?"

"No! Your FACE is dying!"

"You mean … crying, don't you?"

"Yes! Your face is dying. You said det."

"Det?"

Catherine whispers in his ear, "She heard you say the gift of death."

"You said det is a gimp! I heard you!"

"Mom, is my face crying or dying?"

"I could go either way."

"Thanks, Mom. Please make us all hot chocolate."

"You're not helpless, Conte."

"Just hopeless."

"Just lazy. I'll make it for you two. Causes me extreme constipation."

"ConsterNAtion, Mommy!"

"Yes," Cruz says, "it certainly is," and exits to the kitchen.

"Mommy said in the telephone we striked it BITCH."

He says, "*On* the telephone. Not *in*. *On*."

"BITCH!"

"We struck it rich, is no doubt what she said, dear."

"I'll cut you, Daddy! We'll put his malls in a nice. In the telephone she said."

"Don't say you'll cut me, dear. Or anybody. Or shoot me. Or anybody."

"We'll put his MALLS in a NICE!"

"Your mother and I are terrible models."

"His MALLS!"

"Annie, malls are where we go shopping and to gaze in horror into 3-way mirrors. On the other hand, what you're trying to say is … uh, never mind."

"Stop dying, Daddy."

"At this time, I'm neither dying or crying."

"When are you dying, Daddy? Can I die too? Daddy? Stop looking at the ceiling."

"Your mother didn't say malls or nice. I'm … I'm afraid those are not the words she said."

Catherine stands at the threshold with 2 cups of hot chocolate.

"Why are you afraid, daddy? Because you are dying?"

"Among other reasons."

"Who brings you the present, Daddy?"

"Present, Annie? Who brings it? Why, ourselves. It's good to be present. It's the only hope. All else is doom."

"What did you say, you silly?!"

"Uh."

"Silly! The presents of SANTA Claus! The gimp of det. DET! I want det too!"

Catherine mumbles "goddammit" and comes to the bed.

Ann points to the hot chocolate that Catherine offers her, and says, "I don't want that SHIT! I want MAMA Bunny."

Conte says, "I swear to God, Catherine."

"You believe in God, Conte? Since when?"

Catherine fetches Mama Bunny, formerly white, now gray and frayed, like her husband, but Ann is fast asleep. A miraculous first. Because the demon does not nap.

Catherine, now with quiet intensity: "We have to be proud of our daughter's insights. Why are you crying, daddy? She has to ingest your grief at 3 years of age? Our only job, now that she's in our life, is to hide our grief from her. I did my job. Do yours. You want to die? Because you have heart trouble the seriousness of which you exaggerate? Because your dick doesn't work the way it so-called used to? It did 3 weeks ago. Because you're spending your time online driving yourself into daily rages about political garbage? But you don't vote. You are without politics. You don't have cancer. Two months ago we checked out your paranoia for 52,000 dollars at Sloan Kettering. Because, I'll tell you why. You let depression the last 2 years steal your appetite. That's why you lost too much weight."

"Norman Mailer said depression causes cancer."

"Conte, who the fuck is Norman Mailer?"

"Some writer who in 1968, at the height of the Vietnam War, wanted to participate in the levitation of The Pentagon."

She makes the sign of the cross and says, "I don't know what to say about that. You admire this Mailer quack? Because you identify with writers? You're all a bunch of quacks. (She makes air quotes.) Artists. (She makes air quotes again.) Artists. I love you anyway in spite of your (air quotes) artistry."

"Thanks, Cruz."

"Get serious. Let's not contaminate our daughter. You're saying, you don't care one way or the other if you live or die. Show your darkness to me. Because in the end, I don't matter, one way or the other. Does any wife to any husband?"

"You matter. No one ever mattered more. But no one saves anyone, especially in intimate relationships, where salvation is routinely expected and salvation is bitterly and routinely thwarted."

"Okay, Professor. If you say so."

"Go ahead, mock me, but Annie needs one invulnerable parent and I don't measure up. Be happy to go to your grave without letting The Fiend ever see you in your darkness."

"You mean, Eliot, don't let her see us in our complete humanity?"

"Exactly what I mean. But I've already failed her."

"So, Eliot, as she moves into the awful teen years of sensitivity and then adulthood and from time to time feels hopelessness, as everyone does from time to time, she can think of her long-dead parents as gods who—"

"Not me, Catherine, *you.*"

"Those god-like parents who rode the bucking broncos of life without ever falling off and—"

"Bucking broncos of life? Catherine, are you writing? Becoming (air quotes) an artist? If you are, be afraid. Be very afraid."

"Shut up, Eliot. And then she feels like a loser who let her parents down? And then she spends the rest of her life and tens of thousands on shrinks?"

"I have nice hair."

"What?!"

"So, Cruz, she says to me, You have nice hair."

"Who said that to you?"

"Someone."

"It's true. You do."

"Aren't you jealous?"

"I don't have that gene."

"So then, she runs her fingers through my hair."

"Who?"

"Be jealous. Fake it if you must. It'll help restore my manhood. It was the audiologist adjusting these vanity-destroying devices. These markers of my mortality."

Conte strokes his chin. He says, "If I grow a beard, it'll beef up the appearance of my chin and I'll feel better in the crisis of the 3-way mirror."

"Did she, this hot audiologist—"

"I never said 'hot,' although, as a matter of—"

"Did she inhale your musk?"

He laughs a true laugh, from the belly, which wakes The Fiend who says, "Daddy, I want one of those little BIG things for Christmas. Like the one you got. Can I have yours until Santa comes?"

"Santa hasn't … come lately, I'm afraid."

"What did you say, silly? I want Santa to COME!"

Conte tickles Annie. Catherine tickles Conte. Conte tickles Catherine. Annie tickles her mother. Annie tickles her father. They each try the impossible—to tickle themselves. This goes on for some time, as they laugh themselves to death.

Three weeks to surgery.

4

CATHERINE CRUZ AT THE BREAKFAST table brooding on the memory of her husband and herself in conversation: how they used to be like long-time tennis pals at opposite sides of the net, nice and easy, back-and-forth—neither trying to hit an outright winner—neither unleashing a silence-enforcing conversation-killer, because they only wanted to keep the ball in play. For as long as possible. Just keep it in play. Forget the mechanics of the strokes. Forget everything. Including yourself. Because in the rhythm of conversational back-and-forth you become the rhythm, and life outside the rhythm disappears. That's the way it was, before he was hit by the news of heart disease.

On this, as on many recent mornings as she butters her wheat toast and stirs her coffee, she's on edge, anticipating rupture. They'd been chatting about their daughter's gifted pre-K teacher. How Annie couldn't wait to get to school to see her. How reluctant Annie was to leave her playmates at the end of the day. And what a comforting sign it was for Annie's future as a self-sufficient adult in a nasty world. In the absence of her parents, for six hours, Monday through Friday, at age 3, she was showing signs of fierce independence.

"She will grow up to be strong," Catherine said.

"Stronger than her father," her father said.

Then without taking a breath and without the briefest of pauses he says:

"It's female fear, isn't it?"

(She thinks, Here we go again. To what end, not even God knows.)

"It's the primal smile of female fear, isn't it? Meet someone you barely know, she smiles. Pass someone on the street you never saw in your life, she smiles. Why do women do this? Fear of men?"

(He said to me last week, Catherine, my face has collapsed. I told him, Not true, but it's true. My face too, a little. My tits now, a little. He said his worthless balls were dragging on the floor and fears stepping on them. We laughed. Talks crazy talk so he won't have to think thoughts he doesn't want to think, but thinks them anyway. Don't step on my balls, Catherine. Sometimes we laugh. Mostly we don't anymore. In 20 years I'll be playing soccer with these tits.)

She swallows her concern and reacts as if he were playing the game they used to play before his troubling diagnosis, but she can detect no hint of play in his demeanor, as he shifts his gaze from her to his coffee cup, and holds it there, as she responds:

"Not women in general, Eliot. Only those countless ones attracted to you. That's why they smile."

He replies, peevishly, "Don't mock. Women have never been much interested. Name me one name. With the exception of Cora Kaplan."

"Who's Cora Kaplan?"

"Long ago and far away."

He lifts his gaze directly to Catherine: "One name."

She says, a little sadly, "Catherine Cruz."

He says, "You don't count."

She pauses. She says, "I don't know what to say about that."

"You don't count. Because you're the deluded exception to the rule. So let's not get personal."

"Let's not," she says, "but I am a person."

(Does he see me? Got my hair cut 2 inches shorter, 2 weeks ago. He never said a thing.)

"Catherine, you're lethal. You're an erotic no-smiler. Men and women want you to kill them."

"You don't seem slain."

"I dropped dead the day I first saw you."

"I should be flattered, Conte."

"You're not. Why not?"

"More coffee?"

"I charge you with involuntary manslaughter, Cruz."

"May I pour you more coffee, Eliot?"

He doesn't respond.

"More coffee … dear?"

(He shuffles now when he walks. Looks at floor as he shuffles through the house. Suddenly aged.)

"In restaurants, Catherine. Constantly in restaurants. All women under 80. They smile. From taxis in midtown Manhattan, stuck in grid-locked traffic they stare out at all the lonely people on the sidewalk and smile radiantly and cause all the ages and the numerous genders on the sidewalk to yearn hopelessly because they know they will never see her again. Rodge. So forth."

"Rodge?"

"Obviously. Rodge. How many times have we seen it? Rodge. The U.S. Open? Watching the finals when the bored cameraman who loves Federer, but hates tennis, pans to the spectators until he finds a long-haired blond, beautifully tanned and wearing 380-dollar Prada sunglasses, who smiles with thrilling sophistication, and without a shred of feeling. Where does she get off?"

(He stares. He showers twice a week. Doesn't reek, somehow. Combs his hair occasionally. We have a 3-year-old, I tell him. She needs you. He just stared at me.)

Catherine withholds her response to the Roger Federer nonsense and then decides to say: "You've not touched your cinnamon-raisin bagel."

"Because I don't want my cinnamon-raisin bagel."

"But you love cinnamon-raisin bagels."

"The thought of a cinnamon-raisin bagel gives me nausea. A feeling right here, tight in the throat. I feel a gag coming on."

(Trying to be funny? Good sign if he is. I'll try too.)

She says, "Far above the surface of the earth, at 38,000 feet, in a transcontinental jet, Scarlett Johansson is sipping champagne in first class, in the window seat. Where is Scarlett going? Only Scarlett knows. You stand on Mary Street as her plane passes overhead. Scarlett is smiling down upon you, on Mary Street. You look up. Scarlett is waving. You wave back to her 38,000 feet above and belt out *Some sunny day, we'll meet again, don't know where ... don't know when ...*"

He's not amused. Says nothing.

"What? You don't care for Scarlett?" She mimes an elegant backhand slice. She says, "Hit the ball back, Conte."

He says, "The bionic ear."

She does not, because she cannot, respond.

He says, "673 dollars. This afternoon. FedEx. The bionic ear."

She cannot respond.

He replies to her silence by hitting another ace: "479 dollars and ninety-five cents. The Nikon Monarch 7. With your God's help, in the same FedEx truck. Binoculars. High-end bird-watching equipment, like the bionic ear."

She says, "I see."

"Do you?" he says. "Do you really?"

"Am I making you angry, Eliot?"

"375 dollars," he says. "Deadly up to 25 yards. In other words, the depth of our backyard. This afternoon, I pray. An extremely high-powered pellet rifle with a scope. With your so-called God's help. FedEx."

She says, "To kill birds, Eliot?"

"You'll see."

She stands and says, "Someone with an accent that I can't place left a message on the answering machine at the agency. I need to go now or I'll be late for the meeting."

(Is shuffling a sign of oncoming Parkinson's?)

Unable to help him in his distress, she leaves, in distress. She's out the door. He picks up his cinnamon-raisin bagel, slathers on butter and blueberry preserves, and eats with gusto.

Two and a half weeks to surgery.

5

HAD THERE BEEN AN ELEVATOR at 663 Bleecker Street where the agency is located one door west of The Florentine, in a four-storey brick with a neo-Renaissance façade, Catherine Cruz would not have taken it. On old Bleecker, no elevators and only 663 sports an elegant façade: 9, 13, 15 living in a single apartment. Welfare. Food Stamps. Social Security. For those with jobs: yearly salaries of $25,000 and hopes to last beyond a year without health insurance.

She's flying two steps up at a time on a morning already at 90 degrees at ground level—the temperature rising and the air dying as she ascends the narrow stairwell, the air less and less breathable at the top, at the fourth-floor office, but except for a fine bead of moisture along the hairline she's not broken a sweat. She's breathing easily. Catherine Cruz is fit—and not just for stair-climbing in crushing weather.

A Vietnamese woman in her early 60s awaits at the door:

RINTRONA & CRUZ FOR DISCRETION
PRIVATE INVESTIGATION

Three cigarette butts at her feet and a fourth in hand mostly smoked down. "Smoke screen," literally. Cruz, a former two-pack-a-day, shows no repugnance. She shows nothing.

She says, "Here to see me? You left a message?"

"You are a special policeman?"

"That's a way of putting it."

"The normal police laugh when I call 911."

"You are?"

"Lilly Thieu. You will help me soon?"

"Put that thing out and we can talk inside."

"No cigarette inside?"

"No cigarette inside."

Lilly Thieu steps on the cigarette, pulls out the pack and says: "You want one too? Outside?"

"No."

"No smoking in your life?"

"Formerly."

"Formerly? Special American brand? Very expensive?" Lilly-with-a-sad-face laughs.

Catherine is amused, but shows nothing.

"I don't have too much money to pay."

Catherine shrugs her shoulders. She says, "Let's not worry about that now."

"When do we worry? You are serious in your face. Like a judge. Your honor, are you Rintrona?"

Turning the key: "Cruz. Catherine Cruz. After you."

The one bedroom apartment on the fourth floor—now the office of Rintrona & Cruz—was formerly occupied by a 102-year-old woman who had lived there alone for 37 years with a series of cats, the last of which whose body—and hers—was discovered in putrefaction, one week after death. Rintrona said after they signed the lease: "Cat murder and suicide." Barren except for the rusty metal desk and swivel chair—phone, fax, computer, legal pad, cheap ballpoint pen, two chairs for clients, a mini-fridge (empty), and a large floor fan which Catherine switches on. The ancient hardwood floors are scarred everywhere and discolored here and there by cat urine, perhaps the 102-year-old's piss as well, and maybe blood and other bodily fluids best understood and described by a forensic pathologist. On the wall behind the desk, hung against gaudily-flowered wall paper, a 14 x 16 photo of a woman in her early 20s, with big carrot-colored hair: Midwestern wholesome, the pretty girl next door of the 1950s.

Catherine goes down the hall and opens the window to let in the non-existent breeze. Then comes back to open the two front windows with a view onto Bleecker, for non-existent cross-ventilation.

Lilly Thieu, an aficionado of an earlier Hollywood, thinks the carrot-top looks like somebody. She says, pointing to the photo on the wall: "She reminds me of that Maureen O'Hara, that's who. Is she that Maureen O'Hara who was in love with John Wayne in that movie I can't remember the name?"

Cruz wants to dismiss this woman quickly, but how? She says, "Maureen, yes. But not the one in the movies. How can I help you?"

"Do you know the movie I'm thinking?"

"Tell me how I can help you. Please."

"Which Maureen is she? On the wall over there?"

"Irrelevant. State your business. Somebody's wife. She's deceased. Now let's—"

"She died? What a shame."

"Please."

"She's your wife, maybe?"

Cruz thinks she's funny—someone worth playing along with on another dead morning in Utica. Maybe this lively Vietnamese will lighten her week. She needs the week, the last month, the last 2 years, with Conte in persistent mid-winter mood, redeemed. She tries to suppress a smile, but fails. She says: "She's not my wife. I don't have a wife. I have a husband. Now may we—"

"Is your husband male or female? Because I'm thinking you are very contemporary, a sexually open-minded person of intelligence. You want a cigarette and we can go together outside and smoke together outside in peace and discuss your husband? Whose gender you keep to yourself?"

"Mrs. Thieu."

"I am no more married. I had enough of that."

"Please. State your business."

"Are you already charging me 100 dollars per hour and every fracture thereto?"

"Any *fraction thereof.*"

"How much do I owe you already?"

"No charge until we take your case. What do you wish to talk to me about? Spit it out, Lilly."

"I spit out my daughter, who won't talk to me."

"Lilly. We don't at this time, nor will we ever in the future offer family-counseling services. What we offer here is—"

"And now my daughter has disappeared."

Cruz says, "How long has it been since you've seen your daughter?"

"One day."

"I gather your daughter is not a teenager?"

"43 years old."

"Her address?"

"The same as mine. 663 Bleecker Street. The third floor."

"How long since she ceased talking to you?"

"Two days she ceased."

"She stopped talking to you 2 days ago and you haven't seen her for 1 day. What was your last interaction like?"

"We became cats and dogs."

"Lilly. I'm sorry that the police laughed at your situation. They shouldn't have laughed, but they do have a point. A woman of 43 living at home with her mother is not considered missing after one day unless there is clear evidence of—I don't like to say this—of foul play. Contact us in 4 or 5 days. If she hasn't ... Has she ever gone miss—has she ever not come home for the night?"

"Never for 13 years."

"Her name?"

"Rhonda Thieu."

(Cruz makes a note.)

"Thank you. Contact us again if you need to. Wait 4 or 5 days. I know it will be hard."

Lilly, her face fallen in grief: "I think you are saying between the words that I am hysterical."

"Lilly. We're both mothers. I understand your worry. My advice—don't sit at home smoking alone. Go out and do ordinary things. Get your hair and nails done. Have a coffee at Caruso's. Have a smoke in the open air with others. I'm confident Rhonda will be back soon."

"You are giving me now family counseling for free?"

Lilly takes an envelope from her purse, pushes it across the desk and says, "You will need this, in 4 or 5 days. Picture of Rhonda."

Lilly Thieu is at the door when Catherine says, "The title of that movie we couldn't recall. It just came to me. *The Quiet Man*."

Lilly responds, "After what I had, I could use one, but the best quiet men are under the ground and very happy to be there."

* * *

Catherine goes to the window to gaze down on what Conte calls "ex-Bleecker Street"—the Italian-American main drag through the East Side whose sole traces are preserved at Caruso's and The Florentine, twin oases of nostalgia and rueful comic banter.

Catherine Cruz, child of illegal Mexican immigrants, gazes down on new Bleecker with no nostalgia and with some pleasure. There they are: the pants-saggers of all races, the densely tattooed, the earringed teenage boys and young men of all races with rainbow-colored hair. Puerto Ricans and other Hispanics, African-Americans, actual Africans, Bosnians (whose pants never sag), Vietnamese, and sporadically they come too, the Florentine Faithful—the Italian-Americans and Lebanese pushing 80, and beyond, seeking cappuccino and distraction at the end of their lives.

Lilly Thieu down there now smoking at the curb as she leans against an idling, new Mercedes-Benz, whose driver checks her smartphone in air-conditioned comfort. The driver is dressed on this blistering morning as if for a night out at the sort of restaurant or elegant night spot nowhere, anymore, to be found in Utica.

Catherine at the window, Who is that rail-thin man approaching Lilly as she lights up off the butt of the one in her mouth? He's saying something. She offers him one. Bastard! Snatched the pack, he's running. Bastard! Lilly takes off her shoe, rears back, but thinks better of it.

Catherine leans out of the window cursing obscenely—watching the bastard disappear east on Bleecker, out of sight—shifting her gaze now back to Lilly Thieu who's frozen with shoe held high in her left hand behind her head—Lilly still as a picture—right arm extended and lifted, elbow crooked slightly—a statue of a left-handed quarterback whose mouth is agape in amazement, Lilly rendered stone-like by what she sees in the direction of the absconding thief and forgetting utterly that she has a shoe held high in her left hand, as she stares stunned by what Catherine cannot now see: the absconding thief running east fast toward a man walking west on Bleecker—a big gaunt man with uncombed hair, six days unshaven and grinning ear to ear, so delighted because he's seen the incident unfold with Lilly frozen still, the forward pass unreleased and he, this gaunt man, delighted doubly, deeply, because an email from the surgeon in Syracuse has delivered strangely consoling news— and the absconder converging now on the gaunt man and this is what he, the thief, sees: a crazy-looking grinning giant unwilling to relinquish his position in the middle of the sidewalk and coming forward heavily in a lurching gait intent on violent collision, who, this big gaunt man, seeing nothing now before his eyes because he's abstracted from the actual scene as he reflects contentedly on looming medical disaster (his) grinning ear to ear as Lilly sees this—the absconding son of a bitch dropping the stolen pack of cigarettes and in the same moment attempting a sharp dodging move toward the curb in order to avoid the oncoming crazy big man, which is how he sees him, a big gaunt grinning mad man, but the son of a bitch absconder can't accomplish the sharp darting move to his right to the curb because he's incapable of the agile moves of a slashing running back eluding the onrushing huge vicious tackler because he's just a rail-thin uncoordinated brittle fifty-year-old miserable bastard whose maneuver to the curb fails him totally as he crashes to the sidewalk three yards short of the lunatic, this Avenging Angel who comes from the nether region to punish him for his crime against an old woman bereft of cigarettes and daughter—this Avenger who does not break stride—who no longer shuffles—whose vitality has somehow been restored—who without breaking stride and with surprising nimbleness for a sixty-five-year-old heart patient stoops and scoops up the dropped pack of smokes in one continuous motion without slowing down or breaking stride as he approaches the Statue of Lilly, who begins to relax as the Guardian Angel arrives, she's dropping her passing arm and the football to her side, dropping her shoe to the sidewalk, stepping into her slip-on, her mouth still agape—and this is what Catherine can now see—a gallant man presenting Lilly Thieu with her crushed pack of smokes and Lilly accepting it with amazed incredulity.

Eliot Conte and Lilly shake hands. They talk.

Catherine shouts down, "Eliot!" to no avail because her voice is covered by the long boom under a darkened sky, of sudden rolling thunder.

She shouts again, "Hey! Conte!"

He looks up, waves, gives her the thumbs up.

Lilly is asking him a question. He nods. She asks another question, pointing up to Catherine at the fourth-floor window. He answers.

Lilly responds, "You are her male husband?"

Conte says, "I'm her husband, with intermittent male potential and even less actualization."

She says, "Oh! What a shame! Myself, I am just the mother."

Ninety-five degrees, intense humidity, a few sprinkles of rain, then a downpour as they duck into 663 and begin the ascent to the fourth floor.

Newly vitalized Conte is nowhere now in evidence as he labors on the first and second flights, sweating, short of breath on every step. At the third floor landing, Lilly says, "You need rest in my apartment." He nods. They enter. He sits. She offers coffee, "No thanks." "Tea?" "No, thanks. Just water." She notices the light flashing on her answering machine. She delays listening until she brings him a glass of water. She plays the message:

Mey [Mom], it's me, Rhonda. I love you. In a few days, I'll come home to leave home permanently and pack my stuff. I met a wonderful man from Iraq and will live with him until one of us, him or me, passes. Don't worry about a thing. I'm safe and sound. I'm very sorry I was mean to you. As I stated, don't worry. I love you and hope you still love me.

Lilly says, "Now we can tell your female wife my detective problem is solved free of charge, but my family counseling needs to begin soon because I have lost my child," which is what she says, verbatim, in tears, to Catherine in the office of RINTRONA & CRUZ, then adds, "I'll leave you two lovely birds by yourselves," and Conte says, "You mean love birds, Lilly?" Lilly replies, "I hope so," and leaves.

Catherine says, "You look chipper. Something wrong?"

He laughs—an unusual occurrence for the last 2 years—and replies, "It all arrived an hour ago. My birding equipment."

"Tell me Conte, what is a bionic ear?"

He explains that it was an invention intended to aid the severely hearing impaired, the functionally deaf, but that birders use it to pick up bird chatter and song at distances of 400 yards: "The bionic ear leads us to the eye candy."

"And those expensive binoculars?"

"They bring birds 300 yards off to 20 feet."

"So you intend to wander the East Side seeking far-off eye candy, but the pellet rifle with a scope that you say is deadly up to 25 yards, the depth of our backyard, what's it for?"

"Squirrels who defeat all squirrel-proof bird feeders which I've yet to buy and set up." He pulls a piece of paper from his pants pocket saying, "These are my options from reputable websites: pest-off, squirrel-buster, squirrel-be-gone, squirrel-stumper, squirrel-baffle, squirrel-defeater. Then there's those advertised on a Bulgarian porn site, which may not in fact be intended to thwart squirrels: ram-and/or ream-a-squirrel and my choice, fuck-a-squirrel-hard. Then, of course, there's always Mickey."

"Who's Mickey?

"The next-door cat."

"You know his name? Who pisses nightly on our car tires and the back door? The stench is ineradicable."

"I once saw Mickey get one in his teeth by the end of its tail. If Mickey loosens his grip and lets go in order to pounce and crush its neck, the squirrel can make a getaway. Mickey knows this. So there they are in a hopeless standoff. The squirrel leaning and straining forward, Mickey pulling back. The squirrel escaped. Know why? Because the entire tail detached from its body. Broke off at the base."

"How awful!"

"Nah—squirrels' tails grow back, but until they do their ability to execute perilous leaps, safely, high up in the trees, is compromised. They tend to forget their aeronautic disability. They tend to take great falls to death and I say hurray for Mickey! Not long after the incident of detachment, Mickey's hiding under a bush in our yard. I saw this: a robin swoops low near the bush, Mickey springs out of hiding and snags him with one hand. I surmise that the robin was a daddy looking for a worm to bring back to the nest in the tree at the rear of our property. Which is now a single parent nest. The mother can't feed herself and the 3 nestlings. She will abandon her babies and they will die. Because of Mickey."

"Tell me you don't intend to shoot Mickey. Those kids next door would be heart-broken."

"Mickey will be spared. I intend to shoot the squirrels who can't be baffled, stumped, rammed and/or reamed, and who escape Mickey's lethal jaws."

She says, "So you're in a chipper mood because of this whole bird adventure you're about to embark on?"

"Something else too." He pauses.

"Spit it out, Conte."

"I got a message from Syracuse. From my heart surgeon." He looks at her.

"And?"

"A corrected MRI report from the radiologist indicates not only aortic valve insufficiency, but also something else, more interesting. The ascending aortic arch. Basically a blood channel. It's dilated. They call it an aneurysm."

"What's that? The aneur ... What?"

"Aneurysm. A hard word to spell. What it means, a part of the arch is ballooning out. Dilating. My valve insufficiency gives me shortness of breath. This aneurysm is symptomless and always will be until it ruptures, at which point unless I'm very near an ER, where emergency open-heart can be done, it's over."

She's speechless.

He says, *La commedia é finita.* He says it serenely. "Right now I am very close to where rupture happens. The surgeon will replace the valve and repair the arch with indissoluble Dacron. Six hours under the knife."

"So he'll do the scheduled surgery for the valve in a few weeks and at the same time do the aneurysm."

"He's pushed up the surgery. Two weeks from now. Because of the dangerous condition of the aneurysm. He said, 'We don't want to get burned deep down field.'" Conte laughs.

"You're in danger for your life and this lifts your spirits?"

"I'm certain of the beginning, less certain but certain enough of the middle, and now I can see the looming end—with my entire life before me like a well-made literary plot."

"This lifts your spirits?"

"I'm grateful for the clarity."

6

S HE WANTS TO BELIEVE THAT her husband's sense of humor is
a life-affirming sign. That he could not possibly be in despair.
Can you be funny and not want to live? Comforting thoughts,
when she has them, until she doesn't and is slammed to the floor by
the unshakeable belief that he'll be defiantly witty even as the plat-
form upon which he stands collapses beneath his feet, the rope tight
around his neck, plunged broken-necked to his death.

She imagines now two weeks hence walking beside the gurney
to the door of the Operating Room. Does he then, at the door, let
her in? Does he say, "I'm afraid … don't let my hand go. Don't let
go." The truth she fears at the O.R. door is this: he doesn't drop his
shield, doesn't let her in, and she's left there never again to see him
alive.

In a pre-emptive strike against the imagined pain at the O.R.
door, she says, "Give us all a break, Shakespeare," as the violent
storm intensifies, the power at 663 Bleecker fails, the fans meant for
non-existent cross-ventilation die and Catherine and Eliot sit there
in stale 100% humidity-saturated airlessness at 101 degrees. This
was the August storm predicted to usher in a cold front and break
the heat wave, but this storm will break nothing except the spirit as
it rains down not drops but rivers.

She removes from the desk drawer a small flashlight. He takes
it, switches on, points the weak beam under his chin, makes a crazy
face in ghost light—teeth bared, eyes wide and bugged out. He says,

"Why not? Let's do it on the desk." She unbuttons and removes her shirt. He drops his trousers and briefs. Footsteps on the landing just outside the door, an outraged voice saying, "You motherfucker! You cocksucker!" He of the outraged voice attempts but fails to enter—it's their family friend, occasional babysitter, her partner Robert Rintrona, whose curses are directed at the great umbrella, wide enough to shelter a family of eight and which by malignant intention refuses to collapse, forcing him with difficulty, and just barely, to slip through the doorway sideways, as power is restored at 663 Bleecker, with Conte's bare ass on display and Catherine's bra unhooked as both fumble too late to recover as Rintrona is saying, "Can I watch? My friends, tell me, what is a hard-on? An event of the male body? This is what I hear."

Rintrona turns his back to them and says, "Do it on the desk or get dressed. Personally I have no interest in the pleasure of the flesh, in loving memory of my dear wife who claimed headaches on a nightly basis for the last 15 years of her time on this bastard earth. Did I complain? No. Are you in, Eliot? Did I press the issue? No. Did I go outside for something on the side? No. Did Maureen presumably have something outside on the side, which explains the headache claims? Who can tell me? Are you in, Eliot? Are you all the way in? Or was she innocently turned off by my exceptional body? The pot belly. I stand sideways to the mirror and look at it in disgust. Did she get turned off 15 years ago when I became 8 months pregnant? Look. They swing when I move my head side to side. The jowls. The swinging jowls. The pecs? Fuhgedaboutit. They became tits. Plus the rosacea-schnozzola of a veteran drunk, which I am not. Can you believe it? I actually went bald downtown. Believe it or not 15 years ago I went bald in the pubic area. A genetic disaster and who can blame my old man for not revealing it to me? Are you ready for this? It humiliates me to acknowledge the yellow-stained underwear, thanks to the leaking plumbing of my fuckin' 60s. Who wants to look at that as a spouse, however loving, which is what Maureen was, a loving spouse who did the washing with surgical gloves. Hello? I don't hear the classical grunts and groans of hot love behind my back. Are you still in, Eliot? Are you quiet in the act of love or are you just spent?"

He turns to the lovers. They're dressed and grinning from ear to ear because it's play time again with Bobby Rintrona, whose presence in their lives had always given them leave (as now) to forget themselves, to lay by their troubles and to be, however briefly—no other word will suffice—"happy." They had not done it on the desk, but with those unceasing grins were pleased to give Rintrona the impression that they had completed a quickie.

Rintrona says, "What's so humoristic? In my 42 years with Maureen we were old school. So let's leave it at that at the end of the fuckin' day."

He tosses the fuckin' umbrella into the corner. He says, "So what's the story, Katie, in the private dick department? You two are chained to each other, whether you like it or not. Me? I sit in my house on Harrison Ave with take-out and television. Last night I porn-surfed the net. Masturbation? It never crossed my fuckin' mind."

Catherine says, "I have something for you, Bobby."

Conte says, "We have something for you, Bobby."

Catherine says, "Lilly Thieu."

Conte says, "Lilly Thieu."

Catherine says, "Interested?"

Conte says, "Interested?

Rintrona says, "Stop with the back-and-forth. It's an aggravation."

Catherine says, "Her daughter has gone missing with a mysterious Iraqi."

Conte says, "Lilly Thieu heard from her missing daughter this afternoon by telephone, so in a way she's not technically missing, though her whereabouts are unknown at this time."

Rintrona says, "A ransom call with a gun held to her head by the Iraqi?"

Catherine says, "Apparently not."

Conte says, "Apparently not. She says she met a wonderful man. The mysterious Iraqi."

Rintrona says, "So what's the problem? Lilly Due wants her daughter located?"

"She never made that request," Catherine says.

"But it's a reasonable inference from the situation of this mother, who never made the request," Conte says.

"Bobby, it's more than reasonable."

"Yes, Bobby, a mysterious Iraqi. More than reasonable."

"This fuckin' ping-pong turns you two on? It's a pain in the ass. You want me to locate Vietnam and Iraq? There are Iraqis living in Utica? Since when?"

Conte says, "At least one. He's going to open a restaurant on this block next month."

Catherine says, "Her name is Rhonda Thieu. The thought here is you find her and the Iraqi on behalf of Lilly."

"On behalf of the grief-struck mother," Conte says, "whose tragic visage antedates all worldly experience, even as her sadness stands in stark disjunction to the comic patter she delivers as easily as breathing."

Rintrona glares at the dripping umbrella in the corner, then turns to Conte and says, "What you're saying in plain English, which you should try talking sometime, is that the mother is fucked up and funny. In other words, a normal person who deals with a familiar family dynamic, the nasty offspring. Don't get me started on my kids."

Catherine says, "Lilly Thieu likely lives on social security. Likely the minimum, 650 per month. Likely no savings, while smoking a couple of hundred a month."

Conte says, "Likely Lilly Thieu does not eat breakfast in order to save money. Likely a peanut butter and jelly sandwich for lunch. Likely a barely adequate dinner of unappealing elements."

Rintrona says, "Likely I do the work for this Auschwitz victim gratis out of the fuckin' goodness of my heart."

Catherine says, "She stands about 5'3", fine-boned. Must have been as a young woman what they call drop-dead beautiful, who in her early 60s can still turn heads on Bleecker Street. Maybe yours too, Bobby."

Conte says, "So we kill two birds with one stone. You find Rhonda—a P.I. job with the promise of romance."

Catherine: "Here's the photo."

"And you, Bobby—"

"I get set up romantically and cease living alone on Harrison Ave, the boulevard of this broken-hearted widower, who porn-surfs the net without erotic after-effects."

Conte and Catherine: "Why not?"

"Where does she reside, this tiny Vietnamese sex bomb?"

Catherine: "This building. One floor down."

"After your description of her finances, I don't relish sitting without a/c in a squalid apartment."

Conte: "It's not squalid."

"How would you know?"

"I've been there."

Rintrona, raised eyebrows, glancing at Catherine: "Under what circumstances?"

"I gave her something she desperately needed."

"You and Katie have an open marriage? Since when?"

Catherine laughs.

"A pack of cigarettes. I'll fill you in later. Like Lilly herself, the apartment is fine-boned. Sparely appointed with furniture and objects of fragile beauty."

Catherine: "Meet her in air-conditioned comfort at Caruso's, in 30 minutes. Eliot will escort her over. Introduce you. Mediate. Buffer the situation."

"It's America's worst nightmare. You're throwing it in my lap."

"What's that, Bobby?"

"The alliance of Iraq and Vietnam."

* * *

The storm rolls out, but the wind blows hot and humid as Lilly and Conte emerge from 663 Bleecker for the 100-yard stroll east to Café Caruso. For Conte, no stroll. He's shuffling again. He's laboring. Where has he gone, the gallant and nimble savior of Lilly

Thieu's cigarettes? Halfway to their destination—for Lilly, her destiny—when the wind stops—doesn't, as the saying goes, "die down," but dies absolutely and as if born full-blown from its death a chilly blast of cold front bears suddenly down upon them and the temperature in a few seconds dips 20 degrees.

Conte, shivering, says, "This is what it's like, Lilly. The weather of hell itself."

"Your Pope changed his mind? Hell is no longer hot?"

"This Pope doesn't speak of hell. Probably doesn't believe in it."

"You believe hell exists? I am personally a Buddhist once in a while."

"This is hell, now and in Utica. Quick changes of hot and cold."

"Have you been in Vietnam during the war?"

"No. Student deferment."

"Good. You were not in hell."

"I wasn't there. Others were."

"I don't think of the weather, like thinking of Vietnam where my parents were not deferred. Where they were slaughtered. I think of my missing daughter if she loves me, which Buddhism, which teaches the peace of not thinking, is not helping me to not-think because when it comes to family troubles Buddhism is what my daughter calls a 'fucking joke.' Is Catholicism—you are a Catholic?"

"Raised that way. No more, no less."

"Does Catholicism heal family disasters or does it cause family disasters left and right? Is it a fucking joke? When I say the fuck-word I quote my daughter. I do not myself say it. I hope Mr. Rintrona will help me to find her who said I was a 'pain in the ass.' Maybe she doesn't want me to find her. Maybe she is sick of me."

"Mr. Rintrona will help."

"You breathe too fast. Shall we stop for a cigarette? Where did you learn this idea of hell-weather?"

"Let's step in this alley out of the wind while you light up. You can't smoke at Caruso's."

"There is something low moving in that alley. Look! More than one! Let's keep walking. Where did you learn this idea of hell-weather?"

"From a book. By a poet. Who wrote of heaven and hell."

"Does heaven exist according to your nice Pope? Mr. Conte, may I take your arm?"

"Of course."

"Does heaven exist according to the Pope?"

"Not in the traditional sense."

"I think you have a Buddhist Pope. Would he permit me to have communion?"

"He'd probably give it to you his Papal self."

"This good Pope will be assassinated."

Drivers in their cars, cyclists, and pedestrians all slow down to a crawl on Bleecker to take in the spectacle of a man, well-known in East Utica as the son of a deceased political king-maker, and a little woman who has taken his arm, inching along, toward Caruso's. The man stands 6'3", with the frame of an NFL lineman. He's lost 45 pounds over the last 2 years and is no longer robust but still weighs 190 pounds. The little Vietnamese immigrant, 5'3", 102 pounds. Such a twosome, arm in arm, has never before been seen on Bleecker or anywhere else in Utica. A man in the passenger seat says to his driver, his wife, "Welcome to the 21st century, Rosie. This sight over there on the sidewalk relieves my tensions, don't ask me why."

The little Vietnamese says to big Conte, who leans over to lend her his good ear, "My husband who dumped on me for another woman never let me take his arm from the beginning of our marriage. A sign of martial discord as they say."

She laughs.

"I knew it was marital. I just wanted to make you laugh, but you do not laugh. Do you have too much sadness? I think you have too much sadness."

They enter Caruso's. No Rintrona in sight. Just one table occupied, at the back near the cash register: An off-duty policeman, well-known as one of the tragic clown brothers: Victor Cazzamano.

Victor waves, says: "From the way you're walking, Eliot, I surmise you haven't had the surgery yet. Have no fear. I had the same operation last year and look at me now. One leg up to my knee in the grave and sinking. I'll be seeing Ronnie sooner rather than later, that is my prayer."

Conte and Lilly sit several tables away.

Lilly whispers to Conte, "Ronnie? He's married to a man?"

Conte whispers, "His partner in the police."

"He's dead?"

"Murdered in the line of duty. They were friends from childhood and best man at each other's wedding. He never got over it."

Marilyn Caruso approaches: "Mr. Rintrona called to say he's running late and'll be here soon. What can I get for you two?"

Victor shouts, "On me, Marilyn."

Lilly smiles, mimes "Thank you." Palms together. Slight head bow.

Victor shouts, "Anytime, anyplace, sweetheart."

Conte whispers, "His wife left him a year ago. For another woman."

"Maybe this Ronnie would have been a better wife. What is that man's name?"

"Victor Cazzamano."

"You Italian people have interesting names. Does that name mean something?"

Marilyn says, "Does it ever. His male privates in his hand is what it means."

"A bad thing or a good thing? For you Italian people? For Vietnamese, a very good thing if you have no one to love."

Conte asks for a cappuccino. Lilly says, "You don't make Vietnamese coffee. I can show you. Then many Vietnamese will come. Am I the first to come to you?"

"I don't keep track, dear. Not my style. Maybe, maybe not. What can I bring you?"

Lilly says, "I don't know Italian pastries. You pick the best one. Thank you."

Marilyn proceeds to describe cannoli vocally and with precise hand gestures. She says, "I'll bring you two. They're small."

Lilly says, "What you do with your hands reminds me of something that I have not seen for many years."

Marilyn says, "A cannoli is always good in the hand but better in the mouth."

Conte says, "Clean it up, girls."

Here comes Rintrona. An hour earlier, at the agency office, he'd been dressed in a t-shirt, shorts, sandals, needing a shave and dripping sweat. Now: shaved, showered, cologned, wearing a flowered shirt, tan dress slacks and brown tasseled loafers in high gloss. The promise of meeting an attractive female, his age, who'll be looking to him for brave masculine help, so he mused in the shower, spurred fantasy, and fantasy triggered a transformed appearance.

As soon as Rintrona enters, Cazzamano says, loudly, "Here he is, friends! Shylock Holmes."

Marilyn pipes up, "*Sherlock*, Victor. *Sherlock.*"

"What I said. Exactly. Shylock."

Conte: "Victor, are you hard of hearing?"

"You prejudiced against the hearing challenged?"

As soon as Rintrona entered he was smitten, Thank Christ I went home to get spiffed up and didn't come directly here in my disgraceful state. He doesn't even glance in Cazzamano's direction because Lilly Thieu—whose surname he'll forever pronounce "Due"—fills his vision and desire.

Rintrona approaches Conte and Lilly, holds out his hand to Lilly, who takes it in both of hers. He says, "May I sit, Ms. Due? I am Robert Rintrona."

She responds, "Oh, dear me. Yes. You will find my daughter?"

He says, "Please excuse my late arrival." Then adds, absurdly, a Utica impossibility: "I was tied up in traffic. Definitely, I will find her."

Conte says, "You look terrific, Bobby. Almost as good as Lilly."

Marilyn says, "What'll you have today, Detective." Cazzamano shouts "Whatever he wants, on me." Rintrona requests San Pellegrino and insists on paying with a gesture of the forefinger pointing to his chest. Cazzamano reads the gesture correctly, speaks up too loudly again, as the hearing impaired tend to do: "What have I done to earn his hostility? Someone explain this to me."

On the way to fill the orders, Marilyn stops close to Cazzamano and whispers, "This is not a saloon, control your voice."

Cazzamano, again with too much volume: "When Ronnie passed I started losing my hearing."

She brings the cannoli, coffee, and San Pellegrino to Conte's table. Returns to Cazzamano, sits with him and says, "How can I help you, Victor? Feel free to confide."

He says, "Be honest. Am I hideous? This is a word my wife used every 7 weeks when I tried to extend my passion in her direction. Am I really hideous?"

"Victor. Oh."

"If we were a twosome would you find me hideous, Marilyn? Would you constantly every 7 weeks rebuff?"

She puts her hand on Victor's and says, "No. Speculatively speaking, Victor, because my husband and I are strong together, I would not rebuff."

"I appreciate in a speculative vein. I'm not a looker like Ronnie was. I grant. I finally googled this word hideous after she dumped me for Marla. If you are hideous are you doomed to be lonely? Is that why I am lonely?"

"She was hideous to say you were hideous. You have nice realistic looks. Why compare yourself to Ronnie who was an unbelievable looker? Who could compete in this town?"

(Rintrona to Lilly: "I was in Vietnam '68 to '70. Marines. Khe Sanh.")

"In Ronnie's company, which we were constantly in since we were 8 years old, I never felt hideous or lonely. Did I turn my wife into a lesbian?"

"Victor, she was a lesbian from day one. Your passion for her every 7 weeks had nothing to do with it."

"At 55 I'm too young to make a move on that Vietnamese broad over there who's in her 60s for sure, but who can tell their age, just like who can tell the age of black people, who always look good no matter."

She says, "I'm going to set you up with my cousin's cousin's husband's older sister on my mother's side. Soon. Okay?"

"I hope to Christ she's not too much of a looker, because I'll sink into myself in her vicinity. I'll lose my voice."

"I guarantee Teresa will relax you."

(Lilly to Rintrona: "1970 I lived in Saigon. An American soldier said he would bring me to America.")

"Guess what Ronnie and I used to call each other?"

"Tell me."

"Cretins."

"Really?"

"Since we were 9 years old. What does that mean? We never knew. We never looked it up."

"Where did a 9-year-old hear such a word?"

"From Ronnie's mother's boyfriend's daughter-in-law."

"Why didn't you look it up?"

"Because Ronnie said once we knew the true meaning the magic will be gone from our secret name."

"And you never knew?"

"No. Do you know the meaning?"

She takes out her iPhone: "You really want to know?"

"In memory of Ronnie, tell me."

"Stupid. Vulgar. Insensitive. A clod. A lout. Full of pointless information that makes no sense and appeals only to other cretins. A deformed idiot. Here's a meaning from way back that's not totally bad. A Christian."

"Let's not mention this to Teresa. All the while I was thinking all these years it meant someone who was cute."

"Victor, I think you're cute. Tell me: Were you there when Ronnie ...?"

"We were going to our daily stop at Dunkin' Donuts on North Genesee. For the classic mixed dozen. I go in. Ronnie waits in the car. I pay. Two shots ring out. I run outside with the bag of doughnuts in my hand. Ronnie's on the pavement in a pool of blood. I still have the bag in my hand. I'm on one knee. He says, Victor, am I going to die? I say back, Don't talk like that, Ronnie. We all love you. At the funeral I had a hard time hearing the priest, even though I was only 10 feet away. I was sinking in. The department shrink said reality was too much for me. My hearing loss, he said, was only psychological. Three years later it's still psychological. What's next, Marilyn? Blindness?"

"Victor. Teresa is next."

(Lilly: "We were in Vietnam, Mr. Rintrona, like 2 children in the night. Without parents.")

(Rintrona: "Yes. We were.")

(Conte: "But now you two are here.")

* * *

She says, "Mr. Rintrona ... please call me Lilly."

"Call me Bobby, Lilly."

"Bobby, your wife was Maureen?"

"She was."

"The picture on the wall at your office was your Maureen? A beautiful Irish girl with red hair. Is she your Maureen?"

"She was."

"The one on the wall died according to your partner."

"She did."

"So young!"

"She died 4 years ago at 60. The picture you saw was taken when she was 22. We met when she was 30. I always wanted to meet her inside that picture, if you know what I mean."

"I do know."

Conte says, "My guess, you're both free for dinner, so why not take your client out?"

"Terrific idea."

She says, "A nice idea."

Rintrona blushes.

7

THE INTERNATIONALLY DISTINGUISHED HEART SURGEON in Syracuse has lived alone since the divorce, 5 years ago, when on the last day of cohabitation—the legal instruments signed, initialed, notarized—his ex strode hard to the condominium door as he followed, mumbling polite meaningless words, to which she replied, "Enough, Harry. You know why. You've always known." Then left. Not bothering to close the door behind her.

Home from the clinic, at the condo door key in hand he hears it, the voice from within in steady streaming monologue—mellow, hypnotic, and he's almost comforted. It's been a week since Eliot Conte, the patient from Utica, had unsettled him as no patient had unsettled him before.

He turns the key. Inside, they await him. His close (and only) friends, 3 chilled bottles of Polish vodka not available in the United States, Żubrówka, given to him by a wealthy Belarussian patient whose life he had saved. He'll knock back his ritual 2 shots, then shower, then go meet his new friend for dinner at Happy China. Will she be a friend? Should all go well, he'll invite her back to the condo for a very special dessert.

The surgeon enters the 2-storey 3600-square-foot condo, deluxe beyond a real estate agent's imagination, and is bathed by T.S. Eliot's looped reading of *The Waste Land* just as Victor Cazzamano in Utica pulls to the curb at the 2-storey house on South Street, 3 blocks east of Mohawk: a narrow structure, 500 square feet per storey—built in the 1920s and common in Lower East Utica, where many are badly in need of exterior painting and re-roofing and which, thanks to flimsy flooring, afford no tranquility to first-floor residents, who are bludgeoned nightly by every step of the second-storey tenants—houses where even the light-footed among them seem to those below to be furious Rumpelstiltskins about to stomp through—houses where secrets cannot be kept because voices, even at whisper levels, penetrate walls and floors with the ease of classically-trained singers filling a cavernous opera house.

In the car still, Cazzamano checks his cell for God only knows how many times that day, which for cell-checking frequency in the life of Victor Cazzamano is no different from any other day. Nothing. Again nothing. Always nothing. He'd given his number to the compassionate Marilyn Caruso, who would be contacting Teresa, her cousin's cousin's husband's older sister. To propose what, exactly? A date? Do people go out on dates anymore? Do they even say the word "date"? Would you like to go out on a date with me, Teresa? Even though we never met? How can he call a woman he'd never met or seen?

He has a plan. He'll write out a phone-script. His opening words, her six possible responses. His six possible responses to her six possible responses.

"Hello. This is Victor, who if I'm not mistaken Marilyn—

"Marilyn?"

(Long pause.)

"How are you?"

"Uh. Okay."

"Good! I'm pretty okay myself," he says.

"Good for you," she says.

(Long pause.)

"I was wondering if you would like to uh—"

"What?"

"Have a drink or get a coffee or ..."

"I don't drink alcohol and I take coffee only in the morning."

"How about a soda or a milkshake, Teresa?"

"My name is Nancy, asshole."

Victor rests his forehead on the steering wheel in anticipation of telephone-humiliation as Robert Rintrona turns onto Mohawk on his way to fetch Lilly Thieu and take her back to Harrison Ave, where he has prepared lasagna, his mother's brother-in-law's sister's recipe. A Utica legend, known as *lasagna l'ultima*. He'd opened a bottle of chianti too, to let it breathe, as the conno—what are they called? The wine experts. The winos. They say breathe, though truth be told the quality of this chianti is unbreathable. Two years since his wife Maureen passed. He thinks he may be ready to live again. With this Lilly? By the way, how does a Vietnamese get that name? How did her daughter get the name Rhonda? Maybe I'll bond for life with this pretty little woman through mutual recollections of the horror of that country, whose name the American Secretary of Defense, Robert S. McNamara, mispronounced "Veetnam," even decades after the American debacle.

He'll have to guard against the obscene language that spices every one of his sentences. Forget, but how can he, "gook" and "slope cunt?" The last woman he romanced was his wife, more than 30 years ago. Does he know any longer how to talk to a woman? Did he ever? Maureen had had her doubts. He pulls to the curb at 663 Bleecker, feeling again like a teenager about to meet a girl he's nursed a crush on from afar, for months. He, Robert Rintrona, who has known Lilly Thieu for about an hour and is already in the throes. There's Lilly waiting outside.

Like the surgeon in Syracuse, like Victor Cazzamano and Robert Rintrona, Antonio Robinson is lonely. He's Conte's best friend, since childhood, but now they're alienated. What had they argued about 3 months ago? He doesn't want to think about it. Unlike the others, Utica's African-American Chief of Police is without hope for romantic adventure, as he sits in his contemporary ranch-style home high up on Utica's south edge, on Valley View Road, where he faces the glass wall of his living room with a beer and salted peanuts and takes in the sweeping view of the sad little city below. Not much visible in mid-August. There's the bank with the gold dome—not the whole bank itself, just the gold dome. It's really a huge piece of chocolate in gold paper wrapped, he told the kids when they were young enough to believe it, and he half-believed as he told it. Far to the north, atop Smith Hill, the TV towers. Closer in, the New York Central railroad yard near the city center, no longer a center of anything. Over there on the former Polish west side, eyesores galore, the saddest side of town. Mostly what he sees is the green canopy of tree tops, an illusion of rural peace hiding the postindustrial devastation of Rust Belt America. Utica has lost half of its population since the mid-1950s. The textile mills, Savage (the arms manufacturer), the 3 General Electric plants, the Bendix plant—all departed, leaving mainly subsistence-level jobs in the service sector.

Antonio Robinson's empty dream house on Valley View Road comprises his entire happiness. Elegance and acreage fenced with white split railing: a touch of wealthy Virginia horse country, as now just outside the window his mare and pony foaled in the Spring munch good grass and swish their tails against the tireless flies, as crows glide in to peck at their manure.

He wants to call someone. But whom can he call? Not Eliot. Millicent had left for good, neither seeing the point of a formal divorce, and she'd gone to Florida where she knew no one. The kids, grown and educated, saw no point in staying in this desert of jobs and had taken their lives a long plane ride away with 2 stops. And Marilyn Caruso? (Sexy Marilyn?) With whom he (and she!) played at romantic flirtation whenever he frequented the Café—Marilyn, 35 years his junior and happily situated. Call *her*? An *actual* call? He loved playing for her the macho romantic clown. He played, but was silently and privately smitten long before Millicent left. He suspected that Eliot had an inkling about his secret feelings (Eliot did), but Marilyn did not, surely, could not, he hoped not. (Marilyn knew.)

His marriage had gone cold many years ago. Not even a memory of original marital bliss. He called the kids every weekend. Never failed to call. It was necessary to take the initiative because they never called. He thought he'd been an attentive father, but maybe—no doubt not attentive enough. He wasn't all that attentive, ever. Millicent never knew about the affair with Eliot's godmother's daughter, he was pretty sure, but he was probably wrong about that too. (You are wrong about everything, Mr. Robinson.) Millicent, who was never one for making cutting remarks, began making them frequently around the time he'd started stepping out on her.

He doesn't want to think about it, but he thinks about it—the bitter fall-out with Eliot on that late afternoon at Café Caruso amid the comical banter until he, Antonio, made the request on behalf of his nephew, Le Grant, a straight 'A' student at Proctor High in his senior year. He wasn't asking Eliot to do physical damage to the racist white teacher who was giving Le Grant almost failing grades on American literature. Just make a looming appearance, bro, at her classroom at the end of the day. Catch her alone at her desk at the end of the day. Lean over the desk in your emaciated hulk. Tell her Le Grant is your godson, which he is. Tell her you're an Italian who takes his godfather responsibilities very seriously. Say, Know what I mean by 'serious'? Encourage her to purchase a home security system. Remind her that the security system is useless outside the home. All the while leaning over her desk at the end of the day. And Eliot said, No, he would no longer indulge his impulses to violence. Not even of the psychological kind. He was changing. These 2 best pals since childhood who always had each other's back and who together, Antonio as Chief of Police, Eliot as Private Investigator, had made some very bad people pay a very heavy price. And Eliot out of the blue decides to *change*? Since when does anybody *change*? Who is this new Eliot Conte? My so-called all-but-in-blood brother?

Antonio Robinson tonight in his dream house has no desire to cook. Another beer and another handful of salted peanuts will do it. (Bad for my BP, the salt, but I'll double up on the med before I go down and that'll do it.) A few months back he started turning in on the early side. 10. Then it was 9:45. 9:30. Checks his watch. 8:15. Why not? What's the point?

The point? The surgeon thought he knew the point of inviting the newly minted gynecologist to dinner. Attractive, he thought, but only objectively speaking. He was certainly not attracted in a romantic way. She was reserved with a gentle tone in her voice. The thing about her that drew him strongly was her way of being with others. You knew you were in the presence of a person with sympathy at her core. For 5 years he had not seen anyone in a way that might be characterized as "dating," a word still in his vocabulary. What prompted him to ask her to dinner was the experience a week past with the man from Utica. He needed to tell someone, not so much about the man from Utica as about his own bizarre reaction to him. She would listen kindly, he had no doubts. She was the one.

He feared that the consultation with Eliot Conte had revealed something about himself he had never known before. Something, what was the proper word? Unsound? Which was a genteel way of saying deranged? Nuts? Was he headed somewhere that would undo everything he thought he was? When he invited her back to his place, there was nothing in her reaction to the invitation that bespoke, What is this man really up to? Is he safe? She had no fears. He was a very big deal in the medical world, but had no airs. A very big deal who did not act like one. For his part, he had intuited what he was sure was the truth: She was a lesbian, who had been raised on one of the most exclusive streets of Manhattan's Upper East Side. She had heard a rumor about his condo and just wanted to see for herself if such extravagance was possible in the hinterlands of Upstate New York. She would go. Because she thought he was safe.

A restrained person though she is, she can't restrain herself as she enters: "Oh, my! This is beyond words."

He responds, "Ah! But not beyond my words. Regard the gleaming hardwood floors. Like sunlight flaring off a lake still as glass, on a windless day."

"Yes," she says. "The lake is on fire. Do you write poetry?"

"No."

"A pity."

"Look! The floating staircase of metal and wood. Without visible support."

"Magic," she says.

"Come this way to the kitchen and note the floated slate floor. Like walking on a cloud. Touch the granite counters. Like the cool feel? The stainless steel appliances. The custom wood cabinetry. The subzero fridge. The Asko dishwasher. The Miele espresso maker. May I fix you a cup at no charge?"

She laughs. She's relaxed.

"This wine-cooler here—I don't drink wine. My ex-wife's disease. A factor in the divorce. It's empty. A 178 bottle capacity. For my ex, a 3 month supply of solo boozing. I told her before I went to a conference in Venice it was an unnecessary extravagance. Don't buy. When I returned, it was here, installed. 7000 dollars. As you can see, how could you not? The floor to ceiling glass walls. The exposed brick. Those support columns wrapped in stainless steel. I have a balcony on the second floor. A 600-square-foot patio which sports a raised garden bed with an irrigation system. I don't garden. Might you?"

"I might," she says.

He likes her answer.

"The two-car garage has a heated indoor car wash because in winter, in upstate, we don't want to transform my Porsche and Cadillac SUV into high-speed icebergs."

She thinks he's funny. She says, "Do you do stand-up comedy?"

"No."

"A pity, Harry."

"Behold! The master bath is masterful, featuring an 8-head walk-in tiled shower and an 8-jet Jacuzzi. Regard! The double glass sinks. And heated towel racks, it goes without saying. What say you, Kim? Would you mistake me for a gay real estate agent to the Hollywood stars?"

"Yes, Harry. I would. It goes without saying."

"I'm not gay."

"Clearly."

Victor Cazzamano enters the 2-storey house on South Street. It doesn't need painting. The roof is sound. Before his parents died, he and his wife occupied the second floor. Now, alone, he has the first floor and peace above with no tenants up there—nothing up there except an elliptical machine and some free weights. The furniture downstairs belonged to his parents. He kept it in their honor. Circa 1955. He'd had the decayed rugs removed. He had hardwood floors installed—more than he could afford but wanted to do something top class on his own behalf. He liked the way light flashed off the floor. He tried, futilely, to think of a word to describe the effect. The apartment is exceptionally clean. Spic and Span, as his mother used to say, who washed the walls monthly, and he does too. In her honor.

A light flashing on his phone. A message. He plays it: "Hello, Victor, this is Teresa. I go by Terry. Marilyn's friend. I'm open this weekend, if you are. Give me a buzz whenever. Bye."

Marilyn's kids are at her sister's for a sleepover. Marilyn is exhausted. Joey Caruso has prepared a tuna pasta with a side of broccoli. They'd talked about a special romantic evening for months, but she is virtually asleep at the table, her pasta barely touched. She looks good to him. She looks good. He'd purchased the Major League Baseball package and will content himself with the romance of a beer and the Cubs game. He hasn't watched the Cubs all season. They say the Cubs will be like the Yankees of the past. He switches on the TV as—

The surgeon pours Żubrówka over vanilla ice cream. The surgeon has almost forgotten in the pleasure of her company what he wanted to tell her, to unburden himself of the fear that he was cracking up. But why did it feel good, if he was cracking up? Did he not have fun with the patient from Utica? Do lunatics have fun? If he unburdens himself after dessert on this first evening with Kim, a virtual stranger, it would prove to her and to him that he had stepped over the edge. Another time. He hopes there will be another time. (Does she?) He lifts his dish of ice-cream and toasts her. She returns the silly gesture. He's thinking thoughts that trouble and excite him. He, who doesn't pray, prays silently now that she's straight.

She says, "I'm not either."

"What?"

"Gay."

Meanwhile on Mary Street, Conte, Catherine and Annie play the game of who can spell spaghetti. Conte has almost forgotten himself even as he now resumes the habit he tried to eradicate when Annie was born, of digging his fingernails into his cuticles, making them bleed—making them bleed now as 3-year-old Annie, this very child, mispronounces spaghetti, but miraculously, for the first time, spells it correctly.

Jolted (2)

CATHERINE AND CONTE SIT IN the center section of the Stanley Theater on Genesee Street. The orchestra is tuning up. Directly behind Conte a man says, pointing to Conte, not whispering, "Remember him?" His companion says, "Do I ever, Ron." Ron says, "We were in our naked glory. He bursts in." The companion says, "He did us a favor, Ron. The divorce was a blessing for all involved. Thank God you had no kids." Ron says, "I wonder, Greg, if she knows?" Pointing to Catherine. "Did he tell her he walked me to the window of Hotel Utica at gunpoint? Nine floors up? Made me open the window all the way? Made me sit on the ledge? Told me he needed a photo for his client of me going down on you? Either that or out the window." Greg says, "It turned out very nice for us, Ron. Why dredge up the past?" Ron says, "The woman he's with? What must it be like to be involved with a psycho?" The first violinist takes her place. The conductor appears. Conte turns to Catherine and says, loud enough to be heard by Ron and Greg, "I'm happy for them both." Catherine brings both of her hands to her face.

VIETNAM, VIETNAM

THE DRIVER'S BIRTH CERTIFICATE SAYS Francis Robert Rintrona, who was there at the worst time, in the Northwest highlands of what was then South Vietnam, a few miles from the border of Laos, at a base called Khe Sanh in the earliest months of 1968—when 8,000 Marines were surrounded by 40,000 of the North Vietnamese Army. In January of 1968, this former altar boy from Albany, New York was 3 months shy of his 19th birthday and learning to curse. At Khe Sanh saying words that he had never had to confess to his favorite parish priest, Father Guerra—yes, that was actually his name—because he'd never before said them.

At almost 19 years old, Francis Robert Rintrona was about the age of most of the Marines of Khe Sanh, one of whom, a 20-year-old—his best buddy—said to him in the middle of the siege, "I'm getting too old for this shit," and a few minutes later ceased getting too old for this shit when he was cut in half by an artillery shell.

The buddy's name was Jones, sometimes called Jones, more often than not called Jonesey, more often yet called Red, not because of the color of his hair, which was not red, but because he was beset by acne. Jonesey referred to his acne as The Pimples of War. Rintrona thought it unfair that Jonesey was called Red because 50% of the youngsters at Khe Sanh were beset by The Pimples of War. Jonesey himself didn't give a shit what they called him because he knew who he was.

All of these not-quite-men addressed each other by their surnames or nicknames. Rintrona was The Golden Dago. Who knew anyone's first name? What was Jonesey's first name? He could never remember. He meant to write to Jonesey's parents after his death, but couldn't do it. What could he say that would make a difference? I'm sorry for your loss? I really liked your son? He was a good guy? He would have to say the terrible word "was." What words of his could possibly make them feel better? Your son had a terrific sense of humor? He told himself, and believed, that nothing he might say would alleviate their pain. He prayed to God that Jonesey's parents would never be told the brutal fact of the manner of death. Prayed that the undertaker could hide the truth of their only child's corpse. The Golden Dago told himself many things, except the deepest truth of his inability to write to his friend's parents. That he was afraid to write. Afraid to look at the words on paper, each one of which said secretly to him, I loved your son and he is dead and I can't get over it. What good would it do to tell Jonesey's parents *that*? I am in pain, but less than yours? The Golden Dago needed someone to make him feel better—still did, decades later, who couldn't remember Jonesey's first name until he forced himself, drunk, who wasn't much of a drinker, to go to the Vietnam Memorial Wall in D.C., where he found many Joneses, but only one Timothy. And he remembered, and saw, the sly grin on the acne-beset face. Timothy. He touched the name. Leaned on the wall to keep himself from falling. "Tim," he said aloud, whom he had never called Tim. "Tim," he said again, aloud, as those near him stepped back, not in fear but in awe of his grief. "Tim."

When he returned from Vietnam he slept with the lights on for 2 years. When alone, and no one could see or hear him, he cried for Tim and himself and all the Marines of Khe Sanh whose names he never knew, and who left Khe Sanh in body bags. Father Guerra told him it would help to cry, to cry desperately, without hope— "You may curse God Himself, my son, if it helps." So he cursed God, and wept without hope, but it did not help.

* * *

She sits in the front passenger seat beside The Golden Dago and holds a potted African Violet in her lap. She is known in Utica as Lilly Thieu, though in truth she is known in Utica only a little, and mostly not at all. She too was there in the worst of times, never in the highlands of Khe Sanh, but only in Saigon. Her birth certificate says Phuong Thieu. In 1968 she was 16, orphaned and living with an aunt and uncle and working for the U.S. Army's Inspector General, whose quarters, staff, and facilities were located at the Saigon airport, 4½ miles from where Phuong Thieu lived. Her duties: making beds, laundering, and shining the shoes of the officers. Her transportation: like that of most Saigonese, by bicycle. She biked in the time of the heavy wet heat of summer, she biked in the season of the monsoons, when it rained for weeks in dense sheets, and she biked in the forgiving cooler (never cold) time of the winter months. Always she carried in a waterproof sack a change of clothes and shoes. The Inspector General's son, Steve, 24, his father's special lieutenant assistant, told her one week after he met her, as she shined his shoes, and every week thereafter, that he intended to marry her.

The worst of the worst times for Phuong Thieu were those rides to and from the airport, not because of the traffic—bikes wall-to-wall with six inches of separation and a frenzy of pedicabs and a few cars bullying the bikes. Not because of the weather, either, but because of the scene looping daily in Phuong's mind: The scene of two years past when she was 14. Her father a clerk at the post office, her mother a teacher of teenagers. In their living room, that Friday night, the stack of long-playing records, of Viennese waltzes, still playing as she entered and discovered her mother and father in their blood, their throats cut.

Phuong Thieu loved Friday nights better than all nights, when it was thrilling to watch her parents and applaud and flip the records as they danced with mesmerizing formal grace, in their finest clothes, and their movie-star looks. The Fred Astaire and Ginger Rogers of Saigon. She, who was never absent on Friday nights, was absent the night of their murder. She had made quite a fuss, but they insisted that she go to the celebration of her cousin's birthday, to the home of the aunt and uncle who were partial to foreign customs and would the next day become her step-parents. Her parents had taught her in the sternest tones: We Vietnamese do not celebrate birthdays. We celebrate the Day of the Dead. But then why, she asked herself a million times, had her parents so strenuously insisted that she go?

* * *

In the car, she who calls herself Lilly lifts the potted flowering African Violet—one of several that she nurtures at her kitchen window. "Look," she says, at the traffic light. "You like it?"

He wants to say, "I like you." He says, instead, "For me instead of the classic bottle of wine?"

"For you. African Violet."

"From Africa?"

"Like everybody. From Africa."

"I don't mind being more or less black."

"Me more, you less."

"I made lasagna. Hope to Christ that's okay. Are you a vegetarian? It's got meat in it."

"I love Italian with meat."

"I'm Italian with—"

"When I was in Vietnam, Italian food did not exist. We had French. Too rich. Too expensive. Too French."

"Maybe us? We open an Italian restaurant in Saigon. Good idea?"

"Saigon is Ho Chi Minh City. I prefer to say Saigon."

"Beautiful sound. Saigon. What's it mean?"

"I don't know. A beautiful sound is enough maybe."

"Hey! I do the cooking, you're the mayder dee. What do they call the mayder dee in Vietnamese?"

"In Saigon we said *maître d'hotel*. They were wrapping our language. They were wrapping my country. The French."

"Raping?"

"No. Wrapping. I know the word rape. They were trying to wrap everything French around my country."

"They lost."

"Yes."

"Then we lost."

"Yes. You too. But *maître d'hotel* won."

"We lost."

"I hope this in my lap makes you feel better when you feel bad."

Glancing at her lap, he says, "Absolutely."

* * *

As the lasagna bakes, they sit in his living room. She enjoying the bitterness of Campari and soda, he a Coke. She is eager to assist him in the official purpose of the dinner: the investigation of her daughter Rhonda's disappearance. She has nothing else in mind. He wants to find her daughter, but has in mind a senior citizen's fantasy of last chance romance: this lovely Vietnamese woman sitting near.

She says, "I fear this Iraqi."

He says, a little heroically, "Do not fear. I'll take care of him. Eventually I'll take care of everything."

Never has she inhaled the fragrance of what Rintrona has concocted and she's distracted from the subject at hand. She says, "What you bake—it is in a book of lasagna? Will you write it for me? What is it called in the book?"

"Lasagna *l'ultima*."

"You will write it for me?"

"I'll write it down, but it's not in any book. I invented it."

"You invented lasagna?"

He laughs. He's in love.

"I invented *l'ultima*. Because when you live alone you do things to forget your loneliness, which after Maureen died I'm alone most of the time. When I invented it I gave it the name *l'ultima*—'the ultimate,' Lilly. I laughed out loud in the kitchen when there was no one in the house but me. I laughed and was lifted up a little."

"I am blushing at my age. You think I am ultimate Lilly at my age?"

"I was translating *l'ultima* for you in case you didn't—yeah, you're *l'ultima* too."

"I am just a little old lady, Robert."

"Call me Bobby. Shall we get down to brass tacks? Let's start with the names because I'm curious. 'Lilly' is not a Vietnamese name. Ditto Rhonda. Wait. Wait. I'll confess, first. My actual first name, which nobody knows, is Francis."

"Like the Pope."

"I hate that name. Once I got to high school I become Robert so I didn't have to put up with the language. The taunts. But they remembered. Hey! Francis! How many bras you own? The humiliation. They teased me I had a girl's name. Franny. I had a girl's name and I had fights, which I usually lost, and secret shame, which never went away. The tough guys went to college. I went to Vietnam."

"My Catholic friends in my school in Saigon told me the meaning of Saint Francis. A person of kindness and gentleness. Like your Pope."

"Your turn, Lilly."

"My true name is Phuong."

He makes a note: "F-O-N-G?"

She corrects him.

"It means lovely lady?"

"Phoenix. A special bird. In Vietnam, the Phoenix bird never dies. It does not make a fire out of itself like the phoenix of the west and become reborn. It comes only in times of peace. In times of trouble, it hides. A bird full of grace bringing grace."

"Like the mother of Jesus Christ, the only Son of God. I'm thinking it's a beautiful bird, Phuong."

"I cannot say."

"Don't be modest."

"I cannot say."

"You left Vietnam in times of trouble to hide your grace in Utica, of all places? Why Utica?"

"I left Saigon in 1974 during so many explosions in the bars, the restaurants, the stores, when I was pregnant with Rhonda, who does not have a Vietnamese name. She was born in Los Angeles where her father left us when she was 2 years old. I chose it because of the song. Help, Help me Rhonda. Are there Iraqis in Utica?"

"A few. But why Utica? Why would anyone? Her father's name? Is he alive?"

"Steve. I don't know if he lives. I don't care if he lives."

"Is it possible—when did she last see him?"

"Two years old."

"How old now? Forty-something?"

"Forty-three."

"Maybe they made contact? She and the father got together who knows when and she goes off to California. Together again at last. Have you considered that?"

"Forty years after he dumped on us, he made contact?"

"In the business I'm in? Everything is likely. You can't imagine the human sewers I waded into. Worse than Khe Sanh."

"When you were in Khe Sanh, in the mountains there you are surrounded by beauty. My parents would talk so many times of the highlands where you were. A place to visit for escape from the lowlands of Saigon, but they could not go in the time of the French, and then came the time of the Americans. Just a dream. So many decades of violence. In my mind always a painful wish to go where we could not go."

"When I was a kid, every New Year's Day we watched from frozen Albany the Rose Bowl Parade in Pasadena, California. The Palm Trees. The sun. The girls in shorts. I heard how many times my mother say, Let's move there, Anthony, and get away from this damn winter. My father would say, What's so bad about Albany? Eventually he would say nothing. Once, after she said Let's move there, Anthony, he turned off the TV. It was an awful thing in our living room, the way they were with each other when he turned off the TV. My mother went through her whole life wanting to be somebody else in some place else. The word still gives me feelings I had on those frozen New Year's days in Albany. Pasadena."

* * *

The night before Rintrona's tour of duty would come to an end, he slept as he'd slept through all the days of the siege, badly, as incoming, the high arcing trajectories of heavy artillery and mortars hit the base all day and all night every 45 minutes. And that night it had rained hard and steadily, but the bunker he lay awake in was dry and warm and the big rats of Khe Sanh invited themselves in: sounds of little feet on the floor, in the dark. And one of his buddies screams, when a rat jumps up on his cot and crawls under the covers. And when dawn breaks Rintrona recalls dead Jonesey's voice delivering his chilling wit: "Good morning," he'd say, even to the base commander, "How are you tomorrow?" Once, and only once, he had confessed to Jonesey what he said daily only to himself: "I have a bad feeling that today I gonna get hit." And Jonesey replied: "If you get hit today, Bobby, tomorrow you'll be safe." And dead Jonesey saying now to Rintrona as dawn breaks: "It's tomorrow, Bobby. Godspeed and hope to God you don't get sped off to God."

He recalls, as he awaits his ride out, at dawn in the bunker sleep-deprived, the saddest story of the siege: of a fellow Marine whose tour, like his, was at its end, who was waiting crouched in the slit-trench alongside the airfield, as he soon would wait. Waiting for the biggest bird to land and evacuate him and the wounded and the dead—some in body bags, many barely covered in ponchos because they'd run short of body bags. And they waited too, the NVA waited patiently for this sad Marine's ride out, as it would surely await him, and when it landed the runway was hit by mortars and you had to run about 30 yards through the massive wind-blast of the twin rotors hurling grit and dust and small stones at you, the blast so strong that it felt like you were standing in place as you ran with all your might and you thought you'd never get across the 30 yards to the open door, as the mortars came with the intention of destroying your ride home and you—the mortars hitting in the vicinity of your path just as you were going to sprint out of the slit-trench and the legendary Marine, poor bastard, he just couldn't do it. He couldn't leave the slit-trench. He was paralyzed in the slit-trench. He tried again, 8 days in succession, crouching in the slit-trench, steeling himself to race to the epic chopper, but he couldn't do it. And he said, on the ninth day, to everybody and nobody in particular, Fuck it, I'll stay at the base. I'll re-up. And he did re-up. And those who heard about it kept their distance. And they called him the Colonel of Death.

One morning, the Colonel of Death was patrolling the perimeter wire—you finish the sentence. They found him in eleven pieces. Pathetic motherfucker, who made it harder for those who were ending their tours and who'd heard of the Colonel's failure of nerve, and they all thought about the Colonel while they crouched in the slit-trench, where it took extra balls, thanks to that sad motherfucker Colonel, to bolt across the 30 yards to the open door. Bobby! How are you tomorrow? Godspeed!

Rintrona crouches in the slit-trench alongside the airfield, waiting for the gigantic Chinook to land and liberate those whose tours have ended: the wounded, the dead, and those happy few sound of body, and maybe of mind. The trench is a place of safety "below fuckin' grade," as they say at Khe Sanh, unless a mortar falls directly in. It's just a slit, barely wide enough to shoulder in your body. Death is rare in the slit- trench, but it happens.

The NVA on the hills and the ridge-line know as well as you do when the Chinook approaches: they hear the thunderous metallic rumble, as you do, long before the chopper is visible. They are prepared. They fire round after round even before the chopper is visible in order to tear holes in the runway.

There it is: Jesus! 99 feet long, 16 tons, 5,000 horsepower. Incoming intensifies. The door opens. The wind-blast makes a fast runner like you, Golden Dago (Godspeed!) think you're running backwards. You make it. You're in. The door closes behind you. Your face is bleeding. Lift off before you're seated. The floor is crowded with the dead and wounded shoulder to shoulder on the floor—stepping on body bags and on the wounded who curse you and cry for their mothers as you brush the places on the wounded too painful for morphine to perfectly dull. You stand before the open cockpit: For the view below and beyond. The base itself shaped like a long almond, 12 square kilometers, a plateau surrounded by hills and mountains and out there in every direction what the boys call Indian Country. What a beautiful view at 750 feet above grade. Triple canopy, elephant grass—6 feet tall whose edges razor-like slash your hands as you pass through. You could have worn gloves in the elephant grass, an option you wouldn't take, no one would because your trigger-finger would be a little impeded and you'd be a little dead. And mangroves, thick expanses of it, and bamboo and teak. Most did not know the names of vegetation and trees, but they knew the danger of ambush in Indian Country, when once he, Rintrona, on patrol, saw his platoon commander, Lieutenant Terry Johnson, killed, without a face. And Palm trees. He, Rintrona, knew Palms because he'd seen them every New Year's Day on TV at the Rose Bowl parade. Pasadena.

* * *

"The lasagna'll be done in 20 minutes. Let's get back to brass tacks. Your husband—"

"Don't call him that. I know that word. He never did what that word says."

"This Steve. What's his last name? His last known address. Occupation."

"Bayard. Laguna Beach. I heard he had a car dealership."

"Who told you? When?"

"Rhonda. 10 years ago. Volvo."

"So she was in touch with him after all. I need to talk to him."

"Maybe he is dead."

"You'd like that?"

"Not nice what I like."

"What was your problem with this Steve?"

"Love."

"That's a problem?"

"Of other women. Many. Even in Saigon when he wanted every week to marry me."

"He married you in Saigon?"

"Yes. 1972."

"Four years after he began his big move to get you into—"

"Yes."

"The Americans were preparing to leave. Rhonda came in 1973. In 1974 he was with other women and the baby was one year. Saigon in 1974 was almost belonging to Ho. The Inspector General made arrangements for the 3 of us to fly to Los Angeles. The Inspector General caused the official papers. When we landed in California I was the wife of the American, and I was and Rhonda too, we were automatically citizens. In Los Angeles the shit—I have to say that word—it hit the fan of our marriage all over me and Rhonda, but not him. I stayed with Rhonda in Los Angeles until 1977. He sold cars, used. Like me and Rhonda. My uncle in Saigon told of his friend who had gone to Utica to create a Buddhist Temple for 25 Vietnamese ladies who were sent to Utica because they had babies by American soldiers. Like me. They had to be sent somewhere away from the big cities where there is too much temptation. So Utica. How do you say? Laugh out loud. End of story."

"These 25 Vietnamese and the Monk still here?"

"Many are dead. The others are my age."

"The children of these people? Who Rhonda knew when she grew up to become a grown woman? Did she have … uh, any significant relationships with these Viet-American kids? In recent years?"

"I don't think so. Many of the male children made a criminal gang."

"Did she have a romantic relationship in Utica that you know of? Someone, excuse the bluntness, she was seeing on a regular basis at all hours of the day and night?"

"She was very serious when she was 25 until 30 with Stanley, a boy with a Polish name."

"He still around? She broke up with him? Broke his heart? His last name?"

"He left her, Bobby. In the cold. Stanley Dujek."

"He left her in resentment and rage because she was seeing someone else?"

"He left her because he died from cancer when she was 30. 13 years ago. Testicular cancer."

"Phuong, I'm a detail-type detective. I'm big on detail. Cancer was enough without the locale. Relationships since then of a carnal—a romantic nature?"

"No."

"She had a job?"

"At the mall in New Hartford. Cleaning. Like me."

"Still does?"

"Not since the Polish boy died. Home with me."

"Since?"

"13 years."

"Cooped up with you in a tiny apartment and now the mythical Iraqi. She's in love again and shacking up you think?'

"I hope so. Better than other things that make a person disappear out of the blue."

* * *

From the Chinook well above grade he will not see what he'd on occasion saw on patrol in Indian Country. Actual elephants. Tigers. 25-foot pythons. Creatures whose names he never knew. Bugs the size of your foot. Exotic birdlife that made you forget the danger you were in. He'd heard that a patrol of bored and pissed off Marines, eager for contact, to "get some," as the boys liked to say, made contact finally only with an elephant, which one of the boys proceeded to blast from a distance of 50 yards. The beast was not fazed and went crashing through the bamboo and disappeared. Eleven days later the stench of putrefaction hangs like a blanket over the base, causing mass nausea and vomiting. The elephant had died and rotted in a creek, upstream of where the boys would bathe and swim.

* * *

In Spring and Summer she would stroll along the malodorous canal, the one that ran by her uncle's house, bound (she and the canal) for the Saigon River and the warm breeze that made the humidity and heat a little bearable, but did nothing but intensify the odor which is nameless: From the mango trees laden with fruit and the stalls of the soup vendors decorated with flowers, the too sweet perfumes of the tropics mingled with the stench of sewers emptying into Saigon's many canals, the flow of human waste making its way to the river, where on its banks many fine restaurants and hotels offer outdoor seating for drinks, dinner, and the view. Phuong strolling over the network of hidden Vietcong tunnels, where Charley stored food, ammunition, cared for their wounded and launched attacks in the countryside and in Saigon itself against the Americans and those Saigonese whom they suspected to be sympathizers. Bombs in public places where the soldiers congregated, bullets and slashed throats for the local sympathizers, privately delivered.

The familiar foulness of Saigon never offended or even registered when she took her long weekend ambles to the river. Phuong Thieu, like all locals, was immune to the sewage-inflected air. But on this hot morning on the 11th of June, a Saturday, a unique fragrance, at once awful and pleasant would register—even with the locals.

The rumor had flown everywhere that an important event would occur, at noon, in central Saigon, at a busy intersection outside the Cambodian embassy, 2 blocks from the palace where President Ngo Dinh Diem, a Roman Catholic, had 2 months ago imposed harsh laws of discrimination against Buddhists, who comprised 80% of Vietnam's population. Two days before the event of the 11th of June, President Diem struck harshly again by banning the Buddhist flag and dedicating Vietnam to Jesus and the Roman Catholic Church.

Thich Quang Duc was his name, a Buddhist monk, who had decided at dawn on the 11th of June that Diem's oppression needed to be fought on equal terms. At 11:45 a.m. Thich Quang Duc drives to the intersection with a fellow monk beside him who clutches an empty 5-gallon container and a siphoning device. When they arrive, already a crowd of monks and nuns (Buddhists mostly, but a few Catholic nuns too) has gathered, blocking all traffic, except for the rusted old Renault which Duc drives. Phuong Thieu is there, 9 yards from the center of the intersection. Duc steps out of his vehicle. Duc's passenger monk, the helper, lays a cushion at the center of the intersection so that Duc would sit in comfort. The good helper monk siphons gasoline from Duc's car, leaves the hood up, as Duc in his flowing robes sits on his cushion at the center of the intersection, in the traditional lotus-position. Cross-legged. Feet on opposing thighs. On his cushion. She, Phuong Thieu, like Duc, arranges her hands in the ascribed way: before her midsection, palms upturned, one beneath the other. She is standing, as are all on-lookers. In her hands, nothing. In his, a string of wooden beads. She takes two steps forward, separating herself from the encircling crowd—she's now 7 yards from the center of the intersection, where Duc sits. She sits. Assumes the full lotus-position. She will tell no one. The good helper monk approaches Duc. The good helper monk pours 5 gallons of gasoline over Duc. Without changing the position of his hands, Duc rotates the string of beads and chants in a quiet monotone, just a murmur. The crowd is silent, inhaling the stench of gasoline. She knows the chanted words. Her lips move, her murmur floats across the space to where Duc sits chanting. She will tell no one. He, the martyr, strikes a match and drops it on himself and in an instant is enveloped, as the flames begin to consume his flowing robes, as he chants, as she chants, as he and she maintain the elegant lotus-position, as the flames lick and begin to consume his flesh, his face. He ceases to chant though his lips move as he maintains beyond all human understanding, to perfection, the lotus-position, as black oily smoke emanates from his burning body.

Phuong Thieu ceases to be Phuong Thieu. She has been eaten by the spectacle before her. She is the black oily smoke, the leaping orange and blue flames, the burning body. Later, years later, she will recall the odor of Duc's burning flesh in a backyard in Playa del

Rey, California, as her husband barbeques steak and pork chops. How quickly he burned, never moving a muscle, never uttering a sound. How still he was in the elegant lotus-position. Not a twitch, or a flinch, how terrible the head held high, how terrible the back, ramrod straight, until 10 minutes after the match was struck, burning black, he topples, smoking, backward, dead, his withered and shriveled limbs retracted and thrust up as if climbing the air toward the other world that Duc does not believe exists.

The crowd wails and moans. She, like Duc, is still as a statue and silent to the end, when she too topples backward, arms retracted at the elbows and thrust up, climbing the air toward nothing.

* * *

He serves her and himself considerable slabs of lasagna from the oven-hot Pyrex. Enough left for 4 more of the famished in body and soul. He pours her Chianti Classico, water for himself. She asks if he doesn't like wine. He answers that he does, but as the "designated driver etcetera." They dig in.

She says, "How good. My God."

"You believe in God?"

"Only love. Only burning love. What is all this in it?"

"Red onions. Garlic. A lot. Pancetta. Red wine, don't go too overboard. Tomato paste. Ground sirloin for the meatballs in there. Pecorino Romano. Eggs. Parsley. Flour. 56 ounces of Italian plum tomatoes. Italian sausage. Is there another kind? Don't tell me Kielbasa. Sweet and hot. A lot of mozzarella. Ricotta. So forth. 16 sheets of lasagna noodles. Preferably Antica Pasteria."

"You will write it down? With the amounts of each?"

"The amounts go by how I feel at any given time. My moods."

"You felt good in your mood when you made this."

"Phuong, I've come to some tentative conclusions for your case. The chances of Rhonda and your ex being in touch are remote. I'll talk to the family of this Polack who died. I'll talk to her supervisor at the mall. These interviews likely give me nothing. Did she just sit home every day for 13 years? I don't think so. She went out here and there."

"She went to Café Caruso in the afternoon for coffee and to read the newspaper they keep for customers. Lately in the evenings, I don't know where."

"This Iraqi story. You believe it?"

"Yes."

"I mean, why make up an Iraqi, which we don't have many in this town. I'll make inquiries. Phuong! You made short work of the lasagna. How about another chunk? Why not?"

"A small piece. Not too big."

He duplicates the slab she's just annihilated.

She says, "This is too small."

They high-five.

He says, "The young people think they own everything, including certain things. We're so old we don't even blush anymore."

They blush.

He pours her more wine.

"Phuong, shall we share memories of your native ground?"

"My secret name for Rhonda I tell no one is Giang. [Yiaang.] It means 'river.' It's good to be a river. The river can't be killed, not even by pollution."

"Like the Phoenix, no?"

"Better."

"How?"

"Unlike the Phoenix bird, the river is real. You call me Phuong. May I call you Francis?"

"Please, don't."

∗ ∗ ∗

This is what Rintrona remembers, sometimes in daylight hours, but mostly at night, when alone and sleepless: He's never told it to anyone. He'll tell it to Phuong now as they sip espresso and nibble almond cookies:

How he was never hit, except once.
His company assaulting Hill 881 South.
5 Kilometers from the base.
45° angle steep. Dense brush, big sharp rocks.
Heavy fire from summit.
I'm attacked. I'm hit. I was hit.
How he crawled screaming for cover.
Behind a large rock.
Screaming.
Jonesey rushing to his aid.
A swarm of bees, Phuong. It was bees.
Screaming, but not Jonesey screaming.
How Jonesey lay over him.
How Jonesey took bees in the face.
5 comrades dead. From summit fire.
Jonesey's face more red than ever. Swollen.
Acne oozing.
Jonesey saying homeopathic. Fight fire with fire.
Weirdly. How strange. Two days later. Jonesey's acne
   diminishing greatly.
Three days later: No acne.
Jonesey: pointing to his cleared-up complexion.
Jonesey: pointing to his face: The miracle of Hill 881 South.
Jonesey: pointing to his face: Blessed be Our Lady of 881
   South.
Not bullets. Bees.

When he returned to the States, he tells her he told no one
about the bee attack and what Jonesey did to protect him. Because
he was ashamed of his reaction to the bees while 5 of his buddies
were killed. Saw their bodies after the bees. Bullets, not bees, had
torn them apart.

She says, "You are brave to show me your shame. Men do not
usually do this."

She wants to tell him something she has told no one, not even
Rhonda, all the years she's lived in the U.S.A. She asks him to bring

his laptop to the table. She tells him that she can only do Google. Nothing else.

Rintrona fetches the laptop. She googles an iconic photograph, together with video. Of a man executed in Saigon. On the street.

He says, "I've seen that. What's the deal?"

She proceeds to tell him the story of the Friday night in 1966 when at 14 she discovered her murdered parents: Phuong and Rintrona side by side at computer. He, speechless. Takes her hand and says her name. She says, "Thank you, Bobby." She tells him that the execution on the street took place mid-day on February 1, 1968, while she was working at the airport. That when she returned from work to her uncle's house, he told her of the execution and why this man was executed: Because he was the leader of a Vietcong revenge squad that operated in Saigon. Killing police officers and their families. Killing suspected sympathizers of the capitalist enemy with their Western social values. Her uncle said that the leader of the revenge squad had made an effort to have his life spared by confessing to unsolved murders. Yes. He had personally slit the throats of the wife and six children of a police officer that very morning. Yes. He would give the names of squad members and their locations and families. Yes. The postal clerk and his school teacher wife, Phuong's parents, were his personal mission because one of her students had reported to him her fondness for Western music and literature, especially Viennese waltzes and the novel, *Huckleberry Finn*. A foul work of anarchy, not solidarity.

They stare at the iconic execution-photo, taken a fraction of a fraction of a second after Nguyen Ngoc Loam, the National Chief of Police, fires his .38 at point-blank range into the head of the captain of the revenge squad, Nguyen Van Lem. In the real time of video, the .38 is raised, the executed man falls to the pavement, a river of blood runs from his head. The photo of frozen time tells us more. The man, hit, but still standing, his face in a grimace that reminds anyone who knows it of a famous American photo, the face of Lee Harvey Oswald as he is gut-shot by Jack Ruby. The video shows what the photo cannot: the man being led to his executioner: bare foot, in shorts and short sleeve shirt. He looks like a teenager. A full head of dark hair. Handsome by any measure. His executioner is older, in his early 30s, hairline in retreat. The Chief of Police executioner is the godfather of one of the children who that morning had her throat slit. She was 3 years old.

Rintrona tells her this execution-photo went viral all over the world and energized the anti-war movement. The movement of the Left, he says. She says nothing. He says the youth of the American Left spit on the soldiers who came home from the war. Greeted them at the airport in San Francisco, when they came off the plane, yelling that they were war criminals. Moral monsters. Yelling at these soldiers who would get no parades. Ever. They got contempt. My Jonesey was spared, thanks to an artillery shell, of the spit and the contempt of the idealistic Left, which saw the executed Viet Cong captain of revenge as a victim of capitalism. They hated the capitalist tool, this executioner who fled to Australia where he was shit on—this executioner who said at the scene of the execution that the Buddha would forgive him because this man he killed had murdered many unarmed civilians.

She says nothing. She cannot say to Rintrona that when she looks at the Viet Cong captain of revenge she sees a child. Who seems gentle. Who has parents who grieve and who once rocked him to sleep. She cannot say that she forgives him for murdering her parents. She cannot say that she feels toward him sadness or pity or hatred.

She speaks. She says, "Who deserves this," her finger pointing to the man who killed her parents? "Look how small he is." She points to the executioner and says, "Look how tall he is for a Vietnamese. Google told me he moved from Australia to Virginia. To Burke. Near D.C. He opened a pizza restaurant. In Rolling Valley Mall. I think a rolling valley is a place where you feel good. Google says, reviled, a world-wide villain. Someone wrote on the toilet wall of his restaurant, 'We know who you are, fucker.' He did not feel good in the rolling valley where he died of cancer. Bobby, tell me. Who were these Left people?"

"Types with smart brains and no hearts. College kids and their professors."

"Are we friends, Bobby?"

Rintrona nods. Holding her hand still, saying, "You have a computer at home?"

She shakes her head.

"Rhonda?"

"Yes."

"You two shared her computer?"

"Yes."

"If she left the computer when she disappeared, I could get a forensic examination. We could learn who she was in contact with."

"The computer is gone with my daughter."

"That's a good sign, Phuong."

"Why, Bobby?"

"One more question and I'll tell you why. Did she ever take the computer with her to Caruso's?"

"No. I don't think so."

"Then she took it with her when she disappeared because she had a destination planned in advance. My theory that it's a good sign is this: She wasn't kidnapped. She didn't take her computer with her if she had in mind to do—uh, serious self-harm. That's my theory. I'd bet on it. She took clothes? Right? Did you check her closet? Her bureau? Her toiletries?"

"Yes."

"And?"

"She took nothing."

"Not good news for my theory."

"Will I see my Rhonda again?"

"I guarantee it."

"Alive?"

"Absolutely."

What does Francis Robert Rintrona know that allows him to guarantee absolutely? Nothing, except his desire to free a mother of anxiety for her missing child.

"Does she have a cell?"

"No."

"Do you?"

"No."

"So she called you on your landline. Did you check the origin of the call?"

"I did."

"Did you call that number?"

"I did."

"And? Come on, Phuong. Don't keep me in suspense."

"From Joey's Restaurant on the corner of Mohawk and Lansing."

"The two of us should have lunch there. But they don't have a pay phone. Angelo must've let her use his because Angelo Raspante is a good guy. I'll talk to him and his staff. This is a real lead. How about it, Phuong? Lunch at Joey's tomorrow? I'll pick you up."

"I accept."

She points to the wall: "I like that picture over there. Did you create it?"

"No. My neighbor. Bob Cimbalo, the artist."

"Very expensive, I think."

"A gift for helping him shovel 2 feet of snow. It's a lithograph. One of Bob's specialties. *Embrace*, he called it. Embrace is what you see in a lot of his work. A beautiful idea."

"Yes. The most beautiful."

"What do you see, Phuong?"

"A man sitting in a chair and a woman sitting in his lap. They are hugging."

"The woman is big. Very big."

"He is small in comparison, Bobby. He is hard to see underneath her big body, which is not fat."

"He's more or less disappearing under her embrace. Her bigness. Which is what a man needs to do."

"Disappear in a woman's love."

"Whatever her body-size, her love surrounds him. That is the deep meaning of Bob's art."

"You like this meaning, Bobby."

"Totally."

"There is one more photograph of the Vietnam War. The most—the most worst of all."

"I know what you're referring to, Phuong, but I think we shouldn't look at it. Ever."

"We have already looked. I think you and I have."

"Let's never again."

"Let's never again."

* * *

He has taken her home. He's sitting in a chair facing Cimbalo's *Embrace*. Remembering what he heard, but did not see. Maybe no one at Khe Sanh saw. Maybe it was just rumors without foundation. What the besieged imagination of soldiers created: more real than real: The Marine who cut off the ear of a Gook and mailed it home to his girlfriend. The Marine who cut the heart from a Vietcong and fed it to his noble scout dog, a beautiful and hungry German Shepherd. The Marine who was hoarding body parts of the enemy because he intended to build his own Gook. The Vietcong who was said to be immortal, ubiquitous in space and time, who appeared—on sworn testimony—simultaneously in all regions of battle. The Khe Sanh base commander who was said to have said, "I am a great believer in planting flowers."

Said to have said: two black Marines:

"I ain't never gonna get hit in Vietnam."

"Oh, no? Okay, motherfucker, why not?"

"Cuz it don't exist."

Actual fact, not fevered imagination: Bobby did piss his pants, more than once. He did see and applaud and cheer until his throat was sore: the beautiful displays, in Indian Country, of Napalm strikes. How fucking beautiful. Burn those midgets. He did see the torn bodies of Marines, not looking all that different from what he'd seen on his summer job, when 15 years old, at a slaughterhouse in Albany. He did hear, and enjoy, and cheer the blood-curdling screams of the enemy when our artillery struck gold. And how he cheered, they all did, when our B-52s rained down cascade after cascade of 500-pound bombs—killing everything, human, animal, vegetable within 1000 meters in all directions from ground zero, by force of concussion alone. Totally beautiful. No fucking tooth-brushes for 3 weeks: the real tragedy. The rumors that the babies, the tactical field nukes, would be used on the NVA who surrounded Khe Sanh. Yes! Yes! Yes! Please God, let it be! And no shelter from the rain, and his clothes rotting in the rain and humidity. And the trembling of the earth when our sexy B-52s fucked them brutally. And the human sounds of battle: crying, screaming, cursing, cry-ing, crying.

And the worst thing. Not imagined. What he, The Golden Dago, does after the bees hit him on 881 South as he proceeds toward the summit under heavy fire and jumps into a mortar crater to find 2 children in there. 13 or 14 years old. With rifles. Children, but NVA, fucking little Gooks 5 feet tall and skinny, who freeze when this big American joins them in the crater. Where is she? Our Blessed Lady of Hill 881 South? They drop their rifles. They huddle. They em-brace. They stare at the former altar boy, Francis Robert Rintrona, who does not hesitate. Two little kid Gooks dead in their embrace. He told no one. He will tell no one.

* * *

Francis Robert Rintrona, a fanatic for Italian opera, rises from his chair to fetch the bottle of Chianti Classico, three-quarters full. He stands before Cimbalo's *Embrace*, hoists the bottle and intones the nihilistic words of Iago, in Verdi's *Otello*:

CREDO IN UN DIO CRUDEL'

* * *

Rintrona had slept badly. Last night, worst of all nights, he twisted and turned as they refuse to let him go—images like tiger claws in his head—two surrendered boy-children, soldiers maybe

14 years old—embracing and shivering in 95 degree heat and heavy humidity—their discarded rifles at their feet on Hill 881 South— then dead and bouncing and quivering as he poured round after round.

What was he supposed to have done differently? Tell me. In the midst of an intense fire fight? The enemy within 40 yards and above. Take those two NVA kids prisoner as the Geneva Conventions demanded? Listen, asshole, this wasn't fucking Switzerland. Turn his back on the NVA fire from above? Walk his prisoners back from the hill to the base 4 miles off and leave his platoon on Hill 881 short yet another man? He, the sixth man, 5 others dead who he'd seen dead and he alive and safe, walking 2 children up to the perimeter wire gate and through, sporting a few bee stings as the sign of his bravery on the field of battle. Or take the time to disable the little bastards' rifles? Weapons he had never before seen, much less handled? While they shivered and embraced and watched him fumble ignorantly and the battle raged on? In the mortar crater, with the 2 children, he did not think. He killed them a few times over.

What chance for a peaceful and intimate relationship with Lilly Thieu if he doesn't confess to her? Who would want to live with such a brutal animal? Can't imagine telling her and asking for forgiveness, as if asking all of Vietnam on behalf of all of America. Can't imagine keeping it to himself. In the middle of the night he sees himself living with Lilly, his secret intact. Self-conscious, guarded. Impossible life. He must confess.

* * *

In 5 minutes he'll knock on Lilly Thieu's door and she'll play Rhonda's 2-day-old message, the content of which Cruz and Conte had already summarized for him. He has no interest in the precise wording of the content. His only interest lies in the precise tone of Rhonda's voice.

He listens. Says nothing in response, except "Let's go to lunch." His no-response upsets Lilly, who says nothing, and now they're in the car heading to Joey's for a late lunch and to quiz Angelo

Raspante, proprietor and chef, about the phone call made from his premises by Rhonda Thieu, presumably in the company of an Iraqi male.

They ride in silence—Rintrona because he's thinking too much about how she sees him—she because she fears that he had heard something disturbing in Rhonda's message.

He breaks the silence, "72 degrees and dry, a rare thing in this town in August."

She answers, "You heard a clue in my daughter's message that you are afraid to tell me?"

"We'll see down the line. I'll take care of everything."

"Take care of everything? How? You scare me."

"Don't be scared."

"Why not?"

The answer that he suppresses: Unless she's the Vietnamese Meryl Streep, who's capable of perfectly hiding the truth of a frightening situation, I heard the relaxed and natural voice of an ordinary person, without a trace of strain or awkwardness. The voice of a 43-year-old woman who is not "missing," but who has somehow, we don't know how yet, made a connection that she thinks will change her life from boredom and constant low-level misery to romantic adventure and the promise of a life worth living.

He won't say the truth: Lilly, I doubt Rhonda is a "case" for this private dick working gratis. She's only my excuse to stay close to you so that you'll be the cure of my own loneliness, if you'll have me in spite of what I've done and that I'm afraid to tell you.

He says, "Rhonda claims she'll return in a few days to pick up her stuff. That was 2 days ago. Let's wait before we jump to conclusions. Let's not leap into the dark where the monsters lurk. A few days more."

"She *claims*? Monsters? You don't believe her?"

"A few more days and we'll see."

"How much is a few?"

"If after a week from today—"

"Then we worry and fear?"

"Try not to imagine the worst."

"I am afraid of the monsters in the dark."

"Because you're the mother."

"Bobby, are you afraid too?"

"Of lots of things, but not necessarily at this point for Rhonda's welfare."

"You are scaring me more."

She had heard of Joey's, but had never been there. If she had passed by on her walks she never noticed the weather-beaten brick store without a parking lot on the corner of Mohawk and Lansing. They enter and she's happy to see that it's not anything fancy to look at. A dozen or so tables, many forever unbalanced, on the tilted floor, which the waitress will balance upon request with a book of matches. The tables covered—this is what catches the eye—with vinyl green-and-white checked tablecloths, periodically switched out for blue-and-white ones. The hardwood floors dark and scuffed-up. The ceiling white-painted tin. The big wooden bar—bar stools but no one comes to Joey's to drink at the bar. The bar there since the restaurant was founded by Joe Giruzzi in the 1930s, darkly stained and scarred, like her, and featuring one tap: Utica Club. The lighting is soft, weak, inadequate, which suits the weathered seniors who come to Joey's, who feel they look better in such lighting. The interior of Joey's is a sepia-toned movie.

She hasn't been able to afford a beer in months. Maybe Bobby will say, "On me, Phuong." If he does, should she, at 1:30 p.m.? On an empty stomach? One wall was decorated with cooking utensils she'd never seen: cheap antiques bought by Joey in the 1930s that once served their function in 19th-century farmhouses. On another wall, family pictures. Alongside the bar an autographed picture of an old time baseball player. She will ask about him. Bobby will tell her, "That's Lou Gehrig, who died at 37 from a disease they named after him. In his honor. They called him the Iron Horse. When he knew he would die, he said on a day to celebrate him at Yankee Stadium, "I consider myself to be the luckiest man on the face of the earth." And she will think back to the martyred monk who self-immolated and ask Bobby if this dying lucky man was a Buddhist. Because this is how Buddhists think. No, Bobby will answer, he was not a Buddhist. He was a first baseman.

The lunch crowd has cleared out and only one customer remains, sitting looking at his smartphone, at a table beneath the picture of Lou Gehrig. It's Eliot Conte, who doesn't look up until they approach.

He says, "My lucky day. Please join me." He goes back to his fucking phone.

Rintrona says, "Join you so we can look at our phones together?"

Conte puts his phone down.

"Know why she doesn't have a smartphone, Conte? Because she's already smart."

She bows her head. They sit.

Lucille comes to the table with menus. She's an East Utica girl, 21, Angelo Raspante's daughter. Angelo worked as Joey's assistant, then bought the restaurant, had the ceiling repainted, and bought the photo of Lou Gehrig in Joey's honor, a melancholy Yankee fan who once said that there can be no happiness unless the Yankees go undefeated for an entire season.

Lucille has worked at the restaurant since she was 17 and knows all the customers, except one, by name. She says, "You guys hungry?" Holds out her hand to Lilly, they shake, and she says, "Welcome to Joey's. Your first time, am I wrong?"

"You are not wrong."

Lucille excuses herself, goes to the kitchen and emerges with Angelo who holds out his hand to Lilly, "Angelo Raspante, call me Ang, an honor to have you here. You're the first Vietnamese to walk through that door and in your honor lunch on the house for all three, Utica Club for Bobby and the pretty lady, Lucille, and a Coke for Mr. Conte, unless the lady would prefer something of a lighter variety?"

Lilly gives a little head bow and says, "I am Lilly Thieu. I prefer whatever you prefer. You are very kind."

Lucille says, "Dad, hey, I hate to break it to you, but this pretty Lilly isn't the first Vietnamese to come here. She's the first to *eat* here, which we hope she'll enjoy, but not the first to come in, which was 2 days ago to use the phone, who was sort of Vietnamese, which I didn't mention because she didn't eat."

Rintrona says, "Sort of Vietnamese?"

"She was tall for one of those."

Conte says, "Rhonda."

"And lighter colored, unlike present company."

Lilly says, "Her father was a white American and tall. You saw my daughter."

"Wait a minute," Angelo says, "so this first so-called Vietnamese I let use my phone was half and half, nothing wrong with that, don't get me wrong, so she's not the first pure one. Lilly is. I say in her honor she eats here free lunch and dinner every day for a month."

Lilly says, "Oh, dear."

Angelo says, "Don't hesitate to put out the word to your community, Lilly, how much we appreciate their contributions to Utica. You people are all welcome at these tables, though of course your deal is unique to you."

Lilly says, "And I appreciate the Italian people," glancing at Rintrona who, sadly, happens at that moment to be looking at Angelo and Lucille.

Rintrona says, "This half and half. She come in with someone?"

"A strong-looking dude," Lucille says, "in a black shirt and black pants, who eats here a lot and leaves a nice tip. I once asked him where he was from and he says to me, From the country I helped America to destroy. Which I laughed and I go, Wyoming? We had a good laugh. He seems nice but who knows."

Rintrona says, "He pays with a credit card?"

"Never. Only cash."

"So you don't know his name?"

"No. The big mystery of Joey's."

"Did you see the car they left in?"

"Barely. It was black with writing on the back window, which I couldn't read."

"Make?"

"Oh, my God! I don't know cars."

"License plate?"

"Don't be crazy."

"I'll bring you a book of car photos tomorrow. You're my chief witness, Lucille."

"Mr. Rintrona, I don't want involvement."

Angelo says, "Bobby, this is an up-and-up business."

Conte says, "Lucille, Ang, take it from me. No one disrespects Joey's. What this is about is trying to locate Rhonda Thieu, Lilly's daughter. In all your dealings with this guy she came in with, Lucille, anything worrisome about him? Out of line in any way? Any oddities? Any shadows?"

"A good guy as far as I'm concerned. You should talk to Cara tomorrow. She's waited on him. I think she'd serve him after hours, if you know what I mean, don't mention I said that."

Rintrona says, "If you see him in here again do me a big favor and call me right away." He hands her two cards. "The other one is for Cara."

"No problem. Cara's about his age."

"What's that?"

"Early 40s."

"He had an accent?"

"Yes."

"Could you place it?"

"Sounded like a Russian I extremely briefly dated, back in the day," says 21-year-old Lucille.

"Maybe Iraqi?"

"A what?"

"Just a random thought, dear."

She draws 2 Utica Clubs and a Coke as they look over the menus. She brings the drinks, says, "You need a little more time?" Nods all around. She says, "I'll be back in a bit."

Rintrona decides on Greens and Beans in a garlicky broth because he is partial to foods that encourage ease of movement. Conte wants Eggplant with Peppers, Provolone, topped with a Marinara sauce. Lilly is captured by Sausage and Peppers with Mozzarella and a side of tomatoes. The price of the meal for three, including the beers, the Coke, and coffees all around will be $29.75. When Conte attempts to pay he will be told "No way" by Angelo in the kitchen via Lucille. Rintrona will drop a 20 dollar tip.

As they wait for the food, the conversation turns to cell phones. Rhonda doesn't have one. Lilly doesn't either. The reason they don't is obvious and will not be stated in Lilly's presence. The mysterious Iraqi with a car surely must have one because if he can afford a car—but, then, why didn't he permit her to use it?

Conte says, "Traceable and he doesn't want to leave a trace, unless it's one of those cheap disposable ones which can't be traced, in which case why wouldn't he let her use it?"

Rintrona says, "He doesn't want to leave a trace? So he brings her to Joey's and comes in with her in the open? Where he is well-known except by name? And parks out front on the Mohawk Street side where the car is totally visible thanks to the big window? Give me a break. If it's one of those untraceable pieces of junk and he doesn't let her use it, I haven't the foggiest what he's up to."

Conte says, "Maybe he's up to nothing. Because it's an innocent situation and he has nothing to hide. There's no problem folks, he's found the girl of his dreams. Rhonda's safe. We don't have a 'situation,' Bobby, what we have here is a love story. He brings her into Joey's to make the call because he wants to introduce her to Italian-America at its best."

Angelo pops in from the kitchen, says "15 minutes." They notice a limp and a grimace.

Rintrona asks, "What gives, Ang, with the limp? You've had it for a year at least."

Ang says, "The left hip is shot. I need to go in for a false hip, but who takes over in the kitchen?" Goes back to the kitchen.

Lilly says, "I have nothing to worry about, you say, Mr. Conte, but why can he not let Rhonda use his phone and introduce her to Italian-America at its best another time, when they can have a meal here together?"

Lucille pops out of the kitchen excited: "I just called Cara. She knows cars, she says it's a Lexus SUV RX350, pretty new and she knows what it says on the back window. She tells me. I tell her to spell it out because I don't get it." Lucille produces a slip of paper, hands it to Conte, who reads silently then out loud: "Allahu Akbar Airport Service. So he runs a cab service to the Syracuse and Albany airports. You need a license for that, which would require contact info and an address."

Rintrona says, "So we more or less cracked the case which isn't a case. We're on the verge."

Lilly says, "A new Lexus SUV is expensive, I think."

Conte says, "Depending on the model and the extent that it's loaded, in the 50-grand plus range. Or more."

Rintrona says, "Airport service can't be that lucrative unless he's transporting contraband, which I doubt, let's not get carried away. But where is the money coming from?"

Lilly wants to know when the address can be acquired. Conte tells her this afternoon, then calls Catherine, who gets on the task. Lilly should be relieved, but she's not.

The food arrives. They dig in. After a few bites Conte says, "You need to see this." He holds up the screen to his smartphone: a photo of himself with a twisted wire sticking out from the back of his head and binoculars around his neck.

Rintrona turns to Lilly and says, "He's gone extreme for birds, according to his wife. That thing is the bionic ear sticking out of his head and in his ear so he can hear birds, who knows how far away. Long-range artillery for bird-quarry. Did you buy a selfie-stick?"

Conte says, "I'm shuffling along Mary Street when none other than Patrolman Victor Cazzamano pulls up in the cruiser. Somebody in the neighborhood, he tells me, called 911 to report a man wired with a bomb. A terrorist on Mary Street. After I tell Victor what it's all about, he says, Thank God your father's not alive to witness your descent. Then he takes the picture with my phone."

Lilly says, "You should visit Vietnam and then you will see birds! Here in Utica only those little brown things that hop on the sidewalk."

Conte does something with his smartphone and shows them the screen, saying, "Like these in Vietnam? Exotic. I'd like to visit."

She says, "Not exotic. Normal in Vietnam."

Rintrona says, "Especially in the Khe Sanh area."

Conte says, with a touch of self-laceration, "My deferment was my birding loss."

They resume eating.

Conte says, "Student deferment and then a teaching assistant deferment at U.C.L.A. kept me on the home front."

Rintrona and Lilly do not respond.

Conte says, "I escaped."

Rintrona says, "Except for the big shot officers, nobody at Khe Sanh wanted to be there. Get over it. Did you protest the war with the students on the West Coast? Disrespect the returning soldiers?"

"No. I was indifferent to the student radicals. As for returning soldiers, I didn't know anyone except a guy in a wheelchair I knew a little, who wanted to be an actor, who said things like Yo! Marie! I had no feelings one way or the other about the soldiers. The guy wanted to be Sylvester Stallone in a chair."

"You know another Vietnam Vet. Me."

"Yeah."

Rintrona makes the crucifix gesture looking at Conte and says the Latin words he heard at the end of confession: "*Ego te absolvo a peccatis*—I can't remember the rest. In other words, Eliot: I absolve you from your sins of deferment in the name of the Father, and of the Son, and of the Holy Spirit. Amen."

"Thanks. Now I can die in 2 weeks in the O.R. and be guaranteed a place in Heaven after 3000 years in Purgatory. How about you, former Marine Rintrona? Need absolution?"

Rintrona does not reply. Lilly puts her hand on his arm, as if she knew what he needed and why.

Conte says, "*Ego te absolvo* so forth."

Rintrona says, "Thanks, pal."

Conte says, "*In nomine Diabolo.*"

Rintrona says, "You got that right."

Lucille comes to the table, "How's everything?"

The guys say, "Good." Lilly says, "I am very happy."

Lucille says, "Mr. Rintrona, I remembered something about that man whose name I don't know. So okay: He's parked right over there on Mohawk facing toward Bleecker. So when they leave he makes a fast U-turn and the tires make that sound. You know what I mean? So okay: He pulls up to Lansing and makes a right turn!"

Conte says, "He went the wrong way on a one-way street? He went west?"

"Oh, yeah! Is that a clue? That's all I remember. Ang says have dessert."

Nobody wants dessert.

Rintrona says, "This is getting interesting."

Lilly says, "I am more scared."

Conte lies: "Lilly, I can't tell you how many times I've sat here for lunch and seen cars go west instead of east. An innocent mistake, believe me."

"I want to," she says, "but I can't."

And then the three of them: gripped by sudden self-consciousness and silence and isolated in thoughts of Vietnam and the fate of a missing daughter, at mid-afternoon at Joey's when the only sounds are those of sporadic traffic on Lansing and Mohawk and some broken chatter from Angelo and Lucille in the kitchen, the restaurant empty but for the silent three.

Conte turns to Lilly and says, "You are brave to sit here with the upstate slaughterhouse boys," and she is pulled away from her fears, she giggles, the Utica Club having done its work and she says, "Who have you killed, Mr. Eliot Conte? Who have you killed, Mr. Robert Rintrona?"

Rintrona rises and goes to the restroom.

Conte says, "The two of us as teenagers worked summer jobs in slaughterhouses. Bobby in Albany. Me, here. But we didn't kill anything because you had to be a skilled union knifeman to kill. We did the grunt work. We hauled the beheaded and eviscerated calf-carcasses to the big coolers."

Rintrona returns. He says, "The slaughterhouse was our preparation for life. Me for Vietnam. Him? Did he tell you he watched live open-heart surgery for preparation for his own? Because knowledge reduces fear, he thought. Yeah. Now he goes to the O.R. with a clear image of himself opened up wide on the table. He's scared shitless, excuse my vulgarity, Lilly. The slaughterhouse didn't help me in Vietnam. Even though they look the same. Human and animal guts and blood. You'd think spending your teenage summers in a slaughterhouse would harden you for what's down the road. Laugh out loud. He's scared shitless, I'm sorry, Lilly. Nothing helped me in Vietnam except a good friend whose name was Tim Jones. I saw Tim's guts. When he was gone nothing helped me in Vietnam."

Rintrona rises and goes again to the restroom. Conte and Lilly are speechless. He returns red-eyed and says, "Let's change the focus, shall we? There's a sentence my friend Tim Jones, my friend Jonesey quoted many times to me. He once quoted it to the Commander of Khe Sanh, who held his tongue. From the preamble to The Geneva Conventions. I still hear Jonesey in his sly voice: 'The human dignity of all individuals must be respected at all times.' Laugh out loud. Let's change the focus, shall we?"

Lilly says, "After your surgery you will allow me to make you a special Vietnamese dinner? Will you come?"

"You'll need to drain the formaldehyde before I sit down."

"Got his sense of humor back. Good sign. Maybe."

"Mr. Conte," she says, "here is a new focus: You will know happy death many years in the future with Catherine and Annie holding your hand."

"You can't know that."

"But I do."

"What else do you know, Lilly?"

"Why we celebrate the Day of the Dead in Vietnam and not birthdays. Why we worship our ancestors. Because they are sources of our lives when they are dead, who we the grandchildren imitate their gestures, so that when we become the grandparents, we who repeat their gestures pass them on to our grandchildren who repeat and pass them on. Through the generations passing on the ways of the hands and the ways of walking and sitting and bending deep in the flooded rice paddies, sowing and reaping. Mr. Conte, in this Vietnamese passage of time there is no rushing forward into death.

No end for the dead grandfathers and grandmothers. We bury them in the rice fields which sustained their families. In death they give life to the rice fields, and there, in the rice fields, they continue to live in the bodies of their children and grandchildren, in the rice they eat, in the ways of the hands, the ways of walking and sitting, sowing and reaping bending deep. Time is not an arrow, but a flow wrapping around itself like the flow of water in the rice fields. The Day of the Dead is a celebration of life without end, in time without change. Without history. In America, with your birthdays, you live flying forward on the arrow. Never in the eternal circle."

Conte says, "The Vietnamese think, and live, in this way?"

"Oh, Mr. Conte, less and less."

"Why?"

"We all become modern now."

"You too?"

"I live in East Utica, do I not?"

JOLTED (3)

CONTE RECOGNIZED VINNY, BUT DIDN'T want to let on. It had been 47 years since that summer when he worked the slaughterhouse job as an unskilled laborer. Hosing down the blood-flooded killing floor. Shoveling guts into barrels. The guts sliding off the shovel. Picking up the guts with gloved hands. Then not bothering, after a point, with the gloves. Vinny was skilled. Vinny was a knifeman. Vinny-with-one-eye said, "This eye? I thought you'd recognize me." They had crossed paths at the gas station on Broad. "I think you recognize me, Conte." Vinny was an attendant. Conte was filling up. Vinny says, "I probably shouldn't've given you the knife on coffee break. Good thing I did. You said you just wanted to feel it in your hand. The heft, you said. That vicious steer with the horns from here to Syracuse breaks free. Remember? It's charging the crew. You jump on his back near the neck. You crazy fuck. You stick it in. You got the jugular. Then they treat you like a hero for 2 weeks." Conte says, "How are you, Vinny?"

THE IRAQI

LILLY THIEU RETREATS TO THE kitchen, where she's almost out of earshot of Catherine's second re-telling of what was learned that afternoon at City Hall: that among Utica's cab drivers only one appeared to qualify as their man: Tariq Al-Chobani, who had registered his company as Allahu Akbar Airport Service. The vehicle: a black Lexus SUV RX 350. His address: a long-abandoned and thoroughly-vandalized bungalow in West Utica. Number of drivers employed by Al-Chobani: one: Tariq Al-Chobani. There could be no doubt: Al-Chobani is the man they seek and Rhonda Thieu is in his company. Or is "possession" the correct word?

Rintrona says for the second time, "I don't get it."

Conte says for the second time, "Makes no sense."

From the kitchen, she, who never raises her voice, does so now in anger: "I will tell you what makes no sense. His name."

She returns to the living room. Rintrona says, "Why not, Lilly?"

"A fake name! Chobani! Greek yogurt! What shall we do beside talking?"

It's a warm August evening. No need for a jacket, but Conte is wearing one with some bulk to it at his upper right chest.

Smiling, hand-in-hand, they enter the apartment: Rhonda Thieu and a thick-bodied man wearing black pants and a black short-sleeved shirt. Massive forearms. The top 3 buttons of his shirt unbuttoned.

"I thought something bad," Lilly says, rushing to embrace her daughter.

A little peevishly, Rhonda responds, "Bad? I told you I'd be home soon to gather my stuff. Mey, did you forget I'm not a teenager? This is Tariq, Tariq, my mother, Lilly."

He bows, takes Lilly's hand, kisses it. Lilly suppresses her repulsion.

Six in the tiny living room. On the couch, Rintrona, Conte, and Cruz. Lilly paces. Motions Rhonda and the man in black to the chairs facing the couch.

This man who calls himself Tariq Al-Chobani says, "Are you prepared for comedy? I will tell you who I am. Once upon a time in Baghdad, when I translated for your country for the very first time, in the Green Zone of safety, in Saddam's Republican Palace at the top floor, in a room with silver and gold fixtures and tiles you would not believe—a room with a sweeping view of the River Tigris winding below us like a strong brown snake. Tea and delicate sandwiches and delightful pastries. In that room sat a high-ranking official, who did not manage to escape with Saddam, who vomited his sandwich before even one question was asked, who sat facing the great window giving on to the Tigris and the damaged city below. The ancient city of smashed bridges. The city of exploding and smoking power stations at the city's edge. Outside the temperature was 116 degrees. In the air-conditioned room, 72 degrees. And I stood at the window, staring at the river. Wishing to be the river. I turned to my chair opposite the prisoner and sat heavily and the chair of the Saddam regime died beneath me with a crash. From the floor I laughed until tears came, but the high-ranking prisoner who was to be interrogated did not laugh. He said, Please, in God's name. He had bepissed himself. I laughed again from the belly and said to him, We have not yet begun and you have bepissed. I warn you, I said, not to beshit, because if you do you shall face consequences that not even Saddam himself dreamed in his finest rages. We had a very successful interrogation. The highest-ranking American had observed. He was pleased. He made me his man in the room with a sweeping view. He was my faithful audience."

"That's a funny story?" Rintrona says. "I forgot to laugh."

"You speak," Conte says, "like a writer writes. A writer of the high style. A little forced."

"Rhonda," Lilly says, "you have chosen such a man?"

Rhonda nods. Caresses his forearm.

The man who calls himself Tariq Al-Chobani closes his eyes and rests his head on Rhonda's shoulder. He says, "I have run out of options. Even here in America, the land of options. I need help. Rhonda too, my fiancé."

"You will be married, Rhonda?" Lilly asks.

"Yes, Mey. And also—" She cuts herself off.

"Also what? Don't make me imagine."

Catherine says, "No kidnapping. No crime. The mysterious Iraqi is no longer mysterious. None of this is any longer our business, Eliot. We should go now."

Rintrona says, "What's the point of your story? Why did you tell it? Like Eliot says, you talk like a book."

Conte says, "Are you in danger?"

"Rhonda too."

Rintrona, who will seize any excuse to remain in Lilly's company, says, "We should hear these lovers out."

Conte says, "Allahu Akbar Airport Service? Do you mean to—"

"Yes. I do mean to evoke what you have not said. The 9/11 leader, Atta, who exclaimed when his airport service was about to smash the North tower: Allahu Akbar. God is great!"

"Sick joke," Rintrona says.

"You smiled a little, sir. I saw the little smile."

"Mey, I am pregnant."

"You are pregnant?!"

"I think I am pregnant."

"Have you seen a doctor?"

"No."

"Why not?"

"You know we can't afford a doctor."

"They have a test you buy cheap at the pharmacy. You pee on a stick."

"How would you know, Mey?"

"Never mind."

"I'm pretty sure I am."

"Why?"

"I missed my period for 3 months."

"I think we should leave," Catherine says.

"They call you Eliot," Tariq says. "How many 'l's?"

"What?"

"In your first name. How many 'l's?"

"One."

"Like the poet who pleases me most. T.S. Eliot. Unreal city. I had not thought death had undone so many. He saw the future of Baghdad."

Rintrona says, "What's poetry have to do with anything?"

"At university I studied English and American poetry and wrote it myself. I received highest honors. Upon graduation, a letter of commendation from Saddam, who fancied himself a poet and novelist. His writings were clichés, but let it be said competent clichés. Between wars and domestic terrors we lived a little and died much. The people of my Shiite faith, who resisted Saddam the Sunni, lived less and were found in mass graves, if found at all."

"Cut to the chase," Rintrona says.

"I did not resist, unlike my father and sister who spoke bravely and foolishly in the cafés. They disappeared. Then I disappeared, into the writers I loved. I was not brave. Instead, I wrote 3 poems in praise of Saddam the artist and received another letter from him, and money too. I cultivated detailed loathing for my spineless life. Then the Americans came to topple the regime and I lost my cowardice and offered my services to their cruelty. Where was Saddam? Where were Uday and Qusay, the sons who made the father seem like Saint Francis of Assisi? Your army wanted answers. They thought someone so sensitive to language would be a very fine translator and interpreter. For basic training, they sent me to observe at the palace of horrors called Abu Ghraib, which Saddam founded but your army perfected."

"The chase, Tariq, the chase."

"The prisoners at Abu Ghraib were low-level. What they knew, if they knew anything at all, was of no value. What was of the greatest value to me were the methods of torture. Wasted torture of the body. The body shuts down at a certain point. But the mind? You are eager for the juicy part of the narrative, Mr. Rintrona? At Saddam's Republican Palace, in the room where we interrogated high-level people of the Saddam regime, I redeemed Abu Ghraib. I transferred from the insulted body to the mind, where terror has no limit. What did Satan say, according to the poet? Myself am Hell. In that room, which I thought of as Room 101—"

"Orwell," Conte says, "*1984*."

"Yes. You too are a literary man. Like all true literary men, a connoisseur of violence? In that room, I directed the Theater of Interior Hell."

Lilly says, "What is your true name? Did you tell my daughter the truth?"

"Mey!"

"Did he, Rhonda?"

He says, "My passport, my driver's license, my birth certificate, my citizenship documents, my social security card—all say, thanks to my U.S. handlers, Tariq Al-Chobani. They do not say, Tariq Al-Masri, which Rhonda knows to be my truth."

"Your handler went to the grocery store and saw Greek yogurt and decided to give you that name?"

Catherine says, "So you collaborated with the American military and we brought you here with a new identity to save you from Saddam's assassins?"

"Yes."

"They have such a long reach? Not credible."

"The American private contractors have long reach, who once worked for your government."

"Your mother is here?"

"No."

"Your mother is still in Baghdad?" Lilly says. "Are your handlers stupid or cruel?"

"Bet on stupid," Catherine says.

Conte says, "Tell us more about your theater of mental Hell. You were its sole creator?"

"You have an appetite for hellish details, Mr. Conte? I was writer, producer, director, and co-star. Do you know the name Tariq Aziz? My greatest theatrical triumph. Tariq Aziz was closest to Saddam in Saddam's inner circle. The equivalent of your Secretary of State. I had been elevated to the double role of interrogator/translator. I ordered that his chair face the great window open to the city and the river. When he was brought into the room I escorted him to the window. I asked if he loved, as I did, the traditional Iraqi poets also much loved by Saddam. He did, and quoted a famous passage flawlessly. I quoted another passage and he responded with yet another. Back and forth we went. Two poetry lovers shoulder to shoulder. The room was cool. I had ordered the thermostat set at 65°, but he perspired profusely and malodorously. Here, I said, we are not vulgar. We love the poets. You shall not be physically harmed, unless you so request it. Why would I request it? he said. Here, I said, everything is possible. I said at the window, pointing out, The dead land. The broken jaw of Saddam's lost kingdom. I took him by the arm and gestured to a chair without arms. I nodded to the guard at the door who opened the door and gave a hand signal. A waiter came with tea and pastries. I sat opposite Aziz. Very close. My foot brushed his. I said nothing of this indelicacy. He held the tea cup and saucer in one hand and the pastry with the other, in his chair without arms. Unlike me, he had no small table beside him and when he attempted to put the pastry in its napkin on the floor so that he might sip his tea, I spoke. I said, You recall that vulgarity is not permitted? He did not put his pastry on the floor and his hands began to shake. Tea spilled onto his lap. I said, Allahu Akbar! A man like you of such elegant formation. Let me assist you, I said. I took his pastry and ate it. Then I ate my pastry."

Lilly says, "My God, Rhonda."

Rintrona says, "When does Aziz vomit?"

"He doesn't. He begins to weep and does not cease until our session ceases. I nodded to the guard who opened the door and signaled. I said to Aziz the Arabic equivalent of, Do you catch my drift? He nodded. Are you catching it well? He nodded. A tall and beautiful woman entered holding a leash, at the end of which, a bejeweled collar around his neck, a man on all fours, with a bag over his head. Naked and barking."

Lilly says, "Rhonda. My Rhonda."

Rhonda says, "Be patient, do not judge."

Conte, Cruz, and Rintrona are swept up in the teller's tale.

"Then she, the tall and beautiful woman, walks the dog, circling us several times. I said to Aziz, Has your tea gotten cold? Would you like a pastry? He did not respond. I said, I understand completely, my friend. She is—I said the Arabic equivalent of drop-dead beautiful. I said, Focus! I said, Do not be distracted by the woman and her dog. I said, Do not drop dead. Are you happy, I said? Be careful how you reply. The woman and the dog leave the room. I nod to the guard. A different tall and beautiful woman enters holding a leash tied to a naked man's genitals. A bag over his head. The woman instructs him in Arabic. The man begins to masturbate. For many minutes without success. I say to Aziz, Would you like to lend a hand? Or in your infinite generosity perhaps some aperture of the body? Might you conceive of your aperture as the door to your infernal Sunni soul?"

Rhonda takes Tariq's hand. The others sit in silence, by turns enthralled and disgusted.

Lilly moans.

Tariq Al-Masri asks Lilly why he and Rhonda have been denied the courtesy of a proper introduction to—he points to the 3 sitting on the couch.

Lilly says, "They are nice people who are detectives."

"From the Utica Police Department?" Al-Masri asks.

"No," Lilly replies, "Private. They were helping me to find Rhonda."

Rhonda says, "For God sakes."

"Perhaps," Al-Masri says, "before this night is finished, we will all be on the same squad. God willing." Lilly introduces the nice detectives.

"After the failed masturbator and the lovely woman left the room," Al-Masri says, "Aziz said, Please, I beg you, ask me questions. I replied, You do not approve of masturbation? You understand, Al-Masri says to the gathering in Lilly's living room, I had only one goal in my work: Never to forget my father and sister and to rid Iraq of the missing Saddam and his sons. All methods to those ends are sound. Everything is sound in defense of family, and occasionally even of country."

Conte says, "No methods are unsound that rid of us those the law cannot eradicate. I agree."

Rintrona says, "He's your man, Tariq, believe me."

Catherine says nothing. Shakes her head.

Conte says, "How can I help you?"

"To help you must forgive the horrors of my measures in The Republican Palace. Because the horrors of my imagination belong to me and I suspect you, Mr. Conte. When Aziz asked, pitifully, for questions, I offered him the *pièce de résistance*. I said, Most Honorable Aziz. God loves most those who are patient. I nodded to the guard. He enters, unleashed and unattended. His head bagless. Naked. Face, neck, chest and belly, genitals, legs, back and backside, smeared thickly with feces. He chants softly and constantly words I had written for him: Touch me, love me, touch me, hold me, heal me now. I said, BEHOLD! SHITBOY! Aziz collapsed to his knees, facing Mecca, and chanted, There is no God but God, Mohamed is His messenger. Then he arose and embraced and kissed Shitboy on both cheeks, turned toward me—himself smeared—and said, I do not need questions, I will tell you what you seek to know. One day later, Uday and Qusay were found and shot to death. Two days later, Saddam was captured alive in a spider hole near his hometown of Tikrit. When the Americans pulled out, they extracted me."

Rintrona, incredulous, says, "They planked you down in Utica? They chose Utica?!"

"Oh, no. First Los Angeles, then Phoenix, then Salt Lake City, then Miami, Chicago, Philadelphia, New York. Always one step ahead of my pursuer. I am sick of running. Utica is the last resort."

* * *

They leave Lilly's apartment at the same time, minus Rintrona, who was quick to accept Lilly's offer to stay for Vietnamese coffee. On the street, Catherine asks where Rhonda and Tariq can be reached and Rhonda replies, "We can't. We're spending our days and nights here and there in Tariq's SUV." Tariq gives them his cell number.

Conte asks, "Have you seen this man—I assume it's a man—who's pursuing you? Can you describe him?"

And Tariq tells of the appearance of a male of slight build, Caucasian and blond, always wearing a red windbreaker zippered to the throat. First sighted in Los Angeles in the parking lot attached to a vast complex of movie theaters, at twilight, standing behind Tariq's vehicle and apparently taking down the license plate number. When he, Tariq, approached, the man moved swiftly off and disappeared in a sea of vehicles. In Chicago, the same man, in the parking lot of the Jewel supermarket, in the suburb of Westchester, circling Tariq's vehicle. As Tariq approached, the man without haste walked away after giving the thumbs-up gesture. In the New York City suburb of Bronxville, there he was, leaning on Tariq's car, spotted across from the house that Tariq was renting, as Tariq stood at the window with his coffee at 6:15 a.m. The man nodded, ambled off and has not yet been seen again, but was heard from—it must have been him—in Lebanon, New Hampshire, where Tariq was renting, where he received a postcard postmarked Clinton, New York. In block letters: I WILL CARVE YOUR BABY FROM YOUR WOMAN'S BODY. THEN I WILL CARVE YOUR BABY.

Tariq said that Utica was the move he'd planned after Lebanon, New Hampshire: "The final move to obscurity."

Catherine says, "Clinton is 4 miles from Utica. As if he knew your next move. As if he knew that you'd meet Rhonda. As if he knew she'd become pregnant."

* * *

Home again on Mary Street, Conte and Cruz relieve the baby-sitter and put Annie down for the night.

She says, "A miracle. The Fiend went out like a light. Let's go over his story."

He says, "I need to google something first."

"Can't it wait? If we're going to help Tariq and Rhonda we need to be clear on the details while they're still fresh."

"I need to google something."

"Pertaining to Tariq's story?"

"No. I need to do this now."

He sits at the computer. She taps her ballpoint pen rapidly on the legal pad. Six minutes later he says, "He's dead."

"Who? Who died?"

"Vincent."

"Vincent? I don't recall any Vincent. An old friend?"

"From back in my U.C.L.A. days. 1968, '69. Vincent O'Brien. A Vietnam Vet in a wheelchair."

"You were close?"

"In a way. Let's do Tariq's story."

"You want to talk about Vincent?"

"Later. Let's do Tariq now. Find the opening. Because I'm not totally sure about this guy."

"Me neither."

So that night on Mary Street they comb through Tariq Al-Masri's story many times, in search of the detail that hides what he won't reveal, but they can't find it. Around midnight, Catherine exclaims, "It's obvious! Here's the key—the highest-ranking American official in Iraq is in the room for the interrogations. This is what Tariq told us. It was staring us in the face all along."

An easy internet search leads them to Paul Bremer, Administrator of the Coalition Provisional Authority of Iraq, the man who ruled by unrefusable decree. Hated by Saddam's Baathist party, which he'd outlawed, and a target of assassination attempts, one of which nearly succeeded. Bremer, they learned, reported directly to Secretary of Defense, Donald Rumsfeld, who in theory reported directly to the President, but who in fact was filtered by Vice President Richard

Cheney, who, in turn, reported in his own ways to President George W. Bush.

"The order to protect the Iraqi translators while they were in Iraq and then evacuate these opponents of Saddam and company, when we left, it had to come down from The Pentagon," Conte says, "not from Bremer, whose presence in what Al-Masri called Room 101 Bremer would need to keep hidden. Rumsfeld's order to evacuate the collaborators was rooted in the principle that if we do not protect these people our national security interests will in the future be compromised."

Catherine says, "Because who in Iraq or any other foreign country would in their right mind work for us if they knew they'd in the end be deserted?"

He says, "Betrayers beheaded."

She says, "Did Rumsfeld know that Bremer was an eyewitness to torture? Would he want to know?"

"Unlikely. Because after Abu Ghraib the strategy was at the highest levels to deny knowledge of torture. No doubt after Abu Ghraib the effort was made to add even more layers of insulation and quarantine torture to the lowest levels, to those at Abu Ghraib with the leashes and the pails of feces. Otherwise, Bremer, Rumsfeld, and Cheney give press conferences with shit-smeared faces."

"Better," she says, "to throw her in prison."

"Who?"

"Lynndie. Specialist Lynndie England. Make an example of her sad little ass. This nobody who took pictures at Abu Ghraib, and posed in them too, thumbs up, holding the leash on the head-bebagged failed masturbator. This tiny girl from somewhere far below even the working class in the dirt-poor backcountry of West Virginia, whose boyfriend at Abu Ghraib knocked her up in the torture palace."

Conte says, "A child conceived in the ecstasy of torture. Yeah."

"She was fucked every which way."

"But here's the question, Catherine: Why would Bremer, who needed perfect deniability, have let Tariq leave Iraq, knowing what he knew that Tariq knew? Makes no sense. He needed to eliminate Tariq. With extreme prejudice, as the boys in the CIA say. He had the power to have Tariq murdered, but didn't. Why not?"

"You think Tariq is holding out on us?"

"We need to talk to him."

* * *

The next morning in Catherine's office on Bleecker: Tariq, somehow crisp in dress and looking rested after another night in the SUV. Rhonda one floor below, visiting her mother. A large thermos of coffee and 3 plastic cups on the desk. Also on the desk, a legal pad and a ballpoint pen. Catherine rapidly tapping the pen on the pad.

Catherine starts: "We asked for this meeting because we need blunt answers."

Conte: "Because we don't intend to drive blindfolded. That's the long and the short of it."

"Why do you speak to me in this manner?"

Catherine: "Because we're not your friends. We're investigators not interested in cuddly chit-chat. Especially if there's danger. Which you claim there is."

"I don't 'claim': There *is* danger."

Conte: "Consider the coffee a friendly gesture. Help yourself."

He does not. They do not.

"Good. Let us then be cold, but let us also be effective. Let the interrogation commence. Am I sitting in Room 101, Utica style?"

Conte: "Time will tell. You met Rhonda when and where?"

"At Café Caruso. Three months ago. She was alone. I asked if I might join her. A request that surprised myself because I am not bold with women."

Catherine: "How long have you been in this country?"

"Nine years."

Catherine: "How many times have you seen the man in the red windbreaker?"

"Three times, as I told you last night. Until yesterday, the fourth time, when I saw him on Mohawk Street as we were leaving Joey's."

Conte: "According to an eye witness, you made a U-turn laying rubber on Mohawk, and then sped off the wrong way on Lansing."

"He was walking on Mohawk in the red jacket. Toward us. I panicked and turned the wrong way."

Catherine: "Let's get back to the first encounter. L.A. 9 years ago. What did you conclude at that time?"

"This I knew: I was a target of assassination. As a Shiite born in Iraq, in paranoia, it was the only conclusion. I knew also that he was not an Iraqi. No blond men in Iraq. Do you know that your word 'assassin' is from Arabic?"

"Even the stones know that."

"Who did you surmise he was?"

"An American, of course. Hired by the famous private contractor who worked for America and was paid by America. Who did murder for America in Iraq of noncombatants. You know Blackwater?"

Catherine: "What did you do about this perceived danger to your life?"

"Perceived? The next morning, as soon as the car dealerships began business, I sold my car and bought a new one. Later that morning, I broke my lease on my small apartment in Westwood and forfeited a month's rent of 5,000 dollars. I moved that afternoon into a cheap apartment in a dreary neighborhood far from Westwood, at the northern edge of the San Fernando Valley."

Conte: "What make car did you sell and what did you replace it with?"

"I sold the BMW and purchased an Audi A8."

Conte: "Were you gainfully employed at the time?"

"No."

Conte: "Since you moved 9 years ago, have you ever been gainfully employed?"

"No."

Conte: "The next question is obvious."

"Yes. The money. For 3½ years I worked for your government and was admired and valued. I was the ace of my department, as you might say. I was paid very well and living day and night in the safety of the Green Zone. Paying of course nothing for a luxurious room and excellent food living in The Republican Palace. Some of my money was sent underground to my mother. Most I kept, which I did not spend. How was I to spend? When I left Iraq I had a most lovely sum. For 9 years every month I am paid 10,000 dollars tax free by your government in gratitude for my service. My first vehicle, the BMW, was purchased by your government. Since then several new vehicles purchased by me. I have lived here well, quite well. Thanks to your government. Have I answered to your satisfaction?"

Catherine: "In the parking lot of the supermarket in Chicago, you said the man in the red windbreaker walked away casually. You didn't confront him when you had the chance?"

"Would you confront your assassin unarmed?"

Conte: "This assassin, so-called, had the opportunity to take you out in L.A. and Chicago. He didn't. Why not? Doesn't make sense."

"Perhaps the fiendish torturer of the Republican Palace must himself be fiendishly tortured, for years, before he is executed. If we capture him alive, Eliot Conte, before he achieves his purpose, we will find a way to make him happy to answer your intriguing question. I foresee your decisive contribution."

Conte: "I hope to make you a prophet in your own time. Tell us, how much time between the windbreaker's appearances?"

"I was living in Los Angeles for 3 years, my first stop in America, when first he appeared. Chicago was 3 years after Los Angeles. Bronxville 2 years after Chicago. New Hampshire 1 year after Bronxville. The event of Mohawk Street, 6 months after New Hampshire. I changed vehicles in Chicago from Audi to Buick. I changed apartments in Chicago from Lake Shore Drive to Melrose Park. I left Bronxville the day after I saw him and I changed vehicles from Buick to Volvo. In New Hampshire, after the event of the postcard, I purchased my current vehicle and left for Utica. In between Los Angeles and Chicago I moved 4 times. Salt Lake City, Phoenix, Miami, Philadelphia. Let me answer your question before you ask. How does he locate me? No idea. I suspect your country's intelligence agencies have a mole who works for Blackwater. Just a suspicion, you understand. Speculation without ground, driven by fear with solid ground. How does he know in advance that I would come to Utica? No idea. He made a guess. He said to himself, America has many unappealing places, too many to count. Where is more unappealing than Lebanon, New Hampshire? Utica, he guesses. Absurd speculation, yes, I understand. I find Utica deeply appealing and wish to live my life here with Rhonda and our child. I have no idea how he knows. A tracking device in my vehicle? Is it still on the Lexus? Which must be electronically compromised. Tomorrow I will trade it for a Ford, the most American car of all. You see, I am prudently paranoid. How can he know that Rhonda when we had not yet met would become pregnant? Such a shot in the dark, even when it misses, produces terror. This is what I observe: the times between encounters grow progressively shorter. It will end here. In Utica."

Catherine: "It adds up. You almost add up."

"You speak harshly."

"My first allegiance is to my client, Lilly Thieu, her daughter, and the unborn child. Let's just say you almost pass the test."

"I agree with my wife. I find it prudent to agree with my wife, believe me. It is difficult to pass her test, believe me."

Catherine: "Why didn't you offer your cell to Rhonda to call her mother? Why take her into Joey's to make the call? Didn't she ask to use your cell? Don't bullshit me, Tariq."

"She did ask. I said, I wish to take you into Joey's where I eat so often, to meet kind people. I said, I have been living abnormally for 9 years. I want us to be normal people. I said, We will now act like normal and ordinary people and perhaps become normal and ordinary people, who need to use a phone and the good Angelo will let you call from his private phone. What I have said to you, it is not bullshitting."

Catherine breaks her pen in half.

Conte: "She's the bad cop, believe me. Answer this: Paul Bremer was under Pentagon orders to extract people like you. But Bremer was compromised in your presence. And if he's compromised, potentially so are others way up the food chain. What you did in the Aziz interrogation is only done by those at the bottom of the food chain. That was the official defense of the Bush administration. Why did Bremer let you go? Bremer should have had you eliminated. Had my wife been in Bremer's shoes she would have had you eliminated. Believe me. Why did Bremer let you out? Doesn't add up. If that doesn't add up, you don't either."

"I answer that Paul Bremer found himself between a rock and a hard place, as you say in this country. Between the rock and the hard place is always the Iraqi condition. By coming to Room 101, Paul Bremer became an Iraqi. A Shiite Iraqi, no less, like me. He was as you say here, a saying I like very much, of beautiful vulgarity, Bremer was royally fucked over. He had fucked himself over by coming to Room 101. Seen there by the guard. Seen there by the tall beautiful women who escorted the victims. Seen there by the so-called victims who were in truth most courageous volunteers from your army. Actors. Shitboy was an American soldier of Christ-like character. What was Bremer to do after he eliminated me? Kill all those witnesses? And all those that they might have told, who would have told others of this spectacle of torture? He would have needed to initiate a carnage worthy of Saddam himself. The most florid version of the American saying is best. Paul Bremer had fucked himself over every which way to Monday."

"Sunday," Catherine says. "Not Monday. Sunday."

"Thank you. Forgive my error."

"Like I could give a fuck."

"Thank you, Catherine. So he facilitated my extraction, then played his Blackwater card and prays, and it continues to be played long after Bremer leaves Iraq. To this day."

"You don't and can't know that about Blackwater."

"Do you have a better theory, Catherine?"

"Mr. Al Masri, I prefer facts."

"Let the facts, God willing, be those which will be excreted from the red jacket."

Catherine: "I think we're done here."

Conte: "I'm curious about one more thing. How did you decide on Lebanon?"

"A 5-minute drive from Hanover, where a rich archive of Robert Frost is housed at Dartmouth College. Since my student days in Baghdad, I have dreamed of sinking into Robert Frost."

"Utica? Why Utica?"

"I liked the classical-sounding name and imagined meeting here a woman like Rhonda. 9 years. No friends. No intimacies. There is no woman like Rhonda."

* * *

"When you broke the pen in half? I thought, Do I know this woman? She's *that* strong? Will she break me in half?"

"Got his attention. He needs to know we're serious people. It was an act. Me, the bad cop."

She opens the drawer to her desk and removes Conte's .357 Magnum. She says, "You brought this here this morning, which tells us what we need to know about you. Keep in mind you have a family. We need you for the long-term. Especially Annie."

"With my heart condition, I'll only be able to squeeze the trigger, when it's time."

"*When*?!"

"Sooner or later. Absolutely. I see myself sitting. Maybe standing. Not running, because I can't. Not in physical contact. With my condition?"

He touches the gun. He says, "This takes the place of my unhealthy heart. This easily propels ordinance in and through any car-engine block. Much less Tariq's stalker."

"You'd like that, wouldn't you?"

"More than you'll ever know."

"While you're fantasizing killing the man in the windbreaker, here's our problem: Protecting Rhonda, getting her to a safe place. I'm proposing that after midnight tonight Bobby picks her up and takes her to his house, until the danger to her and Tariq has been eliminated."

He points to his gun: "That's the eliminator."

"Only if his life or yours is in immediate danger. No reason now to think that'll be the situation. I guarantee you won't be in danger."

"Guarantee?"

"You'll see. This stalker has shown no signs of violence. He's had his chances to take Tariq out. He didn't because he has something else in mind."

"Which is what, Sherlock?"

"Very slow psychological torture and finally assassination."

He points to the gun: "That's for the baby-killer."

"He's not killed anyone. That we know of."

He points to the gun: "And won't. What about Tariq? What have you in mind for him? Let me guess. He's the lure? The bait?"

"Yes."

"He keeps the Lexus, am I right? No Ford in his future."

"Yes."

"What's our first move, Sherlock?"

"We go down to Lilly's apartment right now, where Rhonda is visiting and where Tariq no doubt has joined her, and we present the plan."

"What about Lilly?"

"Lilly goes with Rhonda to live at Bobby's until it's all sorted out."

"Bobby will sprout the wings of eagles."

"For Bobby, everything comes up roses."

"No roses for us, Catherine. If this stalker learns that we're his pursuers? You're telling me to think about my family? What about Annie? If he discovers where we live? What about Annie?"

"He's only interested in Tariq and Rhonda."

"And the child who will come out of her womb. How could you forget the unborn baby? Put this in your plan: Until the problem is eliminated, you stay home with Annie and your .38 Special at the ready."

"I stay home with Annie. Yes. Bobby, fully armed, stays at his house with Rhonda and Lilly. Then you and the red windbreaker zippered to the throat face each other off on Bleecker Street at high noon. Is that your fantasy, Mr. Gary Cooper? Let's go to Lilly's."

* * *

The meeting at Lilly's was a fiasco. No sooner did Catherine begin to unveil the plan for Rhonda's and Lilly's removal from Bleecker Street than she remembered that Lilly knew nothing of Tariq's American odyssey and therefore the entire story had to be told. Once told, Lilly lost her native nobility and restraint. She said to Tariq, in tones approaching hysteria, that a "man like you has no right to be with Rhonda or any woman, or any human at all," because "you will bring catastrophe and death to all that you will be attached to." And Tariq replied, "You would condemn me to a life of solitary confinement and ceaseless self-laceration?" And Lilly said, "Yes!" And Rhonda said, "Mey, I choose Tariq. Keep talking like that and you'll never see me again. I will spit on your grave!"

The mother-daughter ugliness escalates rapidly, far beyond "I will spit on your grave." Lilly says, "I should have died with my parents in Saigon and then you would not be born!" Rhonda with equal cruelty says, "Not Saigon! Ho Chi Minh City, Mey! Ho Chi Minh City, Mey!" And Lilly replies, "You bitch!" Through it all Conte, Cruz, and Tariq sit in silence, desiring to crawl under the couch. Until Tariq speaks: "Your mother is right. I am a danger. You should not be with me." At which point Rhonda rises and sits in Tariq's lap and strokes his chest. Then Lilly rises and, near hysteria still, says, "I don't make American coffee! Who wants American coffee can't have it here! I will make Vietnamese coffee for all, whether you like it or not!" And Conte says, "You Vietnamese are worse than Italians." Laughter. Even from Lilly. Then Lilly says, "But what will happen to Tariq? My brave son-in-law? Who will save him from the madman in the red coat?" At which point Catherine and Conte, having learned their lesson, say, "We will speak to Tariq privately."

* * *

The three of them sit in Caruso's sipping espresso, at a safe distance from other customers. Conte has yet to hear the details of Catherine's plan for Tariq. Bait, she told him. Bait, he thinks, is another name for dead meat.

She says, "You want it to end here."

"Yes."

"To live in peace in Utica with Rhonda."

"Yes."

"Good. We think he's here. We're fairly sure."

"Yes."

"We need to draw him in. Close to you. In a place which we can control. With Eliot near. Are you willing to take the risk?"

"As soon as possible."

"Good. Let's assume he has a way of monitoring your movements. Maybe a tracking device on the Lexus. Maybe not. But he has a way."

"I am sure of it. You are saying do not trade the Lexus."

"What I'm saying."

"I will have no means to protect myself, but Eliot?"

Conte says, "You know what this is?" Pointing to the bulge at the front upper right side of his jacket.

"I can guess."

"You don't have to." Flashes open the jacket and closes it.

"You are willing to use, God willing?"

"Oh, yeah."

"To protect a stranger?"

"Rhonda and your baby. You're part of the package."

"If I were just me and not Rhonda and the baby and me? No package? You would care?"

"You want my answer?"

"Not required."

"Here's the plan," she says. "Your daylight hours starting this afternoon will be spent driving around town and out of town. Get tired of Utica? Up north to Old Forge and the Fulton chain of lakes. You'll love the Adirondacks. Checking the rearview mirror frequently. Then go to Clinton and see the college on the hill, Hamilton, picturesque. Consider a leisurely drive south to the Cooperstown area. Highly recommended. Beautiful. Rolling hills. Small lakes and ponds. You're enjoying Upstate New York. Checking the rearview mirror frequently. East to the Green Mountains of Vermont, so different from the Adirondacks. Not severe. Rounded. Like breasts. What will you do as you drive?"

"Checking of mirror if I am followed."

"Excellent. At about 4:30, starting tomorrow, you will drive to Lilly's apartment. You'll be living there until the problem is eliminated. I'll lay in groceries for you. Do you drink?"

"No."

"Splendid. Once there you don't leave until the next morning. Where will you park your car?"

"In front of Lilly's building."

"Correct answer. In the morning you begin touring the countryside. I will change the name on Lilly's mailbox to Tariq Al-Chobani. After you arrive at Lilly's at 4:30 p.m. or so you will never lock the door until you go to sleep. You must not arrive before 4 or after 5. At 11 sharp you lock the door and turn off all lights. And sleep if you can. If followed on your tours, do not speed up or try to evade. If when you pull up to Lilly's building you see him on the street, in the vicinity, pretend you have not seen him. Unlock the door. Enter. What else, Tariq?"

"Leave door unlocked."

"Very good. What do we hope for?"

"That he climbs the stairs and enters the apartment to find me there. But should I hear, as I climb, footsteps climbing behind me?"

"Breathe deeply. Keep climbing, don't look over your shoulder because you suspect nothing. You enter. He finds you there, but not alone. Eliot will be living there day and night."

"With his impressive gun. Is it legal to shoot someone who enters? A stranger? What will be the excuse to shoot? What will happen?"

"Tariq," Eliot says, "at the point he enters, we have an extremely unstable situation."

"What do we do?"

"We improvise."

"For what purpose?"

"In order to restore extreme stability."

She says, "Tonight you will park the Lexus in the visitors' lot of the Utica Police Department on Oriskany Street. And sleep in the Lexus. Beginning tomorrow night you sleep at 663 Bleecker, apartment 3A."

Conte says, "Can you really commit to this, Tariq?"

"It is the only way."

She says, "Time to hit the road, Tariq."

"I will go south to Cooperstown. To the Mecca of Baseball. For 9 years I have learned this subtle game of America and have loved the Yankees, who have ceased to be strong. I am now loving the Cubs. Goodbye."

"I'm confused. I'm disturbed. You say you want me to be sensible and think of you and Annie, but you want to put me in a dangerous situation? Where who knows what might happen? What's wrong with you?"

"You'll not be in danger. Relax. The red windbreaker will never make it inside 663 Bleecker. Last night while you were re-reading *Moby-Dick* yet again, I was emailing with our dear Patrolman Victor Cazzamano. He's off duty for the next 2 weeks. On vacation. He'll be sitting in his car outside Lilly's building. From 3:45 to 11. Every day. He has the description. Victor will stop him cold with no holds barred. Since Ronnie's murder, he tells me, he wants to do something in Ronnie's memory. He's been taking martial arts for 3 years. He hits the shooting range 3 times a week. He's strong and his eye is deadly. The stalker won't get in 663. Victor was happy when I made the proposal. He won't accept payment because money, he said, would dishonor what he wants to do in honor of Ronnie. Okay?"

"Victor wants to be a hero? Better him than me."

"Would you like to talk now about Vincent O'Brien?"

"Some other time."

Marilyn comes over to ask if they'd like something else and to say, "That Iraqi guy? He's been in here with that Vietnamese girl a few times. They make a good-looking couple. Hey! Is Utica diverse or is Utica diverse?"

* * *

Lilly's apartment: Conte and Tariq:

"Do you cook, Tariq?"

"I do not,"

"All your meals taken out for the last 9 years?"

"Yes."

"Does Rhonda cook?"

"I am afraid so."

"I cook extremely well. Assuming we'll be here for a few days, you will too."

"You will teach me the Italian way?"

"Tonight I'll teach you a pasta sauce in the style of the great whores of Naples, where they place big pots of it hot in the open windows. Which is how they suck in men. *Puttanesca*. Put this apron on."

"The woman's way. I will not do it."

"Here's your options, Tariq. You put the apron on and I put you through your paces and you learn to cook in the style of the whore, or you go out on the street and risk your life."

He puts on the apron saying, "I do not understand this necessity of the apron."

"To add the female dimension. To make us less stereotypical males. Less assholes."

"Less, but still assholes?"

"Of course. Without preparation we're doomed. Let's prepare. Pour a quarter cup of the olive oil in that big skillet there."

"How will I know a quarter?"

"This thing here is a measuring cup: one quarter precisely. Good. Open the cans of the chunky and diced tomatoes."

"They are not opening, Eliot."

"That thing in your hand, have you ever used a can opener before? Didn't think so. Squeeze the handles hard until you achieve penetration. Yes! Now turn the thing. Be careful of the lid. It'll sever off your fingers. Okay. Fetch the container of oil-cured black olives from the refrigerator, which can't be used as such or we'll crack our teeth. They need to be de-pitted. That thing over there I brought from home? It's my special de-pitter."

"It looks like an instrument of sexual torture."

"You would know. De-pit 20 olives, chop them up roughly on the cutting board and set them aside. Good. Now take that thing there—"

"What is it?"

"A box cutter. The protruding razor blade is good on boxes and human throats. You might recall the 9/11 hijackers slit the throats of a few flight attendants as a lesson to any passengers who might have thought of intervening."

"I am sorry to know."

"Now use the box cutter to shave 6 cloves of garlic extremely thin. Be careful. Don't sever your finger off. Thinner! Thinner! Good! Set it aside on the cutting board. Now drain the tin of anchovies and set aside half of the tin on the cutting board. Heat the skillet, our prep is almost finished. Hey! Don't turn up the gas so high. A little lower. Lower. Good. Do nothing for 60 seconds. Use your fancy watch. Don't lose track of time. Tariq! Look at the watch! Okay? Ready? Now scrape the garlic shavings and the anchovies into the skillet. Quick! The hot pepper shaker. Shake some in. More. More! Reduce the heat. Do you know what you are doing at this point?"

"I am cooking."

"More precisely, you are sautéeing. Observe. When the garlic shavings and the anchovies have completely dissolved, you're almost there. Quickly now fill the big pot with hot water and dump a little olive oil in and turn it on high. Look! The garlic and the anchovies have transcended themselves. Dump the cans of tomatoes in gently. Gently! No splashing! I hate a dirty stove. Shit! We have forgotten the capers and the parsley. Not too many capers, I get a rash. Take your time, Tariq, you have time to rough-chop the parsley. Don't chop your finger. When the whole skillet starts bubbling—it'll take awhile—you lower the heat and let it simmer for 10 minutes. Now you can say it, Tariq."

"What may I say, Eliot?"

"That you're cooking."

"The aroma is from God."

"Don't inhale too deeply, you'll lose your appetite for 3 days. You'll desire nothing, like after the best orgasm you ever had."

"Such a great volume of sauce for 2 people!"

"What we don't use, we freeze for later in the week. If there is a later. I have a feeling it all ends soon."

"God willing."

"God wills that we sit down and enjoy the cooking you've done like a veteran whore. Tariq?"

"Yes?"

"You're a good student."

Tariq laughs. He likes Eliot.

Another perfect August twilight in Upstate New York. 75 degrees, light humidity, the front windows open to the sounds of Bleecker. The .357 on table. They eat in seriousness. They eat a half pound a piece, smothered in the luridly wonderful sauce.

Conte says, "I screwed up. We should've had a salad. Arugula and radicchio with a tart oil and vinegar dressing. To be eaten after the spaghetti puttanesca. As my father used to say, Salad is best afterwards to cleanse one's mouth, especially after given the pleasure of the whore."

Tariq says, "My father used to speak similarly. A bitter salad at the end in order to purify the mouth. We Iraqis and Italians are the same."

Conte says, "As we were eating, I thought, what if he enters now, the fork at my mouth, partially in, sucking it in, what do I do, pick up my gun and blast with my left hand, I am a leftie, while my fork continues in the right hand on its journey to the promised land?"

"The desire to eat and the desire to shoot my stalker would be equal? You paint a comical picture."

"He's not coming through your door tonight or any night. My man on the street will destroy him. Neither of us exposes our self at the window. Understood?"

"*Capito.*" (Understood.)

"You know Italian?"

"A little. From the guard in Room 101."

"An Italian?"

"No. Black. Very black."

* * *

The second dinner: Night #2.

"Utilize 8 sweet Italian sausages. Utilize 8 hot Italian sausages. Utilize 10 Italian frying peppers, known to American white bread as bell peppers. Yellow, orange, red, green. Cored, seeded, halved. 2 large onions, very large, thinly sliced, and halved. 6 garlic cloves, lightly smashed with the flat side of a big wide knife. Don't sever your finger off, Tariq. Salt and pepper. ¼ cup of olive oil. Preheat the oven to 400 degrees. Put it all in a roasting pan and drizzle democratically with the olive oil. Roast for 1 hour and imagine what is to come. Turn the sausages every 15 minutes until they're nicely browned all over. We rip off the unsliced Italian bread frequently to mop up at the end."

"You talk like a cookbook."

"Have a problem with that, Mr. Al-Masri?"

"You will have a long life, Mr. Conte."

"I already have."

"Much longer."

Tariq says, "Enough for 8 normal people."

Conte says, "We're not normal. We're fully masculine men."

"And," Tariq says, "at least partial assholes?"

"Yes. Of necessity."

They drink water. Tariq asks Conte if he likes wine, like all Italians.

Conte says, "I love wine, beer, and hard booze. Johnny Walker Black on the rocks, but I don't partake because I'm a former booze-bag. An alcoholic sentenced to a life of hard recovery."

Again spumoni for dessert.

Again no action on the street.

Tariq says, "My religion forbids drinking. May Allah be merciful and change the rules. And may He protect me from red jacket."

* * *

The third dinner: Night #3.

Conte says, "It ends tonight. You've been like a dead man for 9 years. Tonight, the third day of Italian gorging, I predict that like Jesus Christ you will arise from the grave."

"What will we eat tonight, Eliot, before I convert to Christianity?"

"Utica Greens, which no one in Utica calls Utica Greens. We were the origin of this dish—it was invented here by someone's grandmother at the dawn of Italian-American time—long before it spread to upstate cities, Albany, Syracuse, and around the country. Tampa, Chicago, Las Vegas, New York City. In Utica, Utica Greens, as it is known everywhere, is known here by the restaurant that serves it. Joey's Greens. Ventura's Greens. Giorgio's Greens. Morelle Greens it's called at The Chesterfield, where Joe Morelle was the chef years ago. Joe invented a special version in the 80s and it spread all over town and eventually across the nation. Joe Morelle was the God of Utica Greens, which if you want to piss him off call Morelle Greens Utica Greens in his vicinity."

"I would not wish to piss off Mr. Morelle."

"Let's go to the kitchen."

"For The Last Supper?"

"Outstanding. Tariq, you are outstanding."

But before they can reach the kitchen, a high-pitched scream from the street, maybe female, maybe not, followed by the blast of a gunshot or is it a car backfiring and they rush to the open window to look down and see a man—it's Victor Cazzamano—rising and cursing from the pavement and another man—slight, blonde in a red windbreaker 5 yards away and facing Cazzamano and firing a handgun, the second shot, and Cazzamano knocked down again, this time rising but not cursing, his handgun drawn and trained on the blond and the blond, in terror, having fired point-blank, twice at Cazzamano's chest, he couldn't have missed, the blond now turning and running a zigzag pattern, and Cazzamano in pursuit who won't fire, there are too many people on the street, some paralyzed in fear, standing, others lying on the pavement, others in the act of falling as the blond darts into the street between 2 parked cars where he is immediately slammed hard by a girl riding her bike fast and the girl on the bike flies tumbling over the handlebars as the slight blond male seeming almost weightless is sent spinning and almost floating from the collision toward the other side of the street, falling and sliding now into the lane of oncoming traffic, where there is none except for a city bus heading east, the driver braking hard, grinding to a slow rolling stop, the huge, fat wheel on the bus's left front rolling near the blond head, rolling and stopping atop the blond head exploding—blood spray, among other things, across both lanes.

They rush down the stairs, Conte is saying, "You know nothing, say nothing. You're an innocent bystander."

The passengers on the bus exit to stare and point. The foot traffic at the scene crowds into the street, staring, murmuring. A tall heavily-muscled man cries. Cazzamano, gun in one hand flashes his badge with the other and waves them all back. He's about to call 911, but one of the bystanders has already beaten him to it and the faint wail of sirens of ambulance and squad cars grow loud and louder. The bus driver exits the bus moaning. Cazzamano tells him to back the bus a few feet: "Get it off the fuckin' head!" The bus driver refuses, saying "I'm quitting this job, I'm going home," and begins to walk away. Cazzamano hollers, "You want me to arrest you for obstruction of justice?" The bus driver returns, backs the bus a few feet and jogs away.

Conte approaches Victor and asks if he's okay.

Victor gestures to his chest and says, "The force knocks me down, but no penetration. The prick must've thought I was fuckin' Superman. This cocksucker tried to kill me." He points to the body: "Now look at you."

Conte whispers, "May the man you were here to defend approach?"

Victor says, "Wait," and approaches the body, finds no wallet, nothing in pants or jacket, and says with a wink at Conte, "The unknown stalker, let's bury him in the dump on Wertz Ave."

Tariq says, "There is no doubt. The jacket. The body form. The blond hair. No face, but I do not require a face to know what I know."

The *Utica Observer Dispatch* will run a front page story the next day with this headline: *Heroic Off-Duty Officer*. The story will not report on the curious fact that the off-duty hero just happened to be wearing a bulletproof vest, as he lounged outside 663 Bleecker.

Conte whispers, "You're the man, Victor," then takes Tariq by the arm and guides him back to the apartment, asking him: "You, like me, lost your appetite?"

Tariq nods.

"I was going to teach you Morelle Greens tonight. I owe you. I'll cook it for you some time soon. Should I not survive to deliver on my promise, consult the *New York Times*, February 28th, 2017. "Utica Greens." A story with a recipe at the end. You'll like the picture of Sal Borruso, who owns The Chesterfield Restaurant, he has a plate of the greens in question in his hand and Joe Morelle by his side has his arm around big Sal's big shoulders. May we eat Morelle's Greens together ... on the other hand ..."

"You see death nearby waiting for you?"

"I go in soon for open-heart surgery."

"We will eat Morelle Greens together. After your surgery."

"You speak confidently, Tariq."

"Because God is willing."

Jolted (4)

Rintrona and Conte finishing a late lunch at The Chesterfield. Alone in the dining room. Rintrona says, "Give yourself a break after 3 years. We had the bastard who terrorized this town with 4 killings. We had him, but we couldn't prove squat. Me an ex-cop? You a private dick? A good lawyer makes mincemeat out of us. We know this. So cut yourself some slack. The guy is on the floor. You put him down for the count. So you get down on this bastard and force your .357 in his mouth. So you blow his fuckin' brains all over the room. I say you did deep justice for this sad little town. You did good. Know what surprises me to this day? After the mess you make of this psycho's brains, no one could be more dead, you get up and kick the liv—the shit out of him. I almost said living shit. LOL. I'm still hungry. I could go for another plate of Utica Riggies. How about we split a plate?" Conte says, "I don't remember the kicking."

PREPARATION FOR SURGERY

THIS IS KNOWN: ON DECEMBER 5th of 1969, Eliot Conte purchased and read the account in *Life* magazine of the slaughter at May Lai 4, liberally illustrated with appalling color photos. This is not known: He put the magazine away on the night of December 5th, but did not throw it away when he drove back home nonstop in 72 hours to Utica, New York, having been given a terminal M.A. degree at U.C.L.A. after the fiasco of his Ph.D. orals, where he was frozen, question after easy question, only finally to say at the exam's conclusion, "I need to get my hands dirty." To which his supervisor responded, "I don't understand, Mr. Conte." To which Conte rose to reply, "Don't worry, you'll never understand," as he left the room.

On the following day, he began his sleepless caffeine-fueled trek home to Utica, with a trunk full of books (the *Life* issue on the front passenger seat in a large manila envelope) and only the clothes on his back. Home to the Italian-American enclave of his upbringing—home to friends from childhood—home where he left behind the "Styrofoam California marriage," as he would call it years later, when he met Catherine Cruz, whose love would make him almost whole—home to steady and unsatisfying adjunct teaching of American literature at Utica College—home to get his hands dirty as a driven Private Investigator who packed a massively lethal handgun.

The words printed in *Life* were terrible: "the exposed viscera of children lying in the weeds of a shallow ditch." Terrible words, but words, just words, far surpassed by images in color, whose invasive vividness made the words seem insulated from the world they would evoke.

Had he only been there at My Lai 4, not draft-deferred, would he have intervened? He? A lover of beautiful sentences in great books? Who, for the heck of it, had memorized Keats's major odes? This man given to observation and contemplation? Catherine Cruz knew him at home as mild-mannered, at times even timid—this bruiser at 6'3", 235 pounds. Except for that one time, just once, as they disagreed at low key over a triviality—who can remember what it was about?—the pot of pasta water reaching a boil when he flung the box of linguini hard against the wall and raw linguini exploded everywhere. In Vietnam, he feared, he'd have stood by, a true man of letters, in a vacuum of moral action—just another betrayer of the innocent.

He had never shown Catherine the *Life* that he stowed at the bottom of his lowest desk drawer, under a chaos of old utility notices, old tax documents, old newspaper clippings of his teenage baseball exploits. He hadn't looked at it once since December 5th, 1969. Nor had he ever talked to her about it. Vietnam, Vietnam: the bill he did not pay.

Like the outstanding bill for his failure to protect the lean, small newspaper boy, black, maybe 12 years old. He had driven to the front of the pharmacy on Santa Monica Boulevard at 7 a.m. sharp to pick up his Sunday *L.A. Times*, before hunkering down later that morning at the end of his fourth month of preparation for the Ph.D. orals he would fail, the following week. He will see forever the small boy untying his stack of Sunday *Times*, about to begin his route. The small boy who anticipated the arrival of this generous customer who appeared at 7 a.m. sharp each Sunday, unfailingly to pay him double for a paper. This big white man who will say that morning, "Are you studying hard at school?" And the boy responding, "Yes, sir, school is easy for me. I get straight As," as Conte takes a ten dollar bill from his wallet, as a powerful blast of bone-dry wind from the desert bears down hard on the boulevard—bending the palm trees and scattering the untied stack everywhere. For a full three seconds, Conte stands frozen before he bolts to help the boy retrieve the papers moving fast toward the boulevard, and onto the boulevard, and this is what he will see forever: The boy darting toward and into the street to be struck flying through the air across the boulevard—dead before he hits the pavement by a speeding driver who does not stop, whose license plate Conte could not identify.

And caffeine-fueled across the country he will say to himself at 75 miles per hour, I should have said forget about the newspapers. I should have said I'll buy all of them at triple price. I should have said I'll pay for your college education if you don't win a scholarship, which you most definitely will because you're smart and I'll applaud you at your graduation and take a picture of you and your happy parents. I should have said forget about the papers because they were never blown away because I stopped the cruel wind which ruined your parents for life. And he did understand in a one-diner little town in Oklahoma that he mustn't feel responsible and guilty. It was absurd to feel responsible and guilty. No one on this wretched earth would blame him except Eliot Conte, himself, the hanging judge who delivered the irrevocable sentence.

He never told Catherine about the small boy on Santa Monica Boulevard. He never told anyone.

* * *

It's 2 days before surgery, in warm late August at twilight, as Conte and Cruz sit on the top step of the porch, with the front door open behind them. Annie is asleep. The house has been secured: back door checked, all windows checked. He's thought for weeks that he'll not survive the operating theater and has decided to confess tonight what he's surmised she may have suspected via rumor. He will make his hidden history known before he goes under the knife. Trust his darkness to her love and hope for the best.

He had never stepped out on the California wife, though he should have—it would have made the Styrofoam marriage less destructive to the both of them. In his years with Catherine he had never felt the urge to go outside, but nevertheless believed that withholding from her his secret history was a betrayal, the act of a philanderer.

She says, "More fireflies tonight than ever. An underrated goodness in this world, don't you agree? I read once they flash to signal availability for mating. Or maybe I didn't read that. Maybe I'm just imagining. Once when I was little I trapped one in a jar. It kept flashing. I never did it again."

He says, "I did that once when I was a boy. Then I dropped a lit match into the jar. Never again. Live and learn. Sometimes you live and don't learn. I need to tell you I haven't learned."

"Hear that?" she says. "In the house?"

He's been through this moment with Catherine many times. He's heard nothing, but does what he must and goes quickly inside to check on Annie. Check every room. Try the double-dead bolted back door. The windows again.

Fear for Annie's safety had been the irresistible undertow of their lives ever since the end of the eighth month of the pregnancy, when Catherine received two anonymous letters. The first, printed in large block letters, said that the pregnancy would end in the birth of a dead baby. The second said if the birth "by any chance" was live, it would be "short and violently concluded." They'd initially alerted the police, who told them it was a matter for the FBI because such letters are considered implicit ransom threats—a federal crime. Give me money and your child will not be harmed. Typed on an old manual upright, the FBI agent said of the second letter, who wore dark glasses even inside the house. He told them that people who write such letters do so to destroy you mentally—they don't follow up with violent action. Try not to let this dominate the rest of your lives, which is what they want you to do. They want you to destroy yourselves with obsessive worry and fear. You two are in for hard times, but eventually time is your friend. It will ease your troubles, though of course there will always be a panic attack here and there out of the blue. Trust time. Your child will be fine.

For a year and a half, one or the other hovered in Annie's close vicinity. Insomnia plagued them both. Each night, Annie was placed between them in bed. Very slowly their fear moved to the edge of consciousness, sometimes dipped below out of mind, sometimes for no immediate cause fear abrupted into the center in a seizure of anxiety for Catherine, who heard voices in the house at night, and in suppressed rage for Eliot, who felt the need to do damage to someone deserving of his fury, long-simmering since December 5, 1969. Catherine's anxiety would manifest itself in an inability to eat. Conte's suppressed rage manifested itself in a fondling of cool metal. The heft of it. A .357 Magnum. Eliot Conte has a gun.

He returns with a large manila envelope. He says, "All secure within. She's safe. Annie's safe."

She says, "I know. I can't help it ... What's in the envelope?"

He says, "I need to tell you something about me you don't know."

She makes a lame attempt at humor: "You wrote the anonymous letters?"

He shows her the *Life* of December 5, 1969. He says again, "I want to tell you something." He opens the magazine to the article entitled "The Massacre at My Lai."

She says, "Tell me something. Tell me everything."

So they sit side by side, amidst flashing fireflies, without a word, as she reads and pauses over the photos, without expression, as Conte takes in the photos for the first time in almost 40 years, his fury flashing hot and cold. When she finally speaks she asks why he's kept this magazine for all these years, and he replies, "Because of what we did to children in Vietnam," and she says, "Because you opposed the war and this was the reason?" And he says, "I had no feelings at the time, one way or the other, about the war. I was politically disconnected. I kept it for the pictures, which once you see them, they're in your head forever, what adults do to children. Because there is no greater crime than to cause the suffering and murder of children—or to see it happen and do nothing. I did nothing." And she, "Think of the terror of these children. Annie is never in terror—oh, she cries when we discipline her and make her sit in the time-out chair because the punishment comes from the parents who feed her, who play with her, who tell her stories, who dance with her, love her, who she knows intuitively will continue to love her and care and play and dance and cancel the time-out chair after a very short while." And he says, "It breaks my heart when we tell her to go to the time-out chair and she goes quickly and sits there without a peep. When I see her do that it breaks my heart." And she says, "Because you love her, but these kids in Vietnam, before they died they watched in terror as strangers descended in thunderous helicopters and butchered their brothers and sisters and parents without the possibility of a safe return to love, because there was no love. You weren't there. You didn't do it and didn't watch them do it and didn't let them do it." And he says, "Butchering adults is awful, but to do it to children, to babies, sucking at their dead mothers' breasts at My Lai—if there is a God, but there isn't because it was done and continues to be done even now at our Mexican border, the tearing of children from the arms of their parents, as the God of Cruelty sits back in his paradise and lets humans do these things here and everywhere." "But what does this My Lai story," she is saying now, "have to do with you now? With us? So many years after it happened?"

So then he told her about what he witnessed on Santa Monica Boulevard and she teared up and said, "But you weren't responsible—you were victimized by your witness. If only you slept late that morning, you wouldn't be carrying this grief." And he said, "If I'd been born 50 years after My Lai and Vietnam—if I'd not gone to Santa Monica Boulevard that morning—if I were not me in those times and in those places—all across the country as I drove home to Utica I felt something and it wasn't grief rising and to call it 'rage' doesn't do justice to what I felt and wanted to do. Rage is hot. What I felt was cold. I needed to strike back, but no targets presented themselves. As I drove back east from L.A. I thought, What can I do, because the law is slow and doesn't save anyone and the military is beyond the law and beyond all decency and I thought I would work on the edge of the law, legally and illegally as a Private

Investigator—I would take cases of children who had run away or were in the custody of Social Services, like orphans, because they were abused by their fathers, whose wives would contact me—and as I drove across country I had fantasies of my heroism on behalf of children—I would be the savior who atoned for being deferred from Vietnam. Home and working as a P.I. who wanted to get his hands dirty—to get my hands out of the books which I loved—still love—but I never got such cases of children whose fathers I would punish as judge and jury and cold-blooded executioner." And she: "You wanted to punish the bastards for the guilt and helplessness you felt for the horrors you did not create?"

And he: "I have another story for you. You don't know about this. Shortly after I met you when you pulled me over for speeding in Troy—the luckiest day of my life—we were dating for a few weeks—I'd drive down to Albany, sometimes take the train down to see the Troy cop who I couldn't get out of my mind. I never told you about what happened, what I did on the train back from Albany to Utica after a night with you. About a man and his wife and baby, a few months old." And she says, "This is a story where you are there and you are not helpless to help? Where you act?" He says, "Yes," and proceeds to tell her about the crying baby, the man and the wife who had a bruise under one of her eyes. How the crying was piercing, hard to take. No one would disagree. How the man who was sitting across the aisle from Conte began to pinch the baby's thighs. Leaving purple marks. How he continued to pinch. How the wife said, Stop hurting her, Jay. How the man said, You want something under the other eye? And reached over and slapped her. How he pinched the baby's cheek, making it purple. The baby's screams reach new levels. How he, Conte, looked over to say, You must not do that, sir. And the man replied with a middle finger, thrust up and the hand thrust across the aisle close to Conte's face. And Catherine said, "You spoke civilly to this animal? You restrained yourself." And Conte said, "In a cold, restrained way, I stood, stepped over to him, grasped his neck with both hands and lifted him straight up over the seat and shook him like a rag doll. He lost control of his bowels. He urinated. I carried him, feet in the air, to the restroom, deposited him there and told him to clean up and not come back to his family or I would kill him. When we got to Utica, he came from the restroom and took his family off the train. I followed. This time I did the right thing. I took down his license plate and told him some night I'd greet him from behind with a knife. I said, "I know anatomy. I know the location of your kidney. I'll help you to pee more easily—directly through the side of your body. You'll no longer have to unzip your fly. You'll pee without control 20 times a day through the hole in your kidney. Beware, sir, of the dark, because I'll be behind you when you least expect it." And Catherine said, "This is you? Where has this Eliot been hiding? Did you feel better after?" And he replied, "Better after and during." And she: "You actually did this, didn't you? Hot or cold when you gave him what he had coming?" "Cold." And she: "Your manner of talking, much less the prodigious strength you finally unleashed, would be enough to scare any bastard shitless. As it were." They laugh. And she: "Or any innocent bystander. Like me. Did you feel that you had discharged the guilt you were carrying since Los Angeles?"

He says, "Somewhat."

"Annie needs you. We need you. You can't—you could go to prison for this. You can't risk—we'd be destroyed if you went to prison. This thing of yours must end. Have you done this often? Have you gotten it out of your system since that time—what? Six plus years ago?"

"Yes."

"Did you just lie?"

"Yes."

"What have you done since that time on the train?"

"I scared some people."

"Child-abusers?"

"No. Different kinds of assholes."

"Physically?"

"I never hurt anyone. I needed to hurt the right person. The one who sent the letters, but I couldn't find him. From the time of the letters I needed to find him and free him from the earth. For 3 years, from Annie's birth until she was 3, I discharged my desire for revenge against the unknown perpetrator by scaring ordinary assholes, once blameless innocents, but the perpetrator, who promised to hurt Annie, eluded me and the FBI. He promised to hurt not children I didn't know, like those at My Lai, but my child. It built in me to do something and—"

"Three years ago you actually killed someone. A cop-killer who killed 4. In a dangerous situation, according to the Chief, your best friend. Also according to the story in the media. According to what you told me, you took him out before he could kill again, which he was about to do, but you killed him first because you were there at Caruso's when it all came to a head. But that was legal, what you did. It had nothing to do with a child-abuser. What am I missing here?"

"The truth. What you don't know, because I never told you, he was disarmed and pinned to the floor, by me. He was in custody, in effect, when I forced my gun into his mouth and pulled the trigger. Since those letters, I wanted to do someone in, needed to, who deserved to be done in, and I did it and it felt good as I did it. My desire had built up for many years. My desire got onto the fast track to do a killing after we got the letters, and it finally exploded like the best orgasm when I finally did it. And since then I've felt peace, except for the fact that until tonight I'd kept you in the dark about this violent theme in my history. Do you still love me?"

"Of course."

"Do you want to say more, Catherine?"

"Just one question. Before you learned about My Lai, were you never overcome with desire to do violence? Strong impulses, which you never acted upon? To get your hands dirty? You felt these impulses for years but never acted before My Lai? No violence before My Lai? You want me to believe that?"

"Never before My Lai."

"Are you telling me the total truth?"

"Almost."

"I don't need to hear anymore. You're a good man who can't bear injustice, I've always known it and loved you for it. One more question, I promise this is the last one, and then let's go to bed in pursuit of orgasms better than the one you had at Caruso's."

"I'll answer the question that you want to ask. Since I killed at Caruso's, 3 years ago, I'm no longer taken over by impulses which possessed me after I learned about My Lai. After what happened on Santa Monica Boulevard. After the anonymous letters. Unlike the reformed alcoholic who makes amends to those he's hurt, I made someone else make amends for my madness, with his life, and that has made all the difference in mine. I'm a dullard now. A man at peace."

"Annie must never know anything."

"No, never. In two days, my chest will be opened up and what is truly hidden in my heart will be revealed."

"Your sense of humor tells me that you're likely in a good place."

"Likely."

She says, "One more question."

He says, "There will always be one more."

"Did you tell me the total truth—or only the truth you think I can bear?"

"Yes."

"Clever, Conte. Now tell me what you think I can't bear to know."

"The impulse to lash out violently goes back as far as I can recall, a part of who I always was. I don't know why. It was a malignancy cut out of me on the kitchen floor of Caruso's three years ago, when I pulled the trigger. I seem to be in remission."

She says, "Let's embrace remission."

* * *

They will arrive at 1318 Mary to be greeted at the door by the perpetual jumping jack, Ann Cruz Conte. It's Annie's father's idea: A dinner party for friends, on the evening before he's to check into the Upstate Medical Center in Syracuse. He tells Catherine that he

165

looks forward to his "pre-Wake Wake," at which as "corpse-to-be" he'll listen with quiet pleasure to memories of himself, as the guests snack on spicy Sicilian olives, imported salami, sip full-bodied red wine, all the while chatting with bleak humor and sporadic belly laughs about his life and times as husband, father, and sometimes scarily temperamental friend.

And she replies, "Not bad, Conte. Write it down and I'll quote it at your interment. Calvary, yes? The only cemetery in Utica for the Dago Christ, who died in the O.R. for his sins."

"I'll remember that, Detective Cruz, as they wheel me into the O.R. But Annie won't sleep. With all the commotion in this jewel box we call home? She'll never sleep."

And Catherine replies, "She'll make demands on the guests. Nonstop."

"She'll get the guests," he says with a twinkle in his eyes. "She'll jump up and down making immense demands. She'll drive everyone crazy."

"They'll love it," she says.

"We will too," he says.

"Especially you, Conte."

"Annie'll spoil my Wake. All that good feeling in this house will obliterate the undertow of melancholy that would tell me they all care. They all miss me."

"You joke, but you don't joke."

"I'm sort of complicated."

"You're sort of obvious. You've always been obvious, and if you kick the bucket in Syracuse—you better not. Because if you do Annie and I—our lives become narrow and lonely."

"After I'm gone, do this in memory of me: like old Italian ladies, you and Annie wear black, head to toe, daily, the rest of your long lives."

* * *

The party is his idea, but she has made the calls of invitation, except for one. She calls Rintrona and Lilly, Tariq and Rhonda, Victor and Terri. And they insist that it wouldn't be right if Eliot, master chef of Italian cuisine, does the cooking. Each will bring something sufficient for 9 serious eaters. Rintrona would do his third lasagna *l'ultima* of the last 10 days. Lilly would make *Bi Do Xao Toi*, stir-fried pumpkin with garlic, onion, fish sauce, and sugar. Tariq would make Morelle Greens according to the recipe published in the *New York Times*, which drew many raves from readers as well as, Joe Morelle said, many pain-in-the-ass phone calls from people across this dying country, who didn't trust what the *Times* printed and wanted it straight, as he put it to one caller, from the horse's ass. Rhonda would make the Iraqi version of Kibbeh, but (she says apologetically) it's not going to be any different from the Lebanese, the Syrian, the Moroccan or the Israeli versions, because she tried but failed to find in the United States a distributor of reasonably fresh camel meat. Victor Cazzamano and Terri Brindisi would bring dessert from Caruso's and Terri would make a huge salad of fennel, tomatoes, and cucumbers. When they tell Marilyn Caruso of the occasion she fixes a large box of 30 pastries and will accept no payment. Catherine isn't supposed to cook either, but she makes chiles rellenos, anyway, for the Mexican dimension.

The call she doesn't make is to the alienated friend, Antonio Robinson. That call is made by the alienated friend Eliot Conte, who lies when Antonio answers, and says "Robby, what went wrong? I have no memory of what happened 3 months ago."

And Robinson lies in response, "I can't remember either."

And Conte says, "So why don't we see each other anymore?"

And Robinson says, "A mystery of the fucked-up male ego over something we can't even remember."

Then Conte explains about the party and Robinson says, "You're finally having that heart surgery where they open you up wide? You're calling me now because you're worried you'll go to your grave with me on your conscience? And I'll be left alone on this fucked-up earth with *you* on my conscience?"

"I'm calling because I miss you."

"Yeah. Me too."

"You miss my company, Robby?"

"Didn't you hear what I just said? I said me too. Shall we cut the fag talk?"

"If we talk like fags, we're not necessarily fags. On the other hand."

"I'll bring black food. Ham hocks. Like Mama taught me to make. Ham hocks and mustard greens. 5 hours in the kitchen in your honor."

"Not African-American food? You don't call it that?"

"Back in the day, Mama called it Negro food. Black was a white put-down back in the day and we insisted on Negro for respect. But once we had Negro for awhile, we wanted black again in order to throw Honkey America for a loop."

"Black is beautiful. The Panthers, Handsome Huey Newton, so forth."

"Then we decided we needed parity with you people, the Italian-Americans and all the other hyphenates. So we went for African-American. But I'm not bringing African-American food for The Last Fuckin' Supper. I'm bringing it black."

"Any of the brothers call it n-word food?"

"You can say nigger, El."

"I don't."

"Not even in your mind once in awhile? I say wop, dago, guinea, greaser in my mind and out loud in your presence. I'm thinking once in awhile you say nigger in your private mind."

"Hey, bro?"

"Lay it on me, El."

"Fuck off."

"El?"

"Yeah?"

"I miss you."

"Robby. Truly. How have you been lately?"

"I resisted so far the urge to eat my gun."

"But you're over it now?"

"El. Why do we talk like fags?"

"You have a problem with that?"

* * *

What Conte fears will subvert his living Wake does not imme-diately come to pass. They arrive between 6 and 6:15 in the midst of another August thunderstorm, but the jumping-jack is asleep at a depth achievable only by the very young and the very dead—in a bedroom at the end of a short hallway that runs off the all-purpose front room (TV room, writing-room-with-desk, dining room).

The guests are gathered, the feast is about to commence. A small table accommodates 5, 2 others sit at the couch, 2 others on folding chairs. This is an East Utica front room. The quarters are tight and the guests speak (not quite the word) like those in a crowded res-taurant, alcohol flowing, in voices that parents try in vain to teach their little uncivilized ones not to use inside the house. The guests speak in what parents tell the little beasts are "outdoor voices," with elevated volume just short of shouting—and still Annie sleeps un-disturbed as violent thunder and good feelings shake the house. In about an hour, the food-charged 9 adult bodies will have driven the thermostat from 75 to 82 degrees.

Robert Rintrona proposes, Tariq Al-Masri seconds the motion, "That we eat slowly for 3-4 hours—we annihilate this international array, enough for a company of Marines just returned from a 2-day hill assault, under intermittent fire from the enemy we rarely saw, which is the way it was at Khe Sanh. A lot of the guys couldn't eat when we got back to the base. They tried. They vomited. Too much stomach tension. Me? I went at it like a starved lion."

As Rintrona holds the floor the others, with the exception of Antonio Robinson and Rhonda Thieu, eat with sustained vigor. When he finishes, silence, except for the sounds of chewing and smacking of the lips.

Victor Cazzamano looks up from his plate of lasagna and Morelle Greens and says, "I support Bobby making speeches. He's like in the opera when one guy sings for awhile and everybody else's forced to listen, like it or not until he drops dead."

It's Victor's second date with Terri—they are fatally smitten. She's a stranger to the group. She looks down, blushes. Rhonda at the couch, a full plate on her lap, untouched, stares at Rintrona but sees nothing. Tariq leans over and whispers inaudibly in her ear. Still staring straight ahead, blankly, she nods almost imperceptibly. He's asked her if she feels good enough to stay.

Antonio Robinson, barely picking at his food, says "Rintrona loves an audience. Khe Sanh, Khe Sanh. A shit-storm you survived. You forced that reference on us. Make you feel good to lay it on us? My football knees kept me on our shit-storm home front with the long-hairs and the bra-less. Your turn, Eliot. Let's hear it now from the knifing-victim to be. He didn't go either, Rintrona. Me and my bro, Eliot—cowards and slackers together forever."

Rintrona replies, "I never thought going there made me any better than anyone who didn't. You think I wanted to go? It made me worse. I did an inhuman thing over there."

Robinson says, "Tell us about the inhuman thing, son, and I'll absolve you."

Lilly says, "You are mean how you talk to Bobby."

Robinson says, "Forgive me, mother, for I know not what I do."

Lilly says, "Don't be snotty, Mr. Chief of Police."

"Enough, Robby," Catherine says.

Robinson says, "There's too much bullshit. El thinks he's coming home from Syracuse in a box. If he does, the bullshit ends."

Tariq says, "If food be the music of life, eat on!"

Eliot says, "I'll eat to that."

Robinson says, "I can be an asshole. Like tonight."

Lilly says, "Everybody once in awhile is that word you just said. If you dwell on that word against yourself, you become that word."

Robinson says, "I go to doctors 6 times a year. Every time I go the nurse asks me, Are you a Vet? No, I say, 6 times a year. I am not a Vet. I went to no war except in my marriage."

Eliot says, "First I got deferred because I was a student. Then, once I started teaching at U.C.L.A., I got deferred again because the government considered what I was doing to be vital to our national interests and the defense of our country. I defended the U.S. of A. with James Joyce and T.S. Eliot."

Everyone laughs, except Rhonda.

The thunderstorm is over but the rain, a steady drizzle, continues. Conte raises the windows for the cool air. They eat, except Rhonda, praise the food and the cool air, make small talk, until Robinson says, "My guess you all know what the general public doesn't concerning the disaster on Bleecker last week, in relation to Tariq here. I want to bring you up to date. No I.D. on the body, but we found a car with Florida plates ticketed for illegal parking on Blandina. When the car wasn't moved for 3 days, we traced it to a rental agency in Albany. The vehicle had been washed, thoroughly wiped down and cleaned on the inside before it was rented to a driver who was described matching exactly the bus victim, minus the head. The prints taken from the steering wheel were digitally sent to the FBI. As were the prints taken from the body itself. They have a database you wouldn't believe the vastness. Trust me, this guy wasn't a virgin before he stalked you. They'll know who he was, who he associated with, who was behind his action. Even if the sponsor is high-level government sensitive, a message will be sent to the contractor in question. Assuming no funny business at the FBI, I'll have an answer in a few days. Tariq, the terrible time you've had in this country is soon over."

Tariq responds, "Iraqis do not expect the terrible times to end. I will not be surprised if in time another is sent in a red jacket. But now I have friends and most of all a woman named Rhonda I did not dream could exist on my behalf, to bring gratitude to be alive, whatever comes in any color of jacket."

Rhonda says, "Bad men in jackets, or no bad men, we are embracing Utica and the people in this room."

Rintrona says, "How do you say it? Alla what?"

"Allahu Akbar."

Rintrona says, "On behalf of us all, your new family, Allahu Akbar."

* * *

"They let you eat the night before?"

"Not after midnight."

"Pack it in!"

"How many days in the hospital?"

"Four or five assuming no complications."

"Such as?"

"I could come home the day after. Or even the same day."

"The same day after open-heart?"

"Absolutely."

"How so?"

"I croak in the O.R."

* * *

The door to the short hallway opens noiselessly and there she is, clutching her frayed fringe blanket, still as a statue—her parents' backs to her: Rhonda goes to her and holds out her hand. Annie takes it and Rhonda leads her to Catherine. Annie breaks away and climbs instead on her father's lap and says to the room, "Daddy won't throw me up in the high air and catch me no more because he's sick! He says he's sick! Damn God!" Much laughter. She hugs her father. He's happy. She points to Tariq: "You throw me in the high air up and catch me! Now!" He does. Points to Rintrona, saying "Uncle Bobby! You do it!" He does. "Uncle Tonio!" He does. She says, "A girl! Not mommy. You! You're little like me." Pointing to Lilly. Lilly does. She climbs back up on Conte's lap and says, "When are you not sick anymore?" He says soon, and with that she puts her head on his chest and falls asleep.

Then they're eating again with unclassifiable good feelings of no name that this child brings to a room of complicated adults. The feelings that come when you, Conte, and the others in the room let yourselves go out of sight and forget all that has gone by and do not imagine what lies just ahead, and you sink into the uncomplication of her innocence, and do not think that it cannot endure, this moment, for you and for her. You don't say to yourself that you know what lies ahead and Annie does not, but that soon she will. You, Eliot Conte, do not think in this shielded moment that she will soon grieve periodically for the rest of her life: The words "rest of her life" shatter you. When they push your gurney into the O.R. you will imagine a world where children never die and you will hold that vision tight as they administer deep anesthesia.

They speak unnecessarily in a stage whisper—she's safe and deep in the place that older adults don't get to without medication.

Victor says, "What will she be when she grows up? Hope to live to see it."

Rintrona says, "After that, what is there to say?"

Terri finally speaks, "If you ever need a babysitter, here I am."

Victor says, "Two for the price of one."

Rintrona says again, "After that, what is there to say?"

Robinson says, "This, Rintrona: We need a change of subject. The theme of the amazing child is played out and overdone. How about you confess your inhumanity in Vietnam? You confess, we absorb your sin and guilt and shed our infinite mercy upon you."

Lilly puts her hand on Rintrona's and says "Are you unhappy, Mr. Chief of Police? Is that why you speak the way you speak? Do you need mercy? What he did in Vietnam, he told me."

All eyes on Rintrona. They want a dark war story. He stands. He sits. He stands, walks over to Conte, sits at his feet. Points to the sleeping child. His hand shaking a little as it points. He says, "How old is she now?"

Conte says, "3 and 7 months."

Rintrona says, "They were about 10 years older than Annie. 13, 14 at the most. Little, like Lilly, but thinner than Lilly, who's pretty thin to begin with. We were assaulting up Hill 881 South. The NVA, the North Vietnamese Regulars were shooting down on us through the mist drifting in and out that morning. It was hot, 90 degrees. The fog was not dense. You could see through the mist which made everything look distorted. There were sharp boulders. There were big thorny brushes. There was mud everywhere. We had rain that came down in sheets all week. Mud. I was filthy. A little bloody.

Bruised. On my hands and knees most of the time scrambling up 881 South. The noise. The noise. Rifle fire and grenades constantly. Mortars. I have ear plugs in but they do no good. As a neat person, I couldn't stand my personal filth that morning. I wanted to kill somebody. One of our guys in front of me crouches down. He never got up. I was screaming. I got to a point about my personal safety, excuse the language, ladies, I got to the point I didn't give a shit. I needed to blow someone apart. I felt this need under fire and even when I wasn't under fire. I was more pissed off than scared. I was extremely pissed off they were trying to constantly kill me."

He looks up at Annie. He says, "Jesus, Eliot. My daughter was her age once. I know what to do as a babysitter. There was a big rock I didn't go around. I jumped up on it and stupidly exposed myself and jumped off and landed in a hole. It wasn't a natural hole. It was a crater made by one of our artillery shells, when the day before they tried to soften up the NVA on 881 South. Here and there NVA bodies that had been softened up and crawling with bugs, rats. The crater hole I jumped into was not empty. Skinny. Short like Lilly. 13, 14 at the most. 2 of them. I must've looked like a giant monster. They throw down their rifles. They hug each other. They look at me. I shoot them. I shoot into their small bodies more than once at point-blank range. I kill them 8 or 9 times because I was the special delivery babysitter from hell."

"In that situation," Robinson says, "I can't see you had a choice. Did you think you had a choice, Bobby?"

"Choice? Think? What thinking? I jump into a hole and 2 seconds later I mess them up. Only later, at the base, I had thoughts that I couldn't spare them with their rifles. I couldn't confiscate their rifles and let them live, I thought. I couldn't carry their rifles up the hill, I thought. Take them prisoner, like you're supposed to with surrendered enemy? Not possible, I thought. Possible, I thought, sure, but put my life in danger on that hill? For them?"

Tariq says, "I am sorry that you judge against yourself. What I did in Iraq was worse."

Victor says, "If I had been where you were, Bobby? I'd be nuts for life. I guess you could say I caused that guy on Bleecker to get killed, who shot me 3 times. My conscience is more or less clean and I hope to God yours is more or less."

"There's one more part to the story. At the base, a day later, a guy in my company who fought on 881 South, he says to me, he says while he's eating, he's wiping his mouth on his sleeve, he says he saw a pathetic thing on that hill, he's sorry for the rest of his life he had to see it—he went home in a body bag 2 weeks later—that was the rest of his life—two children, he called them, dead in a shell crater. Their bodies a total wreck. He says he checked their rifles. Empty. No ammo. No ammo on their bodies. No sidearms, he says. No knives. Not even a canteen of water. Know what I think, he says to me? Kill all politicians, what I think."

Rintrona, who was sitting at Conte's feet, lies down at his feet in the fetal position. Lilly sits on the floor beside him. His eyes are closed. She rubs his back.

Robinson says, "It wasn't inhuman what you did. You had to. Forgive yourself."

Rhonda says, "You tell us about the heavy bag of garbage you carry since Vietnam, and now we help you to carry it."

Catherine says, "But if we help carry each other's garbage, we're still carrying garbage. Other people's garbage is lighter because it's not ours? What am I saying?"

Victor says, "You're saying we can't be our own garbage men? We don't have our own garbage trucks? What's next? Recycling? Compost bins for the garden we never plant in the spring?"

From the fetal position, giggling or maybe crying, Rintrona sits up. "Victor," he says, "we never got along, but if I ever get married again, God and Lilly willing, I want you as my best man."

Lilly says, "You are asking me or God?"

"You."

"I accept."

Tariq says, "Rhonda and I will get married next week. Perhaps Eliot Conte will be my greatest man."

Conte says, "God and my surgeon willing."

"3 days ago," Rhonda says. "3 days ago. My baby. Where my baby was inside of me, now there is nothing."

Robinson breaks a long silence: "Forgive me for asking, Rhonda. Was this your first pregnancy?"

"Yes."

"My wife," he says. "We lost our first one. It was hard. Especially on Millicent."

"Before Annie—Annie was our second pregnancy," Catherine says. "When I lost the first one I was inconsolable for 2 weeks. Eliot felt helpless to help me. I didn't let him in. Let Tariq in, Rhonda."

Terri says, "I was the second try. They had a name picked out for the first one which my mother refused to tell me what it was. After my mother died, my father told me what it was. It was Teresa. She wanted a girl and finally got me. Teresa the Second."

"The doctor told me," Rhonda says, "it's common what happened to me. The female body, he said, for many women, needs to practice first before the real game starts. He said 'real game.' Why do men always think in sports? The miscarriage was practice, but I'm 43 and my time is running out."

Tariq says, "Would you like to leave, Rhonda?"

She smiles for the first time in 3 days. She says "Let's stay for as long as possible. May I have a cannoli?"

Lilly says, "A happy pregnancy is not far off."

"You know this how, Mey?"

"I know this."

"But how?"

"You'll see."

"This is what I know: My new family in this room helps me to feel less alone, but when we leave I will be alone in my grief and closed off to Tariq. Tariq will not be able to make me feel better and the knowledge of the miscarriages of so many other women will do nothing. I will remember that I had life inside. Then the inside of me killed my baby. I became my baby's coffin."

Conte speaks: "Until much time has passed and a new pregnancy, but even then—closure is a word for people who don't want to feel."

Robinson says, "It'll never roll off you like water off a duck's back."

Tariq says, "This is why I love you."

"Because I am not a duck?"

Everyone, even Tariq, laughs.

"Yes. No. What am I trying to say? What are the correct words?"

Rhonda laughs a true laugh. She says, "Unable to speak the correct words, is this how we sometimes speak most clearly? What am I trying to say? No idea. I am not a duck. I am perhaps a crow." She laughs again.

Robinson says, "We don't need the words. The words are—"

Rhonda, cutting him off, says: "Quoting you Mr. Police, the words are too much bullshit."

Robinson crosses to Rhonda. They exchange a fist bump.

"A famous philosopher," Conte says, "I studied him at Hamilton College, he wrote: Whereof one cannot speak, thereof we must be silent. I think he might have been referring to the biggest things. Love, death, grief. We talk about these things, but in the immortal words of Utica's Chief of Police, there's too much bullshit. This philosopher I studied in college—"

"Whereof? Thereof?" Victor says. "What language is that? What was this guy's name?"

"He would answer you, What *is* his name. He's dead, but his name is not. 'Ludwig Wittgenstein' *is*."

Rintrona wants to know if "this kraut" had anything to say about miscarriages or the slaughter of children."

"Not that I know of."

Annie stirs, lifts her head from Conte's chest, looks at all the people, puts her head back down, and returns to perfect sleep.

* * *

After the guests have departed, and the dishes have been done, and the living room returned to its pre-party order, he opens the large envelope that he keeps in the bottom drawer of his desk: The *Life* issue of December 12, 1969. Clipped to its front cover, what he's recently discovered and printed from the Internet: the story of Cathy LeRoy and her photos of the Vietnam War. "Cathy," as he thinks of her, as he re-reads for the fourth time—as if she were an intimate, an unsettling intimate, born and raised in Paris, who at the age of 20 determined to go to the war as a photojournalist of no formal training and no experience and no media contacts, who saved enough for a one-way ticket to Saigon. At 21, she arrived in 1967 with her Leica M2 and 100 dollars and marched directly to the offices of the *Associated Press*, where Horst Faas, the legendary photo-editor, gave her 3 rolls of black-and-white film and promised 15 dollars for each photo he used—never, likely, expecting that she'd ever give him anything worth using. She told him she had combat experience. He didn't believe her. He believed that she lied. She did. He didn't care.

What could have moved Horst Faas, except pity for this pip-squeak girl with 2 long pony tails, hard to call her a woman, who stood before him at 5 feet and 85 pounds. When he asked her in French if she could speak any English—she would need some English if she was to live among rough American warriors—she nodded and spoke perfectly the 7 obscenities she knew, because that's all she knew. He arranged for her to acquire combat fatigues and boots for her size 4 feet. But size 6 was the smallest boot available.

In her first week in the field, a senior officer said something to her which she understood correctly as sexist condescension. She replied, looking up at his big face, "cunt," and was promptly barred from the fields of action for six months.

Conte is in love with her unarmed courage, who died from lung cancer in Los Angeles in 2006. Too many Gauloises. She at 5 feet, 85 pounds, doing what she did under fire, while he, at the same time, 6' 3," 235 pounds, teaches modern literature at U.C.L.A. Could he have handled the stress of fire on Hill 881 as she and Rintrona had? What had he ever risked? How was it that they'd been able, in battle, on that hill, or on patrol—actually been able to move *forward*? Not been paralyzed with fear? Not said, Fuck it! I'm walking back to the base. Then I'll swim to California.

After her suspension was lifted, she returned to hot engagement, to live with the soldiers and Marines, to accompany them in combat, never to be sexually harassed or abused. "We were all filthy, we stank," she said years later when asked about being a cute young girl in the midst of lonely and testosterone-heavy young men.

Cathy LeRoy, the first photojournalist, male or female, to take part in a combat parachute jump. They joked that she was too light to come to earth and would float forever away. Captured briefly by the North Vietnamese Army which permitted her to take photos of their warriors, the first of their kind. Hit by mortar fragments, covered in blood, and saved, barely ("I think she's dead, sarge," she heard, and thought those would be the last words she'd ever hear) but was saved, but of course she was, how else? by one of her cameras, which deflected the largest fragment that would have penetrated her chest. What would Cora Kaplan, Conte thinks, have said about Cathy? What does *he* think? Cathy was more man, he smiles, than I was. Though knowing she is dead, he wants to meet her.

It was Rintrona's identification of the scene of his horror and guilt, Hill 881 at Khe Sanh, that motivated Conte to look again at Cathy's most iconic photos, a triptych set at Hill 881: Two figures above her on the hill, just a few feet above, she shooting from flat on the ground.

The first panel of the triptych: a fallen Marine, his feet uphill, helmeted head close to her. No face visible: helmet and chest. A corpsman (a medic) his helmet off, on his knees over the fallen Marine. The medic's right arm embraces the fallen one. The medic's right hand gently on the fallen one's shoulder. In the medic's left hand a white cloth pressed to the chest. The medic looking down at the wound-stancher, his lips slightly parted.

The second, the middle panel: Cathy has moved a little closer. The medic with his ear to the chest of the fallen Marine. Listening for a heartbeat. No heartbeat.

Third panel: still stanching the wound of the dead Marine, the medic looking up at the sky. The medic in anguish. A Marine is dead and the medic is looking at the sky where the clouds go, nevertheless, in their direction. The sky, Conte thinks, not the heavens. Just the sky.

No photo of this: the medic, Vernon Wike is his name, breaking cover, running toward the summit of entrenched North Vietnamese Regulars. He's shouting: "I will kill them all."

Vernon Wike survived his rage, but not his anguish. He lived long and lived badly—haunted, ill in body and mind, in poverty. At the end, in a chair, paralyzed from the waist down.

Conte has spent a lifetime giving into periodic surges of rage, mostly suppressed but felt within, churning in his chest. Mostly suppressed. How many times has he fantasized doing violence? He's done terrible things. He is certain that his rage-surges damaged his heart. In recent years, it's mainly surges of sadness.

From rage to sadness to grief. That's progress, isn't it? Progress in his seventh decade.

Conte once read a sophisticated meditation on photography by a New York intellectual, who contended that photos of war violence de-sensitize us to violence, do not make war less frequent or less ugly. Do not make us less ugly.

He says aloud, as he and Catherine get into bed, "They changed me. I've changed."

"What changed you?" she says.

"They didn't de-sensitive me. The opposite."

"Who? What are you referring to?"

"It's late," he replies. "I'll tell you about it tomorrow on the way to the Upstate Medical Center. We'll have 48 miles to mull it over. They sensitized me. Ron Haeberle and Cathy."

"Who's Ron Haeberle?"

"The guy who took the My Lai photos I showed you. It took awhile, but he started the ball rolling and Cathy gave it the final push."

"Who's Cathy? Stepping out on me?"

"No. Not really."

"Not *really*?"

He laughs. "A photographer who died 10 years ago."

"You call her by her first name. You know her?"

"Only her pictures and some few facts of her intrepid life."

"You never met her. She's been dead for 10 years, but you definitely have a thing for her. I can tell."

"Jealous?"

"No."

"Just a little?"

"No."

"Say just a little."

"Just a little."

"Thank you."

EPILOGUE

"YOU COME HOME WITH A fully-functioning heart. Then what?"

"I re-invent myself for the final phase."

She turns over.

He switches off the bedside lamp.

He waits.

He eases himself out of bed, moves quietly but quickly to the bookcase in the living room, where he pulls down a yellowing and battered paperback edition of Hemingway's *In Our Time*, the very text he'd used at U.C.L.A. in 1968. Tucked into it, an envelope bearing no return address, postmarked Malibu, California and containing a letter that includes no contact information. Sent to him many years after he'd left California and several years before he met Catherine Cruz. He'd read it periodically since the day he received it, even through his years with Catherine and Annie. He reads it again:

Dear Professor Conte,

Not long after I left U.C.L.A. and inspired by your teaching of *In Our Time* by Hemingway, I read *The Sun Also Rises*. I did not like it. About a week ago, I decided to re-read it because a thought out of the blue nagged me that there was something in the novel personal to me. I was grabbed (at last) by the end, where Lady Brett Ashley says, Oh, Jake, we could have had such a damn good time together. Jake says, Yes. Wouldn't it be pretty to think so? They didn't believe in God. I don't either. Do you? I'd guess not. For a long time politics was my god, but now politics is nothing to me. After all these years I wonder what is the point of writing to you, except to think about loss beyond my power to rescue. I would like to say beyond our power. How suddenly vulnerable I feel, as I write this, after all these years. I recently had double knee-replacement surgery and require a walker to get around. Like the old lady that I am.

Always,

Cora Kaplan

He tears the letter in many pieces. Places the pieces inside the envelope and stuffs the envelope inside his briefcase. The briefcase dating from 1968. He needs a new briefcase. Tomorrow is garbage pick-up day in East Utica.

He goes to Annie's room.

He carries Annie to the middle of the big bed.

Catherine is asleep.

Annie is asleep.

"I am content," he says.

In the dark, he says, "I am content."

ACKNOWLEDGMENTS

Georgia Cool.

Dr. G. Chad Hughes, thoracic-heart surgeon, Duke University Medical Center.

Melissa Menacho, ACNP at Duke University Medical Center.

Lt. Colonel Harold McKinney, second in command at Khe Sanh.

Mackie McKinney.

Holmes Bryson.

Dan Duffy.

Chris Cox.

Jeff Jackson.

John Prados and Ray W. Stubbe, *Valley of Decision: The Siege of Khe Sanh*.

Michael Herr, *Dispatches*.

Frances Fitzgerald, *Fire in the Lake*.

Thomas H. Bass, *Vietnamerica*.

Lieutenant Calley: His Own Story, as Told to John Sack.

About the Author

After groundbreaking work as a literary critic and theorist, Frank Lentricchia changed his focus in the early 1990s. Since then he has written a number of novels that explore the complexities of ethnic and artistic identity, often within the context of contemporary disasters—the Vietnam and Iraq wars and the diseased glamour of the American Mafia. Lentricchia was born in Utica, New York—the setting of many of his novels which evoke the working-class ethnic family in its pleasurable and stressful vitality.

Fiction By Frank Lentricchia

The End

Printed in May 2020
by Gauvin Press,
Gatineau, Québec

THE GLAMOUR OF EVIL

GUERNICA WORLD EDITIONS 27

THE GLAMOUR OF EVIL

A NOVEL

Frank Lentricchia

GUERNICA
World
EDITIONS

TORONTO—CHICAGO—BUFFALO—LANCASTER (U.K.)
2020

Michael Mirolla, editor
Cover design: Allen Jomoc Jr.
Interior layout: Jill Ronsley, suneditwrite.com
Guernica Editions Inc.
287 Templemead Drive, Hamilton (ON), Canada L8W 2W4
2250 Military Road, Tonawanda, N.Y. 14150-6000 U.S.A.
www.guernicaeditions.com

Distributors:
Independent Publishers Group (IPG)
600 North Pulaski Road, Chicago IL 60624
University of Toronto Press Distribution,
5201 Dufferin Street, Toronto (ON), Canada M3H 5T8
Gazelle Book Services, White Cross Mills
High Town, Lancaster LA1 4XS U.K.

First edition.
Printed in Canada.

Legal Deposit—Third Quarter
Library of Congress Catalog Card Number: 2019949199
Library and Archives Canada Cataloguing in Publication
Title: A place in the dark ; The glamour of evil : two novels / Frank Lentricchia.
Other titles: Novels. Selections (Guernica) | Glamour of evil
Names: Lentricchia, Frank, author. | Lentricchia, Frank. Glamour of evil
Description: Series statement: Guernica world editions ; 27 | Two separate works printed
back-to-back and inverted (tête-bêche format).
Identifiers: Canadiana (print) 2019017451X | Canadiana (ebook) 20190174595 | ISBN 9781771835312 (softcover) | ISBN 9781771835329 (EPUB) | ISBN 9781771835336 (Kindle)
Classification: LCC PS3562.E57 P53 2020 | DDC 813/.54—dc23

For Jody McAuliffe

THE READER

A T THE HIGH-SECURITY PRISON CALLED Attica in Upstate
New York, an inmate I would come to know well—and
even, so to speak, to love—recovered the small child that
he once was—the very child who told his father that he wanted to
"learn reading." The child's request was answered by daddy's thick
black strap, swinging hard on the child's bare back, as daddy informed him that reading was for girls and would cause him to grow
un orecchione, a big ear, and thereby become a *finocchio*. Because in
the imagination of southern Italian peasants large ears were understood as the male equivalent of a vagina and the inescapable cause
of homosexuality. At blessed Attica, the magical life promised to the
child by words on a page was at last married to the prisoner's long
and easy practice of savage violence. He became, at Attica, wholly
himself, a reader of serious literature and philosophy, a poet and
a painter, as well as the man that he was and always would be: the
dedicated assassin of dangerous men.

The abusive father, himself a criminal—though never at his son's
storied level—was startled, then puzzled, but ultimately enraged
when his son fell from the womb blond and piercingly blue-eyed,
in a Neapolitan family of the uniformly swarthy and racially ambiguous. The genetic history of the south of Italy was unknown to
the father and his neighborhood in the poor Red Hook section of
Brooklyn. They would not have known that, many centuries before, vigorous Viking males had slid with erotic impunity into the
southern gene pool. The blond and blue-eyed boy was a remote possibility, actualized, not the issue of adultery, but the father's friends

1

whispered among themselves that the milkman was the cause. That fucking blond Polack from down the street. Soon, the father—a cartoon of male villainy—heard the rumor and his wife Angela suffered the pain of the thick black strap, until one of the whisperers repented and told him that he himself had a blond and blue-eyed nephew, still in Naples, who was given life by his nun-like sister-in-law. When the father scoffed and said this nun was certainly a *putana* (a whore) the good neighbor replied, No. Believe me. No. The father said, You tried to get in? And the good neighbor said, Yes. With great firmness, but I failed, though my firmness did not.

In his teen years and through young manhood the prisoner of Attica was known as Joe the Blond. Though never to his face. In its obituary of April 8, 1972, the *New York Times* reminded its readers, who needed no reminding—because they were long-smitten by his legend—that in his maturity he was known as Crazy Joey Gallo. Though never to his face.

* * *

It is possible that you may wish to ask me, as it was said in my old, dead neighborhood of Little Italy, Where the fuck do you get off? My bona fides—"these are my bona fides," which was never said in the neighborhood except once, when I heard Joey say, "These are my bona fides," as he broke a man's arm across a table at the Luna, his favorite restaurant on Mulberry, just south of Umberto's Clam House. My authority—to use a word I detest—from whence doth it derive? I once heard Joey say "doth" with a stone-cold stare directed at an enforcer from a rival family, who spoke with a speech impediment and promised Joey, sooner than later, bloody doth (death). And Joey replied, "Doth be not proud, Carmine," as he placed a knife on Carmine's throat and added, "John fucking Donne, Carmine."

My authority to tell the story from the inside? Where doth I get off? I was a neighborhood boy in Joey's time who had heard all the Joey stories, mythically enlarged, perhaps. Or perhaps not, because Joey did not need mythic enlargement. For a bookish and

bespectacled asthmatic like me, Little Italy was a brutal neighbor-hood, through which I moved warily along its edges, until my sudden acceptance at its center.

At Umberto's, 129 Mulberry Street, just before Joey's fatal dawn, 4:30 a.m., April 7, 1972, Joey Gallo and his party continued the celebration, begun the previous evening at the Copacabana, of his forty-third birthday. Happy shouts. I hear them still. I, the waiter. I, the only waiter at that hour—as wine glasses were raised. *Cent' an'*! (100 years more!)

Two years prior to that singular dawn at Umberto's, I passed the Luna and he, Joey Gallo, happened to emerge and notice me just as I passed—me, carrying a book. It was a boy bearing a book, I am convinced, that caught his attention and his sympathy. I could not know then that I was beginning my journey to become an insider of the gravest consequence.

This is how it begins: I bear a novel called *Knock On Any Door*, whose central character is a young Italian-American, who lives a life of crime, kills a corrupt and bigoted Irish cop, and dies in the electric chair at twenty-one. This is how it goes: Just as Joey emerges from the Luna and I cross his path—at that moment a familiar neighborhood bully, who I had hitherto successfully avoided, puffs on his cigarette alongside the Luna entrance. The bully strikes: He says, "You faggots prefer books to cunts and when you don't have a book in your hands you have a dick in your mouth." Joey Gallo is a blur of unreal speed smashing the bully's head repeatedly on the pavement into a mess of blood—and something else that I cannot describe. Joey says, "Would you like to kick his face, kid? Give him one in the balls?" I cannot speak. Joey wears an expensive-looking white suit and black shirt open at the collar. Not a spot of blood on him. Not a wrinkle in the suit. Not a drop of sweat on his forehead. He laughs in an unsettling way, which much later I will hear in a favorite film of his, *Kiss of Death*, featuring his favorite actor, Richard Widmark. He says, "Kid, I understand. You won't kick his face. You keep your rage bottled up, which makes you good, and un-happy and unhealthy. Me? I am not good, but I am healthy (so far)

3

and happy." I cannot reply. He points to my book and quotes the doomed hero's motto: Live fast, die young, and have a good-looking corpse. "My philosophy," he says, "and my future in a few terrific words. I love books and I act harshly on the world. One day may you do the same."

I manage to force out, "Pleased to meet you, Mr. Gallo."

He says, "Only judges call me Mr. Gallo. Judging me, kid?"

"No sir," I say.

He laughs that laugh. He says, "You have good manners. Had dinner yet?"

"No sir, Mr. Gallo." Good manners make for good self-preservation, I thought, but did not say.

He says, "Call me Joey," as he escorted me into the Luna.

I say, "Thank you, Mr. Gallo. I accept your invitation, but I'd rather stick with calling you Mr. Gallo, Mr. Gallo."

He laughs, like Richard Widmark. Many years later I heard from one of his associates, who was run over by a truck, not by accident, that he modeled himself after Widmark. He practiced Widmark's Tommy Udo before a mirror. He created his image derived from the image created by an actor. The violence he did was real. The truck that ran over his associate backed up and ran over him again.

In the pre-dawn of April 7, 1972, at Umberto's, Joey had four guests with him. One of them a twelve-year-old girl named Lisa, his stepdaughter, who adored him. She was the daughter of the wife he had married just two weeks prior to that day in the apartment of the well-known actor, Jerry Orbach. They had begun at the Copa six hours before: his new wife, her daughter, his sister, and two bodyguards. Word on the street had it that there was an open contract on Joey's life. One of the bodyguards, the most lethal of Gallo enforcers, did not accompany Joey to Umberto's. Why not? A question that detectives never asked. And they did not question me, who answered the phone at Umberto's at 4 a.m., thirty minutes before the birthday celebrants arrived. At Umberto's, Joey was short on fire power.

I've read and heard many accounts of his life and times, but in none of them is the question asked: What is a twelve-year-old,

much less a twelve-year-old girl, doing at 11 p.m. at the Copacabana to take in the obscene Don Rickles show at midnight? At the *Copa*? In that risqué atmosphere and with that fast crowd until 4 a.m.? And then she is driven to Lower Manhattan with four tipsy adults to experience there what she experienced. Lisa. Dear Lisa.

I left you suspended in narrative time—I have difficulty these days, at my age, staying on track. Joey was about to escort me inside the Luna, where I'd never been before. Made from two storefronts, the Luna was wide and deep, with dark wood-paneled walls and a black and white tiled floor, sloping from each side of the restaurant to the center to form a shallow channel that marked the gap that once separated the original two stores. At the back wall, two large tables. At one of them, always, three old women, dressed in mourning black with black kerchiefs covering their heads, peeling every day mounds of garlic cloves. The other table was Joey's. Reserved for him at all times. It was known as his office, where he conducted business within easy earshot of the mourning garlic-peelers. When asked by an investigative journalist what they had heard, long after the event at 129 Mulberry, one of them said, "That is their life they lead. It is not our life we lead. Joey bought us Christmas presents for 20 years. That is what we know. And we know this," as she held up an unpeeled clove.

Prior to our chance encounter on Mulberry Street, I had seen him a few times in the neighborhood only at a distance—entering and exiting a black Cadillac. Of course, I had seen his photo in the sensational dailies, but until I sat opposite Joey in his office at the Luna, the full impact of his visage did not register. I say "visage," not "face." "Face" would only indicate the physical configuration of his features. I mean "visage"—what comes through the physical, which is not itself physical. What was pushed out into view from his unseeable interior life was pure force. Joey's impact was impact itself. Looking at him across the table I felt myself succumb to the charisma of his violence. The head was too large for his body. The head needed, and had, a powerful neck to keep the head from toppling off his body. A sizable mole on his left cheek. The sheer physical face had a muscular look—as if the face had been lifting weights three

times per week. If a handsome face can entail brutality among the possibilities of handsomeness, then Joey Gallo was brutally handsome and I couldn't look away.

His first words across the table were these: "We don't kill cops, we don't kill FBI agents, we kill each other: Relax. The trouble with that kid in the novel you're reading? He killed a cop. They call me crazy, but I'm not out of control. They fear me, which is what they mean by crazy."

He reaches across to shake my hand. "No more Mr. Gallo. Just Joey. Do you fear me?"

"No, sir. Joey."

"Those who fear me want me dead."

"I don't fear you." I was, in truth, strangely relaxed and content in the company of this legendary killer. I was falling in love, not with love, as the song goes, but with Joey. I was enchanted, caught by surprise.

"Ever going to tell me your name, kid?"

"Roger Castellano."

"Any relation to Constipated Big Paul?"

Big Paul Castellano, the Don of all Dons, was known in New York Mob circles for his constant complaints about his bowels—"I can't move my bowels"—as well as his unwillingness to spread the bread around to his soldiers and closest associates. Big Paul stood 6-3, 270 pounds. I told Joey that Big Paul was a distant relative, who I had never met.

He said, "'Distant' is too near."

Joey and I were the same height, at 5-6, but in his presence I not only felt that I was shorter—I *knew* that I was significantly shorter and noticed that when his associates or rivals, who were objectively taller than he, and stood in his company, their eyes were trained above his head. Not, I believe, because they could not bear to meet his gaze, but because in their fear they were actually meeting his gaze somewhere above his physical head. He was taller than Big Paul. Joey Gallo—*Il Gallo*, Italian for the Rooster, the dominant male among men whose terrible violence paled beside his. In Joey's vicinity, they were all his hens.

The question that anyone not Mob-affiliated might pose—any reasonably nice person—is the question that I once posed—I, who was a reasonably nice person until the hours just before dawn at Umberto's, on April 7, 1972: What exactly made Joey's acts of violence special? What did he do uniquely that set him apart from the knifers, the shooters, the wielders of lead pipe, the swingers of heavy chains, the garroters who practiced their trade with piano wire, the punchers, the kickers, the chokers-to-death who delighted to use bare hands? Joey performed all of these actions—and others that I must not specify. But it was not the medium of his violence that made them all afraid and caused them to call him crazy. Like the greatest of Americans among all Americans—Henry David Thoreau, Martin Luther King, Junior—Joey was a man of defiance, whose most outrageous act of defiance was of time itself.

Imagine a pole-vaulting competition. Bear with me, please. For normal vaulters, a beginning, a middle, an end. A past, a present, a future. We hear a vaulter's name announced. We see the vaulter appear at the top of the runway. The vaulter runs hard, high-stepping down the lane and slides his long pole into the vault box and lifts himself with the aid of his flexible pole up, up, and over the bar. The moment of ecstasy is that smallest of moments high up when the vaulter knows he has cleared the bar. Then flop-down, and spent, into the protective netting, where he wishes someone would offer him a post-coital cigarette.

Now imagine a vaulter who is not normal. His name is Joey Gallo. We do not see him walk to the top of the runway. Because he does not do so. We do not see him run hard to the point of takeoff, inserting his long pole. Because he does not do so. Nor is he seen swinging high up to the bar. Because he does not do so. Because he has no pole. He does not fall to the other side, into the protective netting. There is no protective netting. He abominates protective netting. He does not fall.

Nothing transpires for the viewer of vaulting Gallo, or for Gallo himself, but the moment when he is seen high and afloat above the bar. No past of preparation as he races down the path, no dismal future of flop-down death. There is only the split second of suspended

7

and frozen clearance of the bar. For the viewer, a cinematic freeze-frame never forgotten. For Joey, the moment when he comes to life in the no-time time of full presence to himself, in the present, when he becomes Joey Gallo.

Like vaulting Gallo above the bar, the real Gallo's violence abrupts without prelude and triggers the fear of those for whom anticipation of violence is the fragile guarantee of immunity from murder. He was called, in tired language, unpredictable. I thought of him as instantaneous, the man of no transitions, who *was not* until he achieved existential identity in a flare of action, in the ecstasy and terror of violent suddenness above the bar. That is what it means to say Joey Gallo was dangerous as no mobster ever was.

At the Luna, once a week for two years, we conversed about books. No small talk from Joey—how are you, the weather, the Yankees. He was just an immediate rush of talk. He was immediate man, whose time was running out. Talk fast, Joey. Thirty minutes with him was like three hours with an ordinary person.

Talk faster, Joey.

The difference between Sartre and Camus was his obsession. He wanted to know my philosophical position. I didn't have one, I said. He replied, "I thought you were a serious person." He found Camus a pathetic life-denier, because why else drive a car at that speed over a narrow winding road unless he was courting death in a crash, which is how he died. But Sartre affirmed life, he said.

Whenever Joey said "Sartre," his face brightened and never looked happier: "Because Sartre wrote," he said, "grab the freedom to make yourself and become who you are in the rip and slash of the street." (I did not ask if Sartre actually wrote "rip and slash of the street.") "At birth," Joey said, "we're like pigs, goats, and monkeys. We become human only when we make ourselves, whereas" (a word Joey liked) "pigs don't become pigs in the power struggles of the pig pen. They are who they are at birth and they all get along in the sty. The day a pig *chooses* its pighood, that's the day it transcends piggery and becomes human," Joey said. "On the other hand, Mr. Roger The Reader Castellano," he said, and laughed his Richard Widmark

laugh, "I'll cut off your hand. As it were, kid. As it were. Listen: Most so-called humans root in the sty of their environment. They suck it in and become what they suck in. Goats, pigs, and monkeys—birth until death. So let's not monkey around." (Widmark again.)

"Forget the liberal whining peddled in *Knock on Any Door*. Red Hook Brooklyn didn't make me. Throw that novel in the garbage before it destroys your power to make yourself in the unfolding of time. To live, to die, in what *you* made. Me? I choose who I am daily. I know my end. Not the time and place, but the *how*. I know the *how*," Joey said, Joey sang, at the Luna, as his face brightened.

That theatrical man—I knew him well.

* * *

My father was blessed with a liquid baritone voice. Every morning, as he prepared breakfast for me and my mother, he would sing along with the radio. The station of the golden oldies. His favorite was, "You Always Hurt the One You Love." Unlike Joey Gallo's father, my father did not hurt me. And neither did Joey.

CONTE

1

T HEY SAID, MR. CONTE, DON'T push it. Start with a short walk around the block. Don't push it? I don't want to leave the house. Doctor's orders, said Catherine Cruz—my wife, my specialist in tough love. The one and only Cruz.

The day after I'm discharged from the Upstate Medical Center in Syracuse, and return to Utica, I take a short walk around the block. They hadn't warned me about the incessant chirping of the sparrows. Or the cracks in the sidewalk. Or the oil stains in the street, where cars had leaked while parked overnight. Much less the wind through the summer trees—like fingernails crawling down a chalkboard.

Has general anesthesia damaged my brain? Do I suffer cognitive dysfunction, but only outdoors? In a vacant lot, a broken tricycle cut through me like a hot knife through butter. I won't tell Catherine, whose father lost his mind, that the world bears down on me hard.

I open the door. The phone. I shouldn't pick up because I don't recognize caller I.D. I pick up. A ravishing voice says, "Is it you, Mr. Eliot Conte?"

I reply, "More or less."

The voice says, "Very nice. I have chosen the right man."

I don't respond. A scam-caller, but I can't hang up.

The voice says, "I am a friend of your father. From New York. Lower Manhattan. In the vicinity of Umberto's Clam House."

"My father's been dead for five years."

"Who was to tell me, Mr. Conte?"

I don't respond.

The voice says, "How does it proceed, your post-surgical recovery?"

I am unable to respond.

The voice says, "My dear Eliot, our friends push away the nearness of the world. Are you acquainted with Umberto's Clam House? I believe that you are."

"Who are you?"

"You have desired my call. For many years."

"I get eight scam-callers a day. You're the best."

"When you were four years old, you said to your father, Daddy, why do you put up the seat when you do pee-pee with that little big thing? Why, daddy?"

"My father said before he died that 'why' was my middle name."

The voice says, "You shall be known amongst our friends as Eliot The Curious. Amongst dear friends—our comfort and our shield."

"What are you trying to sell me?"

"My life. Buy it and it may cost you yours."

I don't respond.

The voice says, "Release yourself."

"Say your name."

"Amongst our friends, I am known as The Reader."

The line goes dead.

* * *

I retrieve his number and call back. An automated voice says, "We're sorry. The number you called is no longer in service." I've punched in an incorrect digit. Try again, with concentration. Same result. Again: We're sorry ... I conclude that he'd bought one of those cheap throwaway phones, made the call, then threw it away. Nothing to be done but wait, confident that he'll call again with another throwaway, that he'd bought many throwaways. We'll talk again when he wishes, not when I wish, but my desire is urgent. The

situation requires patience—a virtue I never had. He said that I've been waiting for his call for many years.

I don't mention the caller to the formidable Catherine Cruz. Because she'd only say that it was one of my girlfriends from decades past. They never get over you, buster, she'll say, and I'll say the caller was male, and she'll say, So how is Maryrose what's-her-name these days, Marlon? Over the years, Catherine and I have cultivated this brand of banter. Never fails to bridge the gap. Especially in times of trouble. I consider myself lucky to have found Catherine. When I tell her so she delivers a swift and not-quite-playful jab to the solar plexus.

Two days after the call, no call back. Catherine says, I forgot. When you were in the hospital, a call came from someone who said he was a friend of your father. He wanted to speak to Mr. Eliot Conte. So I tell him, Marlon's in the hospital for major surgery. I probably should've kept that to myself. He says, Marlon? I say, Forget about it. A private joke between Utica's greatest lovers. He says he'll call back. I say, Would you like to leave a message? He says something about a clam house. I ask for his name and the line goes dead. This guy's cracked, Els. Don't get involved.

* * *

The caller's references to Lower Manhattan, to his circle of friends, "our friends," he insisted, the repeated reference to Umberto's Clam House—site of a Mafia hit—I took them all as a deliberate performance of bad acting—what theater insiders call "indicating"—self-conscious hints of his identity. He wanted me to know that he was connected, but a rarity among the connected— a well-spoken Mafioso, a man of books as well as a man who had killed—"made his bones," as "our friends" put it in the poetry of Cosa Nostra. He wanted me to believe that he was a connoisseur of fine writing, who never peppered his conversation with obscenities, who claimed that he knew my father, the upstate New York political kingpin based in Utica, who I knew—my father, I mean, who

I knew not well, but without doubt knew him from my teen years forward, my father—to be involved—which was the rumor swirling in Utica, which I took as fact as I listened from my teenage bedroom at 2 a.m., as he, my father, spoke an incomprehensible Sicilian dialect—spoken only in an isolated spot in isolated Sicily, 70 years ago, when he sailed to America in steerage. I listened to my father speak weekly on the phone at 2 a.m. in the persistent, quiet drone of unrequited rage.

How did the man who called himself The Reader lead the connected life as a man of books, speaking daily, in dryly witty and formal English—a little forced, a little phony—to men who never smiled and who appeared at their social clubs in sweat clothes at 5'6", 250 pounds, clutching the second super-sized chocolate milkshake of the morning? Why did he think of me as "the right man?"

* * *

His call came the day after I'd come home from the hospital, where I'd been for six days. Five and a half hours on the table. Openheart. Where was I for five and a half hours that passed as if no time at all had elapsed, from the moment they administered general anesthesia to the moment in Cardiac Intensive Care when I awoke?

"Not even a second," I said to the attending anesthesiologist, when she checked on me at intensive care. "You put me into a timeless realm. Isn't that what death is like, Corinne? Corinne," I said, "this is my wife, Catherine Cruz, who doesn't like to be called Katie. I'm warning you, don't call her Katie."

Corinne smiles a little. Catherine does the same. Then my wife gives me one of those looks.

"Or maybe," Corinne says, deadpan, "not death but the sudden onset of romantic love. The Thunderbolt. The timeless early stage of romantic love."

I say, "I'm too old to be flirting with you. Or anybody."

"But he flirts," my wife says.

I say, "I love my wife." I give my wife one of those looks.

My wife says, "He says he loves me now in here, with all those tubes in him, in order to continue flirting with you. It's his old age. He's afraid."

We laugh. They, easily. I, with difficulty. My chest hurts, where they had sawed me open, as does my head. They hadn't sawed my head open. Maybe next time. For the autopsy.

"I'm not really flirting, Doctor."

Corinne says, "Do you wish to deny it?"

Catherine says, "We're all on to you, Conte."

I say, "What do we contact in deep anesthesia? Tell me, if you know."

Corinne is tall and attractive in the Scandinavian way, younger than Catherine, who is much younger than me, twenty years younger than me. Catherine is forty. Catherine is not so tall. She's attractive in the dark Latin way.

Corinne said, "I have yet to experience death itself or the onset of that other death called romantic love."

I say, "The passing of romantic love, like the passing of deep anesthesia, drops us back into time. Where we don't want to be."

"Wait till I get you home, buster."

They laugh. I start to, but stop. The chest. The head.

"Drops us back in time?" Corinne says. "Dumps," she says, "is the word."

My wife says, "Amen, sister."

I said to Corinne, "So you *have* experienced the onset of the other death called romantic love."

"Stop," my wife says, "or I'll use this sharp knife right here in my purse on your you-know-what."

Corinne grins and says, "Mr. Conte, you're married to a beautiful surgeon."

"Slasher is the word."

Corinne says, "But I haven't experienced death and returned, as you believe you have. I've never been under general anesthesia."

I say, "If death is what I experienced, a time of no-time for five and a half hours in the O.R., then what's there to fear? What can you give me for this headache?"

"How about another round of general anesthesia?"

"He doesn't faze me," my wife says. "He never fazed me. Which is why I fell for him."

I point to my head: "It's killing me. It's splitting."

Corinne says, "Only the living have head-splitters."

"He flirts, which is how he gets rid of the old age thoughts he can't deal with. But they come back anyway. Why dontcha try flirting with me, sometime, geezer?"

They laugh. I don't hold back in spite of the chest and the head. My face must've been grotesquely contorted, as I laughed through the pain, because they looked at me in horror.

The contorted face that Corinne and Catherine saw in Cardiac Intensive Care was the face of a vomited soul. Mine. The hidden face of another man of books. Mine. The caller had chosen the right man.

Corinne leaves. Catherine shuts the door. She says, "You shouldn't be talking so much. Don't talk. Rest. Listen, don't respond. We're happy with the comic back-and-forth, but I'm thinking we do it because it avoids the elephant in the room. Don't respond. Ever since your heart issue struck, two and a half years ago, we stopped having sex and you started flirting with all kinds of women. Don't think I don't notice. I notice. That over-the-hill sixty-plus opera star you met when she came to Utica. Marilyn at Caruso's, constantly. Our baby-sitter, Gertie, a grandmother in her 80s. The hot waitresses at Joey's and The Chesterfield. Plus when you're not flirting you're checking out all ages on the street, at the market. Now Corinne, who I grant is a knockout. You look happy when you flirt. All the while ... I'm sad. Don't talk. Speaking of Gertie. I better get home to relieve her. Anything special I can bring from your library? *Moby-Dick*? How many times can you read that thing? Tomorrow, back to the comedy, Marlon, or we're lost."

2

CATHERINE AT 8 A.M. TAKES Annie, our six-year-old, to school, after which she meets her partner Robert Rintrona for coffee at Caruso's, where they chew over two new clients in need of discreet private detectives: a recently married woman, whose husband is cheating on her with her sister, and a policeman whose fifteen-year-old daughter is eagerly screwing his forty-six-year-old brother. Two clients possessed by homicidal desire and convinced that private eyes Cruz and Rintrona will do what's necessary, because they'd heard wild rumors that Cruz and Rintrona are connected to an ex-P.I., yours truly, who had once done a gruesome killing on the kitchen floor of Caruso's itself. Rintrona knows the truth. Catherine does not.

I don't take any more walks around the block, but tell Catherine, when she returns with Annie at 3:15, that I have. I don't tell her that I tried just once when I opened the back door, very carefully. I don't tell her that I stood at the threshold. That I stepped quickly back inside and closed the door because the grass moved in on me.

What I do between 8 and 3:15 is await The Reader's call, as I perform rituals of distraction and read for the first time, slowly, with pleasure, the nonsense of *The Godfather* and write frequently in the margins BS, even as I sink into its presiding fantasy of charismatic Italian-American mobsters—the only free people of America—virtuosos of revenge, thugs of robust individuality—who do whatever they want with impunity. Because they embody the dark logic of

the founding American myth. As I read, I indulge the hottest erotic dream of timid, law-abiding, male Americans—initiation into the realm of freedom, where liberation is granted by a *capo*, in whose presence those who do not please him lose control of their bladders—as urine puddles about their feet. I see him, my imagined *capo*, my desire, put his arm around me and say, "Join us. Save yourself," as he offers me an elegant decanter of Grappa and the complete pirated recordings of Pavarotti.

I have long been intimate with the wound of unrequited revenge. It has festered in me daily since one month before our daughter Annie's birth, six years ago. Six festering years of a lethal disease of the heart that could not be healed by my cardiac surgeon's knife—this disease whose only cure is a righteous act of violence on behalf of my family. Not in fantasy by a fantasy *capo*. Not by a real world *capo*, either. Or by one of his real-world soldiers. But by me, and only me, at whatever cost to me.

* * *

I google "common side effects of general anesthesia:" *nausea* (no), *vomiting* (no), *dry mouth* (no), *shivering* (no), *sleepiness* (let it be), *mild hoarseness* (yes: Brando in *The Godfather*). I scroll down to "less common side effects" under the heading, "Post-Operative Delirium:" *visual hallucinations* (the green grass moves in on me), *anxiety* (the green grass moves), *distress* (the grass), *motiveless aggression* (I have motive. I have serious motive.) I scroll down to the acronym POCD: Post-Operative Cognitive Dysfunction. A list: None of which apply, but one, should it eventually apply, "problem with memory," will be my death before my death. I find nothing concerning chirping sparrows, oil stains on the street, wind through the summer trees, broken abandoned tricycles, or grass wanting to enter my house.

I speculate agoraphobia. I speculate that the medical establishment has suppressed the link between general anesthesia and agoraphobia. All my googling comes to nothing.

In the meanwhile, Catherine grows impatient. She asks if I'm really too weak to "at least throw out the garbage." With all of her domestic duties she's now forced to add *this* one too? She says, "The garbage barrel is what, Eliot? Fifteen feet from the back door? You walked around the block the day after you came home from Syracuse. You're telling me you're in decline since then? We're going back to Syracuse."

I fear to tell her about the proximity of the garbage barrel and the grass. Instead, I say, "I don't want to go back to Syracuse."

"You have to."

"It's not physical, Catherine."

"Jesus, Eliot."

"That's why I didn't want to tell you because I—"

"Don't start with my father that I married my father."

"I never said that."

"Listen, Els, that thought haunts me ever since we got involved."

"I have to tell you something, Catherine. Why I can't throw out the garbage. I'm afraid to go outdoors."

"Jesus Christ, Marlon."

"Marlon won't get us around this one. No use anymore calling me Marlon. Or me calling you Stella."

"You never called me Stella."

"I'm in trouble, Stel."

"You go outdoors the day after you come home from Syracuse and suddenly you become my father?"

I'm on the verge of telling her everything: starting with the incessant sparrows. But I only get as far as the incessant sparrows when she interrupts: "That's not crazy. That's aggraphobia."

I don't have brass balls, which is what it would take to correct her pronunciation.

She says, "Don't worry about the garbage."

"I'm not worried about the garbage. I'm worried will I ever leave the house."

"Corinne," she says, "this tall blond anesthesiologist? She gave you her card with her cell if you needed advice in an emergency, if

you started to lose it, which she figured you might because you told her you knew what death was from the inside of death. Let's call her now, because sooner or later, Els."

"Sooner or later what? I totally become your father? We can't call now—it's quarter to midnight. I'll call the hospital tomorrow. I'll email in addition. I'd text her, if I knew how to text."

"You call the hospital and they'll transfer you to a triage nurse, who will pass on your message to Corinne within 3-4 business days, or maybe never. More likely they alert the psych ward about your problems with grass. You email Corinne—I know how high you are on her, this hot Scandinavian, but she's a doctor foremost and you know how they are? You put 'urgent' in the subject line? She'll get back to you next week, because that's how they are. It's almost midnight? Good. She'll be home."

I agree to Catherine's request to activate speakerphone and call Corinne.

First thing Corinne says, "There's no need to apologize for the late hour, Mr. Conte. I've in fact been fearing that you might not be doing well in the mental department."

After I explain my symptoms she asks, "Are you perhaps a vet who experienced traumatic injury in battle?"

When I say no, never served, why do you ask, she says, "There is evidence that vets who experienced traumatic injury in battle will show symptoms of agoraphobia, even years later upon emerging from general anesthesia. Anything at all in your history akin to having experienced traumatic injury?"

When I say no, Catherine says, "How about if he gave traumatic injury to someone *else*? Will that set you up for aggraphobia?"

Corinne says, "That's an interesting question, Catherine. Very interesting. It raises another question: Can traumatic injury be transferred psychologically from victim to perpetrator? Conventional thinking assumes not, but my intuition says I think you're on to something major."

I ask Corinne how long my condition will last and she answers, "For some unfortunate souls, forever, but for most up to six months

according to the best studies. In the meanwhile, you can manage the situation by taking Catherine or a friend with you when you leave the house. Studies indicate that companionship helps alleviate the symptoms of the agoraphobics among us."

"Six months for most, but for some?"

"The life-timers usually begin in their early teens. For the late-bloomer types like you, no need to over-worry it. You'll likely be normal after you serve your six-months sentence."

Catherine jumps in: "So we throw out the garbage together? For six months?"

Corinne says, "One more thing, Mr. Conte. There are no double-blind studies to support this, but you might try wearing the darkest and sexiest sunglasses that you can purchase—you know, Mafia glasses—every time you leave the house. Even on overcast days. And if that doesn't work, blindfold yourself and"—Corinne begins to giggle like a little girl—"get yourself a seeing-eye dog."

3

TWO DAYS LATER. THE PHONE. Caller I.D. registers The Reader's out-of-service number.

The voice says, "I am never out of service."

I say, "I assumed you bought one of those cheap throwaway things."

The voice says, "The term of art, Mr. Conte, is 'burner.'"

I say, "You're calling from Lower Manhattan? Near Umberto's?"

"No," he says. "From Utica."

"You're here?"

"I am."

"In *Utica*?"

"I do not care to repeat myself."

"When can we meet?"

"Soon," he says.

The line goes dead in the prison of 1311 Mary Street, deep in Utica's former Italian-American fortress.

* * *

They had warned me sternly upon discharge: No driving for six weeks. Now that I am agoraphobia-trapped, Catherine walks me arm-in-arm, once mid-morning, once mid-afternoon, but even with her protection things press in, though a little less insistently. As Corinne predicted, Catherine's company calms me. I tell her, as we walk, "The meaning of our marriage is revealed at last in my post-surgical condition. You save me from myself."

"But not from me, Marlon," she says, as she delivers a more-than-playful punch to my shoulder.

Every day, three times, she calls from the field:

"How's it going, buster?"

"I am alive."

"Any more calls from that man?"

"No."

"Are you BS-ing me?"

"No."

"Hope you're not trying to arrange a meeting."

"I'm not."

"BS-ing me?"

"No."

"I think he's dangerous, Els."

"Don't worry about me."

"But I do. Gotta run. Talk tonight."

"I'm your house-bound, house-broken pet."

No response. She'd already hung up.

* * *

In every room of this lonely house I see a beckoning decanter of Grappa—the mirage of many piercing shots offered to me by the frightening *capo* of my fantasy. This morning I gave my *capo* a line of dialogue: "*Alla tua salute*, my friend," he says, as he raises a tulip-shaped glass of amber-colored paradise.

I am an alcoholic, in year eight of my newly-challenged sobriety. Grappa-less, I continue my slow-reading of *The Godfather* and sink ever-deeper into its nonsense of freedom inside the ideal family, three pages per sitting, before I resume my daily rituals of distraction, as I await The Reader's next call and the promise of a meeting. The fantasy *capo's* voice always in my head: *Join us. Save yourself.*

In the month prior to surgery, I had lingered late into the morning in pajamas and robe, shuffling aimlessly, apparently at times mumbling, through the house. In her kindness, Catherine said nothing, but our six-year-old began asking questions. The formidable

Catherine, a Mafia history buff, has only scorn for *The Godfather* (novel and movies), and refuses to watch *The Sopranos* with me. She loses her patience. She says, "You've become the Vincent Gigante of Mary Street. Eliot the Chin Conte. Eliot the Robe. Eliot the Grass Conte. Do not go out on the street in that ensemble. Or the front porch. And forget about fetching the mail. Because soon Annie will be calling you The Oddfather.

Now, each morning, upon waking, I shave, shower, splash on cologne, put on crisp, clean clothes—crispness being the key to my precarious tranquility—and lace up shoes shined and buffed to an elegant dull gloss the previous night. Each morning, I prepare coffee and breakfast for Catherine in an effort to respond to her care for me and to ward off victim-syndrome of patients who have undergone multi-hour, major surgery of the heart. Upon discharge, a hospital psychologist told me that being there for others puts the blues in retreat, though not, she was quick to emphasize, out of sight. The blues are out there, Mr. Conte, on the far horizon. Try not to look.

Mid-morning and mid-afternoon, I douse my face with cold water. The psychologist said I should return to the habits I had before surgery. I said, I totally agree and returned to the habits I never had. Cold water is not the cure. Late afternoon, just before Catherine returns, a change of shirt.

No matter how light the load, I launder daily and iron—including socks and underwear. Wash bathroom floor. Shower. Tub. Toilet—thrice daily. Dust pictures on walls and tables. Such pleasure.

My mind dissolves into the movements of my body. The strategy of distraction works well until the actions become habitual and my dissolved mind gathers itself, congeals, separates itself from the movements of my body—free to think of my house-chained self—free to brood upon The Reader. Where in Utica does he live? Or should I say holes up?

A knock on the door. It's only Bobby—Robert Rintrona, my wife's partner in private investigation.

He says, "Katie gave me the low-down. I'm here to stage a fuckin' intervention."

Bobby is the only one she allows to get away with calling her "Katie." Should I be jealous?

He says, "What's with the cologne in the isolation of your house? Gone homo on me?"

"Yes."

"Good answer," he says. "They legally knife you in Syracuse, but you emerge with your sense of humor intact. You suddenly became a three-dollar bill?

"Yes."

"Good answer. We're going for a drive."

"Not sure I can handle that."

"You're in a plane. 38,000 feet. Answer me this: Are you outside? Same difference in a car. We cruise the broken neighborhoods of this dying city, have lunch at a drive-in, you're never outside."

"What about to and from the car?"

"This so-called agoraphobia? It's only mental."

I say, "I tire easily since they sawed me open."

He says, "Take a nap while we cruise."

I take his arm as we walk to the car.

He says, "You're the first man who ever took my arm. It's a special feeling. Don't tell nobody."

* * *

Bobby was right. Inside the car I wasn't afflicted. I was bored. A high school teacher of mine loved to say, Familiarity breeds contempt. She married six times. Except in death, how else is it obliterated from memory, my origin as a son of Utica? Obliterated. I'd seen all the neighborhoods too many times. All the sad people, too familiar. Utica is the unappetizing wife who starved me from the first date forward. Utica: three-day-old salad.

The upside of my agoraphobia: formal separation from the moribund Utica wife. Better to be locked up at 1311 Mary Street than to go out seeking the boys of my generation at Caruso's, for coffee and pastry. Sam's dead. Babe's dead. Buddy was cremated. Tootsie.

Nicky. Dates is missing. So is Hindoo. Gene. Where is Gene? Gene is gone. Gene went. I can't say the other word about Gene, my oldest friend who supported me in my 20s when I wanted suicide like an obliterating orgasm. My father, the political boss of Upstate New York, is dead. Never more so to me than when he was alive.

With death so close and ever-present, what's the point of struggling?

Gene died.

Bobby, a good and profane man, thinks he has cancer: "Internal cancer, Eliot, in the bowels. Blood every time on the paper. It's not piles. Or those hemorrhoids either, as they say these days. It's old blood from deep up inside. Dark, black, like tar."

This conversation in the car about Bobby's anal bleeding, as we ate McDonald's, was good—it obliterated, I keep repeating that word, "obliterated," don't I?—Bobby's talk obliterated the stale life of Utica. Bobby's conversation is always good—makes me forget myself, especially when he gets into a groove about his failing body.

"Are you in pain, Bobby?"

"I sense its approach."

"Have you gone to the doctor, Bobby?"

"They'll want surgery, it's the default option. Let's say I let them do it. They open me up. They take one fuckin' look and they gag. They immediately close me up. Internal cancer gives off a stench which even these hard-assed knifemen never get used to. Shortest surgery on record. When I come out of anesthesia they'll tell me to get my affairs in order. I'm thinking the affairs of my 20s. I get one more shot? They're saying before I die I bang women now unrecognizable in their wretched senior years? Who, when these old broads, they take one look at me, in my present state of decomposition? They think, He changed. Can you believe it's Rintrona? What a change, Marie! I had one affair, Eliot, which was an affair erotically, though not technically. Because we were both single. She's dead and I miss her worse every day. The wife. I still miss Maureen."

I tell him about the phone calls. He says, I advise you don't answer if he calls again. Get involved with these people? You owe

27

them for life because they'll do you the favor which you asked for, and the debt cannot be paid. Forget the interest: the principal is fuckin' infinite. Obviously I'm talking here to the wall."

* * *

Home: two calls waiting. The first asks me to email my bank account numbers to Nigeria so that 500,000 dollars can be deposited in my account. The second is the one I've been waiting for:

> *Mr. Conte: I trust that you and Mr. Rintrona*
> *had a pleasant sojourn about town. I must say*
> *that it warms this old man's cold heart to*
> *observe you mid-morning and mid-afternoon,*
> *arm-in-arm with Catherine Cruz.*
> *Your dark beauty. Detective Catherine Cruz.*

4

S HE COMES THROUGH THE DOOR looking ashen—if a Latina like
Catherine, a decidedly brown person, can look ashen, or even
remotely ashen. Somehow she did. I ask, "What's wrong?" She
replies, "Later," with a gesture toward Annie, who ran up to greet
her. The meal was a success, even with our six-year-old, who hitherto would only eat Rigatoni in the lightest of butter sauces.

With Annie put to bed and asleep I assumed Catherine would
immediately grill me about the mysterious caller's second call, but
she didn't. She had something to tell me about Rintrona. She says,
"I think we're going to lose him."

Fireflies in the August twilight, as we sit on the top step of the
front porch, our backs to the open front door. I understood her implication, but replied with my go-to fear-killer—the comic stance of
my senior years: "He's finally made up his mind to move to Florida,
where all Utica Italians long to die?"

She said, "For once stop with the deflections. After Bobby
dropped you home, we met at the office to compare notes on our
new clients. We were speculating which of the two was most likely
to do murder. The wife tells Bobby she's going to kill her husband,
who's screwing her sister. She says seven times in their half hour in-
terview that she'll use the 12-gauge shotgun when he's asleep. Close
up, in the face. I tell Bobby when they talk crazy they do nothing.
I say to Bobby, the cop is reserved. He's having trouble getting out

of bed in the morning. I tell Bobby he'll stalk his fifteen-year-old daughter and his forty-six-year-old brother until he catches them in the act. Then he'll kill them both. Suddenly Bobby stands, screams, and drops to the floor grabbing his abdomen."

"His gut," I say, "taking revenge on the double Big Mac, the double order of fries, the thick chocolate shake you need a spoon-not-a-straw to consume, and the massive chocolate chip cookie."

She says, "Stop. He's your friend too. Annie loves him. We all love him. He was in tears. I never saw a grown man—not to mention of Bobby's temperament—crawling and moaning like a dying animal. He digs his fingers into his gut like he's trying to give pain to his pain. So I drove him to St. Elizabeth's. They're doing tests. When I left he said, "Bye bye, Katie. See you on the other side. Don't let them do an autopsy. Don't let them chop me up, Katie."

She says, "Hear that?" as she looks over her shoulder at the open door.

I'd heard nothing. She tends to hear things. I rose quickly to go back inside to check on Annie. I check every room. I try the double-deadbolted back door. The windows. Fear for Annie's safety had been the undertow of our lives ever since the beginning of the ninth month of Catherine's pregnancy, six years ago, when she received two anonymous letters on successive days. The first saying that the pregnancy would end in the birth of a dead baby. The second that the child's life would be short and violently terminated.

Back at the front porch, I say, "Nothing."

"I know," she says. "Always nothing. But I can't help it sometimes. After six years I'm still—you don't ever seem to be."

"I'm afraid too."

"When does it end?"

"One hundred percent? Never."

"Let's say," she says, "we ourselves go all out to find the sender that the FBI with all their resources … and by some miracle we—"

"Yeah, miracle."

"Let's say he's found. Charged. Convicted. Put away for life."

"Not for life, Stel. Maybe a short stay in the bughouse. Or a few

years in prison. Three to five. Out after eighteen months for good behavior. Converted to Christ. Maybe does no time at all with a shrewd lawyer. Why do you assume the doer is male?"

She says, "What good does it do to talk about this? I need a cigarette after seven good years."

"Not talking is worse." But I didn't talk to Catherine about what I saw in the vacant lot on my first walk around the block. What haunts me, in the daylight hours and in the dark: The thrown away, broken tricycle.

"So he called you again," she says. "Talk to me about that. He knew your father? Talk to me about that. What's his name? No BS."

"Don't know his name. He called himself The Reader."

"Like you. He didn't call you. He never called you. You called yourself. You with your nose constantly in a book."

"He told me that he knew my father from when I was a child. He had a detail about me he could only have gotten from my father. A funny story that my father told me when I was an adult."

"About putting the toilet seat up? Your insatiable curiosity?"

"That one. He said I should be called Eliot The Curious."

"He gave you a Mafia-type handle? Tell me more. No BS."

"I think he's connected."

"With?"

"Probably."

"By any chance did he speak of *our friends*?"

"Yes. Likely not by chance."

"Mafia."

"Apparently."

"Your father's old friend?"

"Yes."

"For God sakes, Els."

"Says he's from Lower Manhattan. Vicinity of Umberto's Clam House. More than once he mentioned Umberto's. Asked me if I knew Umberto's. Said I had to know Umberto's. I understood his implication. Umberto's was the site of a famous Mafia assassination of a mobster named Joe Gallo. Crazy Joey Gallo, as he was known,

who loved serious philosophy and literature. I'm guessing you know all about Crazy Joey."

"You guess right, Marlon. Crazy Joey was another reader. Just like you. Crazy Eliot Conte."

"I'm not crazy-violent like Joey anymore. I put all that behind me."

"So far."

"He said I always wanted to make contact with someone like him."

"Is that true, Els? You really wanted involvement?"

Saved by the phone from within.

She says, "Bobby, I hope, with the test results. Is it safe to leave you alone with the fireflies? Can you handle the grass?"

I say, "God only knows and He doesn't exist."

She was gone and I was outside alone. I decided to test myself by shutting the front door. Done. I was truly outside. No glance over the shoulder could give me the comfort of a beckoning interior: Catherine, Annie, the drifting fragrance of a kitchen whose walls breathe out sautéing garlic. The fading light softened the look of things and the fireflies decided not to move in on me.

I had withheld critical facts from Catherine. That The Reader was now in Utica and promises a meeting. Soon. That I had strong desire to meet him, who said he was eager to sell me his life. Whatever that means. And if I bought, it might cost me mine. What that means is clear. I had no fears. I had a plan, rooted in my long-cultivated Mafia fantasy, that would cure once and forever our fear for Annie's life.

She's back. She says, "You survived! Bobby's home and happy. The mass lodged in his colon is not a malignant tumor. Or even a benign tumor."

"I can imagine the cure."

"He loved the cure and urged me not to tell you because you might get the wrong idea."

"Enema, obviously."

"Better. High colonic."

A new white Cadillac SUV rolls to a stop opposite our porch. She points, she says, "Our turn, Marlon."

"What?"

"You don't read Gertie."

"What?"

"Gertie. She alerted the list serve. He's been introducing himself to his new neighbors. Our turn. He bought 1303 Mary. Think of it—a new Caddy SUV on Mary Street!"

The man moving toward us wears a white, loose-fitting track warm-up suit. A.K.A. sweat clothes. He's short. I guess 5-6. And heavy. I'd say 250, but hard to tell. Loose-fitting white clothes cause us to look heavier than we are. He's carrying a super-sized drink of some sort with a straw sticking up, and a plastic spoon in his free hand. What comes waddling toward us is the embodiment of the low-level Mafia soldier I had always imagined. I knew who he was. I was sure of it.

He effects a slight bow and says, "Detective Cruz." The telephone voice but richer, more seductive. He looks at me, raises his cup as if in toast, and says, "Mr. Conte." Then, pointing with the plastic spoon, he says, "Annie, I presume?" And there she is, standing in the open doorway.

The roly-poly smiling man bows as deeply as his vast belly will allow: "Call me Roger Castellano, young lady," he says. "At your service."

Catherine takes Annie by the hand. She says, "Drop in for coffee sometime, neighbor"—as she escorts Annie back inside—as Annie twists and looks over her shoulder at the stranger—as Annie says, "Roger-Dodger."

The door is ajar. I close the door tight. I turn to face the man who calls himself Roger Castellano, but he has disappeared. Another man stands in his place, in a white track suit, holding a super-sized drink with a white Cadillac SUV looming behind him. Pudgy face no more—a hint of hollowness in the cheeks—merry eyes now a corpse-stare—lips parted in slack-jawed horror. A face without pity. Where has he gone? The roly-poly man. Am I crazy?

I say, "And you are?"

From deep inside the folds of his track suit: "Yes."

"And you—?"

"Yes."

And—?"

"Yes."

"Chocolate shake, super-thick? Hence the spoon?"

"I abominate chocolate."

I say, "Catherine may not put two and two together because I never told her that the mysterious caller—that you were in Utica— that he, you—the voice—the mystery—promised a meeting."

"Detective Cruz and I spoke while you were in hospital. Doubtless you know. She may well recognize the voice. Two plus two, Mr. C."

"She has a tin ear."

"Come again?"

"She once mistook Elvis for Sinatra."

"Say no more."

"I told her the voice was connected. Am I wrong?"

"Trust yourself and the whole world will be your oyster, as it slides down your throat."

"She asked me if you said the words *our friends*. I said yes. Who are you really?"

"Think of me, Mr. C, as the *nunzio* of the Genovese family, the most powerful of the five families. And I the *nunzio*."

"*Nunzio*? The messenger for—?"

"Yes. A kind and generous man. A devout Roman Catholic. The only Pope."

"The only God, Mr. Castellano? Isn't that what you mean? And you are His Messenger?"

"You blaspheme, Mr. C."

He lifts his gaze toward the house. He says, "When you turn to track my gaze, she will have closed the blinds and disappeared. The fascinating Detective Cruz."

I turn. The blinds are closed.

He says, "Detective Cruz has put two and two together."

He raises his shake: "Vanilla." A long pause, as he shovels it

in. When he's finished it off, he says, "No. You are not. Not in the slightest. Not at all."

"I am not *what*?"

"Crazy. *Meshuggeneh*. Paranoid."

He pauses. He nods. He says again, "Paranoid." He winks. And the roly-poly man returns to life.

"Meshugg?" I say. "Me? That what you really mean?"

"Yes," he says. "We are."

* * *

At breakfast the next morning, Catherine says, "Guess what? Gertie says that Remo—you know, our neighborhood watchman?—Remo identified our new neighbor's license plate. The vehicle in question is out of Lower Manhattan. Remo knows things. And I think you know exactly who he is, don't you? Our new neighbor."

I say, "Far-fetched coincidence, Stel. I know no such thing."

"Don't Stel me," she says. "Don't BS me. I don't like the smell of this guy. Don't Stel me, Eliot."

I say, "Don't be angry with me, Catherine."

She says, "I'm more scared than angry."

I say, "Forget him. Before Annie started kindergarten last week, she was under the strict protection of her parents. She went nowhere without us. So yesterday I called Victor Cazzamano and said now that you're a melancholy retired cop we need your help for a good fee. So I filled him in. I said we need you to be at school when Catherine and Annie arrive. We need you there at the playground at mid-morning. We need you there at dismissal time. We need you armed. He said he wouldn't take a cent, but he'd take the adventure."

Catherine says, "Annie will need a security guard for life. We're not going to live forever."

* * *

After an uncomfortably silent breakfast, I go out to retrieve the morning paper and find a plain, letter-sized envelope protruding from under the welcome mat at the front door. No address. No return address. No postmark. I quickly unseal it before I go back inside. A type-written message in capital letters:

ANNIE IS SIX YEARS OLD.
HER TIME GROWS SHORT.

THE READER

THE CURIOUS ONE APPEARED AT mid-morning, having partially beat back the terror of his unaccompanied one-block journey from 1311 Mary Street to 1303 Mary. My mid-morning's treasure, Eliot Conte. He came to me to propose a guided tour of Utica's neighborhoods: he the guide, I the driver. I replied that I had read the obscure fiction of the Utica School and had been more than sated with its detailed images—overly detailed images, I thought, but did not say—of the neighborhoods, the streets in relation to one another, the cafés, the restaurants, the ethnic composition and the racial and ethnic enmities, all of it dwarfing the human characters in those novels, as if Utica itself were the only authentic character. I said, "Eliot Conte, I do not require a tour," but he insisted that deterioration had accelerated since the era of Utica's native novelists, especially on his beloved East Side, which he claims to love no more—its original settlers from the south of Italy were long dead, he said, their children and grandchildren had fled and scattered to the suburbs of many distant cities, and many of the children and grandchildren were, like those suburbs, also dead. He insisted that I needed to observe the thing itself, the look of "this dying city," as he put it. The Utica novelists have failed, he said, "precisely where direct and immediate contact succeeds."

In lieu of a driving tour, I said, why not a soft stroll down Bleecker, as you take my arm, as we move easily, I said, toward the storied Café Caruso?

He replied quickly, with quiet cool force, "I prefer The Florentine. Where I don't have to face my dead friends."

"The Florentine? Not what it used to be, Eliot," I said, "so I've heard, but Caruso's has persisted in its excellence down the decades. Indulge my desire for Caruso's, where I was last when you were 10, at our initial meeting in the company of your good father, one of our dearest friends, who was proud of his son's passion for books and would grow ever more proud, as he told me many times—he who never read a book—as you advanced brilliantly through high school—he never attended, it shamed him to say so—then college as valedictorian. Then graduate school. Roger, he asked me, What is graduate school?"

"Proud?" Conte said. "News to me," he said. "So this," he said, "is not your first visit. Not visiting this time? Moved for good?"

"Anything is possible," I said.

He told me that he had vague recollection of being, as he put it, "dragged along with the old man to Caruso's," to meet what his father called "a man of honor," to whom "he owed everything." "My vague memory of this man," Conte said, "does not match the Roger I see before me. *That* Roger was slim, dressed in a form-fitting dark pinstripe suit, with movie-star good looks."

"Ah, Eliot!" I said. "Your memory is not vague. We were once, you and I, slim and handsome with a spring in our step. Now I waddle. Now you shuffle. Where have they gone, the young men of yesteryear?"

We agreed to a compromise. A walk on Bleecker toward Caruso's and The Florentine. On the way we would decide from which of the cafés to take coffee and pastry. I saw us strolling: he, lean, too lean, and towering at 6-3 over my 5-6—taking my arm as the old Italians of old Mulberry Street did, men with men, men with women, women with women, all gone with the snows of yesteryear. After one block along Bleecker, he stopped. Housebound with agoraphobia, he was unable to exercise daily in the open air—steadily, daily increasing his distance. He was spent—mouth-breathing heavily. We took the next bus to our destination at the corner of Bleecker and Mohawk.

As we waited he agreed that Caruso's is superior to The Florentine. He said that the owners of Caruso's were friends from

childhood and treated him like royalty whenever he came in. He spoke with a small smile that expressed deep peace and even deeper sadness. But the boys that he'd gathered with at Caruso's over the years, he said, at 9 a.m. three times per week in unshakable solidarity—he meant "love" but could not say the word—had all fallen "victim to natural causes," to which I replied, "Ah, natural causes, Eliot Conte."

He said, "You're thinking of the truth of your world, Roger: Two in the back of the head by unnatural intention, with malice aforethought."

"On the contrary, Eliot," I said, "such intention, with malice aforethought, is the only purely natural intention amongst those we call human."

"I grant your point," he said, "but it's repressed everywhere by the civilized. You and I, Roger, we're not civilized."

As we took our seats on the bus and rode west on Bleecker, he gazed out the window and muttered New Bleecker, and I thought, but did not say, Like New Mulberry in the vicinity of Umberto's Clam House. And I recalled French cynical wisdom—cynical but not wise—that the more things change, the more they stay the same. The new immigrants, the new colors, the new poor have buried for good what was old Bleecker and old Mulberry. Things have changed and they are not the same. Nor will they ever be. Now they come to New Mulberry, the tourists, seeking bad pizza at six dollars per slice.

I said gently, in a whisper: "Prozac, Xanax, Zoloft, Paxil, Valium, Librium, Klonopin, Buspar. These are the instruments for the maintenance of our civilization. 'Syphilization,' a writer that I love once wrote."

He replied, "You too, Roger Castellano? Intimate with these drugs which I don't take? You know them well?"

We'd reached the corner of Bleecker and Mohawk. "To be continued," I said. "Shall it be Caruso's, then?"

"Let it be," he said.

As we enter, I whisper, "How quiet it is."

He whispers, "Funeral parlor."

I whisper, "Ambien, Trazodone, Ambien."

He nods, he grins. He says in a normal voice, "The cure of cures, Roger, of our civilized discontent: two in the back of the head."

Just two tables are occupied in a silence broken only by the clink-clink of spoon and cup. At a table nearest the kitchen, a woman, not quite Caucasian, baby at her breast: discreetly nursing. At another table, a young man, possibly Hispanic, possibly something else, with rainbow-colored hair—a swivel-head with earbuds affixed, who can't keep himself from glancing at the nursing mother. This now is Caruso's? We are greeted by a beauty of Italian provenance, early thirties, perhaps, with a voice full of embodied life that gives me ludicrous illusions.

"Where have you been sweetheart?" she says, as she hugs Conte. "We haven't seen you since when? What? Three years? Ever since—I won't bring it up."

Conte responds by ignoring the question and introducing me as "Up from NYC, Little Italy section. Roger Castellano. Now one of us in East Utica, where we could use the re-enforcement."

"Amen to that," she says, touching my elbow. Then adds with a wink: "Welcome to the struggle, Roger." We each order a macchiato. Conte takes a seat facing the street at a table nearest the door. I ask if I may have his seat. He rises saying, "What was I thinking? My apologies, Roger." She returns with our coffee and a tray of six pastries. She says, "In honor of Eliot's return and our new East Utican, everything's on the house. Smile, Roger! You're on candid camera! She walks away, a fully-embodied life.

I say, looking at the pastries, "Delicious."

He says, distracted, "She is."

I say, "So this now is Caruso's, Eliot. This is yet called Caruso's."

"Moribund," he says, "in this moribund town. Except for the antique décor. The coffee and the pastries are antique décor. Memories."

"And the lovely Marilyn?" I say.

"Living décor, Roger. Get in line with all the other bitter dreamers who feed on memory."

"You dream of Marilyn?" I say. "Not the incomparable Detective Cruz?"

He says, "I dream of deep anesthesia, beyond dream and beyond time."

"Eliot Conte," I say, "I speak as much to myself as to you: It is not Bleecker Street. Nor is it Café Caruso. No, not Utica either. It is Eliot Conte that you mourn for."

He says, "Fuck it."

"Good," I say. "Let's move on to the questions that surely press you since our first phone call: Why am I called The Reader? Who are my closest associates? What do I hope the two of us can together accomplish? Our lives—yours, mine, your father's. How intertwined? For good or for ill?"

"This," he says, "displaces all the questions." From his pocket he places on the wobbly table a letter-sized envelope. "Read it," he says. "This," he says, tapping hard on the envelope. "Read it."

I do. I turn to him and cannot, even now, upon reflection, describe the look on his face. He's afraid. He's bursting with rage. He needs to act. He's paralyzed. He needs help. He's resigned. He's sad. He's hopeless. He's disappearing inside himself where he finds nothing except a need to kill. I have known stone-cold killers in my time. Eliot Conte would not qualify. He would not be assigned serious work, as I once was. Like me, Eliot Conte will never find peace.

"Six years ago, when your father had entered the late stage of congestive heart failure, he called me distraught, not over his impending death, but to tell me that on Detective Cruz's birthday, one month before the birth of your superb daughter, the good Detective had received two ominous letters. One year later, your father died frustrated and seething over this threat that he could not eradicate with a proper instrument. A broken heart was the truth beneath his medical truth. As my Pope would say of the anonymous sender, 'I'll sever his fuckin' head off.' A favorite phrase of the Pope. Your father had the reason and the passion. We had the proper instruments. But we, your father and his friends in New York, had no target. At that time. *His* head, Eliot, or was it *her* head? Shall we say, *Cherchez la femme*?

"The Boss of all Bosses is not one to indulge critics, but he indulged me. I recall the day I first corrected him. The day I said, Dear Boss, 'to sever' includes in its meaning 'off.' It is redundant to say 'sever off.' And he said, Can you believe this fuckin' English major? The balls? Anyone who fucks with this kid, I'll sever off their fuckin' head. At which point, emboldened by his expression of affection, I said, Actually, dear Boss, your redundancy projects fierce energy and resolute intention to swiftly smite down our enemies. And he said, Smite! Redundancy! The fuckin' language on this kid! Then he points to his two most frightening enforcers, Nicky the Nail Gun and Bernie the Blow Torch—they are goons, the word was created for them, though I never allowed myself to even think such a word in their vicinity. The Boss points and says, You two should listen to the kid and learn how to—what's the word, kid? 'Comport' yourself in the world? 'Comport,' kid? Yes, sir, I replied. Comport yourself properly or be composted. The Boss laughs. The goons do not. Or, if you so desire, Boss, *behave, conduct, acquit.* Then the Boss points to Nicky, goon #1, and says, Get a piece of paper and write those words down the kid just said. Or fetch, sir, I said. Fetch a piece of paper. The Pope is happy. He hugs me. He hugs Nicky as he calls him a 'lazy cocksucker.' The Pope says, This kid brings light and—what's the word, kid? It starts with an 'l'? Levity, I say? Yes, he says, the kid brings levity into our strife-ridden world. How do you like that, kid? Strife-ridden. Thumbs up or thumbs down? I say, Very nice, Boss. Strife-ridden is a nice cliché. Perhaps we might work sometime, in your leisure hours, on a more original phrase. The Boss puts his arm around me and says, My one and only son, who sits at my left hand—now and for all eternity. I say, Seated at the left hand, sir? Kid, he says, do not blaspheme.

He hasn't touched the pastry or even so much as sipped his coffee once. I attack a second cannoli. A small fleeting smile crosses his face and for a moment I see in Conte the Pope of all Popes at his most dangerous. He says, "In other circumstances, Roger, I would be amused. You have a certain comic flair. What was the point of all that?"

"Point, Eliot?" I say. "It gave me pleasure."

"You're the so-called Reader?" he says. "You're the Writer. Making all that shit up, weren't you?"

"Eliot Conte," I say. "Readers would be writers too. Must you begrudge me the pleasures of imagination?"

"*This.*" Tapping the letter hard. "You avoiding *this*, in your flight of buffoonery? Was any of it even true, what you just said? *This* does not amuse me. Does it you?"

"No," I say. "But I must ask you why you wanted me to read it. I suspect you have illusions."

He says, "Six years ago I had illusions about the F.B.I. What else did my father tell you six years ago?"

"That you had called the police. That the police told you it was in effect a matter of implicit blackmail, a Federal crime in the purview of the FBI. The FBI investigated. Tried and failed to acquire fingerprints from the letters. Made a few local inquiries. Questioned friends of yours and Detective Cruz. Asked these friends if they knew who might be hostile. Bearing not-so-hidden rage. Names were given. Further interviews ensued which featured, according to the agent in charge, this overwhelmingly stupid question: Would you, Mr. or Miss Hostile, like to confess to this crime? They asked you and the Detective if you had suspicions and you gave the name of your California ex-wife. The agent, not being entirely stupid, asked how this ex would know of the Detective's pregnancy and neither of you could give a persuasive answer. The agent, a few days later, told you that the investigation would be closed pending a dramatic new development. What have I left out, Eliot?"

"Only one thing, Roger. That Catherine and I have been damaged and that the fear and anxiety for Annie has not, over time, diminished one iota. Time did not heal."

"Our friends, Eliot, have always known that time heals nothing. Only proper action, undertaken without mercy, heals, as it destroys."

"Catherine and I won't recover unless the perpetrator is found and punished."

"By 'punished' you mean?"

"Limb from limb."

"Literally or metaphorically?"

"Literally. With the proper equipment."

"The FBI surely told you that anonymous threats of this sort almost never come to action. They are meant not to kill a body but to destroy a mind. The sender of this third letter sent the first two and intends to damage you two for life. The sender has infected you with psychological cancer: slow, relentless, inescapable."

"Unless?" he says.

"Unless you find a way to cut the cancer from your psyche, your soul if you believe in such a thing. I do. The Boss of all Bosses does. Do you?" He doesn't respond. "Let me tell you this. They never interviewed your ex."

"You know this how?" he says.

"Our friends have tentacles. You should know this. You surprise me."

"Then," he says, "you and your friends—"

"*Our* friends. The son of Silvio Conte was destined to be a friend of ours."

I reach out to shake his hand. He takes my hand.

I say, "You approach your destination within this thing of ours."

"You will cut the cancer from our souls?"

"You think too much of me, kid."

"You," he says, "and your—our friends cannot at least make an effort?"

"We don't do this kind of work—it is not what we do. But in honor of your father's loyalty—"

"You will make the effort? The Pope will care?"

"He cares deeply for you and your father."

Conte sits back. He sips his cold macchiato. He nods.

He says, "Limb from limb, Roger?"

"God willing."

The nursing woman is standing and saying something to swivel-head, harsh and with high volume in a language I do not understand. Swivel-head shrugs. She strides to the exit without a glance in our direction. Marilyn comes from the kitchen shaking her head. Swivel-head hands her his credit card. He's walking

toward the exit. As he passes our table, he throws me a quick furtive stare and leaves.

I say, "Eliot Conte, I need a great favor. Please ask Marilyn for rainbow-head's name. Now, please."

He looks at me with incredulity. He says, "Really?"

"It is of the utmost urgency."

"Life and death situation?" he says, joking.

I do not respond.

He says, "Spit it out, Roger. You'll do something for me? No free lunch. What do I have to do for you?"

I tell him that I want him to write my life on the inside: *The Autobiography of a Lethal Reader.* "Good title, if I may say so, don't you think?"

He says, "I once wrote a scholarly book on Melville. I'm not the kind of writer you need."

I reply, "Melville was a man of darkness. Like you and me. A man of the underside of beauty. Of the murderous depths. Like you and me. I cannot imagine enduring the isolating rigors of composition, as you have. I need you."

"If I do it," he says, "it may get us both slaughtered?"

"Yes, Eliot, and should that occur, imagine the posthumous fame."

"No writer," he says, "wants posthumous fame. They want it *now* because they don't believe that after death they'll be somewhere looking down with happiness on the discovery of their world-shattering greatness. They want it *now*. Including those who say they believe in God."

I say, "You will have it in this life when you write my deepest secret into public print."

"If you were a woman," he says, "I'd call you a cockteaser."

I say, "You are aroused? Good. Detective Cruz has a daughter by an earlier marriage, does she not? Now in her late twenties? The FBI never interviewed her."

"Her mother and I are not going there."

"Eliot: Our friends have a finger up inside the Bureau itself. Don't be naïve."

RINTRONA

A T CARUSO'S, 2:30, I'M SUPPOSED to meet Cruz-Control, which is what Conte calls her. I get there at 1:45—you would too if you ever laid eyes on Marilyn, at any age, male or female, but especially at a certain age. Like mine. I'm not referring to eye candy, which Marilyn definitely is. Marilyn is sudden full sun through a break in the clouds. She's just full of life, which I've been running on near empty for a long time. At Caruso's, on any given afternoon, in her presence, a 500-pound bag of garbage is lifted off my back. That's Marilyn.

I asked Katie one time if I could just once call her Cruz-Control, if she would let me get away with it. She goes, Sure, Bobby, if you want your balls to be a fading memory. My what, I said? She goes, Good, Bobby. Nice comeback. Just once, though. So you better pick the crucial moment.

Katie's had too much drama the last six years, during which I've become increasingly bored with age. (A solution waits not too far down the road.) The drama in my life used to come from Italian opera, which my wife, R.I.P., couldn't go for. My fantasy was to be an opera star pouring it out on the Met stage. Not just the aria. Myself poured out. Evacuated. She couldn't understand why I played it so loud. I told her the louder, the quicker it eliminates your loving husband. She said, Bobby, what's wrong? Don't you like yourself? The music, I said, it invades me like a lover. Don't take that wrong, Maureen. She laughed. She said, I knew who you were from day one. You were always my red hot lover. Still are, in your own way.

Yeah. My own way.

Since Maureen passed I don't listen to the opera. How fucked up do I sound to you? Eventually I'll bore myself to death, a form of suicide not recognized by the Association of American Forensic Pathologists, which held its annual meeting in Utica last spring. Those corpse-gropers came to the right town. Needing to kill time, as usual, I took in a session. Knowledge of the decomposing body will set you free from the unknown, these people say. Their motto. I think my freedom depends on is there maybe something more than my body, which I doubt. If there is, what happens to that extra-Rintrona after *this* Rintrona, this tub of guts, which is what I am, rots away? I'm not one of those eternal soul types. A warm body next to me in bed is all that's necessary. I miss Maureen. Soon I'll miss Lilly, my Vietnamese girlfriend, who I miss already, who's on her way out with advanced lung cancer. Three packs a day for thirty years.

A warm body or a cold body. What else is there? As much warmth as possible because there's nothing else before I'm cold for good. Last night, when I got into bed with Lilly, it didn't help.

I think I'm similar to one of these corpse-groping pathologists. When they showed a film on the proper technique of inserting a gloved hand inside a decomposing abdomen, I wasn't bored. These people are an upbeat bunch. They lose themselves in professional pleasure. So one of them invites me for a drink. I go because I'm curious about the after-hours conversations these types have, which turned out to be technical to the point of total obscurity. One of them tells the table he's eager to take in the exhibit of the latest advances in bone-saw design. This guy says to me, Robert, you have a healthy glow about you. He looked disappointed. Don't worry, Harold, I said. I'm rotting on the inside, including in the mental area. That brightened him up. He laughs. I've used that quip a few times. Always brightens the mood, especially with the older crowd. Including my mood. Possibly I'm not that fucked up.

When I walk into Caruso's, three tables are occupied by people I've never seen before. Youngish. 40, tops. I sit near the door, as far from these people as possible, the only senior at Caruso's. Marilyn

comes over. First thing she says, "Don't ask. I saw them here first time about a week ago. Good sign they came back, don't you think, Bobby? One of them asks me if I could give a discount on two dozen cookies. Another wants to know if we do wedding cakes. So I say to her, 'Who in this town does better wedding cakes?'"

I say, "Happy days are here again, Marilyn." Neither of us believe it. "What happened to your arm? That's some patch."

"Quitting smoking again, Bobby. Trying."

"How old are you, Marilyn? Twenty-eight?"

"Thirty-four."

"Smoke a long time?"

"Seventeen years. How's Lilly?"

"Promise me you'll kick the habit."

"I will."

"How old are your kids, Marilyn?"

"Four and eight."

"Lilly's not going to make it. She's in hospice care."

"Bobby."

"You better quit, Marilyn."

"I'm trying."

"Don't give me 'trying.' Don't break my heart, Marilyn."

"I won't."

"What are—I forget the kids' names."

"Ricky and Mary."

"Ricky and Mary. Four and eight."

"I get your point, Bobby."

"So what's new, sweetheart? So what's the story?"

"Eliot Conte came in this morning. First time in three years."

"Did he check out the kitchen?"

"Not funny. The cleanup took two days."

"Did you take part?"

"Don't remind me. Eliot had someone with him. From the Big Apple. Eliot says this guy moved into East Utica. From former Little Italy down there to former Little Italy here."

"Do you have a name?"

"Roger Castellano. You private dicks never stop."

"We get off on mystery."

She sits down. We're elbow to elbow.

She says, "I want to tell you something. Right up your alley. A customer at the same time they're here—rainbow-colored hair. Mid-twenties."

"You're talking like a Private Dick."

"This guy leaves and right away as soon as he's out the door Eliot comes to me and wants to know the guy's name. I tell him never saw the guy before. Eliot says, He used his credit card, according to Roger. So you have his name. I say I don't know if I—he goes, how long have I known the Caruso family, Marilyn Caruso? So I look over at this Roger and—"

"Describe him."

"Short. Very heavy. Sweat clothes. Expensive-looking shoes with that outfit. Small feet. Weird, right? The shoes? With that outfit? So I look over at this Roger. He's got a great smile. Gives me a little wave. So I give Eliot the name."

"Which is?"

"You really need to know, Bobby?"

"Did this so-called Roger Castellano need to know?"

"And they say we women are nosy. Give us all a break."

"I need to know."

"This part of some case?"

I say yes at a moment when to say yes is impossible. I was imagining far ahead. Hoping for adventure.

"Darryl Riddell. Wait."

She goes to the register and comes back with Darryl R Riddell.

I say, "One more thing, Marilyn. Credit card company and number."

"That would be wrong. That's some kind of crime you're asking me—"

"What if I told you this info might save the future of Eliot Conte and his family?"

"Might?"

"I'm being totally honest. Not saying more than I can say. Think about this: Have you seen my partner lately?"

"Two days ago. I was a little shocked at how she suddenly aged."

"That's my point, Marilyn."

"How old is their daughter now?"

"That's my point, Marilyn."

"You're really starting to scare me, Bobby."

I say more than I can say. Because I need the info: "You should be scared because I am. Listen. This Riddell, he's in Utica. He used his credit card here, am I wrong? So he no doubt used it elsewhere in town. So you're in the clear if you give me the facts because who's going to say it was you, Marilyn?"

She goes to the register. Makes a note and comes back with a slip of paper. She says, "I really have to help Carmen in the kitchen. Don't tell anyone how you got this. Don't let anything bad happen to that nice family."

I say, "I won't." As if it were in my power.

She asks if she can bring me something. I say when my partner gets here in a few minutes. She says, "Don't mention to her what I said about aging." She goes to the kitchen to help Carmen.

It's true. Cruz-Control is aging faster than Conte ever since they got those letters six years back. She's spaced out a lot. How do I protect my child 24/7 for the rest of her life? His face no change, but internal. Cancer, they thought. Unexplained weight loss. Loss of appetite. Night sweats. Fevers at 2 a.m. I asked him, lump anywhere? On the heart, he said. Those letters almost killed him. Internal destruction. I babysat whenever they needed to get away from themselves. Bring your .357, Bobby. Loaded. Check frequently the stuffed animals are not against her face as she sleeps. Now Conte's connected with a connected man from New York. For what purpose? Who wants info about a rainbow-head. For what purpose? Here comes Katie.

CRUZ

S O I SAID TO HIM—TO my husband in bed that night, when he wanted it for the first time since the surgery—the first time in more than a year, a lot more than a year, because he thought he would kill himself in the saddle by doing it with his bad heart, which is the way Nelson Rockefeller went out, he said. I said Bobby told me via Marilyn, who we all love and trust. Bobby said according to Marilyn you and the new neighbor were "creepy cozy," which is how Marilyn put it, according to Bobby. You were intimate with the new neighbor like long-lost lovers, which is how I'm putting it. I said, "You egregious asshole."

I said to him, "You're cooking a special meal for the Fat Man or Annie and I are moving to Albany—we're vacating the premises permanently to live near my parents. Because you are an egregious asshole. A welcome-to-the-neighborhood meal, got it? During which we hash it all out—you, me, Bobby, and the Fat Man, who we give an ultimatum to: Get out of Utica or we get you out of your fat life. So he says to me with his pajama bottoms off and semi-erect, which is better than nothing—semi-erect could work, it could be useful—he says, "I don't understand." I say back, "You know fucking well what I'm referring to. You're cooking for fucking fatso, who you're involved with, or Annie and I are gone. Jerk yourself off with your pathetic Mafia hard-on—you won't die—then pull up your pajamas because I'm not interested tonight or for the foreseeable fucking future, you egregious motherfucker. You asshole."

He pulls up his pajamas, the ones decorated with rabbits and squirrels. He's white as a sheet. In our six years together, he never

heard me use foul language because I don't use it except in my private mind, like Pope Francis does. I think I scared him with my foul talk. I was feeling light and lifted up and over myself in the moment I blew my stack and I cared about nothing. Not sex, give me a break. Not the fat man and what Eliot might be planning with him. Not even Annie, which I'm ashamed of admitting now—I'm feeling guilt now and selfish, but had no shame and guilt then because in the moment I blew up I was just Catherine Cruz alive to the hilt. The Cruz I was in the blow-up felt liberated in rage, but now I ask myself liberated from what? And I tell myself liberated from having to care about others. Care for *them*. Take care of *them*. Isn't that something?

What about me, the mother? The wife? I'll say it: In that moment I didn't give one darn. Except for a few seconds my rage-freedom didn't last. I crashed back down to Responsible Cruz. I'm trying not to sneer at myself. Am I not myself when I'm mother and wife? Don't think I'm insensitive to language. I know what "to the hilt" refers to. The handle is the hilt. All the way up to the handle of the knife. The sword.

He turned over. His back to me and I thought he's trembling. Or maybe it was me trembling. The foreplay game that we used to play: Me, tough bitch, he, dominated male, and the usual hot results? This time no game. No hot result. I was inside an explosion. I *was* the explosion. But now, not even a memory.

His back still turned to me, he says, "*Gnocchi Emiliani*."

"The special meal? Is that it?"

"His last supper."

"I want him out of our lives, Eliot. For good."

"You want him dead, Catherine."

"Gone. I want him gone."

"Charred onion. Brown butter. Rutabaga. You want him dead."

He turns to face me. Not trembling. He reaches under the covers.

I say, "Him or us. Our marriage and your daughter or you with your Mafia hard-on. Choose."

His hand on the inside of my thigh. I say, "Reckless asshole." Push his hand off.

He says, "I choose the connected man because I choose my wife and daughter."

I say, "Talk sense, you idiot."

Then he told me: "Yesterday. After six years. Another letter."

"You didn't tell me, you son of a—"

"I'm telling you now. Gorgonzola dolce. You want it laced with arsenic? Gone, you say. Out of our lives, you say. You want him dead. Say dead. Pumpkin seed is the final ingredient in Gnocchi Emiliani. Shall I substitute something more interesting? Say dead, Catherine. Is that your hand drawing mine closer to the promised land?"

"We need to call the FBI."

"If Annie were Obama's daughter they'd go all out. For us they do pro forma. We're going the alternative path and the Fat Man will get us there. Which is what you want too. We want the problem we've had for six years eliminated with prejudice. Someone, not Roger Castellano, dead. We want the same thing. Death to the letter-writer."

I said, "You are ill: Bobby saw it all. He gave me the details this afternoon because after three years of keeping it to himself he said he needed to tell me that my husband, my daughter's father, his friend—you, Eliot—what you did on Caruso's kitchen floor three years ago—he couldn't carry the burden by himself anymore. So he threw some of it on me. I hope Bobby feels better. You killed a man unnecessarily. You had him disarmed and pinned to the floor. Helpless. A short thin man, who killed six people, under your big body. Bobby wanted to call Utica PD. He said you forced your .357 into the man's mouth. You broke through his clenched teeth. He was choking on his broken teeth—

"Pearly white."

"You are ill."

"Yes."

"You blew brains all over Caruso's kitchen. Bobby said when you stood up over the body your face was flushed and swollen. Your

lips were parted. Like you had a tremendous orgasm. Who am I married to?"

"When you lost your temper with me," he says, "you were having a pale version of what I had on Caruso's floor. Jealous, Catherine?"

"Tell me this, Conte: What does Castellano want from you for this favor which he obviously can't deliver? He's manipulating our fears for Annie. He can't be trusted. Are you naïve or just in love with the thought of deep Mafia-involvement?"

"As told to Eliot Conte. His autobiography. The inside story of how he became a made man."

"You have to kill to become made."

"I'll write it."

"Were you happy when you killed?"

"The word doesn't do justice."

"Who are you?"

"This," he says, and pulls down his pajamas.

A noise, a thump possibly coming from the front porch. We didn't stop. After, he said, "We're fucking sick." How we laughed!

He put his head on my breast, just like old times, and said, "I never heard you say that word. It scared me."

I said, "Motherfucker? Asshole?"

"No," he said. "Egregious."

I said, "What? What's it mean? How do you spell it?"

"When you blew up, you said it."

I said, "I have no memory of that. That's your college-boy word. Not mine. I have no memory of that."

(The other day, I looked it up. It took me awhile because I couldn't spell it right. Eventually I found it: appalling, horrible, terrible, hideous, abominable, outrageous. And I thought in my private mind: yeah, that's the truth, especially when combined with asshole.)

He lifts his head from my chest. He looks at me. He looks extremely scared. Like he doesn't recognize me. He says, "You have no memory of saying that word?"

He gets up and goes to the front room and turns on the porch light. He says, "Catherine, come here. You need to see this."

It was a tricycle. The seat cover torn and hanging. The front wheel gone. The spokes of the back wheels broken. Rusted. I was afraid and couldn't speak or comfort my husband, who trembled as his forehead rested against the window.

THE READER

L ONG BEFORE OUR FIRST ENCOUNTER outside the Luna, I knew that Joey Gallo had made many corpses. Once, with an ice pick, so it was said. A unique surgery, during which the victim's intestines were slowly offered to the light as his screams, starting high up in the soprano range, descended the scale until they were nothing but a basso grunt, fading to silence.

Better the cartoons of simplicity? Better to flee the entirely human? Joey Gallo was entirely human. Joey was many things. Long after his death I heard it said that he had superb verbal skills—which I knew firsthand—and that he was able—this I did not know, to render the gouging of a man's guts with the same eloquent ease he used when discussing classical literature. The emphasis should not be placed on the gouged guts, or the books that he loved, but on his verbal prowess. His eloquent ease. Because Joey was at heart a literary man.

After reading the first twenty-five pages of his autobiography-in-progress, a powerful New York agent agreed to represent him to mainstream publishers. Shortly before his death, she had secured a contract and a six-figure advance from Alfred A. Knopf, which was eager, in the words of its Editor-in-Chief, to acquire the "little guy with steel balls."

At the Luna, Joey showed me the first sentence of his maiden literary effort. He wrote in his elegant hand on the back of the check: "Poor, violent Red Hook Brooklyn, where I was raised, is the only part of New York City with a full frontal view of the Statue of Liberty." Joey Gallo was a sly ironist.

Would it surprise and perhaps confuse you to know, as I knew early in our relationship, that Joey was shy? As the saying goes, Who knew? Who was to tell us that he was vulnerable to those precious few who showed him a kindness motivated only by charitable impulse—rather than the manipulative kindness of those who feared him. To show him kindness in its purity was to wound him gravely and cause him to doubt his philosophy of human relationships. When offered to Joey, the milk of human kindness sent him into deep retreat as the Gallo self he thought he was, and performed daily, died psychically. I surmise that his death by true kindness was more painful than his physical death by the bullets of April 7, 1972.

More than forty years ago, he said to me at the Luna—he announced at the Luna—I recall the words as if I had them on tape: "Any man who is strong enough to take something and hold it, he owns it. If he's not strong enough to take it and hold it against all comers, he's a dead man walking. Nobody gives anybody anything free of charge except two in the back of the head. Tell me this, Roger: Who gave Thomas Jefferson Louisiana?"

He had never spoken to me with such cold tone. After he was gone, I reflected on that harsh moment at the Luna and concluded he was concerned for my safety and did not want me to choose his path because he believed—how wrong he was—that I would not survive in his world:

"Roger, sink into the books, study hard, get your degree and live in a nicer world—I don't say nice, Roger, I say *nicer*. There will be knives, but not real ones. Eventually you get good with word-knives that cut feelings rather than flesh, but at least you won't need two armed bodyguards when you leave the house. Become a professor of literature, because they don't gun you down in the halls of academe. Once they start killing students and profs in schools? Civilization is finished."

How many times had he said that I might be with him when he was killed?

Except for that one hard moment at the Luna, Joey Gallo spoke gently to me like a good and wise teacher trying to help a beginning

but promising student. I couldn't respond to his tough message except by taking from my valise a book I had bought for him. A collection of Hemingway's earliest stories. I slid the book across the table.

I said, "I wanted you to have this. For your library."

He said, "You're loaning me?"

He understood my plain English, but couldn't risk letting it inside. I said, "No. No loan. It's for you as your own. To write notes in the margin. To read at night in bed. Or when you awake, as we all do, in the middle of the night with your head spinning with bad thoughts. It's the Hemingway book you don't have and it will tell you the truth of who he was."

How many times had he told me that I might be with him when he was killed?

He struggled to say words that he may never have said. Words not spoken in his world. He looked down at the book. Touched it and pulled his hand away. He looked up, but averted my gaze. He said, "Okay, kid. Okay." He looked off to the side. Where was Tommy Udo when he needed him? He looked worried. Or maybe ashamed. Ashamed of what? He said again, "Okay, kid. Okay, kiddo." Then he put himself back together and returned to his theme: "Free of charge. No strings attached. Two right here," and pointed to my head. Touched me lightly on the forehead. Then laughed his Udo laugh. He had escaped his vulnerability. The waitress comes over. He helps her clear the table.

She says, "Oh, Joey."

One hot August evening, as a thunderstorm rattled over Little Italy, my mother cooked for us: *pasta e fagioli* and a salad of *scungilli*. She bought the scungilli fresh early that morning from the Fulton Street Fish Market, a two-and-a-half mile walking roundtrip. (My mother waste money on a taxi?) Scungilli resting on a bed of tomatoes, cucumbers, and basil bought fresh that afternoon from the Farmer's Market on Union Square. A three-mile walking roundtrip. That was my mother: fit, vigorous, parsimonious, and—after a half glass of wine—bold in conversation, who loved her son and was happy to cook for the guest he brought to Elizabeth Street.

As she cooked, Joey and I discussed Kafka's *The Metamorphosis*. He was not shocked by Gregor, the young man who awoke one morning to find himself transformed into a man-sized cockroach. I said something in the hip idiom of the day:

"Far out idea, don't you think?"

He quickly responded, "We're strange to ourselves, which is Kafka's truth."

"Your truth too, Joey?"

"Roger. You hard of hearing? I said 'we.' What bothers me? The way Gregor's family treats him. Like garbage. Including the sister he was close to. They throw a half-eaten apple at him which sticks in his scaly back and it stays in there rotting away. For days. In the end they're glad to see him dead and in their post-Gregor lives they're more happy than ever. Kafka is saying to me, Don't look for love from the usual places. Especially home."

At which point my mother comes to the table with two steaming bowls of pasta. Joey jumps up, goes to the kitchen and brings the third bowl for my mother.

She says, "Thank you. You see, Roger, what a nice man does for an old lady? You should learn."

Joey laughs, not the Tommy Udo laugh but normally. He says, "Mamma Castellano, *you* are nice. *I* am something else."

She says, "Oh, a mystery person. Like the Lone Stranger."

We all laugh. I say, "Ma, *ranger*, not *stranger*."

She says, "I know what I'm saying. Don't tell me what I know."

Good feeling at the dinner table that night on Elizabeth Street. We ate quietly, no chatter, the meal was too good to interrupt—until my mother said—she had had her half glass of wine—she was ignorant of who he was, she was a little tipsy, and she said, "My son studies literature books at NYU and you are his professor, Mr. Gallo?"

He replied, "I teach, but not at NYU. I teach certain people in the five boroughs how to behave."

My innocent mother said, "*Dio mio!* We need teachers like you in this neighborhood where the Chinese people are rushing in too

fast. The Chinese people are nice people, but they could be more nice. My son could use a teacher like you. He is nice, but he could be more nice."

I said, "Ma, there's no teacher like Professor Joseph Gallo."

She replied, "My son is lucky to know you. I think you need more *pasta fagioli*. You're a little skinny. You need the weight."

She gives Joey a second large helping. He had lost much weight in prison. His dramatic cheekbones that had made him once attractive were much too prominent. I don't want to say skeletal. He devoured his second helping, then rose and began to clear the dishes.

My mother said, "You should not do my son's job that he never does."

My mother said, "Your friend shows you how to behave after your mother cooks."

She brings out a large double-layered rum sponge cake, topped with whipped cream and filled between layers with vanilla pudding and fresh strawberries. She puts on the espresso.

Joey has cleared the dishes and commences to wash them. She says, "He washes, too! *Madon'*! You don't need to wash."

"Allow me the honor," he says.

"I'll dry," she says, "because my son ..."

"I'll dry, Mamma," Joey says, "you put them away because I don't know where they go."

She points at me and speaks of me in the third person: "He knows where they go. Maybe he knows. Who knows if he knows."

I put them away. When he's about to leave for God knows where, to do God knows what, she gives Joey a hug and says, "You remind me of my husband who died six years ago. He was like you."

Joey Gallo, I did not say, you are wrong about love.

He starts to hug her in return. His arms begin to rise slowly. Halfway to their destination they fall back to his sides.

My mother, who had gone beyond the limit of her half glass of wine, says, "A saint has come into my kitchen on Elizabeth Street. He reminds me of the angel who flew in through the window to

make the big announcement to the Mother of God, before she was the Mother."

She glares at me and adds, "I was the mother, but my son was never baby Jesus. What do you announce about my son? Tell the truth."

Joey replied, touching her face, "He's a survivor, Mamma. He will survive. After certain other people don't."

I watched from our second-floor window as he exited onto the corner of Elizabeth and Hester. No umbrella. Bareheaded. He stands for some time on the corner, still as a statue. Suddenly, he thrusts out his arms, palms up, as if to catch the gentle rain. He tips his head back, feeling the rain on his face, then turns and looks up but there is no light on in my bedroom. He waves. He could not possibly have seen me. Yet he waves, perhaps at the dark itself. After a while, he walks slowly away down Hester, toward Mulberry, in the rain.

CONTE

THE NIGHT OF THE BROKEN tricycle: No sleep for me, very little for Catherine. After she'd seen the thing on the front porch, I had no choice but to confess my initial encounter with it. What it had done to me. What it was doing to me. What it will always do to me.

She said, "Knowing your literary appetite, your interest in Melville's symbols so forth, how could you not see a damaged child? You saw Annie. I saw a piece of junk, not Annie tossed on our front porch around midnight. An aggressive act. It scared the hell out of me. Someone is torturing us, especially you, and unless your Mafia boyfriend comes across we're in the dark with no hope for Annie's safety. Something very ugly, Eliot. Very soon. We need to do something very ugly."

I said nothing. Because I wasn't sure that I could deliver the proper ugly.

She said, "Annie can't leave the house. Don't doubt me. Given the chance, I'll kill this bastard. Please, I need one of those sleeping pills you take every night."

The bedside digital clock said 5:33 a.m. I lurched to the front window and stared at my sleep-killer. The position of the tricycle was changed from what I recalled. Turned around and facing the front door. Hallucination of panic-driven memory? Post-anesthetic paranoia, once more? At 6:44 a.m. I heard a noise that seemed to come from the front porch. I lurched to the window. The tricycle was gone. I went to my desk, unlocked the small safe, removed my .357 Magnum, loaded it, took the weapon to the kitchen and sat

there, my body out of direct line of the window. Could I kill again? I didn't doubt Catherine's resolve.

At 7:10, Grandma Gertie, as Annie calls her, knocks on the door: Our neighbor Gertie Romano, postmaster of the neighborhood list serve and Annie's beloved babysitter, who cooks every Sunday, at her full expense, a major meal for the priests of Saint Anthony, who do not pay but pray for the soul of her dearly departed husband. Gertie was white as a sheet of pristine typing paper. That morning would see our lives—Annie's, Catherine's, mine, and Gertie's—brought to the precipice of ruin, and the danger of something worse than ruin.

My father once said, Eliot, what happens after death is the surviving loved ones with tears in their eyes put your picture on the wall. In the days and weeks after your death, they look at it frequently. After a point, not so much. After a point, just another picture on the wall. Like your mother's on my wall and yours. That's all I know, he said, about the afterlife. I hated what my father said about my mother's picture. He's dead. Now he's a picture on my wall and I see the light of his wisdom.

The man who calls himself Roger Castellano knows something darkly extraordinary about my father. Castellano who refers to "our friends," "our thing." I have yet to hear him say the formal name: *La Cosa Nostra*. The gravity of the Italian has always compelled me. As does the allure of its very sound. *La Cosa Nostra*. This thing of ours. Roger Castellano, emissary of the Mafia Chief of all Chiefs—the *nunzio* of Pope Infernal the First is also my father's *nunzio*. He, my father, was wrong. He lives beyond his picture on the wall. I am my father's not-so-reluctant son, eager to embrace the secret of his legacy known, and held closely, by Roger Castellano.

Gertie Romano was scared. I invited her in for coffee, but she refused and stood frozen at the door. She said, "Let's stay out here so we don't wake up the angel of Mary Street."

Catherine brought Gertie a steaming mug of coffee, which Gertie accepted but did not sip. She was there to tell us a story which she blurted out helter-skelter, but clearly enough for us to gather the facts.

She had arisen just before dawn, as she had for the past six weeks of severe drought, to water her front garden:

"You water during the heat of the day in the upper 90s these days, my God in heaven, you burn up the plants. They die. So I water before Satan's fire, that is the true name of the sun, which they don't put it in the Bible. My head down I'm watering when our new neighbor's big truck, or whatever in God's good name you call it, it's rolling past and I see it stop in front of your house quiet as a lamb and someone gets out quiet as a—it's not the fat man from New York. It's a man with a normal body tip-toeing to your porch and tip-toeing back down with something, a tricycle I think, I'm sure it was, the light is coming up. A tricycle. Tip-toe into the back of the truck, or whatever, he puts it in. He looks left. He looks right. He does that because he's a g-d criminal. He gets back in and backs down Mary. He *backs* down! What kind of person does that, tell me? Out of the corner of my eye I see he sees me, but I don't see him see *me see him* because it's only my sly right corner looking and I'm keeping my head down with the hose, which is shooting into my face because I was so nervous I didn't keep my hose-hand down. So I turn, after I turn my hose-hand down, after he passed. He stops in front of the fat man's house, Fatty R Buckle, I call him. He takes the thing from the back of the so-called truck, or whatever, and carries it in to Fatty's house. Once he's in there for a while I turn off the hose and stroll slowly down the street softly singing, because I'm just an innocent old lady and have not seen a thing, Whistle While You Work, and when I pass the Fatty house whose blinds are up—Fatty must not be so smart, even though he's from New York. He keeps the blinds up! And he's giving something to the other criminal. They shake. I keep walking and softly singing around the block and return to my watering with my hose-hand down for sure this time. They stole Annie's tricycle. We should call the police, although you two are police in your own ways. With guns, I hope. Jesus Mary and Joseph. I wouldn't go near them unarmed. JMJ. Who are these people? Where do they get off? The one who was not fat? I noticed something in the inside of the house he

was in. The hair I'm referring. It looked crazy. I would say inhuman colored hair. It was just a glimpse, maybe I'm wrong about the hair, but I think I'm right about it, the inhuman hair. Thank God Annie didn't see this crime. For stealing Annie's trike they should suffer, Eliot. Vengeance is mine, you-know-who said, but sometimes vengeance is ours."

I said, "You are brave, Gertie. I'm grateful."

Catherine says, "They will suffer. I promise, Gertie."

Gertie says, "Let them suffer, Catherine, worse than you have suffered."

Then I walked Gertie to her house just to give myself five minutes reprieve from the talk that I knew I had to have with Catherine. To tell her that Roger and I had seen a man with rainbow hair in Caruso's. That Roger was eager to secure from Marilyn information that would lead to his identity and whereabouts. That I believed there was a mysterious and worrisome connection between the two which involved the tricycle, involved Annie, involved me and the writing that Roger wanted me to do for his autobiography. That somehow involved my father.

Catherine's response to my revelation was swift and harsh: "Worrisome, Conte? Is that your egregious best? Worrisome? Try 'life-threatening', if you want me to take you seriously. We're going to see your Mafia honey soon for the special meal you're preparing for him. I'll be there and, as they say, packing heat. For his ugly dessert."

Catherine wanted to do the meal that night. She was impatient to face the issue. "To get it over one way or the other," in her words. I succeeded in calming her down by reminding her of our exhaustion after the night we'd had. We needed to be rested and alert if we were going to bring it all to a head. Especially if violence was a possibility.

"Which it is," she said.

"Tomorrow is soon enough, okay?" I said.

"Tomorrow night, Conte," she said. "Not a minute later."

My reasons for delay were sound, but I had a plan to see Roger Castellano that same day. Alone. I wouldn't tell Catherine, who

decided to tell me that for the last few days she had deep googled New York Police Department archives and found the name of Roger Castellano. When I asked her for specifics, she said, "References that say what we already know. He's connected. Nothing juicy, Conte." I believed she was withholding crucial information.

THE READER

I T WAS A CHILLY AFTERNOON in late August, in Utica, New York, when I experienced the first of the headaches that could not be vanquished by the usual means. I had chosen for my living quarters the ground floor of the house at 1303 Mary Street and the second floor for the library, desk, brutal desk chair, and the well-cushioned recliner for my back—not because I am beset by chronic back pain, though I am, but mainly to nurture the memory of April 7, 1972, at about 5:15 a.m., with Joey Gallo on his back, bleeding out un-cushioned on a dirty street, at the corner of 129 Mulberry and Hester.

In my recliner, I enjoy brooding upon Joey's distinction between the styles of Faulkner and Hemingway. "Faulkner," he once said, "forces you to look up words nobody ever saw in print or ever said out loud, or even in their mind. But Papa Hemingway, kid, the father I wish I had, he gives me big emotions with simple words, which they go in quick—they go in easy, they go in deep, like bullets. The other thing I dig? The no-words of death. Ever notice how many times he writes, 'He said nothing.' Write your honors thesis on 'He said nothing?' They say nothing because there's nothing inside except the Big Nothing. Who can forget the end of *A Farewell to Arms*, especially when you need to forget it, when he walks out of the hospital in the dark and rain. Dead, but not dead in body. When I go, I want to go celebrating with friends and leave completely, inside and out. Dead all the way. Papa was a sensitive son of a bitch. Because what could be worse than the living dead of Papa's young guys? Maybe the ex-Boss of all Bosses is worse, Joe Profaci,

slowly rotting from cancer in Florida, America's ugliest state. Dying in Florida, at any age, is worse."

The three last words that Joey took in were simple and direct: quick, easy, deep. Two not life-threatening. One that dissects a major artery and with each beat of his heart, less and less blood to the brain, less and less consciousness, as he lurches toward the glass door at Umberto's, crashes through the glass, his last exit to a dirty street in New York, where he once bloomed in the filthy gutters.

My word is Faulknerian: *Glioblastoma.* Are you looking it up?

* * *

My library consists of two large glassed-in bookcases: each eight feet long by six feet tall. One for the books, mostly paperback, that I had acquired over a lifetime, now rushing to a close in eight or nine months, the other containing the books, all hardcover, that Joey's wife said that he wanted me to have when something happens to him, he said, according to her, before it happens to me.

I asked: "He said *when* or *if*?"

She said: "*When.*"

Joey once joked about which one of us would die first: "Hey, Roger, better you than me."

Once, and only once, I replied: "Joey, Mr. Gallo, I might have something to say about that."

"If you do," he came back in a flash, "in your Sartrean freedom you'll make yourself the son I never had. A father-killer. You Sartrean bastard." He laughed his Widmark laugh.

I said nothing.

He said, "Feeling the Big Nothing inside? Have no fear. I won't kill you. Today." (Widmark again.)

I said nothing.

He said, "Okay. Mr. Well-Read, you know the title of that play they all screw up? About the father-killer who beds his own mother?"

I said, "Everyone knows it. *Oedipus Rex.*"

"Spell the second word, Roger."

"R-E-X."

"Wrong," he said, "Mr. Big Brain. W-R-E-C-K-S. I got that from the fuckin' *New Yorker*. Surprised I read *The New Yorker*? Be careful how you answer."

I said nothing.

* * *

When Eliot Conte knocked hard on my door that morning, I was reviewing notes for my lasting mark on American history: *The Autobiography of a Lethal Reader*. Many notes on episodes in the life of a cultured man, inside a violent world which nice, ordinary people can only fantasize. Notes—more importantly, I thought—on literary strategy. How best to capture and drive the reader without mercy, beginning to end.

I opened the door to a stare that recalled nothing so much as what I had seen from Joey when he was in the company of those for whom he had conclusive plans. Conte carried a valise. I greeted him. He said nothing. I said, *Buon giorno, paesano.* He nodded. I asked if he'd like coffee. He shook his head. I said that I owned the finest of all espresso machines. Six hundred dollars. He stared—and I was afraid.

I said, "Shall we go upstairs to the library? A good time, I trust, to plan our book?"

He spoke. He said, "Trust."

Had he discovered what was to remain hidden? Did he have conclusive plans for me? I gestured to the stairway so that he would proceed to the second floor ahead of me—in order that the opportunity of firing a bullet into the back of my head would, at least then, as we ascended, not present itself. Should it happen, I thought, who will write the concluding scene for my posthumous fame?

I pointed to the desk and took the recliner. He took a laptop from his valise, opened it, and said, "Who'd you kill?"

I asked, "What else do you carry secreted and bulging in your valise?"

He whipped it out and laid it on the desk: A handgun. He said, "Do you know what this is?"

I said, "The opposite of love."

He said, "Who'd you kill?"

I said, "In a way, my wife."

He said, "In a way, we all kill our wives. Who'd you hit in the head like a pig?"

My oncologist at Sloan Kettering had given me eight or nine months. I thought eight or nine minutes was more likely.

I said, "In a way, I killed Joey Gallo."

He touches the gun. He says, "Who cares? He's been obliterated by history. Nobody knows about him except a few Mafia buffs, like my wife, and some old guys in New York City. After they're dead, nobody will remember."

I said, "Let me tell you stories. About your father. About Joey. About Big Paul Castellano. About Lisa, my wife, who is dead. About how Lisa and I met."

He said, "Castellano's 1001 Nights? Give it a shot."

Could I defer the inevitable? Could I tell stories for eight or nine months?

I said, "Your father loved you in the way he could, which was never good enough for you. I think you never loved your father."

He said, "Boredom brings out the worst in me."

I said, "Within this thing of ours, your good father was known as Silvio The Artist Conte."

He looks away. He looks back at me. Does he glimpse the father that he always wished he had?

He points the barrel at me. He pulls the trigger. Click. Nothing. He puts the barrel to his head. Pulls the trigger. Click. Nothing. He points the barrel at me, says "Feeling lucky, Roger?" Pulls the trigger four times. He says, "*Nada y nada.* This isn't Russian Roulette. Never loaded. I came here this morning, not necessarily to kill you, but to invite you to dinner tomorrow night, at 7, at Casa Conte. You, me, Catherine, and our friend Robert Rintrona. Possibly for somebody's last supper."

"And the child," I said, "the daughter in danger? Will she be there to make melancholy adults smile and lose themselves in her innocence?"

He takes a bullet from his valise. Loads. Points the gun at me and says, "Now tell me a true story about a tricycle."

What hope could I have at that point for my project, my reach for posthumous renown, my book, my project, my projection of myself into a future in which I would be no more? Unless I told him all, and by so doing, perhaps, perhaps not, likely not, gain his sympathy and his assent to proceed as my ghost writer. His writing for my ghost. I told him about my brain cancer.

He googled *glioblastoma* and said, "You deserve it."

I told him that I had refused surgery, chemotherapy, radiation, and experimental drugs, all of which would give me sixteen to eighteen more months of a life sick unto death, with horrible side effects worse than death itself, for sixteen to eighteen months of so-called life. I refused in order to have only eight or nine months more, the first five or six of which would be relatively symptom-free, relatively, so that I could work with him with a relatively clear head.

He said, "You should vomit daily every hour on the hour for eight or nine months."

I reminded him that his daughter's vulnerability, which thanks to his father's confidence I had known of for six years, was my—I used the phrase—my "ace in the hole." I took the risk, thinking that naked honesty was now, as I was literally under the gun, my sole chance to survive and save my project.

He rose, gun in hand, and stood behind me. He said, "Do not turn to look at me. Don't even think about it." He pressed the muzzle to the back of my head.

I said, "Hear me out, please. When your wife told me that you had undergone major surgery in Syracuse, one of our friends in the medical profession made an inquiry on my behalf and my plan was suddenly born. You would be advised to walk after your release. A short, slow walk around the block. I knew this. No more than that. I could envisage it, my plan in action."

He came around from behind me and with his free hand slapped my face hard.

I said, "I leapt into action, Eliot. At a junkyard in the Bronx I acquired the ruined tricycle." He slapped me again.

I said, "With the advice of one of our friends in Utica, I made the purchase on Mary Street. I placed—this was my wager—I placed the sad tricycle where I guessed you might see it in your first rehabilitating stroll in the neighborhood. Might. A guess, Eliot. A desperate wager that I needed to win."

He slapped me extremely hard, several times, drawing tears. Mine and his.

I told him that he was a sensitive literary type—he flinched at the phrase. I told him that we were both sensitive literary types, like Joey Gallo, and we, like Joey, love the vicinity of violence. I told him that literature, especially the most beautiful, gives us a taste and need for it, to do it, I said, as you have done it. I believed that the sight of the sad tricycle would cast you deep into your anxiety, your fear, your consuming need to shield her from all danger for as long as she lives. We are sensitive literary types. Like Hemingway. Ruined tricycle, ruined child. Yes. You would kill on her behalf. Yes yes. But had you actually seen the tricycle? I couldn't know.

I needed him to need me if my project was to be secured. We had a deal, I said. You will write for me and I will find the perpetrator of your misery. I am very close to freeing you and Catherine from all anxiety for your daughter. I needed to know if you had been securely hooked, which is why I had my assistant, a new tool of our friends, drop it on your porch and later remove it: As if you were being taunted by the one who would harm your daughter. To bring the danger to Annie to where she lives.

With his free hand he punched my left eye. A black-and-blue topic for dinner conversation on the following night. He said, "Don't say her name again."

I said, "I will deliver what you need. Is tomorrow night at dinner soon enough?"

He returned to his chair and ejected the bullet. He said, "There'll always be time for this," as he held up the gun. "Tomorrow night," he said, "or no deal. If no deal, then this." He held up the gun again.

I said, "The book. How do we begin?"

He said, "With your betrayal of Joey Gallo."

"My fatal tumor," I said, "has betrayed me."

"No," he said, "long before that you betrayed yourself. You will get some readers, no doubt, who carry you in memory. They die. Before they die they'll have recommended you to some other possible readers. Some of them, fewer than the original batch—fewer, Roger, will read and carry you forward in time. They die. This process goes on for quite a while. A light is lit, then snuffed out, until there are maybe one or two lights left and then no more lights are lit and you, who are long dead, cease to be remembered. The memory of you sinks into oblivion. There is no one left who remembers. And if there should be, for the sake of argument let's say there are a few immortals, roaming this dying earth, who have immortal memory of you. What is that to you? Their praise means nothing because you're dead. There is no you. This desire for fame? It diverts you from life in the present—the only life there is. Forget writing, Roger. Flush it down the toilet. Because what is a writer? A person who sits alone in a room, where all who know him fear to tread, to disturb him, hour after hour, day after day he's insulated from the present, insulated from friends and family. From those he never loved well. Or loved not at all. Living in a world of words. Roger: Sausage and peppers. Lasagna. Saltimbocca."

I said, "May we talk about the project now?"

He said, "Salami, prosciutto, provolone, and a good, dark, spicy puttanesca sauce—in the style of the whore. We eat in the present. Embrace the whore whose name is present time. Because she opens wide for all of us."

He looked exhausted. He arose with difficulty. Eliot Conte had emptied his gun of the single bullet meant for me, and then shot himself with a blast of monologue.

* * *

After he left, I watched him from the second-floor porch, binoculars in hand, as he walked home. A distance of perhaps 50 yards.

Walking exceedingly slowly. Lifting his feet barely off the sidewalk. When he stopped twice to sit at the curb, I put my binoculars on him. To see him mouth-breathing. To see him cover his eyes at the curb. To see a car slow, the driver stop, look at him, move on. His recovery from open-heart surgery appeared to be in doubt. I needed to survive for eight to nine months—he longer to complete the writing to see my project through to the light of day.

RINTRONA

"FAXTON," LILLY SAID. "FOR ME the end is bad," she said, "for you worse." I said, "I want you home, with me." "Crazy," she said, "I will do hospice at Faxton Hospital."

Every morning at 10 I visit. Every afternoon at 3. Every evening, 7:30. One hour each visit. Vietnam Marine vet, who did an atrocity at Khe Sanh, and the Saigon beauty, who immigrated decades ago. Her parents murdered in Saigon. The odd couple. Love conquers until death destroys one of us.

I lost my wife—lost Maureen to women's cancer. Now Lilly with lung. The oxygen mask. The voice slowly crushed to a rasp until 10 days ago. Now no voice. The vicious racket of the oxygen tank. The stink the oxygen tank gives off. The legal pad and the pencil by her side how she speaks the last 10 days.

Two days ago I say, "Marry me." She writes: Why? I say, "Because I want to." She writes: Good answer. Lilly and I are Catholics, but no priest that day. Only those Protestant types they call ministers. This Protestant says, "No problem." No problem? That's why they're Protestants. A very good-looking young nun at Faxton, Sister John of the Cross, a redhead, is the witness, which she'll have to keep secret from her Mother Superior. Bipartisan ceremony.

I kiss the dying bride. I open up an ampule and drop liquid morphine on her tongue.

She was wise, she was kind to spare me home hospice. The constant visits got harder and harder. I wanted to be there and I didn't. I stole subtle glances at my watch when I hoped she wouldn't notice. I think she noticed. Fifteen minutes at Faxton the last week was too

long. I was more or less happy when the hour was up. Sixty minutes on the dot.

I'm not afraid of looking at death. Saw plenty in Vietnam. Dead bodies and bodies, like Lilly, on the verge. It wasn't because my mortality was shoved in my face at Faxton. That's not why I found the hours there unbearable. In Vietnam, every day, I saw my mortality. Can you look at your spouse, or your parents, or best friend dying and not want to escape the sight of it? Some can handle it. Not me.

This afternoon I faked courage. I said, "I'm staying for the night." I tell her I'm sleeping in that chair. She writes: No. Go to Conte, save child. I say, "I'm staying." She writes: Tell hospice nurse bring 4 more morphine. B4 she leaves 4 nite. The nurse tells me in the hallway against the rules, but for Lilly, I say, rules make no sense. She says, "Just between us. Only every 4 hours." Lilly puts the ampules under the covers. She writes: Go. Live all you can.

I kiss my dying new wife and go. I go out into the late afternoon sun, wrecked and relieved.

DINNER THEATER ON MARY STREET

THREE IN LEAGUE AGAINST THE connected man from Lower Manhattan. These three: Conte, Cruz, and Rintrona, who gather together at 5:30, ninety minutes in advance of Roger Castellano's arrival. Three whose roles in co-conspiracy are undefined. Who would plan an attack without having secured the proper weapons, in a battle whose terrain of struggle is obscure. Three who had not, absurdly, devised a well-structured plot to hurtle them forward to the ending episode, where no further action is required because the target has been neutralized, with extreme prejudice.

Sometime after 7 pm, someone will be no one, nowhere.

* * *

Rintrona enters. White sport coat, pink carnation. Inhaling with deepest delight the aroma of Gnocchi Emiliani. Sees table set only for three.

RINTRONA: My watch a disaster? It's 7? Where's Castellano? Where's Katie? Where's Annie? Or have I lost my fucking mind?

CONTE: (*Jeans, sweater. Shivering.*) Nothing wrong with your watch, Bobby. No comment on what you call your mind. Castellano arrives at 7. We three eat shortly. Castellano gets nothing for dinner. How's Lilly?

RINTRONA: She wants me here. Insisted. First move? Put the Fat Man on a diet?

Cruz enters through front door. Form-fitting black leather pants display her exceptional form. Blue blouse. Three buttons open, throat to cleavage.

RINTRONA: Where's Annie?

CRUZ: Thrilled with her new sitter.

RINTRONA: New? Who? Gertie been revealed as a pervert?

CRUZ: Need to know basis only. You don't need to know. Fewer the better.

RINTRONA: You can trust me. I went to college.

CONTE: You went to college?

RINTRONA: Harvard of Upstate New York: Troy Police Academy. Who's this new sitter, Katie?

CRUZ: Information that can't be tortured out of you or Eliot. Only me. Only I know.

Conte puts on table bottle of San Pellegrino and bottle of robust red. Two wine glasses. Three water glasses. This alcoholic is still recovering, but after six years in The Program is sometimes strongly tempted, especially tonight. He fills plates generously. They sit.

RINTRONA: You dream this dish up, Conte? In your convalescence? Speaking of which, you don't look good. You regressing?

CRUZ: It's called Gnocchi Emiliani. Eliot's been having trouble sleeping this last week.

RINTRONA: I don't need the name, Katie. I need a second helping.

CRUZ: You haven't finished the first. Bobby, I'd like to visit Lilly tomorrow. She up for that?

RINTRONA: She'd love to see you. Go tomorrow. Don't delay. So what's the story, Eliot? Katie informs me this guy is going to solve the six-year-old crisis that's killing you two slowly. And in your gratitude you're ghosting a so-called book? His life in the Mob? Am I wrong, Katie?

CRUZ: You're not wrong, Bobby.

RINTRONA: What's up with this husband of yours? Not eating. Not talking. He looks bad.

CONTE: I can talk. (*Shivers.*)

RINTRONA: Me too. (*Opens sport coat to reveal holstered handgun.*) You invite the Fat Man to dinner with the intention of giving him jack to eat. You believe this puts him immediately behind the eight ball with you two in the driver's seat? But what's the point of that? What's the plan? Your wife isn't eating either. Pity the man she decides to bring the ultimate hammer down on. What's the plan? Somebody talk to me. This situation is destroying my appetite. (*Continues to shovel it in: finishes his plate of gnocchi.*) You two going to tackle that good stuff? Because here I am, willing, able, and still hungry.

CRUZ: Bobby, wait a while before making a decision that sends you to the floor moaning and back to the emergency room where they insert a lubricated … Your brain doesn't know what your stomach knows.

CONTE: His brain.

RINTRONA: Let's get real. You two have anxiety up the wazoo, which is why you can't eat. What do you think you'll accomplish inviting Fatso for dinner and not feeding him? What's the plan? You can't answer because you have nothing to say. Why am I here in this house except out of my love for you two and Annie? Your husband's pale as a ghost and you, Katie, despite your brown heritage, look all of a sudden totally Norwegian.

Silence.

RINTRONA: Say something. What am I doing? Riding shotgun?

Silence.

You say nothing because you have nothing to say, which I'm repeating myself in my sixties. My watch says The Thug arrives in

45 minutes. Hey! Who am I to refer to Castellano as the Fat Man? When I consider my girth (*grabs the flab*) which I often consider, who am I to body-shame Fatso? Your husband won't give me the time of day. Look at the look on his face. (*Takes Cruz's plate and starts in on it, as if it were his first.*) Talk to me, Katie, I'm approaching the zone of hopelessness, all kidding aside. I sit here with two wonderful people who have abandoned me.

CRUZ: I haven't abandoned you.

RINTRONA: *He* has.

CONTE: No.

RINTRONA: Say more.

CONTE: No.

RINTRONA: Katie. The plan.

CRUZ: I would tell you now what I dug out of NYPD archives, but I'd rather it hit you guys freshly, for the first time, when I reveal to Castellano what I've discovered. What he no doubt wants to stay hidden.

RINTRONA: Don't we need to be prepared when you lay it on him?

CRUZ: I want you unprepared. Reacting in the moment.

RINTRONA: So I'm like what—an actor, who walks in off the street to a rehearsal, gets handed a script of blank paper, and I'm supposed to perform? You, Katie? Who are you? The know-it-all director? Who's Eliot?

CONTE: The lunatic in the audience who leaps up on the stage in order to—

RINTRONA: In order to what?

CONTE: I think I ... I ...

RINTRONA: Spit it out.

Conte is silent.

RINTRONA: What we want at the end of the party—the final solution to Annie's danger. Can we agree on that? The person identified and taken for a ride.

Cruz and Conte do not respond. Do not so much as nod. Rintrona checking his watch: "Thirty-one minutes before he arrives:" Silence. Rintrona continues to overcome his loss of appetite as Cruz and Conte avert each other's eyes and gaze into the hours to come and the end of their troubles. Or the advent of something far worse.

RINTRONA: Three can play this game. Before I zip it up I'll say this and let's see if you can keep yourself from responding. Darryl R. Riddell. Eliot knows the name. R for Roscoe. Eliot knows this Riddell is an associate of Roger Castellano. I assume your husband has given you everything he knows, which is next to nothing: I did the research. I'll tell you every nasty detail of Roscoe's life and times.

A knock on the door. Instead of waiting to be let in, Castellano opens the door ungreeted as he—well, 'strides' is not the word. Striding has been beyond him for decades. He appears, waddling, in a blue pinstripe suit, expensively tailored to his advantage. A white shirt open at the collar. Tasseled Italian loafers too narrow for his spreading size 6 triple E-width feet.

CASTELLANO: *Buona sera,* my friends.

No response.

CASTELLANO: I am somehow too late?

He sees three plates on table. Two empty. But with smears of sauce, the other still gnocchi-laden. Holds out hand to Rintrona, who does not take it. Walking to table, pointing at dish of gnocchi:

CASTELLANO: For me, I presume?

CONTE: Don't touch it.

Conte takes dish of gnocchi and scrapes it into garbage can.

RINTRONA: (*Brandishes handgun. Points it at Castellano.*) Frisk him, Katie, before I lose my patience.

CRUZ: (*Patting him down.*) He's clean.

CASTELLANO: My friends, what have I done to deserve such disrespect?

CRUZ: If you don't deliver quickly on your promise, then I promise you—

CONTE: The worst is yet to come.

RINTRONA: Stop calling us your friends. Sit on that couch. Now.

Castellano complies. Sinks into couch. His great weight and small feet will make it difficult to rise and stand easily and quickly. Rintrona pulls chair opposite him as he continues to point gun.

RINTRONA: Katie, what's that line from *Streetcar Named Desire* you like to say?

CRUZ: Cut the re-bop?

RINTRONA: Yeah. Cut the re-bop, Castellano. We're running out of time. Cut the crap.

CASTELLANO: All due respect, sir, I know killers. You are no killer. On the other hand (*pointing to Conte*) he I fear. She remains a mystery.

Rintrona to table. Picks up dirty fork. Back to couch. Takes Castellano's hand and jabs fork deep. Castellano does not scream. Blood. Castellano thinks Joey would have approved. Says: You show a bit of promise, Mr. Rintrona.

CRUZ: Bobby, a little too soon for that.

RINTRONA: Too soon?

CRUZ: Just a little.

Cruz produces box of tissues. Castellano applies stancher, exerting pressure. Smiling.

CASTELLANO: Mr. Rintrona. Very much short of lethal. You might have chosen my jugular. The jugular. (*Addressing the three of them*) My assistant arrives within the hour bearing information that we all want to hear. In the meanwhile, how shall we pass the time? May I suggest entertaining ourselves with stories? Rather than with displays of petty violence?

CONTE: You're in contact with your so-called assistant. This is obvious. Your enforcer. You already know. You know what he knows.

CASTELLANO: Not definitively. Not yet. Soon.

CONTE: Where is he now? You know.

CASTELLANO: I prefer not to say.

RINTRONA: What happened to your eye, Castellano?

CONTE: He ran into a door called my fist. Where is he now? Answer me.

CASTELLANO: Returning to Utica. From the Albany area.

Cruz and Conte pull up chairs on either side of Rintrona. Castellano has no way out. The words "the Albany area" scare Cruz. Her daughter—from an early disastrous marriage—now 27 years old, lives in Troy.

CRUZ: Mr. Rintrona was about to tell us a story about your assistant when you came unbidden through the door. Ungreeted. The Albany area? Troy?

CASTELLANO: Troy.

RINTRONA: You want entertainment, Castellano? You sure? I have an FBI friend in Troy who gave me the dope on this dope of yours, this Riddell. Born and raised in Rhode Island. Providence, in the neighborhood of Federal Hill, Italian-American stronghold and Riddell a Wop wannabe who wants to impress the remnants of Raymond Patriarca's crime family, which is not impressed by a sixteen-year-old who's arrested for rape of the sodomistic variety. The underage victim's family won't press charges. At eighteen we find him in Philly, where he's arrested for the same crime with the

same outcome. In Philly, a prime suspect in three cases of arson. At twenty-one we find our man in the Big Apple, where he makes his reputation as a freelance enforcer for a genteel gang of black heroin distributers, who give their bloody work to Darryl, whose fee is modest, even for murder. The traditional Five Families take notice. Especially yours, Castellano. How the fuckin' mighty have fallen, to the level where they hire non-Italians, including blacks, to do violence, including assassination, including they hire this ass-rapist with curious hair, who is not black, who likely killed Sally Daz as he waited for his shitty McDonald's coffee at a drive-through window in the Bronx. This is what I know and this is who you pay to solve the crisis of this family and their daughter. God only knows what Roscoe's done in Troy, that shit hole nine miles north up the asshole of America called Albany. Don't look so shocked, Castellano. You're a lousy actor. You stink.

CASTELLANO: Much of what you say about Riddell was unknown to me until you told it.

RINTRONA: You lie.

Castellano's cell rings.

CASTELLANO: Talk to me … How much longer … *C'est la vie* … No … That's life, Darryl … No … French, Darryl … How did you … Nice … Darryl, do not speak to me about your urges … I am not judging you, Darryl … Both hands on the wheel … Yes … Oh, yes.

RINTRONA: Delay?

CASTELLANO: Overturned tractor-trailer. Outside Ilion.

RINTRONA: Who's he have with him?

CASTELLANO: The girl.

RINTRONA: "Urges?" For Chrissakes.

CASTELLANO: Traffic delays bring out the worst in him. To do violence, he said.

RINTRONA: He said that?

CASTELLANO: Yes.

RINTRONA: Take a look at these two. What do you see?

CASTELLANO: Concern. Understandable fear. I promise you three that at the end of the night all will be well. In the meanwhile, how shall we kill time?

Silence.

CRUZ: Her stage name was Lisa Darnell. A child actress of great promise.

Silence.

CRUZ: Your turn, Mr. Castellano.

CASTELLANO: At Attica, in a riot, he saved a guard's life.

CRUZ: Who?

CASTELLANO: Joey Gallo. Crazy Joey as his enemies called him. At Attica, Joey took his haircuts with a black barber. The white supremacists did not approve. They tried to kill him, at Attica, where he became so-called crazy. Radical. At Attica, he wrote po- ems, painted, read widely in modernist fiction. When he got out, he violated Cosa Nostra tradition by diversifying his crew with blacks, Hispanics, and Jews. His great, good heart was with the insulted outsiders of our society ever since a major Don's servant made him, at 17, go to the back door to deliver a message.

RINTRONA: What's the word for that? What do they call it when you have the hots for a dead person?

CRUZ: Later, after she learned the truth, Lisa Darnell divorced Roger and moved to a remote mountain farm in Tennessee. To raise horses. Far from her connected ex-husband, Roger Castellano, who was a deep friend of Joey Gallo.

CONTE: He says he's dying.

RINTRONA: Who?

CONTE: He claims he's dying. (*Pointing.*) That one.

RINTRONA: When does he get taken off the calendar?

CONTE: Claims eight, nine months.

RINTRONA: The cause?

CONTE: Irreversible malignancy in the brain, he says.

RINTRONA: Which you bought that possible BS?

CRUZ: Lisa Darnell, born Lisa Novak. You met her in the early morning hours of April 7, 1972, at the original site of Umberto's Clam House on Mulberry Street. No. You didn't meet her. No. You were not introduced.

CASTELLANO: We were not introduced. We did not meet.

CRUZ: You protected her. You shielded her. You covered her. You literally covered her when—

CASTELLANO: Four of them burst in shooting. Twenty-two bullets. Joey turned over the butcher-block table. I covered her with my body. She was Joey's stepdaughter. He'd married her mother two weeks before. She, Lisa, adored Joey. And he her. The new wife, after just two weeks, knew she'd made a mistake.

RINTRONA: What's it all about, Katie? Where's it going?

CONTE: Into the book he wants me to ghost.

CRUZ: Betrayal. Murder. Suicide. In that order.

CASTELLANO: Joey embraced and taught me the existentialism of Jean-Paul Sartre.

RINTRONA: Who the fuck is—?

CRUZ: Not now, Bobby.

CASTELLANO: Joey insisted quite strenuously, as Sartre did, that we make ourselves. Make our identity day by day. In our free actions, in the unfolding of time, we become who we are. A favorite phrase of Joey's. The unfolding of time. He cared for me. Joey. Unconditionally.

CONTE: Did you care for him? Unconditionally? With total loyalty? Did you love him?

CASTELLANO: To a point. Up to the point when the nice boy from Elizabeth Street. The good student, with good manners. Me. The gentle English major doing beautifully at NYU. Me. On his life's journey to teaching hopeless students how to write a grammatically acceptable sentence, in a two-year technical college in the boredom of Long Island, at a poor salary without benefits. On his way to a

lifetime of living death until he was seduced by Joey and the thrills of Joey's way of life. I graduated with highest honors and took a job waiting tables at Umberto's Clam House, which was owned by a man who never smiled and was called by Joey "one of us," "one of our friends."

CONTE: You were seduced by what Father Guerra warned me against when I was a teenager. The God-fantasy of power free of constraints.

RINTRONA: Castellano went down on evil. Are we surprised?

CRUZ: The glamour of Joey Gallo.

RINTRONA: Which was the start of his so-called brain cancer.

CASTELLANO: The lure of the erotic hidden life. Yes.

RINTRONA: Which I'm warning you, Eliot, for the last time. You have Katie. You have Annie. You even have me. You don't need the fuckin' hidden life.

CRUZ: When exactly did the nice boy from Elizabeth Street become a new self and betray his friend? How? Where?

CASTELLANO: At Umberto's, a month before his assassination. The word was out: 10,000-dollar contract on Joey.

CRUZ: You betrayed him for 10,000 pieces of silver.

CASTELLANO: I never took a penny.

RINTRONA: He claims he's above money.

CASTELLANO: Not at all. I wanted something else: acceptance on the inside. I chose my new self in the unfolding of time, April 7, 1972, Joey's birthday, when Joey called me at Umberto's from the Copacabana, to ask me to join him and his party for his birthday meal celebration. The call came at 4 a.m. I was the only waiter at that hour, I told him. I could not leave. He wanted me to join them in Chinatown, just a few blocks south of Umberto's. "You of all people, Roger," Joey said, "have to join the festivities." He was thinking of me, "of all people," because two weeks prior I had been his best man at the ceremony held in the elegant Chelsea apartment of the actor Jerry Orbach. Joey wanted Chinese, not Italian. I saw the path open suddenly before me, where I would seize my new me. I informed him that Chinatown eateries close at midnight. Nothing open in Little Italy at that hour, either. Except Umberto's. I said come to your

best man here, Joey, and we'll lift a glass together and shout *Cent'*
anni! May you live another 100 years. He said, "Thanks, kid, but
we'll scout Chinatown first"—and if I turned out to be right, they'd
come to me. He said, "Can we get at Umberto's scungilli as good as
your mother gave me two years ago?" I replied, It's sacrilegious to
say better than my mother made for you. But I'm telling you, Joe,
better. May she rest in peace. The police were correct in their theory
of the hit. It could not have been a setup because everyone in Joey's
party affirmed that they had no intention to come to Umberto's.
They had driven around Chinatown for some time before giving up
the goal of Chinese food. Did the police do the tedious legwork of
checking phone records? Calls from the Copa to Umberto's? From
Umberto's, where I made the call that gave me a new life? Joey Gallo
is dead. May he rest in peace. Did the police care how it came about?
Let those animals kill each other. I was serving them their second
plates of scungilli when four shooters. The girl on the floor screaming. I cover her with my body.

RINTRONA: I think I missed something here. How old at the
time in question was this lovely child actress? Who in your own
words you put your body on her?

Silence.

CRUZ: Twelve. He was twenty-three.
RINTRONA: Let's put that aside for now. I'll get back to that.
CRUZ: He married her.
RINTRONA: Let's put that aside for now. Because I am speech-
less, in so many words.
CONTE: What I'd like to know is how you were not in turn
hit. Later. The civilian, the loose end, who knew the facts of Gallo's
murder, is not himself eliminated?
RINTRONA: I detect something. An unmistakable odor.
CASTELLANO: Your implications disgust me.
RINTRONA: What's that line, Katie? The lady overly protests
his excessive innocence?
CONTE: Close, but no cigar.

Conte laughs, at last relaxed and therefore at his most dangerous. Cruz will attempt to keep the lid on until Riddell arrives. Tell us a true story, Catherine. Quick, Catherine:

CRUZ: Five days after the event, Umberto's re-opened and you resumed your position there. At the scene of your crime. That evening of the re-opening she appeared. To thank you for protecting her daughter and to invite you to dinner. You accepted without a second thought for the following Sunday, when you were met at the door by the daughter. Twelve-year-old Lisa Novak—(*At the sound of her name. Castellano looks away.*) Who hugged you and took you by the hand.

RINTRONA: How can you know these details?

CRUZ: Written into public print. It was a sad but exciting evening. A new start, was it not?

Castellano keeps himself from nodding.

RINTRONA: You writing a bad novel, Katie?

CASTELLANO: Not fiction, Mr. Rintrona.

CRUZ: And so it began. The weekly, then twice a week, then the every weekend invitations to dinner, to console, not the wife, who was well out of that relationship, but the grieving Lisa who'd lost a father-figure, which you became quickly. Too quickly. Within a month, you lifted her out of trauma. The Museum of Natural History. Coney Island. A picnic, just the two of you, in Central Park. The Bronx Zoo followed by a late lunch at Dominic's on Arthur Avenue, where the waiters made a fuss over the pretty girl. Of course, the movies—

RINTRONA: In a darkened theater on a Sunday afternoon. Isn't it romantic etcetera. Did you hold her hand, Daddy? Touch her thigh?

CASTELLANO: You make dirty what was good. The filth lies within you, Mr. Rintrona.

CRUZ: Enough, Bobby. Seven years later, she at 19, he at 30, marry. Roger Castellano had become a special made man in the

family of the grateful Pope of all Popes who was surrounded by foul-mouthed louts and appreciated Roger's verbal sophistication. The Pope of all Popes elevated the well-spoken young man to the position of lead negotiator, in the touchy interactions of the Five Families. Roger Castellano: A man respected and trusted by all. A man of fairness. A reasonable man who defused tensions with what was known as his bipartisan approach. He engineered the peace in New York. He had won the gratitude of all by taking the wildest wildcat, the ungovernable Gallo, trouble for all, out of the game. Do I have that right, Roger?

CASTELLANO: I was very well liked. Never carried a weapon. Never requested a bodyguard. We had no wars. The soldiers of the families lived in tranquility. I did my best and was given too much credit, perhaps, as I became a figure in our dark world. We, Lisa and I, were socially in demand among the Families. She met many of our friends in festive situations and became luminous among the black lights of New York. Eventually, inevitably, a word here, a word there—casually, inadvertently, without malice, sometimes in humor, a picture emerged of the truth of how her husband had achieved his dream of the inside. I told her it was nonsense, that I loved Joey, but she was not moved. My effort to sell my innocence failed. She was three months pregnant and had it terminated. She filed for divorce. She was a loose cannon, but I did not have the heart to ensure my safety. My handsome sinecure.

CONTE: You did not ask the Pope of Popes to issue a contract on her life. How decent of you.

RINTRONA: What more do you need to hear, Eliot? Still want involvement with this guy?

CASTELLANO: She left New York for somewhere in the sticks. I was told the Deep South. That is all I know, to this day.

CRUZ: You lie. She composed a lengthy document which she mailed to the NYPD, which it did not take seriously. I fished it from NYPD archives. Which gave me the gory details. One of your cop contacts leaked it to you from its storage in the department's archive. Let them kill each other and so forth. Less work for us etcetera. The ravings of a distraught woman, who took off much of

her head as she sucked on a shotgun. Like Joey, she does not rest in peace.

RINTRONA: Notice how he's squirming?

CONTE: No remorse. His blood runs cold.

CASTELLANO: I need very much to use the restroom.

RINTRONA: Forgot to insert your catheter?

CASTELLANO: Please, I very much must—

Conte stands, leans over toward Castellano, delivers a swift short arm jab to Castellano's non-blackened eye.

RINTRONA: Atta boy!

CRUZ: What will Roscoe (*smiling*) say when he sees two black eyes on his fair skin?

CONTE: He'll say, Roger Raccoon.

CRUZ: Let's help him up to the bathroom before he soils the couch.

Cruz, Conte, and Rintrona do not move. Castellano struggles to rise. They do not move. He rolls over and falls to the floor. Rintrona helps him to his feet. Castellano says, Thank you, Sir.

CONTE: Better go in with him, Bobby. There's a window. A straight razor in the cabinet.

RINTRONA: Toilet plunger? I'm not going in there with him alone.

CONTE: We'll chance it together.

Rintrona's cell rings. Says he must take the call and walks out the front door, cell to ear. Conte escorts Castellano to bathroom. Conte returns to living room with prostate-impaired Castellano. Rintrona puts cell back in jacket. Stands with his back to front door for many seconds. Returns.

CRUZ: Hospice?

RINTRONA: Yes.

CONTE: Still time to—?
RINTRONA: Lilly's gone.

Cruz says, "Bobby." Conte embraces him. Rintrona collapses. Knees to floor. Embracing Conte's legs. Rises. Falls to knees. Rises. In a flat voice:

RINTRONA: That cop client of yours, Katie? He ate his gun. At the dinner table. Wife and the daughter who's getting planked by his brother were in attendance. His brains were an addition to the marinara sauce. LOL. The woman who threatens constantly to kill her cheating husband? They reconciled.

Conte offers Castellano a glass of wine and to make him a sandwich. Cruz says, Were their checks in the mail, they owed us? Castellano shakes his head to Conte's offer. Suppresses a smile for Cruz's grim humor.

RINTRONA: I saw her, 3 this afternoon. She said, Bobby, don't give up. I thought, What's the point?

Castellano's cell rings.

CASTELLANO: They are at McDonald's in North Utica.
RINTRONA: Sharing a meal. How sweet.
CRUZ: Bobby, we can handle this. You don't need this. You should go. You don't need any of it.
RINTRONA: Where? To watch the mortician do his job?
CASTELLANO: I am sorry for your loss, Mr. Rintrona.
RINTRONA: Cut the phony condolences.
CASTELLANO: Paul Castellano. PC. Big Paul. A name known in this room?
CRUZ: Mob boss assassinated in front of Spark's Steak House, in midtown Manhattan. Spectacular hit at the dinner hour. Many innocent bystanders took it in. Related to you?

CASTELLANO: December 16, 1985. Big Paul was the Boss of all Bosses at the time. Related distantly. Never met him. He wanted my boss dead. My boss struck first. My boss provided the shooters. He thought two would suffice. Eliot's father, the brilliant Silvio, produced and designed the show. As your husband suspected for many years, Silvio Conte was a unique friend of ours. Selfless, really. He permitted, yes, he did, our associates, the Barbone brothers, Frank and Salvatore, to run prostitution and gambling in this town. Naturally, my boss wet his beak. Your father never wanted a cent, but he made my boss one request: that the Barbones not be allowed to cross the line into Utica's legitimate coffers. Tax revenues. He wanted to be assured of that, and was. Frankie Barbone is warned to stay in his lane. Nevertheless, Frankie makes an attempt, then we honor your father's wish, and that is how Frankie gets to be known as Frankie One Hand. With the assistance of two large men, I myself severed the hand. Later, on one of my social visits here to see your father and break bread, I mentioned that my boss needed your father's perspective. To resolve the mortal danger of Big Paul. Through my mediation, we proposed a meeting at Sparks. To dissolve tensions. My boss preferred only two shooters, who would execute Big Paul and his driver as they pulled up to Spark's. No, your father said, eight actors. I relayed Silvio's advice to New York. The Pope wondered, Is our dear Silvio losing it?

CONTE: What is the point of this story? To rub my nose in my father's secret life?

CASTELLANO: Be patient. The good part is coming. Silvio proposed eight actors dressed in long ankle-length white fur coats. White shoes. All wearing the classic Cossack warrior's hat. Black with a white silo atop. Pulled low over the forehead. Just two of them were actual shooters. No innocent bystanders were able to give clear and positive identifications. Or which of the eight lookalikes—that was Silvio's point—did the shooting. Eight milling and circling with gestures as Big Paul pulls up. Bystanders confused by the bizarre spectacle. That was Silvio's point. Your father could have

been something, a major set and costume designer in the world of New York Theater.

CONTE: But what he was, instead, was a political kingmaker who went to bed with people like you. My father, like you and Joey Gallo, had an artistic side that meshed seamlessly with corruption and violence. My father, who art not in heaven.

CASTELLANO: You, Eliot. You too. Art and violence. You are drawn to me, are you not?

CRUZ: Unlike you, Gallo, and Silvio, my husband did not do, or suborn, cold-blooded murder.

CONTE: Not yet.

He goes to bedroom and returns with snub-nosed .38 caliber pistol and a sport coat. Puts .38 in his belt and dons jacket.

RINTRONA: Artists and killers. Who knew?

No One, Nowhere

Rintrona's last words—"Artists and killers. Who knew?"—will mislead you, unless you can hear the actual voice, as if you were in the room, or as if in a theater, or at a film, and heard the actor's tone. If you read against his dialogue to that point, "Who knew?" registers comically. He's a funny guy, not because he tries to be funny, he just is. His way of delivery suggests an unselfconsciousness, a comedian of the streets. You find him all along funny? Likely because you don't often, or ever, converse with his type. Nothing about him suggests a sophisticated reader of literature, with an elite education, a man of books, a man in part made of the books that he reads. If you were in the room you heard in "Who knew?" not his sense of humor, which his naked words on the page would have conveyed, but a cracking of the voice—like a singer reaching for a note that he can't get to—a feeling in the sound of the voice that the words themselves have nothing to do with. A feeling that has everything to do with grief for the woman he's lived with for several years. Lilly said, in her last days, "Tell them, after I met you, that I had a wonderful life." She said, "The peach marmalade was not bitter. Thank you, Robert." Like his wife who also died from cancer, now this one, now Lilly, his last chance.

When they arrived—Darryl R. Riddell and Ariela Cruz—Riddell said, "Who's the sad sack," pointing at Rintrona? Riddell and Ariela look relaxed. As they entered, she had touched his hand with her fingertips. Without the niceties of prelude (she has not spoken to her mother in three years), Ariela tells Cruz that it was she who sent the letters six years ago, because she was "hurt, jealous, enraged

that you left me when I was three and got to replace me with a new baby. But I did not send the new one. Darryl delivered it on his behalf"—pointing to Castellano. Darryl says, "Oh, yeah," as he places his hand on her back and adds, "Your mother is smokin' hot too," as his hand slides down to her ass. She says, "That's all I ever got from her, who abandoned me. The looks."

How did Catherine Cruz respond? In her guilt, who had left Ariela at 3? In her fear, become real, that it was Ariela who had sent the letters? In her relief, that the threat was nothing to be feared—a fear so unbearable that she never informed the FBI agent that she even had a daughter, a daughter who lived in Troy. What did she say to this daughter, who she would never see again? She said nothing. She had no words for what she felt. She would never have the words.

Darryl is wearing a shirt in the contemporary male style. Untucked. Something concealed under there? Conte pulls his gun and tells Rintrona to frisk him. Darryl is not carrying. Ariela says, "Let's get out of here." Riddell says, "They only call it sodomy when they don't like it. They whine and bitch." Ariela grins.

At the door, Ariela turns. She says, "You were my mother and you failed me. You were selfish." Catherine says nothing. What can she say? There are no fucking words.

They leave, but not before Riddell tells Castellano. "I know where you live here, and in New York. You owe me. You owe me now way more than we agreed or I tell The Pope about the book you want to write with this guy, who looks like he's going to drop dead at any minute."

Conte tells Castellano, "Get out of my house. Before I change my mind. In the unfolding of time." Castellano leaves.

Rintrona says "Okay, Katie? Eliot? Case finally closed?" They nod.

Conte says, "Six years of fear and anxiety. Six years."

Cruz says, "We have Annie, who never was in any danger. That's enough, isn't it, Marlon?"

Rintrona says, "You have me too. If you want me."

Cruz says, "We want you. We love you, Bobby."

Conte says, "Bobby." He shivers. He goes to the sink and pours himself a large glass of water. He says, "Six years. I'm supposed to be like it never happened? Like the terror left no scar?" He drinks long and deep. He says, "I need to go to bed." And does.

Rintrona tells Cruz to get Eliot back to the doctor in Syracuse. He says, "Let's catch up in the morning."

Around midnight, Rintrona's next door neighbor hears the gunshot when Rintrona, alone at home, becomes no one, nowhere.

ACKNOWLEDGEMENTS

Chris Cox
Jeff Jackson
Harvey Aronson, *The Killing of Joey Gallo*

About the Author

After groundbreaking work as a literary critic and theorist, Frank Lentricchia changed his focus in the early 1990s. Since then he has written a number of novels that explore the complexities of ethnic and artistic identity, often within the context of contemporary disasters—the Vietnam and Iraq wars and the diseased glamour of the American Mafia. Lentricchia was born in Utica, New York—the setting of many of his novels which evoke the working-class ethnic family in its pleasurable and stressful vitality.

FICTION BY FRANK LENTRICCHIA

The Glamour of Evil
A Place in the Dark
The Morelli Thing
The Dog Killer of Utica
The Accidental Pallbearer
The Sadness of Antonioni
The Italian Actress
The Book of Ruth
Lucchesi and The Whale
The Music of the Inferno
The Knifemen
Johnny Critelli
The Edge of Night (memoir/fiction)

The End